THE
WALKING
DEAD

By Robert Kirkman and Jay Bonansinga

The Walking Dead: Rise of the Governor
The Walking Dead: The Road to Woodbury
The Walking Dead: The Fall of the Governor, Part One
The Walking Dead: The Fall of the Governor, Part Two

THE
WALKING
DEAD

THE FALL OF THE GOVERNOR
PART TWO

ROBERT KIRKMAN
AND JAY BONANSINGA

TOR

First published in the US 2014 by Thomas Dunne Books,
an imprint of St Martin's Press

This edition published in the UK 2014 by Tor
an imprint of Pan Macmillan, a division of Macmillan Publishers Limited
Pan Macmillan, 20 New Wharf Road, London N1 9RR
Basingstoke and Oxford
Associated companies throughout the world
www.panmacmillan.com

ISBN 978-1-4472-6682-2

1 3 5 7 9 8 6 4 2

A CIP catalogue record for this book is available from the British Library.

Printed and bound by CPI Group (UK) Ltd, Croydon, CR0 4YY

Visit **www.panmacmillan.com** to read more about all our books
and to buy them. You will also find features, author interviews and
news of any author events, and you can sign up for e-newsletters
so that you're always first to hear about our new releases.

For Joey and Bill Bonansinga with Love

ACKNOWLEDGMENTS

More than ever, an extra-special thanks to Mr. Robert Kirkman for bringing me along for the ride of a lifetime; additional gracias to Andy Cohen, David Alpert, Brendan Deneen, Nicole Sohl, Kemper Donovan, Shawn Kirkham, Stephanie Hargadon, Courtney Sanks, Christina MacDonald, Mort Castle, Master Sergeant Alan Baker, and Brian Kett; and the best, as always, saved for last: Deep appreciation and undying love for my beautiful woman and best friend, Jill M. Norton.

PART 1

Battlefield

I am become death, the destroyer of worlds.

—J. Robert Oppenheimer

ONE

The fire starts on the first floor, the flames licking up the cabbage rose wallpaper, unfurling across the plaster ceiling, and spewing black, noxious smoke through the hallways and bedrooms of the Farrel Street house, blinding him, choking the breath out of him. He darts across the dining room, searching for the back stairs, finding them, hurling down the old, rickety wooden risers into the musty darkness of the basement. "Philip?!—PHILIP!?!—PHILLLLLLLLLIP!!?!" He lurches across the filthy, water-marked cement floor, frantically scanning the dark cellar for his brother. Upstairs, the home blazes and crackles, the conflagration roaring through the cluttered chambers of the meager bungalow, the heat pressing down on the foundation. He whirls fecklessly in circles, scanning the shadowy reaches of the smoke-bound cellar, batting away cobwebs and choking on the acrid smoke and ammonia-rot stench of rancid canned beets, rat turds, and ancient fiberglass insulation. He can hear the creaking and thudding of wooden timbers collapsing onto the floor above him as the maelstrom rages out of control—which makes no sense because his little childhood home in Waynesboro, Georgia, never burned down in any fire as far as he can remember. But here it is, going up in a terrible inferno, and he can't find his fucking brother. How did he get here? And where the fuck is Philip? He needs Philip. Goddamnit, Philip would know what to do! "PHILLLLLLLLLLLIIIIP!" His hysterical cry comes out of him like a thin puff of air, a breathless chirp, a fading signal on a radio tuned to some *distant station. All at once he sees a portal in one of the basement walls—a strange, concave opening like a hatch on a submarine, a weird greenish glow emanating from within it—and he realizes that the opening is new. There was never such an opening in the basement of his childhood home on Farrel Street, but again, like black magic, here it fucking is. He stumbles toward the dim, radiant, green gash in the darkness. Pushing through the opening, he steps into an airless cinder-block garage stall. The chamber is empty. The walls bear the marks of torture—streaks of dark, drying blood and the frayed ends of ropes affixed to U-bolts—and the place radiates evil. Pure, unadulterated, preternatural evil. He wants out. He can't breathe. His flesh crawls. He can't make a sound other than a faint mewling noise coming from the deepest part of his lungs, an anguished moaning. He hears a noise and spins around and sees another gangrenous-green glowing portal, and he lunges toward it. He goes through the opening, and he finds himself in a pine grove outside Woodbury. He recognizes the clearing, the deadfall logs forming a natural little amphitheater—the ground carpeted in matted pine needles, fungus, and weeds. His heart quickens. This is an even worse place—a death scene. A figure emerges from the forest and steps into the pale light. It's his old friend, Nick Parsons, gangly and awkward as ever, lurching into the clearing with a 12-gauge pump-action shotgun, his face a sweaty mask of horror. "Dear Lord," Nick murmurs in a strangled voice. "Cleanse us of all this unrighteousness." Nick raises the shotgun. The muzzle looks gargantuan—like an enormous planet eclipsing the sun—pointing directly at him. "I renounce all sins," Nick drones in his sepulchral voice. "Forgive me, O Lord . . . forgive me." Nick pulls the trigger. The firing pin snaps. The slow-motion blast flares in a brilliant yellow corona—the rays of a dying sun—and he feels himself lifted out of his boots, slingshot into space, weightless, flying through darkness . . . toward a nimbus of celestial white light. This is it. This is the end of the world—his world—the end of everything. He screams. No sound comes from his lungs. This is death—the suffocating, magnesium-white void of nothingness—and very suddenly, like a switch being thrown, Brian Blake ceases to exist.*

With the abruptness of a jump-cut in a motion picture, he is lying on the floor of his apartment in Woodbury—inert, frozen, pinned to the cold hardwood in paralyzing, icy pain—his breathing so labored and inhibited that his very cells seem to be gasping for life. His vision consists of a jagged, blurry, fractured view of the water-stained ceiling tiles—one eye completely blind, its orbital socket cold as if wind is blowing through it. The duct tape hanging off one side of his mouth, the tiny inhalations and exhalations through his bloody nostrils almost imperceptible to the casual listener, he tries to move but can't even turn his head. The sound of voices barely registers with his agony-gripped auditory nerves.

"What about the girl?" a voice asks from somewhere in the room.

"Fuck her, she's outside the safe zone by now—she ain't got a chance."

"What about him? Is he dead?"

Then another sound registers—a watery, garbled growl—which draws his attention to the edge of his vision. Seeing through the bleary retina of his one good eye, he can barely make out the tiny figure in the doorway across the room, her pale face mottled with decomposition, her pupil-less eyes like sparrow eggs. She lunges until her chain-link leash clangs loudly.

"GAH!" one of the male voices yelps as the tiny monster claws at him.

Philip tries desperately to speak, but the words catch in his scalded throat. His head weighs a thousand tons, and he tries again to speak with chapped, cracked, bleeding lips, tries to form breathless words that simply won't coalesce. He hears the deep baritone voice of Bruce Cooper.

"Okay—fuck this!" The telltale click of a safety disengaging on a semiautomatic fills the silence. "This girl's getting a bullet right—"

"N-nnggh!" Philip puts everything he has into his voice and manages another faint series of utterances. "D-duh—d-don't!" He takes another agonizing breath. He must protect his daughter Penny—regardless of the fact that she's already dead and has been for over a year. She is all he has left in this world. She is everything. "D-don't fucking touch her . . . DON'T DO IT!"

Both men snap their gazes toward the man on the floor, and for the briefest fraction of an instant, Philip gets a glimpse of their faces gaping down at him. Bruce, the taller man, is an African American with a shaved head, which now furrows with horror and repulsion. The other man, Gabe, is white and built like a Mack truck with his marine buzz cut and black turtleneck. From the look in their eyes, it's clear that Philip Blake should be dead.

Lying on that blood-soaked four-by-eight piece of plywood, he has no idea how bad he must look—especially his face, which feels as though it's been tenderized by an ice pick—and for one fleeting moment, the expressions on the faces of these crude, simple men gaping down at him set off a warning alarm in Philip's brain. The woman who worked him over—*Michonne* is her name, if memory serves—did her job well. For his sins, she left him as close to death's door as a person can be without going through it.

The Sicilians say revenge is a dish best served cold, but this gal delivered it with a steaming plate of agony. Getting his right arm amputated and cauterized just above the elbow is now the least of Philip's problems. His left eye is currently lying on the side of his face, glued to his flesh by drying tendrils of bloody tissue. But worse than that—far worse for Philip Blake—is the sticky-cold sensation spreading up through his entrails from the site where his penis was detached with a flick of the woman's fancy sword. The memory of that little flick—the sting of a metal wasp—now sends him back into the twilight of semiconsciousness. He can barely hear the voices.

"FUCK!" Bruce stares bug-eyed down at the once-fit, once-lean man with the handlebar mustache. "He's alive!"

Gabe stares. "Shit, Bruce—the doc and Alice are fucking gone! What the hell are we going to do?"

At some point, another man has entered the apartment in a flurry of heavy breathing and the clanging of a pump-action shotgun. Philip can't see who it is, or hear the voices very well. He floats between consciousness and oblivion while the men hovering over him continue their terse, panicky exchange.

Bruce's voice: "You guys, lock this little shit up in the other room. I'm going to run downstairs and get Bob."

Gabe's voice next: "Bob?! The fucking drunk that's always sitting downstairs by the door?"

The voices begin to fade as the dark cold shroud draws down over Philip.

"—what the hell can he do—?"

"—probably not much—"

"—so why?—"

"—he can do more than either of us—"

Contrary to public opinion and the mythology of the movies, the average combat medic is not even *remotely* as skilled as an experienced, credentialed trauma surgeon or, for that matter, even a general practitioner. Most medics receive less than three months of training during boot camp, and even the most prodigious of these individuals rarely rises above the level of a common EMT or paramedic. They know basic first aid, a little CPR, and the rudiments of trauma care, and that's about it. They are thrown into the breach with battle units and expected to simply keep wounded soldiers breathing—or keep the circulatory system intact—until the victim can be transported to a mobile surgical unit. They are human tugboats—hardened by front-line conditions, calloused by witnessing a constant stream of suffering—expected only to Band-Aid and splint the sucking wounds of war.

Hospital Corpsman First Class Bob Stookey served a single tour with the Sixty-Eight Alpha company in Afghanistan thirteen years ago, at the tender age of thirty-six, getting deployed not long after the initial invasion. He was one of the older enlisted men at the time—his reasons for signing up had a lot to do with a divorce going sour at the time—and he became somewhat of a Dutch uncle to the youngsters around him. He started as a glorified ambulance driver out of Camp Dwyer and worked his way up to battlefield medic by the following spring. He had a knack for keeping the boys entertained with lousy jokes and nonregulation sips from his ever-present flask of Jim Beam. He also had a soft heart— the grunts loved him for that—and he died a little bit every time he lost a marine. By the time he shipped back to the world one week after his thirty-seventh birthday, he had died one hundred and eleven times and was medicating the trauma with a half-quart of whiskey a day.

All of this Sturm und Drang of his past had long been drowned by the horror and clamor of the plague, as well as the excoriating loss of his secret love, Megan Lafferty, and the pain has grown so malignant within him that now—tonight—*this instant*—he is completely oblivious to the fact that he is about to be wrenched back onto the battlefield.

"BOB!"

Slumped against the bricks in front of the Governor's place, half-conscious, dried spittle and ash across the front of his drab olive jacket, Bob stirs at the booming voice of Bruce Cooper. The darkness of night is slowly burning off with the dawn, and Bob has already started shaking from the chill winds and a restless night of fever dreams.

"Get up!" the big man orders as he lurches out of the building and comes over to Bob's nest of soggy newspapers, ratty blankets, and empty bottles. "We need your help—upstairs! NOW!"

"W-what?" Bob rubs his grizzled face and belches stomach acids. "Why?"

"It's the Governor!" Bruce reaches down and grabs hold of Bob's limp arm. "You were an army medic, right?!"

"Marines . . . H-hospital Corps," he stammers, feeling as though he's being levered to his feet by a block and tackle. His head spins. "For about fifteen minutes . . . about a million years ago. I can't do shit."

Bruce stands him up like a mannequin, clutching him roughly by the shoulders. "Well, you're going to fucking try!" He shakes him. "The Governor's been taking care of *you*—making sure you're fed, that you don't drink yourself to death—and now you're going to return the favor."

Bob swallows back his nausea, wipes his face, and gives a queasy nod. "Okay, take me to him."

On their way through the foyer, up the staircase, and down the back hall, Bob is thinking it's probably no big deal, the Governor's got the flu or something, fucking stubbed his toe and now they're overreacting like they always do. And as they hasten toward the last door on the left, Bruce practically pulling Bob's arm out of its socket, just for an instant, Bob catches a whiff of something coppery and musky wafting out of the half-ajar door, and the odor sets off warning bells in Bob Stookey's head. Right before Bruce yanks him inside the apartment—in that horrible instant before Bob clears the jamb and sees what's waiting for him inside—he flashes back to the war.

The sudden and unbidden memory that streaks through his mind's eye at that moment makes him flinch—the smell, that protein-rich stew that hung over the slapdash surgical unit in Parwan Province; the pile of pus-ridden bandages earmarked for incineration; the drain swirling with bile; those gurneys washed with blood cooking in the Afghan sun—all of this flickers through Bob's brain in that split second before he sees the body on the floor of the apartment. The odor raises his hackles and makes him hold on to the jamb for purchase as Bruce shoves him into the vestibule, and Bob, at last, gets a good look at the Governor—or what remains of the man—on the desecrated plywood platform.

"I locked the girl away and untied his arm," Gabe is saying, but Bob can hardly hear the man or see the other guy—another goon named Jameson, now crouched across the room, hands clasped awkwardly, eyes hot with panic—and the dizziness threatens to drag Bob to the floor. He gapes. Gabe's voice warbles as if coming from underwater. "He's passed out—but he's still breathing."

"Holy sh—!" Bob barely makes a noise, his voice squeezed and colorless. He falls to his knees. He stares and stares and stares at the contorted, scorched, blood-soaked, scourged remains of a man who once prowled the streets of the little kingdom of Woodbury like an Arthurian knight. Now the mangled body of Philip Blake begins to metamorphose in Bob Stookey's mind into that poor young man from Alabama—Master Sergeant Bobby McCullam, the kid who haunts Bob's dreams—the one who got half his body torn off by an IED outside Kandahar. Overlaying the Governor's face, in a grotesque double image, Bob now sees the marine, that death mask of a face under a helmet—parboiled eyes and bloody grimace tucked into a chin strap—the terrible gaze fixing itself on Bob the Ambulance Driver. *Kill me,* the kid had muttered to Bob, who couldn't do anything for the young man but load him into a sweltering cargo bay already crammed with dead marines. *Kill me,* the kid had said, and Bob was helpless and stricken mute, and the young marine had died with his eyes locked onto Bob's. All this passes through Bob's imagination in an instant, pulling the gorge up into his esophagus, filling his mouth with stomach acids, burning in the back of his throat, erupting in his nasal passages like liquid fire.

Bob twists around and roars vomit across the room's filthy carpet.

The entire contents of his stomach—a twenty-four-hour liquid diet of cheap whiskey and occasional sips of Sterno—come frothing out, splattering the rug. On his hands and knees now, Bob heaves and heaves, his back arching, his body convulsing. He tries to speak between watery gasps. "I—I can't—can't even look at him." He sucks air. A spastic shudder rocks through him. "I can't—I can't do anything f-for him!"

Bob feels a hand as strong as a vise tighten on the nape of his neck and a portion of his army fatigue jacket. The hand jerks him to his feet so violently, he's practically yanked out of his boots.

"The doc and Alice are gone!" Bruce barks at him, their faces so close now, a fine mist of spittle sprays Bob as Bruce tightens his grip on the back of Bob's neck. "If you don't do anything, he's go-ing to FUCKING DIE!!" Bruce shakes the man. "DO YOU WANT HIM TO *DIE*?!"

Sagging in Bruce's grasp, Bob lets out a moan: "I—I—I don't—no."

"THEN FUCKING DO SOMETHING!!"

With a woozy nod, Bob turns back to the broken body on the floor. He feels the vise grip on his neck loosen. He crouches down and sees only the Governor now.

Bob sees all the blood running down the nude torso, forming sticky, maplike stains already drying and darkening in the dim light of the living room. He looks at the scorched stump of a right arm, and then surveys the breached eye socket all welled up with blood, the eyeball, as shiny and gelatinous as a soft-boiled egg, dangling off the side of the man's face on tendrils of tissue. He makes note of the swamp of rich arterial blood gathered down around the man's privates. And finally Bob notices the shallow, labored breathing—the man's chest barely rising and falling.

Something snaps inside Bob Stookey—sobering him with the speed and intensity of smelling salts. Maybe it's the old war foot-ing coming back. There's no time for hesitation on the battle-field—no room for repulsion or fear or paralysis—one just has to move. Fast. Imperfectly. Just move. Triage is everything. Stop the bleeding first, keep the air passages clear, maintain a pulse, and then figure out how to move the victim. But more than that, Bob seizes up right then with a wave of emotion.

He never had kids, but the surge of empathy he suddenly feels for this man recalls the adrenaline that flows through a parent at the scene of a car wreck, the ability to lift a thousand pounds of Detroit steel off a child pinned beneath the wreckage. This man cared about Bob. The Governor treated Bob with kindness, even tenderness—always making a point to check in with Bob, make sure Bob had enough food and water and blankets and a place to stay. The revelation steadies Bob, girds him, clears his vision and focuses his thoughts. His heart stops racing, and he reaches down to depress a fingertip against the Governor's blood-soaked jugular. The pulse is so weak it could be mistaken for a fluttering pupa inside a fleshy cocoon.

Bob's voice comes out of him in a low, steady, authoritative tone. "I'm going to need clean bandages, tape—and some peroxide." Nobody sees Bob's face changing. He wipes strands of his greasy, pomaded hair back over his pate. His eyes narrow, nested in deep crow's-feet and wrinkles. His brow furrows with the intensity of a master gambler getting ready to play his hand. "Then, we'll need to get him to the infirmary." At last he looks up at the other men, his voice taking on an even deeper gravity. "I'll do what I can."

TWO

Rumors bounce around town that day with the haphazard trajectory of a pinball game. While Bruce and Gabe keep the Governor's condition under wraps, the glaring absence of Woodbury's leadership causes much speculation and whispering. At first, the prevailing wisdom is that the Governor, Dr. Stevens, Martinez, and Alice all stole away before dawn the previous day on an emergency mission—the purpose of which remains shrouded in mystery. The men on the wall each have a different version. One kid swears he saw Martinez taking a group of unidentified helpers out in a cargo truck on a predawn supply run. But this story loses much of its credence by midmorning when all the vehicles are accounted for. Another guard—the young wannabe gangbanger named Curtis, the kid whom Martinez unexpectedly relieved at the end of the east alley the previous night—claims that Martinez lit out on foot by himself. This rumor also loses steam when most of those left behind realize that the doctor and Alice are also missing, along with the Governor himself, as well as the wounded stranger who was being treated in the infirmary. The stoic man stationed outside the Governor's apartment building with the assault rifle has nothing to say on the matter and won't let anyone pass, nor will the guard at the top of the staircase leading down to the infirmary— both situations doing nothing to quell the rumor mill.

By late afternoon, Austin pieces together the real story. He's been hearing rumblings that an escape has occurred—most likely the strangers he saw with the Governor a week and a half ago—and it all makes a lot more sense when he runs into Marianne Dolan, the matronly woman whose boy has been spiking a fever for twenty-four hours now. The woman tells Austin how she saw Stevens very early that morning, before dawn, hurrying across town with his doctor's bag. She can't remember for sure if he was with a group of people. She has a vague memory of seeing a cluster of folks waiting for him under an awning at the end of the street (near the corner where she stopped him), but she's not positive about that. She remembers asking the doctor if he could possibly take a look at her boy later, and he said sure, but he seemed jittery, like he was in a hurry. With a little prodding, Marianne does suddenly remember seeing Martinez and Alice a few minutes later, hurrying down the street with the doctor, and then she remembers wondering who the others were—the strangers accompanying them—the big guy, the kid, the black lady.

Austin thanks her and immediately goes over to Lilly's and tells her the whole story. Through process of elimination, they deduce that the whole group slipped out of town, unseen, at the end of the east alley—the gangbanger's story lines up with this conclusion—and they decide to go over there. Austin brings his binoculars. He also brings his gun for some reason. The tension in the little town is running high by this time. When they arrive at the makeshift wall at the end of the alley, there's nobody there. All the guards have congregated on the other side of town near the main barricades, to continue spreading gossip and smoke and pass around flasks of cheap booze.

"I can't believe they would go with them," Lilly says to Austin, holding a moth-eaten shawl around her shoulders to ward off the chill as she stands on top of the semitrailer blocking the alley from the outer world. A hastily constructed wall of hammered steel plates lines one side of the trailer. On the other side stretches the danger zone of dark side streets, rickety fire escapes, shadowy vestibules, and abandoned buildings given over to the walkers, all of it extending into the lonely outskirts of Woodbury. "Just bail on us without a word?" Lilly marvels softly, shaking her head, staring out at the opaque, black shadows of the pine barrens. The trees sway and flag menacingly in the breeze. "It doesn't make any sense."

Austin stands next to her in his denim jacket, his long hair loose and tossing in the wind. By this point, dusk is setting in, the wind has cooled, and intermittent gusts swirl trash across the alley behind them, only adding to the desolate feeling of the place. "If you think about it, the whole thing makes a crazy kind of sense," he says.

Lilly shivers and looks at him. "How do you mean?"

"Well, for one thing, Stevens hates the Governor's guts—right? I mean that's obvious."

Lilly gazes out at the wasted landscape draped in gathering shadows. "The doctor's a good man but he never understood the situation we're in."

"Really?" Austin sniffs. "I don't know." He thinks about it for a moment. "Didn't you guys try to take over last year? Stage a coup or whatever?"

Lilly looks at him. "That was a mistake." She looks out at the woods again. "We didn't see the . . . practical reasons for the things he does."

"The Governor?" Austin gives her a noncommittal glance, his hair blowing across his narrow face. "Seriously? You call the shit he does 'practical'?"

Lilly gives him another look. "This is our home now, Austin. It's secure. It's a place where we can raise our child."

Austin doesn't say anything. Neither of them notices the dark figure weaving out of the trees a hundred and fifty yards away.

"People have enough to eat," Lilly goes on. "They have resources. They have a future here in Woodbury. All because of the Governor."

Lilly shivers in the chill, and Austin takes off his denim jacket. He drapes it over her shoulders. Lilly gives him a glance.

At first she considers objecting, handing it back to him, but then she just smiles. She finds his constant mothering kind of adorable. Since learning that she's pregnant with his child, Austin Ballard has transformed. He has stopped talking about finding more weed to smoke and has stopped acting like a slacker and most importantly has stopped hitting on any available woman who crosses his path. He genuinely adores Lilly Caul, and he sincerely loves the whole concept of being a father, of raising a new generation as a hedge against the end of the world. He has—at least in Lilly's eyes—instantly grown up right in front of her.

While Lilly is thinking all this, the shambling figure approaches from the distance. It's a hundred yards away now, and coming into view. An adult male clad in a blood-spattered white coat, its dead face upturned and rotating like a satellite dish, it lumbers back and forth across the gravel road, making a winding path toward the barricade as though homing in on some olfactory beacon, some predatory scent drawing it toward the town. Neither Lilly nor Austin notices the figure yet, their thoughts consumed by the exodus of their friends.

"*Alice* I can understand," Austin says at last. "She would follow Doc Stevens into hell if he wanted her to. But Martinez is the one I can't figure out. He always seemed so . . . I don't know . . . *gung ho* or something."

Lilly shrugs. "Martinez is a tough nut to crack. He helped us last winter. I always thought he was kind of ambivalent about the whole thing." Lilly thinks about it some more. "I don't know if I ever trusted him completely. I guess it doesn't matter now."

"Yeah, but—" Austin falls silent. "Hold on a second." He sees the figure approaching. "Hold on." He reaches for the binoculars hanging around his neck. He peers through the lenses at the figure, now closing the distance to fifty yards or so.

"What is it?" Lilly sees the walker shuffling toward them but at first doesn't make much of it. The sighting of an errant corpse weaving out of the trees has become commonplace around here, and Austin has his Glock, so there's really nothing to worry about. "What's the matter?"

"Is that—?" Austin fiddles with the dial on his field glasses and takes a closer look. "It couldn't be. Holy shit, I think it *is*."

"What?" Lilly reaches for the binoculars. "Let me have a look."

Austin says nothing, just hands her the binoculars and stares at the approaching figure.

Lilly raises the binoculars to her eyes and focuses the lenses, and all at once she gets very still and lets out a soft, hissing exhalation of air: "Oh my God."

With awkward, lurching strides, the recently deceased man approaches the alley barricade as though he's a dog being drawn there by a subsonic whistle. Lilly and Austin hurriedly climb down the stepladder and then circle around the trailer to a spot where a narrow gap between the semi and the adjacent building is fenced off with rusty chain link and a crown of barbed wire. Lilly stares through the cyclone fence at the creature lumbering toward her.

At this close proximity—the walker is now about ten feet away—Lilly can just make out the tall, thin physique; the patrician nose; the thinning, sandy hair. The man's eyeglasses are missing, but the drab-white lab coat is unmistakable. Torn and gouged in tufts, soaked in blood now as black as crude oil, the coat hangs in shreds.

"Oh my God, no . . . no, no, no," Lilly utters in absolute despair.

The creature suddenly fixes its nickel-plated gaze on Lilly and Austin, and it lunges at them, arms reaching instinctively, fingers curling into claws, blackened lips peeling away from a mouth full of slimy-black teeth—a horrible breathy snarl vibrating out of its maw.

Lilly jerks back with a start when the thing that was once Dr. Stevens bangs into the fence.

"Jesus . . . Jesus Christ," Austin mutters, reaching for his Glock.

The chain link rattles as the former physician claws and bumps ineffectually against the barrier. His previously intelligent face is now reduced to a road map of livid veins and marble-white flesh, his neck and shoulders mangled to a bloody pulp as if they had passed through a garbage disposal. His eyes, which once perpetually gleamed with irony and sarcasm, are now an opaque white, refracting the twilight like geodes. His jaws gape as he tries to bite Lilly through the fence.

Lilly senses the muzzle of Austin's Glock rising up in her peripheral vision. "No, wait!" She waves Austin back and stares at the walker. "God . . . no. Just wait. Wait. I need to—we can't just—God *damn* it."

Austin's voice lowers an octave, goes cold and hoarse with revulsion. "They must have—"

"He must have turned back," Lilly interrupts. "Maybe he had second thoughts, decided to come back."

"Or maybe they killed him," Austin ventures. "Fucking evil dicks."

The creature in the lab coat hasn't taken its shoe-button eyes off Lilly as it gnashes its teeth and works its blackened lips around snapping teeth, as though trying to bite the air or perhaps to speak. It cocks its head for a moment as though recognizing something through the fence, something important in its prey, something like muscle memory. Lilly meets its gaze for a moment.

The strange tableau—walker and human only inches away from each other, staring into each other's eyes—doesn't last more than a moment. But in that horrible instant, Lilly feels the weight of the whole plague, the enormity of it, the terrible emptiness of the world's end pressing down on her. Here is a man who once ministered to the sick, advised all walks of life, cracked wise and slung witticisms—a man of integrity and humor and audacity and empathy for the weak. Here is the pinnacle of mankind—the highest-functioning member of the human race—stripped of everything that could be called human, diminished to a drooling, feral, neurological bundle of tics. The tears well up in Lilly's eyes without her even being aware of them—the only sign of her anguish the blurring of that livid face in front of her.

At last, Austin's strangled voice wrenches her out of this terrible reverie. "We gotta do it," he says. He has his silencer out now, and he's screwing it on the gun's barrel. "We owe it to Stevens, right?"

Lilly bows her head. She can't look at the thing anymore. "You're right."

"Stand back, Lilly."

"Wait."

Austin looks at her. "What is it?"

"Just . . . gimme a second, okay?"

"Sure."

Lilly stares at the ground, taking deep breaths, clenching her fists. Austin waits. The thing on the other side of the fence sputters and snarls. With a sudden jerk, Lilly spins toward Austin and grabs the gun.

She sticks the muzzle through an opening in the fence and shoots the walker point-blank in the head—the dry clap of the slide echoing off the sky—the single blast slamming through the top of Dr. Stevens's skull, taking off the back of his head.

The monster folds unceremoniously to the ground in a fountain of blood. Lilly lowers the gun and stares at the remains. A pool of black cerebrospinal fluid gathers under the body.

A moment of stillness passes, the thumping of Lilly's pulse the only sound in her ears now. Austin stands beside her, waiting.

At last she turns to him and says, "You think you could find a shovel?"

They bury the body inside the barricade, in the hard earth of a vacant lot along the fence. By the time they get the hole dug, which isn't easy, full darkness has set in, the stars coming out in profusion, a full moon rising. The air turns cold and clammy, the sweat on the back of Austin's neck chilling him to the bone. He climbs out of the trench and helps Lilly lower the doctor's remains into the grave.

Then Austin backs away and lets Lilly have her moment standing over the gravesite, gazing down at the body, before he fills in the crater.

"Dr. Stevens," she says so softly that Austin has to cock his head to hear her, "you were . . . a true character. In some ways you were the voice of reason. I didn't always agree with you, but I always respected you. This town will miss you desperately—not just because of the service you provided but because it won't be the same around here without you."

A pause follows, and Austin glances up, wondering if she's done.

"I would have been proud to have you deliver my baby," she says then, her voice breaking. She sniffs back the tears. "As it is . . . we have a lot of challenges ahead of us. I hope you're in a better place now. I hope we all will be someday. I hope this craziness ends soon. I'm sorry you didn't make it long enough to see that day. God bless you, Dr. Stevens . . . and may your soul rest in peace."

She lowers her head then, and Austin waits for Lilly's tears to pass before he starts filling in the hole.

The next morning, Lilly awakens early, her mind going in many directions all at once.

She lies in bed—the room just beginning to lighten in the predawn glow—Austin slumbering next to her. The two of them have been sleeping together since Lilly broke the news to Austin two days ago that she's carrying his baby. So far, in the wake of the revelation, they have been inseparable, and their rapport is easy and natural. For now, they're keeping the news to themselves, but Lilly is dying to tell others about it—maybe the Sterns, maybe Bob, perhaps even the Governor. She's riding a wave of euphoria and feels for the first time since she arrived in Woodbury that she has a fighting chance to be happy, to survive this insanity. Austin has a lot to do with that, but so does the Governor.

And therein lies the problem. She hasn't seen a trace of the missing leader for forty-eight hours, and she doesn't buy the rumors that the Governor went out on a scouting party to find the escapees. If Woodbury is under the threat of attack—which, Lilly worries, is a real possibility—then it seems to her that the Governor would be needed right here, fortifying the town, preparing to defend it. Where the hell is he? There are other rumors flying around, but she's not buying any of them. She needs to find out what the deal is herself; she needs to see the Governor with her own eyes.

She gently untangles herself from the blankets and climbs out of bed, careful not to waken Austin. He's been a sweetheart to her these last couple of days, and the sound of his low, deep breathing gives her a good feeling. He deserves a good night's rest—especially in the wake of recent events. But Lilly is as restless as a caged animal and has to find out what's going on with the Governor. She walks across the room feeling dizzy and nauseous.

She's had morning sickness from the get-go, but not just in the morning. That high, queasy feeling in the upper GI area has been coming in waves throughout the day—every day—sometimes taking her to the verge of throwing up, sometimes less so, but always churning in her gut like a fist. She has yet to vomit and wonders if that might bring her some relief. She's been belching regularly, and that eases the nausea somewhat but not much. Maybe anxiety plays a part in it—her fear for the future, for the town's safety in the wake of these escapes, for the mounting number of walkers in the area—but part of it, she is convinced, is the normal trials and travails of the first trimester. Like a lot of expecting women riding the roller coaster of hormones, a part of her is grateful for the queasiness—it means on some fundamental level that all systems are go.

Getting dressed as quietly as possible, she practices the deep breathing exercises she once saw on some TV girlie gabfest, a factoid buried in her far-flung media memory banks. In through the nose, out through the mouth, slow and deep and even. She pulls on her jeans, steps into her boots, and grabs her Ruger semiautomatic, which is loaded with a ten-round clip, and nestles it into the back of her belt.

For some reason, a fleeting memory of her father crosses her mind as she pulls on a cable-knit sweater and checks herself in a broken mirror sitting on top of boxes, canted against the plaster wall, reflecting a fractured slice of her narrow, freckled face. Had Everett Caul survived the initial surge of undead that swept across Metro Atlanta last year, the old man would be bursting at the seams with excitement right now. Had he not been brutally torn from the outer door of that rogue bus by a horde of biters, he would be pampering Lilly and saying things like, "A little gal in your condition shouldn't be shootin' firearms, missy." Everett Caul raised Lilly well after the death of his wife from breast cancer back when Lilly was only seven years old. The old man raised his daughter with a tender touch, and had always been proud of Lilly, but the prospects of Everett Caul becoming a grandfather—spoiling her child, teaching the kid how to make fishing lures and soap out of beef tallow—stops Lilly cold at that broken mirror in the predawn light of her bedroom.

She lowers her head and begins to softly weep at the loss of her dad, her lungs hitching with emotion, making strangled hissing noises in the silent room, her tears tracking down the front of her sweater. She can't remember crying like this—even when Josh got killed—and she gasps for air, holding her hand to the bridge of her nose. Her skull throbs. Maybe it's just the "condition" she's in, but she feels the sadness roiling within her like the waves of a storm-tossed sea.

"Enough of this shit," she scolds herself under her breath, biting off the sorrow and the grief.

She draws her gun. Racks the slide. Checks the safety and tucks it back in her belt.

Then she walks out.

The day dawns clear, the sky bright and high, as Lilly strides down Main Street, her hands in her pockets, making note of the general mood of the few Woodburians who cross her path. She sees Gus with an armful of fuel cans, awkwardly negotiating the loading dock steps behind the warehouse on Pecan Street. She sees the Sizemore girls playing tic-tac-throw on the pavement of an alley under the watchful gaze of their mother, Elizabeth, who cradles a shotgun. The vibe on Woodbury's streets is strangely calm and sanguine— apparently the rumor mill has quieted down for the time being— although Lilly detects an odd undertow of jitters threading through the people. She can sense its presence in furtive glances and the speed with which folks are crossing streets and carrying supplies through doors and passageways. It makes Lilly think of those old Westerns that used to play on Sunday afternoons on the Fox station in Atlanta. Invariably, at some point, some old grizzled cowboy would say, "It's quiet . . . maybe a little too quiet." With a shrug, Lilly shakes off the feeling and turns south at the corner of Main and Durand.

Her plan is to try the Governor's apartment first—the previous day she got nowhere with Earl, the tattooed biker guarding the entrance—and if that doesn't yield any information, then she'll try the infirmary. She's heard murmurings among the town gossip-mongers that the Governor sustained injuries during a struggle to prevent the strangers from escaping. But at this point, Lilly doesn't know what or whom to believe. All she knows is that the longer the town goes without a plan, without consensus, without information, the more vulnerable they'll become.

She sees the Governor's building in the distance—as well as the guard pacing across the entrance—and she starts to rehearse what she's going to say, when she notices a figure trundling down the street. The man lugs two enormous thirty-gallon containers of filtered water, and moves with the intense haste of somebody rushing to put out a fire. Squat, broad-shouldered, and bullish, he wears a tattered turtleneck, which is dark under the arms with sweat, and army fatigue pants tucked into his hobnail boots. His big crew-cut head has an awkward forward lean to it like the prow of a storm-rocked ship as he hauls the jugs toward the center of town—toward the racetrack.

"GABE!"

Lilly tries to keep her voice even as she calls out, tries not to appear too alarmed, but the shout comes out tinged with hysteria. She hasn't seen Gabe in forty-eight hours, not since the strangers escaped in such a shroud of mystery two days ago, and she has a feeling Gabe knows exactly what's going on. The big, burly man remains one of the Governor's closest lieutenants and confidantes—an attack dog that has completely sublimated its own personality in favor of serving the iron-fisted town tyrant.

"Huh?" Gabe looks up with a startled, vexed expression. He can hear footsteps but can't see who's approaching. He whirls around with the heavy weight dragging on his arms. "Ww-wha—?"

"Gabe, what's going on?" Lilly says breathlessly as she clamors up to him. She swallows back the jitters and stanches her racing pulse. Then she lowers her voice. "Where the hell is the Governor?"

"I can't talk right now," Gabe says, and pushes past her, hauling the water containers down the sidewalk.

"Wait!—Gabe!—Hold on a second." She chases after him, and clutches at his beefy arm. "Just tell me what's going on!"

Gabe pauses, glances over his shoulder to see if anybody else is within earshot. The street is deserted. Gabe keeps his voice low. "Nothing's going on, Lilly. Just mind your own fucking business."

"Gabe, c'mon." She shoots a glance over her shoulder, then looks back at him. "All I'm asking is . . . is he here? Is he in Woodbury?"

Gabe sets the containers down with a grunt. He runs fingers through his short-cropped, sandy hair, his scalp moist with perspiration. Right then Lilly notices something disconcerting about this barrel-chested bull of a man, something she has never seen before. His hands are shaking. He spits on the street. "Okay . . . look. Tell everybody . . . tell them . . ." He pauses, swallowing hard, looking down, shaking his head. "I don't know . . . tell them everything's okay, the Governor's okay, and there's nothing to worry about."

"If there's nothing to worry about, where the fuck *is* he, Gabe?"

He looks at her. "He's . . . here. He's . . . dealing with some shit right now."

"What shit?"

"Goddamnit—I told you to mind your fucking business!" Gabe catches himself, the gravelly boom of his voice echoing across the far warrens of stone alleyways and brick storefronts. He takes a deep breath and calms down. "Look, I gotta go. The Governor needs this water."

"Gabe, listen to me." Lilly steps in closer and gets in his face. "If you know what's going on, tell me . . . because the town is starting to come apart at the seams not knowing anything. People are making shit up. The guys at the wall are starting to not show up for their shifts." Something inside Lilly hardens then, like a block of ice. All her fear and doubt drains out of her, leaving behind a cold, calculating, ticking intellect. She holds Gabe's wide, shifting gray eyes in her gaze. "Look at me."

"Huh?"

"Look at me, Gabe."

He looks at her, his eyes narrowing with anger. "What the fuck is your problem, lady—you think you can talk to me like that?"

"I care about this town, Gabe." She stands her ground, nose to nose with this nervous, snorting bull. "Listen to what I'm telling you. I need this town to work. Do you understand? Now tell me what's going on. If there's nothing wrong, you got no reason to hide anything."

"Goddamnit, Lilly—"

"Talk to me, Gabe." She arc-welds her gaze into him. "If there's a problem, you need me on your side. I can help. Ask the Governor. I'm on his side. I need him on that wall. I need him keeping people sharp."

At last, the portly man in the turtleneck deflates. He looks at the ground. His voice comes out paper-thin, reedy and defeated, like a little boy admitting to being naughty. "If I show you what's going on . . . you gotta promise to keep it on the down-low."

Lilly just stares at him, wondering how bad it could be.

THREE

"Jesus *Christ*."

The words blurt out of her on a gasp, unbidden and involuntary, as she takes in the entirety of the tile-lined subterranean chamber all at once. Gabe stands behind her, in the doorway, still holding the water containers, frozen there as if held in suspended animation.

For a brief instant, all the information assaulting her senses floods Lilly's brain in one great heaving gulp. The most prominent thing registering with her—overriding every other initial impression—is the pungent mélange of suffering, the coppery tang of blood, the black stench of infection and bile, and the ubiquitous scent of ammonia. But underneath it all, providing an odd counterpoint, is the smell of burnt coffee, an ancient percolator in the corner brewing a pot of bitter Maxwell House. This incongruous odor—a good reason for it, she will soon learn—mingles with other smells of the infirmary in a strangely disturbing way. Lilly takes a step closer to the gurney resting in the center of the room under the big light.

"Is he—?" She can barely speak. She stares at the body lying in the blazing silver light. In its current state, highlighted in that harsh light, the body brings to mind world leaders lying in state, beloved dictators pickled in death and exhibited in glass sarcophagi for the viewing pleasure of endless queues of mourners. It takes several moments for Lilly to realize that the patient is still breathing—albeit shallow, feeble breathing—his lungs rising and falling slowly under the blanket pulled up to his nude, iodine-stained rib cage. His head lolls to one side on a yellowed pillow, his face almost completely obscured by blood-soaked bandages.

"Hello, Lilly-girl," a voice says from just behind her right flank, a blur of movement in her peripheral vision that interrupts her stupor. She turns and sees Bob Stookey standing beside her. He puts a hand on her shoulder. "It's good to see you."

Now Lilly stands paralyzed by another inconsistency—adding to the surreal sights and smells and sounds in that horrible tile room—another weird detail, which also strikes her as incomprehensible. Standing before her with a towel draped over his shoulder, his bloodstained lab coat buttoned at the collar like that of a competent barber, Bob has completely transformed. He holds a Styrofoam cup of coffee, his hands as steady as cornerstones. His greasy black hair is now combed neatly back off his weathered face, his eyes alert and clear and lucid. He is the picture of sobriety. "Bob, wh—what happened? Who did this?"

"Fucking bitch with the sword," Bruce Cooper's voice pipes in. From the corner of the room, the big man rises off a folding chair and comes over to the gurney. The man shoots a glare at Gabe. "What the fuck, Gabe? I thought we were supposed to keep this under wraps!"

"She ain't gonna tell anybody," Gabe mumbles, finally putting the water down. "Right, Lilly?"

Before Lilly can answer, Bruce throws a ballpoint pen at Gabe. The pen barely misses impaling itself in his eye, grazing off the top of his head. Bruce roars at him. "YOU STUPID FUCK!—WHOLE TOWN'S GONNA KNOW ABOUT IT NOW!!"

Gabe makes a move toward Bruce when Lilly steps in between them. "STOP IT!" She shoves them back, away from the gurney. "CALM THE FUCK DOWN!"

"Tell *him*!" Gabe stands nose to nose with Bruce, fists clenched and working. Bob hovers over the patient, feeling the Governor's pulse. In all the excitement, the man's head has lolled slightly, but that's about the only change. Gabe takes shallow breaths, glaring at Bruce. "*He's* the one gettin' his panties in a bunch!"

"Shut up!" Lilly pushes each man aside, staying in between them. "This is not the time to lose your shit. We gotta keep our fucking wits about us—now more than ever."

"That's exactly what I've been saying," Bruce grumbles, meeting Gabe's glare.

"Okay, let's take a deep breath. I'm not gonna tell anybody. Okay? Calm down."

She looks at both men, and Gabe looks down and says nothing. Bruce wipes his face, breathing hard, looking around the room as if the answer to their problems is hidden inside the walls.

"We gotta take this one step at a time." She looks at Gabe. "Just answer one question. What they're saying about Martinez . . . is it true?" Gabe doesn't respond. "Gabe? Did Martinez go with those assholes from the other camp?" She turns to Bruce. "Did he?"

Bruce looks down and lets out a pained sigh. He nods. "The motherfucker helped them escape."

"And we know this how?"

Bruce looks at her. "We got eyewitnesses, saw that cocksucker helping them over the wall at the end of the Durand Street alley."

"What eyewitnesses?"

Bruce shrugs. "The lady with the sick kid, what's-her-name, and also Curtis, the kid guarding the alley that night. Said Martinez relieved him, but the kid hung around and saw them going over . . . saw the black chick splitting off from the group. Bitch jumped the Governor minutes later."

"Where?"

"In the Governor's place—right in his fucking *home*—the fucking bitch bushwhacked him."

"Okay . . . let's just stick to the facts for a second." Lilly starts to nervously pace the room, every few moments throwing a glance at the patient. The Governor's face looks swollen and misshapen under his bandages, the gauze bulging where his left eye socket should be. "How do we know these douche bags didn't have a gun on Martinez the whole time?"

Bruce shoots a look at Gabe, who stares at Lilly skeptically and says, "I wouldn't bet on it, Lilly."

"Why?"

Gabe glares at her. "Well . . . let's see. How about the fact that Martinez is a lying son of a bitch with no loyalty to the Governor?"

"Why do you say that?"

Gabe snorts disdainfully, almost laughs. "Lemme think." He points to an oblong bruise spanning his Adam's apple. "For starters, he waylaid me outside the chick's holding cell, pretty near cracked my skull open." He glares at Lilly. "On top of that, wasn't he part of your little hole-in-the-wall gang last year when you tried to take out the Governor?"

Lilly meets his gaze, doesn't even flinch, just stares at him and says, "Things change—we made some bad choices." She looks at Bruce, then back at Gabe. "I don't know about Martinez but I'm with the Governor a hundred percent now—a *thousand* percent."

Neither man says anything. Both just stare at the floor like children in detention.

Lilly gazes at the patient. "I guess it comes as no surprise that Stevens and Alice went along with the strangers; there was never any love lost there."

Gabe lets out another snort. "That's a fucking understatement."

Lilly paces, thinking. "I think that's what bothers me the most."

Bruce speaks up: "Whaddaya mean? Because we ain't gotta doc now?"

Lilly looks at him. "No. That's not what I'm talking about." She gestures toward Bob. "I think we're covered in that department." She glances back at Bruce. "What I'm worried about is the fact that these assholes have people from our town with them."

Bruce and Gabe exchange another heated glance. Gabe looks at Lilly. "So what?"

"So *what*?" She walks over to the gurney and looks down at the Governor. The man clings to life—one lidded eye visible through an opening in the head dressing, the eyeball shifting slightly under the lid. Is he dreaming? Is he brain-damaged? Is he ever going to fight his way out of this vegetative state? Lilly stares at the slow rise and fall of the man's chest and thinks some more. "Martinez, Alice, and the doctor know this town better than anyone," she murmurs, not taking her gaze off the patient. "They know the weak spots; they know where we're vulnerable."

This sends a paralyzing silence through the reeking tile chamber. Everybody stares at Lilly as though waiting for her to provide an answer. She stares at the Governor's ravaged body for another moment.

At last she turns to Bob and says with a newfound air of authority, "Bob, gimme a prognosis here."

The first twenty-four hours had been anybody's guess. Once they brought the Governor's decimated body back to the infirmary, the main issue was keeping his heart beating, followed closely by stanching the blood loss. Despite the fact that he had a crudely cauterized stump halfway up his right arm at the point of dismemberment—slowing the bleeding from the amputation, which was mercifully clean thanks to the sharpness of the katana sword—there had been massive bleeding at other wound sites, especially the detached penis. Bob had done a lot of hasty battlefield stitching with the storehouse of dissolving catgut Doc Stevens kept on the shelf—reattaching the severed penis at one point with shaking hands. When he ran out of sutures, he used a needle and thread procured from the general store on Main Street.

The old lessons from the war zone came back to him in waves. He remembered the four stages of hypovolemic shock—battlefield medics call it the "tennis match," since the stages of blood loss mimic tennis scores—15 percent loss is minor; 15 to 30 percent is serious, resulting in plummeting blood pressure and tachycardia; 30 to 40 percent is life-threatening, bringing on cardiac arrest; and 40 percent plus is deadly.

For hours, the Governor wavered in between stage two and three, and Bob had to resort to CPR twice to keep the man's heart beating. Luckily, Stevens kept enough electrolytes in the storeroom to maintain the IV drip, and Bob even found half a dozen units of whole blood. He couldn't figure out how to type the Governor— that was beyond Bob's skill set—but he did know enough to get plasma into the man as soon as possible. The transfusions weren't rejected, and after six hours the Governor had stabilized some-what. Bob even found an old oxygen tank that was half-full, and administered it in dribs and drabs, until the Governor seemed to be holding his own. His breathing steadied and his sinus rhythm returned to normal, he settled into a semi-comatose state.

Later, in the fashion of an insurance investigator piecing to-gether the chronology of a fatal accident, Bob Stookey had drawn crude sketches in a spiral-bound notebook of the instruments of torture left in the Governor's living room (as well as the assumed points of entry). The puncture wound from the drill was especially problematic, in spite of the fact that it had apparently not severed any major arteries. It had come within two centimeters of a branch-ing vein of the carotid, and Bob had worked for nearly an hour cleaning out the site. He ran out of gauze, ran out of tape, ran out of hydrogen peroxide, ran out of Betadine, and ran out of glucose. Another issue was internal bleeding—the treatment of which was, again, just out of Bob's reach—but by the second day, Bob was con-vinced that the assault on the Governor's rectum, as well as the profusion of blunt-instrument trauma to 75 percent of his body, had not resulted in any internal hemorrhaging.

Once the man was stabilized, Bob turned his attention to infec-tion. He knew from front-line experience that infection is the silent partner in most battlefield fatalities—the number one tool of the grim reaper once a soldier is out of immediate danger—so he ri-fled through the supplies and ransacked the infirmary cupboards looking for antibiotics. He worried that the Governor was a perfect candidate for sepsis—considering all the rusty, filthy, oxidized tools used on him—so Bob used up every last cc of Moxifloxacin in the IV and administered hypodermically the last drops of Netro-mycin left in Woodbury. By the morning of the third day, the wounds had begun to close over and heal.

"I wouldn't say he's out of the woods yet," Bob now reports, summing up the whole situation as he walks across the infirmary to the trash bin, into which he tosses a wad of used cotton swabs. It's taken him nearly ten minutes to recap the whole timeline, and now he goes over to the coffee urn and pours himself another few fingers of the muddy stuff. "Put it this way, he's on the edge of the woods, holding steady." He turns to Lilly and holds up the coffee cup. "You want a cup o' joe?"

Lilly shrugs. "Sure . . . why not?" She turns to Bruce and Gabe, who stand fidgeting by the door. "I'm not telling you guys what to do . . . but if it were me, I would go check the wall on the north end."

"What are you, the Queen of Sheba now?" Bruce grumbles.

"With Martinez gone and the Governor out of commission, those guys have been deserting their posts left and right. We can't afford to be careless right now."

Bruce and Gabe look at each other, each one gauging the other's reaction to being bossed around by some chick from the suburbs. "She's got a point," Gabe says.

"Jesus Christ . . . *whatever*," Bruce grouses under his breath, then turns and storms out the door.

Gabe follows him out.

Bob comes over to Lilly and hands her a paper cup of coffee. Lilly notices again how Bob's hands have stopped shaking. She takes a sip. "Holy crap, this is bad," she says with a slight cringe.

"It's wet and it's got caffeine in it," Bob comments as he turns back to his patient. Pulling the spiral-bound notebook from his back pocket, he nudges a chair next to the gurney, sits down, and makes a few notes. "We're at a critical stage now," he murmurs while he writes. "Got to keep track of how much Vicodin I've given him—not sure if all the drugs have ganged up on him, maybe in-duced the coma he's in."

Lilly edges her chair closer to the gurney and sits next to the foot of the bed. She can smell the cloying odors of antiseptic and iodine. She stares at the Governor's untrimmed toenails and pale bare feet—as limp and pallid as dead fish—poking out from under the sheet.

For a moment, Lilly is stricken with a strange mixture of impressions—crucifixion and sacrificial lambs—which jolts through her with the strength of a lightning bolt. The unexpected emotion tightens her gut and makes her turn away. What kind of person could do this to another person? Who is this lady? Where the hell did she come from? And the deeper concerns banging around the back of Lilly's mind: If this woman is capable of doing *this* to a man as dangerous as the Governor, then what is her group capable of doing to Woodbury?

"The key now is keeping infection away from the door," Bob is saying, gently palpating the Governor's neck with a fingertip, keeping track of the man's pulse.

"Bob, tell me the truth," Lilly says, looking into the older man's eyes. Bob's face furrows with bemusement as he meets Lilly's stare. He puts down his notebook. She speaks softly. "Do you think he's gonna make it?"

Bob takes in a deep, thoughtful breath, and then exhales with a sigh. "He's a tough cuss, this one." He looks at the Governor's shrouded face. "If anybody can pull through something like this, *he* can."

Lilly notices Bob's gnarled left hand is resting gently on the Governor's shoulder. The unexpected tenderness takes her aback for a moment. She wonders if Bob Stookey has finally found his raison d'être—a channel for all his grief and unrequited love. She wonders if this whole crisis has given Bob a way to stave off the pain of losing Megan. She wonders if this is what Bob always needed—a surrogate son, someone who needed him. The Governor has always been kind to Bob—Lilly noticed that almost from day one—and now she sees the logical extension of that kindness.

Bob has never looked more alive, more at peace, more comfortable in his own skin.

"How long, though?" Lilly says at last. "How long do you think he's gonna be laid up?"

Bob shakes his head with a sigh. "There's no telling how long. Even if I was some highfalutin' trauma surgeon, I wouldn't be able to give you a timetable."

Lilly sighs. "We're in some deep shit here, Bob. We need fucking leadership. More than ever. We could be attacked at any minute." She swallows hard, feeling a twinge of nausea ripple up her gorge. *Not now, goddamnit, not now,* she thinks. "With the Governor out of action, we are *screwed*. We need to batten down the fucking hatches."

Bob shrugs. "All I can do is stay with him, keep watch, and hope for the best."

Lilly chews her lip. "What do you think went down between the two of them?"

"Who?"

"The Governor and that girl."

Another shrug from Bob. "I don't know anything about that." He thinks about it for a moment. "It doesn't matter. Whoever did this to him was a nutcase—an animal—and they ought to be put down like a goddamn rabid dog."

Lilly shakes her head. "I know he had her locked up; he was probably questioning her. Did Bruce or Gabe say anything about it?"

"I didn't ask, and I don't *want* to know." Bob rubs his eyes. "All I want is to get him out of these weeds, get him back on his feet . . . no matter how long it takes."

Lilly lets out another sigh. "I don't know what we're gonna do without him, Bob. We need somebody keeping these people on their toes."

Bob thinks about it some more, and then gives her a wry little smile. "I think you might have already found that person."

She looks at him.

All at once she realizes what he's getting at and the pressure lands on her like a giant anvil, nearly taking her breath away. . . . *No fucking way, not in a million fucking years is it going to be me.*

That night, Lilly organizes an emergency meeting in the courthouse, in the community room in the rear, the doors locked down and all the lights off except for a pair of kerosene lanterns flickering on the conference table. She asks each person in attendance to keep the meeting a secret. The five of them arrive after midnight, after the town has quieted down, and they each take a seat at the table, with Lilly sitting at the head, near the broken-down metal stand bearing the faded, threadbare Georgia state flag.

For Lilly, the room teems with ghosts. Phantoms from her past ooze from the crumbling plaster walls, from the litter-strewn floor, from the overturned folding chairs, from the bullet holes in the front wall, and from the high windows, which are all cracked and boarded up now. A framed portrait of Nathan Deal, the long-forgotten eighty-second governor of Georgia, dangles on the lintel, the glass shattered and stained with rusty blood droplets in the dancing firelight—a fitting testament to the apocalypse.

The memories wash over Lilly that night. She remembers meeting Philip Blake in this room over a year and a half ago—when she first arrived in Woodbury with Josh, Megan, Bob, and Scott the stoner—and Lilly will never forget the swagger, the creepy impression the Governor initially gave off. Little did she know he would become her lifeline one day, he would be her anchor in this sea of chaos.

"Christ on a *cracker,*" Barbara Stern utters after hearing the whole story of the elaborate escape and the condition of the Governor. She sits next to her husband on one side of the table, wringing her slender hands. The gloomy light flickers off her deeply lined face and tendrils of iron-gray hair. "As if we don't have enough on our plates in this godforsaken place—we have to deal with *this* now?"

"I think the first thing we have to do is put out a cover story," Lilly says. She wears an Atlanta Braves cap with her hair in a ponytail poking through the plastic band in back—all business now. The crisis has driven her morning sickness away.

Bruce, sitting at the opposite end of the table, leaning back skeptically in his chair, his lean, cabled arms crossed against his chest, gives her a frown. "A what?"

She looks at him. "A cover story, some bullshit explanation that won't get everybody all excited and stressed out." She looks around the table. "We should keep it simple, make sure all our stories match up."

"Lilly . . . um," Austin speaks up from the chair to her immediate left. He has his hands clasped as if praying, and he holds a pained look on his face. "You do realize, people are gonna find out sooner or later. I mean . . . this is a really small town."

Lilly lets out a nervous sigh. "Okay . . . well . . . if they find out, let's make sure it stays a rumor. People have been saying all kinds of crazy shit."

David Stern pipes in. "Honey, just out of curiosity, what is it you're worried about happening if we just tell everybody the truth?"

Lilly exhales, pushes herself away from the head of the table, and starts pacing. "Look. We have to keep this town buttoned up tight. We can't have people panicking right now. We really have no idea who these strangers are, or what they have in mind." She clenches her fists. "You want to see what they're capable of, go to the infirmary and take a look at the Governor. These people are nuts, they're dangerous as hell. We have to up our defenses. If we're gonna err, we're gonna err on the side of being *too* careful."

Gabe speaks up from over by the windows. "Then I say we go after them." Leaning against the boarded, arched windowpane, his hands in his pockets, he glowers at Lilly. "Best defense is a strong offense."

"Fucking-A," Bruce says with a nod, leaning back against the defunct Coke machine.

"No!" Lilly stands her ground near the flag, her hazel eyes blazing with righteous fervor, her delicate chin jutting defiantly. "Not without the Governor. We don't make any major moves while he's out." Now she looks at every person in the room, one at a time, her voice going low and steady. "We stick to a cover story until he's on his feet again. Bob thinks it's possible he could come out of it any day." She looks at Gabe. "You understand what I'm saying? Until then, we zip this place up as tight as a drum."

Gabe takes a deep breath and lets out an exasperated sigh. "Okay, missy . . . we do it your way."

Lilly looks at Bruce. "You okay with this?"

He shakes his head, rolling his eyes. "Whatever you say, girlfriend. You got the wheel. You're on a roll."

"Okay, good." She looks back at Gabe. "Why don't we tell a couple of Martinez's guys to get lost for a few days, and then we'll tell everybody the Governor's out on a search party with them. Can you handle that?"

Gabe shrugs. "I guess so . . . yeah."

"In the meantime, we keep a guard on the infirmary at all times." Lilly looks at the others. "So that's our cover story. We're gonna need everybody in this room to step up. Bruce, you handle the wall. Keep shifts going all the time, and make sure we got plenty of ammo for the machine guns. Make another run to the Guard station if you have to." She looks at the Sterns. "David and Barbara, you two spread the word, keep your ears open. That group that has coffee in the square every morning, hang out with them. Keep tabs on what they're saying. Austin . . . you and I will take regular walks around the barricade. We'll make sure everything's secure. This is critical, people. With the Governor on his back, we are totally vulnerable. We have to remember—"

A noise outside the boarded windows cuts her off. All heads snap toward the sound of yelling, glass breaking, wood splitting apart.

"Oh shit," Lilly utters, frozen at the front of the room with her fists clenched.

Barbara Stern springs to her feet, her eyes suddenly wide with terror. "Maybe it's just a fight, somebody drunk or pissed off or something."

"I don't think so," David Stern murmurs, standing up and reaching around for the pistol wedged into the back of his belt. He draws his gun.

Austin jumps out of his chair and darts across the room to where Lilly stands staring. "Let's let Gabe and Bruce check it out first."

Across the room, Bruce is already on his feet, pulling the .45 from its holster, snapping off the safety, and shooting a look at Gabe. "You got the other MIG?"

Gabe has already whirled toward the far corner of the room, where two assault rifles are leaning against the wall. He grabs one, and then the other, and then turns to Bruce and tosses one of the rifles as he yells, "C'mon!—Let's go!—Before all hell breaks loose!"

Bruce catches the weapon, chambers a round, and follows Gabe out the door, down the hall, and toward the exit.

The others stand frozen in the community room, looking at each other and listening to the pandemonium rising out on the street.

FOUR

In the darkness, an empty bottle of Jack rolls across the street half
a block north of the courthouse, and Gabe kicks it aside as he barrels toward the southwest corner of town, Bruce right on his heels.
In the night winds, Gabe can see the intermittent muzzle flashes
behind the grove of trees along the town square, sparks as bright
as arc welders bouncing off the sky, the cool night air alive with
screams. One of the guards is already down on the ground by the
curb, his drinking buddies scattering now, their silhouettes receding into the distance. Three walkers have piled up on the
fallen guard, tearing into him, the blood tide spreading in all directions as they feed, burrowing down into flesh, ripping strings
of tendons and cartilage in the flickering shadows. Gabe gets to
within twenty yards of the feeding orgy and snaps the selector
lever on the rifle. His barrel comes up as he charges in and pulls
the trigger.

Hellfire blazes out of the MIG, strafing the top halves of the biters, punching holes through cranial bones in fountains of tissue
and bursts of blood mist. The walkers fold. Bruce roars past Gabe
with his own rifle up and braced on his big shoulder, his booming
voice coming out in one spontaneous cry: "GET THAT FUCKING
WALL BACK UP NOW!!"

Gabe glances back up and sees what Bruce is shouting about in
the darkness twenty-five yards away: A weak spot in the corner of

the barricade—a conglomeration of drywall panels, sheet metal, and roofing nails—has collapsed under the weight of a dozen or more walkers pushing in from the adjacent woods. The men must have been shirking their watch, fucking around, not paying attention, drinking or some such shit. Now one of the young guards on a gun turret frantically sweeps his arc lamp down on the scene—the silver beam crisscrossing the fogbound street—painting luminous halos around the silhouettes of twenty-plus biters staggering over fallen timbers.

Bruce unleashes a barrage of armor-piercing rounds at the onslaught.

He gets most of them—the casings flinging, one by one, up into the air—a row of reanimated corpses doing involuntary jigs in the swirling spray of fluids, ragged bodies collapsing in a synchronized line dance of death. But Bruce doesn't notice Gabe fanning out to the right, going after an errant biter who is dragging toward an alley. If the dead infiltrate the shadowy nooks and crannies of the town before they are all dispatched, there will be hell to pay. In all the commotion—the guards returning with heavy artillery, the shouts, the sweeping beams of arc light, the two machine-gun placements starting to spit fire—Gabe gets separated.

He follows a biter into a dark alley and immediately loses track of the thing.

"FUCK-FUCK! FUCK!—FUCK!!" Gabe hisses loudly, spinning around, scanning the darkness, his rifle raised and ready, the shadows engulfing him. He can hardly see his hand in front of his face. He has two extra magazines in sheaths on his belt, a Glock tucked against his left pant leg, and a Randall knife thrust down the inside of his right boot. He's loaded for bear, but right now he can't see shit. He smells the thing—that rancid meat and toe-cheese odor—infecting the dark. He hears a crunch and jerks the muzzle toward the sound.

Nothing.

He moves deeper into the alley, the sounds of pandemonium out on the street fading in his ringing ears. His heart bangs in his chest. His mouth goes dry. He swings the gun's barrel to the right, blinks away the sweat dripping in his eyes, and then swings the muzzle to the left. Where the fuck did that shit-bird go? He plunges deeper into the passageway. The darkness thickens.

A sudden noise to his immediate right straightens his spine— the clatter of a tin can rolling across pavement—and he pulls the trigger. Half a dozen high-velocity slugs trace through the dark like Roman candles, ricocheting off the adjacent brick in a necklace of dust puffs.

Gabe stops and listens, the blasts echoing in his ears. Nothing moves. Nothing makes a sound. Maybe he has the wrong alley. He could have sworn the thing lumbered into this one, but the darkness works on Gabe now, steals his confidence, sends tremors of panic down his bones.

What the fuck?

He approaches the end of the alley, a dead end crowded with garbage Dumpsters and strewn with trash. He reaches for his Zippo with his free hand, his other hand propping the rifle on his ample hip. He can hear the low putter of a generator nearby—probably inside the wall—as he pulls the lighter out and thumbs the little flywheel, sparking a minuscule yellow flame.

The flickering cone of light illuminates a huge figure with milk-glass eyes in a tattered burial coat standing three feet away.

Gabe lets out a yelp and drops the lighter, jerking back and fumbling for the trigger as the biter lunges at him, chewing at the air. Gabe loses his balance. He falls on his ass hard, hitting the pavement with a grunt. The biter pounces—this one hungry and twitchy and full of fight—and Gabe flails impotently at the thing with the short barrel of the rifle, unable to get a good shot.

The gun discharges once, the muzzle flash capturing a snapshot of the monster going for Gabe's throat with green, mossy incisors. Gabe manages to dodge the snapping teeth but loses his grip on the gun in the process, the MIG clattering to the pavement beside him. He squirms and writhes and lets out a throttled cry of rage and finally gets his hand around the grip of the Randall knife in his boot.

With one violent jerk he thrusts the blade up at the biter's head.

At first the knife merely lands a glancing blow to the monster's jaw, ripping open a flap of mortified flesh. Gabe's eyes have adjusted to the dark enough now to see shapes—wet, fleshy blurs— and he slashes madly at the top of the creature until the knife impales the monster through the left nostril. The point penetrates the nasal cavity and the rotten skull fissures down the middle with the adrenaline-fueled force of Gabe's stabbing blow.

The biter gushes fluids all over him as the cranium splits in half.

Gabe gasps and rolls away, the dead thing deflating and going still in a puddle of its own fluids, which spread on the paving stones like black oil. Gabe manages to roll toward his rifle. But before he can get to the gun—his heart racing now, his adrenaline sparking in his eyes like sunspots—he senses a change in the alley behind him. Movement as black as bat wings floods his peripheral vision as the noise of inhuman growling—a chorus of guttural, rusty gears grinding—rumbles slowly toward him. He smells the telltale stench of rancid proteins and black rot flooding the alley. Dizziness courses over him as he rises up on shaky legs and slowly turns. His eyes suddenly dilate—an involuntary shudder traveling down his spine—as he takes in the horror.

At least ten biters—maybe more—shuffle toward him with implacable dead stares—an entire pack blotting out any hope of escape, an insatiable regiment of monsters moving as one, closing in on him, silhouetted like deadly marionettes by the light spilling across the mouth of the alley behind them. Gabe lets out another garbled, defiant scream, and darts toward his gun.

It's too late. Before he can scoop the weapon up, the lead walker goes for his beefy shoulder. He kicks at its midsection with his jackboot, reaching for his Glock, when another monster moves in from his other flank, clawing at his neck. Gabe puts his head down and raises the pistol and tries to steamroll his way through the center of the pack—firing wildly—the muzzle barking and flashing with the surreal, intermittent flicker of a nickelodeon.

There's too many of them. Dead arms reach for him before he clears the jumble, cold fingers curled into grappling hooks, latching onto him, driving him to the pavement. He lands on the stones, wrenching his back, gasping for breath, his clip already empty, the air knocked out of his lungs. He tries to roll away, but the creatures descend on him—a pack of wolves going for his jugular—and he ends up on his back, wedged against the wall, trapped, staring at the inscrutable starry night sky looking down at him with impassive silence. He can't breathe. He can't move. The shock sets in, seizing up his stocky limbs, and he realizes with an odd measure of chagrin that this is it. This is all she wrote. Fuck. The monsters converge on him. They hover over him, their putrid maws dripping the drool of bloodlust, their eyes as shiny as Buffalo nickels. Everything slows down, as if Gabe is dreaming, as they close in for the feeding. The end . . . the end . . .

He always wondered if the end would be like they say it is in the movies—your life passing before you, or some bullshit woowoo thing like that—but it isn't. Gabriel Harris learns in that horrible moment before the first set of rotten teeth clamp down on him that the end doesn't come in gossamer wings and angelic visions. It comes in a loud pop—like a balloon exploding—and a final image steeped in wish fulfillment. He sees the closest walker whiplash suddenly in a gruesome eruption of tissue and blood, its head coming apart at the seams and raining blood on him in a slow-motion ritual baptism. He stares as the popping sounds continue—the dry, muffled snapping noises recalling a string of wet firecrackers—and more heads erupt.

The monsters collapse around him in a gruesome sequential massacre.

He comes back to his senses in time to see his savior out of the corner of his eye. She stands silhouetted in the center of the alley—thirty feet away—a matching .22 caliber Ruger rimfire pistol blazing in each hand, the muzzles silenced by noise suppressors. The last biter goes down, and the dry clapping noises cease as quickly as they started. The woman with the guns lets up on the triggers. Without any emotion or ceremony, she thumbs the magazine release on one gun, then the other, the empty mags dropping to the pavement with a clatter. The guns lower, dangling at her side now, as she scans the scene with the casual authority of a surveyor taking the measure of a building site.

Gabe tries to sit up, but his back complains, the nerves pinched, his sacrum sprained. "Holy fucking shit," he mutters, kicking away a wet corpse that had fallen on his legs. He rises to a sitting position and cringes at the pain.

Lilly walks up to him. "You okay? Did you get nipped? Did they break the skin?"

Gabe takes in a series of deep breaths, glancing around the alley at the carnage. The dozen or so biters now lie in contorted bundles of morbid flesh across the width of the alley, their heads blossoming with the red jelly of breached brain matter, the paving stones around them running red with their diseased blood. "No . . . I'm . . . no," Gabe stammers, trying to get his bearings. "I'm good."

At the mouth of the alley, an arc light sweeps across the gap and penetrates the darkness. Lilly kneels by Gabe, and she shoves her pistols down the back of her jeans. The light puts a silver halo around her head, highlighting wisps of her chestnut-brown hair. "Lemme give you a hand," she says and helps him to his feet.

Gabe groans slightly as he levers his bullish body to its full height. "Where's my gun?"

"We'll get it," she says.

Gabe stretches his sore neck. "That was about as close as I ever want to come."

"I hear ya." She glances over her shoulder. The sounds of voices raised over the din of gunfire begin to fade. Lilly lets out a breath.

"There's no excuse for this," she says. "We need all hands on deck from now on."

"Copy that," Gabe says.

"C'mon, let's get you checked out and clean up this fucking mess."

She starts toward the mouth of the alley when he grabs her and gently stops her.

"Lilly, wait," he says, and licks his lips. He's not good with words, but he needs to say something to her. He looks into her eyes. "Thanks for . . . you know . . . I'm just saying . . . I appreciate it."

She shrugs and gives him a smirk. "I need you in one piece."

He starts to say something else when he notices Lilly suddenly flinching, doubling over slightly. She holds her tummy.

"You okay?"

"Yeah . . . just a little cramp." She breathes through her mouth, blowing breaths over her lips for a moment. "Girl stuff. Don't worry about it." The pain passes. "C'mon . . . let's go kick some ass."

She turns and walks away, stepping over the corpses of the dead.

That night, Lilly and her inner circle stay up late, working behind the scenes to shore up the town's defenses. Bruce marshals every last able-bodied man on Martinez's crew to reinforce the barricades. They repair the north wall, strengthening the ramparts with extra sheet metal and timbers, and they move more trailers across the weak spots. They keep a close watch on the surrounding wetlands.

All the noise and confusion of the walker attack has stirred more of the dead out of the adjacent woods. Gabe supervises a rotating shift of gunners positioned at the .50 caliber perches off each corner of the wall. Well into the wee hours, the armor-piercing rounds crackle and flare at regular intervals, picking off stragglers shambling out of the trees in groups of two or three, and sometimes as many as nine or ten clumped together in ragged phalanxes. Nobody really notices the fact that the behavior of the dead is changing, their number growing, their movements becoming agitated like schools of fish reacting to vibrations in a vast fishbowl. Nobody pays much attention to the growing threat of herds forming. Everybody is too busy worrying about an assault from the living.

Second-guessing the intentions of these violent strangers becomes an almost obsessive-compulsive activity for Lilly and her comrades that night. They talk about it under their breaths as they work on the wall, they discuss it in secret in dark back rooms, they agonize over it silently to themselves as they perform their individual tasks—taking inventory of their arsenal of firearms and ammunition, making plans for another run to the National Guard station, formulating countermeasures in the event of a raid, laying traps, constructing escape routes, and generally preparing for the worst. Lilly believes they could be attacked at any moment. Since becoming pregnant, she has been vacillating between debilitating fatigue and manic bursts of energy, but now she has little time for food, rest, even a break—despite Austin's entreaties to take it easy for the sake of the baby. Maybe it's the rush of hormones from the early stages of her first trimester. Senses are heightened during this phase, blood flow increases, brain activity sharpens. Lilly channels this surge of energy into a whirlwind of activity—Austin has to pound Red Bull and PowerBars just to keep up with her, following her around like some harried government attaché—and she rises to the occasion with relentless attention to detail.

Nobody says it aloud, but Lilly has almost imperceptibly slipped into the role of surrogate leader. Austin fears that it's too much for a woman in her condition to be taking on such responsibility, but for Lilly it cuts the other way—she's taking all these risks *because* she's pregnant, not just in spite of it. She's not only fighting for her own life—not to mention the future of the town—but she's also fighting for the life of her unborn child. She will do what has to be done until the Governor is back in action. On a deeper level, she's learning what Woodbury means to her. She almost feels as though she understands the Governor on a more fundamental level now. She would kill for this town.

With the dawning of the next morning, Austin finally talks her into having something to eat—he makes her ramen noodles on the Sterno pot—and then convinces her she should get off her feet for a few hours. Gabe offers to take over supervisory duties while she rests, and the town goes about its business of surviving another day.

The rumor mill quiets down—for the time being, at least—thanks to Barbara and David Stern, who assure the townspeople that the Governor is safe, and sending regular dispatches from the hinterlands. No, he hasn't found the escapees yet. And no, there's no immediate danger. And yes, everybody should just stay calm and tend to their families and not worry and take comfort in knowing the town is safe and in good hands and blah-blah-blah.

Of course, during this strange limbo—which continues for days—nobody suspects what's in store for Woodbury—least of all Lilly. Despite her relentless attention to stepping up their defenses and planning for every imaginable contingency, she would never dream in her wildest nightmares what is on the horizon.

"Let's take a gander at that throat," Bob Stookey says with a wink to a little boy sitting on a peach crate in a cluttered studio apartment. The child—a freckled, cherubic eight-year-old in a faded SpongeBob T-shirt with a cowlick of black hair—says "Ah," as Bob gently inserts a tongue depressor into the boy's mouth.

The place smells of liniment and sweat and coffee grounds. Packing blankets drape the windows, and a ratty old sleeper couch in the corner has yellowed sheets on it. The woman of the house—the plump, olive-skinned matron who stopped Dr. Stevens during the escape—hovers over Bob and the child, wringing her hands nervously. "You see how red it is, Bob?"

"Little sore is it, sport?" Bob says to the boy, pulling the depressor free.

The boy nods sheepishly.

Bob reaches down to a medical bag and rifles through the contents. "Gonna fix you right up, little man." He pulls a small vial out of the bag. "Have you screaming at your sister again in no time."

The mother gives the medicine a skeptical look. "What is it?"

Bob hands the pill bottle to the woman. "Mild antibiotic. I'm thinking we got a little bug going around—nothing to worry about. Give him one of these three times a day with food, fix him right up."

The woman chews her lip. "Um . . ."

Bob cocks his head at her. "There a problem?"

The woman shrugs. "I got nothin' to trade, Bob. I can pay you back in food or something."

Bob smiles, closing the bag with a snap. "There's no call for that, Marianne."

She looks at him. "Oh . . . Bob, you sure?"

"This is Woodbury." He winks at her. "We're all family here."

Marianne Dolan once stopped traffic with her olive-skinned French-Canadian beauty, her hourglass figure, and enormous blue-green eyes. A decade and a half of hard housework and single parenting took its toll on her looks, and the plague times deepened the lines around her mouth and eyes, but now, as she breaks out in a guileless, warm smile, the splendor of her once-lovely face returns. "I really, really appreciate it, Bob, you're a—"

A loud knocking on the door interrupts her. Marianne blinks with a start, and Bob glances toward the door.

Marianne turns and calls out. "Who is it, please?"

From the other side of the door, the sound of a clear, forceful, feminine voice rings out. "It's Lilly Caul, Marianne. Sorry to bother you."

Marianne Dolan goes across the room. "Lilly?" she says after opening the door and finding Lilly standing alone in the corridor. "What can I do for you?"

"I understand Bob's here?" Lilly says. She wears her trademark ripped denim and baggy cable-knit, her hair in mussy tendrils, a web belt loaded with mag pouches around her waist. Something about her complexion, the way she's carrying herself, speaks of vigor, sturdiness, strength—the likes of which Marianne hasn't seen in this woman before. The web belt is not a fashion statement.

"He certainly is," Marianne says with a grin. "He's helping Timmy, in fact. Come in."

Bob stands as the two women approach. "Well, well . . . looks like the cavalry's here. How ya doin', Lilly-girl?"

Lilly looks impressed. "Look at you, Bob—making house calls now."

Bob smiles and gives her a shrug. "It's nothing . . . just trying to do my part."

The look on Bob's weathered face—now alert and clear-eyed—says it all. His pouchy eyes glitter with pride, his dark hair neatly combed back. He is a new man, and it delights Lilly.

She turns to Marianne. "You mind if I borrow the good doctor for a minute? Austin woke up a little under the weather today."

"Not a problem," Marianne says, and then, turning to Bob, she adds, "I can't thank you enough, Bob." She looks at her son. "Whaddaya say, Timmy?"

"Thanks?" the little boy mutters, gazing up at his mom and the other adults.

Bob pats the child's head. "Don't mention it, sport. Hang in there."

Lilly leads Bob out the door, down the corridor, and out the exit.

"What's the problem with pretty boy?" Bob asks as they stroll down the brick path in front of the Dolans' building. The sun is high and bright in the cloudless sky, the heat pressing down on them. The Georgia summer isn't far off—the vaguest hints of asphalt baking and miserable muggy days on the breeze.

"Austin's fine," Lilly tells him, leading him into a little alcove of poplar trees for some privacy. "I didn't want to ask you about the Governor in front of Marianne."

Bob nods and gazes across the street at a row of storefronts, where some kids are playing kickball. "He's okay, far as I can tell. Still in a coma, but his breathing seems normal. Color's good, pulse is strong. I think he's going to make it, Lilly."

She nods and lets out a sigh. She gazes into the distance, thinking. "I've done everything I can think of to keep us safe while he's out."

"You done good, Lilly. We're gonna be fine. Thanks to you taking the ball."

"I just wish he would wake up." She thinks about it some more. "I don't want people getting nervous, panicking. They're already wondering why he would be out on the search for so long."

"Don't you worry, he'll come back to us. He's as strong as a bull."

Lilly wonders if Bob really believes this. The seriousness and duration of the induced coma—Bob's best guess is that it was brought on by a combination of hypovolemic shock and all the painkillers and anesthetic administered to the man during the rough patch immediately after the attack—is impossible to predict. As far as Lilly can tell, the man could wake up any day now, or remain a vegetable for the rest of his life. Nobody has any experience with such things. And the uncertainty is driving Lilly crazy.

She starts to say something else when she notices the sound of heavy footsteps on the wind—somebody trotting swiftly down an adjacent sidewalk—the noise interrupting her thoughts. She glances over her shoulder and sees Gus trundling quickly toward them. Built like a fireplug, the little man looks like he just got served with a subpoena, his bulldog features filled with urgency.

"Lilly," he says breathlessly as he waddles up to them, "been looking all over for ya."

"Take a breath, Gus, what's the matter?"

The man pauses, leaning over with his hands on his knees, catching his breath. "They want to use up the rest of that gas we got stored in the warehouse."

"Who does?"

"Curtis, Rudy, and them other guards." He looks at Lilly. "Say they need it for the rigs at the wall. Whaddaya think? That's the last of the fuel; that's all we got left."

Lilly sighs. In the Governor's absence, more and more of the townspeople have been coming to her for advice—for decisions, for guidance—and she's not sure she wants to be the one giving it. But somebody has to. At last she says, "It's all right, Gus . . . let 'em take it . . . we'll go on another run tomorrow."

Gus nods.

Bob looks at her for a moment, a strange expression crossing his deeply wrinkled features—a mixture of fascination, concern, and something unreadable—as though he knows something is different about her. Gasoline has become the lifeblood of Woodbury, not only an energy source but also a sort of morbid gauge of their odds of survival. Nobody fucks around with the rationing of fuel.

Lilly looks at Bob. "It'll be okay. We'll find some more tomorrow."

Bob gives her a tepid nod, as though he knows she doesn't really believe anything she's saying.

Over the course of the next three days, they do find more fuel. Lilly sends a small contingent of guards—Gus, Curtis, Rudy, Matthew, and Ray Hilliard—out in one of the military cargo trucks. Their mission: to scour the auto centers at the ransacked Walmart and the two Piggly Wigglys on this side of the county line. They hope to find one of the underground holding tanks still containing a few gallons of residue. Plan B is to siphon as much as possible from any stray wreck or abandoned car that hasn't been stripped to the bone by looters or two years of hard Georgia weather.

By the time the men return on Wednesday evening, they are exhausted but successful, having stumbled upon an abandoned KOA campground in Forsyth, forty miles to the east. The garage out behind the clubhouse, padlocked since the advent of the Turn, held a couple of rusted-out golf carts and a huge holding tank half-full of the sweet unleaded nectar of the gods—nearly a hundred and fifty gallons of the stuff—and Lilly is delighted with the windfall. If folks are frugal with it and ration it wisely, the fuel will provide Woodbury with another month or so of power.

For the rest of that week, Lilly keeps a lid on things as best she can, oblivious to the fact that events are about to spiral out of control.

FIVE

On Friday night—a night Lilly and her inner circle will later mark as a significant turning point—a warm front rolls in from the south, turning the air as muggy as a greenhouse. By midnight, the town has settled down and fallen silent, most of its inhabitants slumbering on sweat-damp sheets, a regiment of guards quietly keeping watch on the walls. Even Bob Stookey has taken a break from his round-the-clock vigil with the Governor and now sleeps soundly on a cot in one of the adjacent service bays under the race-track. Only the infirmary—still blazing with the harsh halogen light of an operating room—buzzes with the muffled clamor of angry voices.

"I'm sick of it," Bruce Cooper complains, pacing in front of the broken-down monitors and gurneys shoved up against the back wall of the medical bay. "Who made her Queen Bitch? Bossing people around like fucking Cleopatra."

"Settle down, Brucey," Gabe mutters from his chair angled next to the Governor's bed, the wounded man lying as still and pale as a mannequin under the sheets. It's been a week since the Governor tangled with the girl in the dreadlocks, and over the course of those seven days, Philip Blake has remained mostly unconscious. No-body is comfortable with calling it a coma—although Bob has la-beled it as such—but whatever grips the man seems to have its hooks deep within him. Only on two occasions has Philip stirred ever so slightly—his head lolling suddenly and a few garbled syllables coughing out of him—but each time he sank back into his twilight world just as abruptly as he came out of it. Nevertheless, Bob thinks this is a good sign. The Governor's color continues to improve with each passing day, and his breathing continues to clear and strengthen. Bob has started increasing the amount of glucose and electrolytes in the IV, and keeping closer track of the man's temperature. The Governor has been at 98.6 for over two days now. "What's your problem with her, anyway?" Gabe asks the black man. "She never did anything to you. What's your beef with her?"

Bruce pauses, thrusting his big hands into the pockets of his camo pants, letting out an angry breath. "All I'm saying is, nobody made it official that she should be the one in charge right now."

Gabe shakes his head. "Who gives a shit? She wants to be temporary honcho, let her be temporary honcho."

"Some stupid bitch from some fucking gated community?!" Bruce snaps at him. "She's a lightweight!"

Gabe levers himself out of his chair, his back still a little stiff from the debacle in the alley a few days ago. He balls his fists as he comes around the Governor's gurney and stands toe-to-toe with Bruce. "Okay, let's get something straight. That lightweight bitch you're talking about, she saved my fucking ass the other night. That lightweight bitch has more cojones than ninety percent of the men we got living in this place."

"So what?—So fucking *what*?!" Bruce stands his ground, glaring at Gabe with eyes blazing. "She can aim a gun, pull a trigger. Big fucking deal."

Gabe shakes his head. "What the fuck is your deal, man? You get up on the wrong side of bed today?"

"I'm outta here!"

Bruce storms toward the door, shaking his head, disgusted, mumbling obscenities under his breath. He makes his exit in a huff, slamming the metal door with a bang that reverberates through the tiled chamber.

Staring at the door, Gabe stands there for a moment, nonplussed by it all, when he hears a sound coming from across the room that stiffens his spine.

It sounds like a voice coming from the man lying on the gurney.

At first, Gabe thinks he's hearing things. Looking back on it, he will come to the conclusion that he *did indeed* hear the Governor's voice at that moment—right after that door had slammed—the words enunciated so clearly and spoken with such clarity that Gabe initially figured he was imagining the sound of the voice saying something like, "How long?"

Gabe whirls toward the gurney. The man on the bed hasn't moved, his bandaged face still elevated slightly on its pillow, the head of the gurney at a forty-five-degree angle. Gabe slowly approaches. "Governor?"

The man on the bed remains still, but suddenly, almost in answer to Gabe's voice, the single eye, which is still visible on that face—peering through a hatch-work of thick, white, gauze bandages—begins to blink open.

It happens in stages, feebly at first, but fluttering more and more vigorously until that single eye is wide open and staring at the ceiling. Another few blinks and the eye begins to focus on things in the room. The pupil dilates slightly as Gabe approaches.

Pulling the folding chair next to the bed, sitting down and putting a hand on the Governor's cold, pale arm, Gabe fixes his gaze on that single searching eye. His heart races. He stares into that eye with such feverish intensity that he can almost see his own face reflected in the teary orb of the eyeball. "Governor? Can you hear me?"

The man on the gurney manages to loll his head slightly toward Gabe, and then fixes his one good eye on the stocky, crew-cut head looming over the bed. Over dry, caked, chapped lips, the man utters again, "How long—?"

At first Gabe is thunderstruck and can't even form a response. He just stares at that haggard, bandaged face for one endless, excruciating moment. Then he shakes off his daze and says very softly, "—were you out?"

A very slow, very weak nod.

Gabe licks his lips, not even aware that he's grinning with giddy excitement. "Almost a week." He swallows back his urge to cry out with glee and hug the man. He wonders if he should get Bob in here. Even though this man is probably a few years his junior, this is his boss, his mentor, his compass, his father figure. "You were awake a bit here and there," Gabe says as calmly as he can manage, "but I don't think you'll remember anything."

The Governor turns his head slowly from side to side as if testing the limits of his condition. At last he manages another hoarse sentence: "Did you find Doc Stevens?" He takes in a shallow breath as though the very act of posing the question exhausts him. "Force him to patch me up?"

Gabe swallows hard. "Nope." He licks his lips nervously. "Doc's dead." He takes a deep breath. "They found him right on the other side of our fence. He went with that bitch and her friends . . . but he didn't last long."

The Governor breathes through his nose for a moment. He swallows thickly and takes in another series of agonizing breaths. He blinks and stares at the ceiling, looking like a man waiting for the residue of a nightmare to pass, waiting for the cold light of reality to return and chase the shadows away. At last he manages to speak again: "Serves that fucker right." The anger glittering in his eye slowly brings him back, gradually allows him to get his bearings and bite down on the situation. He looks at Gabe. "So if the doc's gone, how the fuck am I not dead?"

Gabe looks at the man. "Bob."

The Governor takes this in, his one visible eye dilating and widening with shock. "Bob?!" Another pained breath. "That's . . . *fucking ridiculous* . . . that old drunk? He couldn't draw a straight line—let alone patch me up." He swallows with great effort. His voice sticks in his throat like a record skipping. "He refused to be Doc's assistant—made that fucking *girl* do it."

Gabe shrugs. "I guess he didn't have to do much—thank God. Said your arm was sealed up good, sterilized enough by the fire, but he still cleaned you up real good, watched over you, gave you antibiotics or something. I'm not sure. The way I understand it is . . . when she cut off your . . . uh . . . when she nicked your thigh, Bob said it just missed a major artery, so there wasn't as much blood loss as there could have been." Gabe chews on his lower lip. He doesn't want to throw too much at the man right now, not in his condition. "It would have killed you for sure if she'd hit it, though." He pauses. "The eye almost got infected—but it didn't." Another pause. "Bob said she must have been real careful. He thinks she *wanted* to leave you alive—like she had more plans for you."

The Governor's right eye narrows with pure, unadulterated hate. "Plans for *me*?!" He lets out a phlegmy snort. "Wait until I hear back from Martinez. I could fill a *book* with the shit I've got planned for her."

Gabe feels his stomach seize up. He contemplates not saying anything but then mutters in a low voice, "Uh . . . boss . . . Martinez went with them."

The Governor cringes suddenly, either from the pain or a surge of white-hot rage flowing through him . . . or perhaps both. "I fucking *know* he went with them." He draws a clogged breath and continues. "I didn't know the doc and his slut would go with them— but this was my *plan*." Thick breathing again, getting air into his leaden lungs. "Martinez helps them escape and then comes back and tells us where their fucking prison is." Pause. "If I've been out for a week . . . he should be here any day now."

Gabe nods as the Governor lets out a long, agonizing sigh and peers down at his heavily bandaged stump of a right arm. His eye registers the horror, the harsh reality. His phantom hand sends ghostly sensations up his shoulder to his brain, and he shudders. Then he presses his cracked lips together, and Gabe sees something glimmering way down in the dark iris of the Governor's deep-set eye. Gabe sees it very clearly. The Governor is back. Whether it's madness or strength or survival instinct or just plain meanness, the luminous pinprick of light in that one eye says everything about this man.

At last he turns his eye toward Gabe and adds in a voice husky with pain and fury, "And when that day comes . . . that bitch is mine."

The rest of that week, the heat of late spring settles into the hollows and valleys of west central Georgia. The humidity presses in, and the brutal sun turns the days into steam baths. Since the air conditioners drain so much energy, most of the inhabitants of Woodbury sweat out the hot spell indoors or in the shade of live oaks, fanning themselves compulsively and shirking their daily labors. The Sterns figure out a way to make ice in the warehouse with an old Frigidaire without sucking too much power. Austin finds some prenatal vitamins in the ransacked drugstore and mothers Lilly incessantly, keeping track of her meals and insisting that she stay cool. People continue to ruminate about the escape, the absence of the Governor, and the future of the town.

Meanwhile, Gabe, Bruce, and Bob keep the Governor's condition under wraps. Nobody wants the townsfolk to see the man moving around with crutches like a stroke victim as he convalesces. At night, they sneak him across town to his apartment, where he spends time with Penny and rests up. Gabe helps him clean his place up— removing as many remnants of the attack as possible, erasing the worst of the gouges and stains—and at one point Gabe mentions how Lilly stepped up during the aftermath of the escape. The Governor is impressed by what he hears, and at the end of the week he asks to see her.

"I know it goes without saying," Gabe says to her that night, after dark, as he leads her through the littered foyer of the Governor's apartment building. "But everything you're about to see and hear stays right here. You understand? I don't even want Austin knowing about this."

"Understood," she says uncertainly as she sidesteps a pile of wet cardboard, following the stocky, thick-necked man through the inner doorway. The first-floor stairwell smells of mildew and mouse droppings. Lilly follows Gabe up the shopworn, carpeted risers, the steps squeaking noisily as they ascend. "But what's with all the secrecy? I mean . . . Austin already knows about the attack. So do the Sterns. And we've kept a lid on it for almost two weeks."

"He's got something in mind for you," Gabe explains, leading her down the fetid second-floor hallway, "and he doesn't want anybody to know about it."

Lilly shrugs as they reach his door. "Whatever you say, Gabe."

They knock, and the Governor's voice—as strong and feisty as ever—orders them inside.

Lilly tries not to stare as she enters the living room and sees the man slumped on his ratty sofa with his crutches canted beside him.

"There she is," the man says with a grin, waving her over. He wears a black eye patch—Lilly finds out later that Bob fashioned it out of the straps of a motorcycle saddlebag—and his right arm is missing, the bandaged stump barely poking through the armhole of his hunting vest. His once wiry form now swims in his camo pants and clodhopper boots, his sinewy muscles reduced to cables under his flesh. His coloring is as pale as alabaster—making his dark eye and hair look almost inky black—giving off the impression of a scarecrow. Despite the emaciated limbs, however, he looks as mean and capable as ever. "Please excuse my manners if I don't get up," he adds with a smirk. "I'm still a little shaky on my feet."

"You look good," Lilly lies, taking a seat on an armchair across from him.

Gabe remains standing in the archway. "It's gonna take more than some crazy bitch to take this man out—ain't that right, Governor."

"Okay, you can both ease off on the bullshit," Philip says. "I don't need stroking right now. Okay? It is what it is. I'm gonna be fine."

"That's good to hear," Lilly comments, and now she means what she says.

The Governor gives Lilly a look. "Been hearing some good things about you, how you stepped up when I was on my back all week."

Lilly shrugs. "Everybody pitched in. You know. It was a group effort."

For a brief moment, Lilly hears a strange, muffled noise from the other room—a rustling, a hissing of air, and the jangle of a chain. She has no idea what the hell she's hearing, but she puts it out of her mind.

"The lady's modest, too." The Governor gives her a smile. "You see, Gabe? This is what I'm talking about. You walk softly and carry a big fucking stick around here. I could use about a dozen more like you, Lilly."

Lilly looks down at her hands. "I'd be lying if I said this town didn't mean a lot to me." She looks up at him. "I want this place to survive. I want it to work."

"You and me both, Lilly." He lifts himself painfully off the couch. Gabe goes to help him, but he waves the man off. Breathing through his nose, Philip hobbles over to the boarded window— sans crutches—and gazes out through a narrow gap in the slats. "You and me both," he murmurs, staring at the darkness and thinking.

Lilly watches him. She sees his expression change slightly, illuminated by a trickle of silver light leaking into the room from a distant arc lamp. The narrow band of light shimmers off the man's one good eye as his face darkens and his gaze curdles with hate. "We got a situation needs dealing with," he mutters. "If we want to keep this place safe, we're gonna have to be . . . what's the word? *Preemptive.*"

"Preemptive?" Lilly studies the man. He looks like a wounded pit bull in a cage, his limp amputation dangling off one side of him, the rest of his body as coiled as a spring. Lilly tries not to stare. His Betadine-stained bandages and scarred flesh call out to her. He is a living embodiment of the dangers facing them. It begs the question: Who could do this to a man as indestructible as this? Lilly takes a deep, girding breath. "Whatever it is you have in mind, I'm there for you. Nobody around here wants to live in fear. Whatever you need . . . I'm totally on board."

He turns and peers at her from under the strap of his eye patch, his good eye blazing with emotion. "There's something you should know." He glances at Gabe and then back at her. "I let those fuckers escape."

Lilly's heart thumps a little faster. "Excuse me?"

"I sent Martinez with them. He was supposed to play spy, get a lock on their position—find this fucking prison they're hiding out in—and then report back."

Lilly nods, letting this sink in. Her mind swims with instant anxieties, variables, and implications. "I understand," she says finally.

The Governor looks at her. "He should have been back by now."

"Yeah . . . you got a point."

"You're a natural-born leader, girlfriend. I want you to organize a search party—you choose your team—and go find out what the fuck happened. See what you can turn up. Can you do that for me?"

Lilly gives another nod, but in the back of her mind she's wondering if this is a good idea for someone in her condition to be doing something so . . . *labor intensive. Labor* is the key. Is she truly prepared for all the sacrifices that go along with being an expectant mother? Walking around with a medicine ball sticking out of her gut? Right now she's in that tender transitional stage—not showing yet, not really handicapped physically, not fully prepared for the slog ahead—but what happens when she starts to slow down? She knows enough about the early stages of pregnancy to know that physical activity and regular exercise are totally safe— even recommended—but what about something as hazardous as going on a mission into plague-ridden backwaters? Over the space of a split instant she thinks it over and finally looks at the Governor and says, "I can absolutely do that for you. We'll leave at first light."

"Good."

"One question, though."

The Governor fixes his one eye on her. "What the fuck is it now?"

She chews her lip for a moment, measuring her words. One doesn't rattle the cage of a wounded animal. But she has to say it. "People are climbing the walls not knowing your condition, your whereabouts." She looks into his one good eye. "You gotta show them you're okay."

He lets out a tortured sigh. "I will soon enough, girlfriend. Don't you worry about that." The silence hangs in the room for a moment. The Governor looks at her. "Anything else?"

She shrugs. There's nothing more to say.

Lilly and Gabe walk out, leaving the Governor to his privacy and the ceaseless, muffled clawing noises in the other room.

Lilly spends the rest of that night gathering her team and supplies for the reconnaissance mission. Austin is dead set against her going on the run and argues with her about it, but Lilly is adamant. She is galvanized by the task at hand—the need to secure the town, the prospects of nipping any potential danger in the bud. She is fighting for two now—three, if you count Austin. And perhaps more importantly, she doesn't want anybody getting suspicious about her condition. She doesn't want to give any indication that she is anything other than a hundred percent. This is her little secret. Her body. Her life. Her future baby's life.

So she prepares for the journey with relentless attention to detail. She considers taking Bob along but decides against it—his services are needed in town a lot more than they're needed on this trip; and besides, he'd probably just slow them down. She also decides to leave Bruce in Woodbury to run interference for the Governor. Instead, she enlists Gabe and Gus to go along with her, and Austin, not only for the added muscle but also because each man is intimately familiar with Martinez's methods and behavior patterns and quirks. Gabe is still stinging from his run-in with Martinez in the subterranean tunnels under the racetrack, but Gabe is also a pragmatist. He knows now it was all part of a bigger plan, and he also knows that Martinez is a lynchpin for them. They need to find these people and intervene before something terrible happens. Plus, Gabe owes Lilly Caul his life.

The last person she recruits is David Stern—mostly for his steel-trap mind and innate intelligence—to help with strategy. Lilly is out of her element here. Tracking human beings across hundreds of square miles of biter-infested wetlands is not exactly a specialty of hers—although she is more motivated than ever now to do what has to be done. Other than Lilly, though, only Gabe and Austin know the real mission Martinez was on. Gus and David are operating under the assumption that Martinez was a traitor and they are now simply trying to catch the escapees.

"It's been pretty soggy out there for a while now," David Stern tells Lilly as he loads a crate into the back of the military cargo truck parked in the predawn darkness near the town's north gate. The truck idles softly—the turbocharged diesel engine burbling and rumbling under the hood—masking the sound of their voices. "My guess is their tracks are still fairly evident."

"Yeah, but how do we know *their* tracks from the boatload of walker tracks that have surely mingled with them over the last week?" Lilly poses the question with a grunt as she lifts a carton of bottled water into the cargo bay. They've packed enough provisions to stay out on the road for twenty-four hours or more—food, blankets, walkie-talkies, the first-aid kit, binoculars, night-vision goggles, extra batteries, extra ammunition, and an arsenal of weaponry from the Guard station—although Lilly wants to get this done as quickly as possible. The walker activity in the woods has picked up this week, and the faster they get answers, the better. "Seems like it's gonna be needles in a haystack out there," she says, shoving the carton on board the truck.

"We'll start where they were last seen," David says, climbing onto the running panel. "Sun's gonna be coming up soon—we'll assume they headed east, at least initially."

They finish loading the truck, and then everybody climbs on board.

Gus drives, with Gabe in the shotgun seat—heavily armed—manning the two-way. Lilly rides in back with the supplies, also on a walkie-talkie, with David and Austin each perched on the rear running board for easy access on and off the vehicle. The sun is just beginning to lighten the horizon as the men on the barricade open up the gap—engines firing up, vertical stacks chugging, a semitrailer pulling out of their way—revealing the primordial darkness of the neighboring forest stewing in the morning mists.

Lilly's stomach tightens as the cargo truck shudders noisily through the opening.

Peering through the rear canvas flap, now beginning to buffet in the breeze, Lilly can see the east side of town passing in the gloomy predawn light as Gus circles around the village. The place looks like Beirut—the territory outside the razor-wire-lined walls littered with wreckage, sinkholes, and mounds of carnage from past skirmishes with walkers. Some of the bodies are headless, scorched, and burned to husks . . . others lying in open graves of brackish water. As the day dawns, the Durand Street alley comes into view—the wall over which Martinez helped the escapees flee nearly two weeks earlier clearly visible now.

Gus grinds the air brakes, and the truck hisses to a stop on a gravel road thirty feet from the outer wall. David and Austin hop off the board and quickly sweep their flashlights across the ground, illuminating the tracks in the mud—now filled with tiny pockets of filthy rainwater—telling the story of Dr. Stevens's attack and the subsequent flight toward Highway 85. Over crackling two-way radios, terse observations are sent back to the truck, and Lilly orders the two men back on board.

Now they proceed down a gravel dogleg toward the highway and then pick up the tracks on the other side of the asphalt two-lane.

David Stern reminds them to ignore all the footprints that mark themselves with long slash marks—the telltale sign of a walker's lumbering shuffle—and keep their eyes peeled for well-defined impressions. Once they get used to the differences, it becomes easier to spot evidence of the fleeing humans. Even two weeks old, the prints—at many junctures along the escape route—have dried into the mire in little perfect boot-shaped puddles.

By midmorning they lose the prints about a mile west of Greenville, and Gus pulls the truck over. Up to this point the escapees have apparently fled in a north-by-northwesterly direction from Woodbury, but now it's anybody's guess as to if and when they changed direction. Luckily, the walker sightings this morning have been few and far between, and as the sun beats down on the cargo truck, turning the interior into a sauna, they sit there for a moment, sweating through their clothes and discussing their next move. Gabe suggests striking out on foot, but Lilly doesn't like the idea of splitting up or leaving the truck unattended.

Then Lilly remembers the crash site—the downed news chopper that sent them on a tangent on their last supply run several weeks ago—and she realizes that they're only about a half a mile south of the wreckage. She asks Gus to drive north a little farther, and he does, and within minutes they've reached the same muddy washout over which they trod three and a half weeks ago.

Gus pulls over and brings the truck to a stop. They all look at Lilly, the realization dawning on everybody all at once: They can't avoid it any longer.

They have to strike out on foot . . . into the walker-infested woods.

SIX

"Okay, David, check this out." She leads him across the muddy gravel shoulder and pauses on the edge of the embankment, gesturing down at the constellation of footprints indelibly stamped in the clay. A cloud of gnats writhes around her head for a moment, and she bats them away as her comrades gather around her. Hundreds of footprints—all shapes and sizes and degrees of freshness—crisscross the mossy ground, many of them belonging to Lilly and her cohorts from earlier that month. But some of them look fresher. "What do you make of those?" Lilly says, pointing at a diagonal row of prints cutting a swath from the road to the woods—a file of people moving fairly quickly—toward the deeper woods.

David stares at the prints. "Looks like somebody knew where they were going."

Gus chimes in. "Crash site?"

"You better believe it," David says. "Maybe Martinez thought they could find something else out there. We didn't get a chance to completely search the aircraft last time. Who knows what we missed."

Lilly gazes out at the tree line in the distance, the dense netting of foliage billowing in the wind like dirty green drapes.

About five hundred yards away, in the cleavage of a thickly forested hollow, they first encountered the wreckage of the helicopter—its pilot dead, its lone passenger clinging to life. Now the smoke has long cleared, but chances are the chopper still lies on its side in the dry riverbed where they found it weeks ago. Lilly makes an instant decision. "Okay . . . everybody knows the drill. Gus stays with the truck. Bring extra ammo and water. We'll stay in touch with the walkies. Let's go."

They load up their packs and strike out across the muddy wetlands.

By midday they reach the crash site. The chopper lies where they left it—crumpled on the banks of the muddy creek bed like a petrifying dinosaur, its rotors torn asunder, its fuselage battered, windows shattered—the riveted hull already beginning to oxidize in the unforgiving sun. Thousands of footprints circle the wreckage in the mud—many, many more than they remember leaving there—and David Stern begins to study them. He doesn't hear the faint crackle of twigs in the middle distance, the collective shuffling of insensate feet churning through the undergrowth toward them from practically every direction. He's too busy extrapolating the narrative of Martinez's journey.

From the profusion of prints, as well as the rearrangement of certain pieces of wreckage, David concludes that Martinez's group not only passed this way but also probably spent the night. The cabin door lies in a patch of weeds and nettle to the left of the nose, a wet blanket draped off one end. Inside the cabin, he finds signs of a bivouac—empty water bottles, wadded wrappers, an empty carton of ammunition. David is shining a flashlight into the shadows of the cockpit when a voice tugs at his attention. "David, take a look at this . . . over here."

He turns and sees Lilly standing on the other side of the riverbed, kneeling, taking a closer look at the leaf-matted ground.

David goes over and sees the footprints embedded in the mud. "Those are fresher, aren't they?"

"Yeah." She points out the deeper tracks that have fanned out from a circle of newer prints near the crash. "Looks like they spent some time here, maybe met up with somebody, and then headed off in that direction." She points to the deepening shadows to the west, where the trees thicken along the creek bed. "I say we head that way."

By this point, Gabe and Austin have joined them, and they have their guns out and ready to rock. Gabe has been hearing noises he doesn't like in the high trees above the stream, and he's jumpy. Lilly checks her .22s and then takes the lead. She follows the dry gulley into the thickets, keeping an eye on both the prints and the adjacent barrier of trees on either side of her. The others follow. Conversation comes to a screeching halt.

The silence blankets them. It's a sticky, droning, heavy silence, full of the implacable vibrations of nature—insects humming in their ears, a distant trickle of water—and it makes their footsteps sound like explosions. Gabe gets exceedingly edgy. Something doesn't feel right. Lilly's heart quickens. After a while, she draws both pistols and then plods along the riverbed holding the guns at her side.

They cross another quarter mile of wooded hollow—the dry creek bed snaking through endless palisades of pines and white birch—before they begin to feel as though the prints are leading them into a trap. The troubling noises have returned. Lilly hears twigs snapping and dry leaves crackling rhythmically from somewhere in the middle distance, but it's impossible to parse which direction they're coming from. They can smell the stench of walkers drifting on the breeze.

Their guns come up, thumbs on the safeties, poised, knife sheaths unsnapping, eyes peeled, hearts racing, muscles coiled, ears pricked, flesh crawling. The woods are alive now with noises and moving shadows and rotten odors rising and it's driving everybody crazy. But from what direction are the dead coming? Lilly slows down and peers into the distant foliage and suddenly raises her hand. "Hold on!" she hisses in a loud whisper, making everybody freeze in their tracks. "Everybody down—GET DOWN!—right now!"

They move as one, each of them ducking down behind a row of mossy boulders embedded in the humus. Guns raised, eyes wide and alert, they all look at Lilly, who gazes over the top of the crags.

In the distance, about fifty yards away, she sees a break in the trees, revealing another clearing—this one a vast, overgrown meadow—crawling with ragged, dark figures. Lilly's pulse quickens. She glances to her right and notices a narrow footpath snaking up an embankment into the higher trees. She looks at the others and points to the path, and then silently gestures at a ridge of deadfall logs higher up.

They follow her up the path—staying low, moving as silently as they can, their breaths stuck in their throats—and Lilly leads them across the top of the ridge. They duck down next to each other behind the massive timbers. From this vantage point—through the cover of trees—they each get a clear view of the huge meadow below.

"Good God . . . it's a fucking convention," Lilly utters through clenched teeth as she takes in the enormity of the primordial pasture.

The size of five football fields laid end to end, the rain-sodden ground riotous with windblown wild grasses and daubs of color from yellow dandelions and red columbine, the immense meadow teems with walkers of every description. Some of them circle a festering carcass of a dead deer, hectic with flies, while others wander aimlessly along the periphery like drunken sentinels. Some can barely move due to missing limbs or mangled appendages, while others look as though their tattered garb has been shredded and spray-painted with gore. The sun beats down on the pasture, the far corners wavering in skeins of heat rays and cottonwood floating in the air like ghostly snow. A faint burr of growling thrums on the breeze from the collective vocalization of at least fifty or more walkers.

"Lilly, honey," David Stern finally murmurs very softly, "would you mind handing me those binoculars?"

Lilly shrugs off her backpack, unzips it, pulls out the small field glasses, and hands them over to David. The older man puts the lenses to his eyes and surveys the breadth and length of the meadow below them. The others gape. Austin huddles next to Lilly, his breathing audible in her ears, his nervousness palpable. Gabe fingers the trigger guard on his MIG, just itching to waste the entire field with a few well-placed bursts.

Lilly starts to whisper something when she hears David mumbling under his breath.

"No . . . not . . . oh God no . . . no." He fiddles with the focus knob and presses the binoculars to his eyes. "Oh Jesus Christ . . . don't tell me."

"What?!" Lilly swallows her fear and hisses the words at him. "David, what is it?!"

He hands the binoculars over to her. "To the left, by the deer," he says. "The one wandering off by himself in the corner."

She gazes through the binoculars and finds the lone walker in the southeast corner of the meadow, and her entire body sags with despair as she identifies the frayed and torn figure shuffling along the cattails and weeds. A twinge of first-trimester cramps clenches her midsection for a moment, and her eyes burn. In the shaky blur of the binoculars' narrow field of vision, she sees the trademark bandanna still wrapped around the tall male's head, the sideburns apparent along the side of the once handsome face—now a nightmare of pallid flesh, cadmium eyes, and puckered, lipless mouth. "Fuck," she utters breathlessly.

Gabe and Austin are both dying to grab the binoculars, so Lilly hands them over.

Each taking their turn, they gaze one at a time through the telescopic lenses at the sun-blanched meadow below them. Each man reveals through body language—a sudden anguished slump from

Austin, an exhalation of air through gritted teeth from Gabe—that they have identified the lone walker.

Austin speaks first, gazing at Lilly. "Whaddaya think happened?"

Lilly looks through the binoculars, muttering as she carefully scans the meadow. "There's no way of knowing for sure, but it looks like . . . I don't know . . . see those deep ruts coming across the field from the east?"

"Yeah, I saw them."

David chimes in. "Yes, I noticed them, too—they look like tire marks from a large vehicle—a truck, a van, a camper, something like that."

Lilly peers through the lens and surveys the ragged circular divot in the ground where the truck or the RV either skidded out of control or came to an abrupt halt. For some reason, she thinks the tracks have something to do with Martinez's demise.

She swings the binocs back over to the lone walker in the corner of the meadow. The thing that was once Caesar Ramon Martinez—a former gym teacher from Augusta, Georgia, a loner with natural leadership skills—now trundles awkwardly back and forth through the dust motes of cottonwood and pale rays of sun with no direction, no purpose, no goal other than to feed. His arms and torso—even from this distance, in the blur of the binoculars—appear completely scourged, eviscerated to shreds by many sets of rotting teeth. Cords of bloody gristle and sinew dangle from his gashed midsection. A slimy white bone fragment pokes through his tattered pant leg, giving his shuffling gate a pronounced limp.

The sight of this man reduced to such a monstrous shell takes Lilly by surprise, the sorrow coursing down her marrow, gripping her insides. She never got to know this man very well—nobody did—he wasn't the sociable type. But over the course of that last year, in quiet moments, Martinez did talk about his pre-plague days. Lilly remembers the details of his modest life. The man never married, never had any kids, was estranged from his parents, but he loved teaching, loved coaching his football and basketball teams at Pope John Middle School. When the plague broke out, the school was overrun. First responders moved in to protect the children, fighting off the early waves of undead, and Martinez tried to save an entire class by locking them in the gymnasium, but that proved futile. Nightmares of that day haunted the man for the rest of his life—the sounds of screaming students calling out for their mothers as the skylights shattered and monsters tumbled into the gym like ragged paratroopers—but the worst part was the guilt. Martinez barely escaped, pushing his way out the loading dock . . . but he would never forget the sounds of the children shrieking behind him as he fled, the biters devouring the class in a ghastly feeding frenzy.

"By the looks of those tire tracks," Lilly utters finally under her breath, "I'm guessing they found him out, took him down, maybe with the vehicle." She looks down. "He wasn't perfect, but he was one of us—he was a decent man. He didn't deserve this."

Austin reaches over and puts an arm around her. "There's nothing you could have done, Lilly. He knew what he was getting into."

"Yeah, I guess," she murmurs, all the confidence draining out of her voice.

Austin lets out a weary sigh. "Can we get outta here now? I mean . . . mission accomplished, right?"

Gabe grumbles at him. "What are you talking about, mission accomplished? Nothing's been accomplished here but Martinez getting wasted."

Austin looks at him. "We found him, right? We found out why he didn't show up. There's nothing else we can do, man. File closed."

David pipes in. "I have to say I agree with pretty boy. For all we know, the entire group of escapees may be dead. Besides, the sun's gonna be setting fairly soon."

Lilly glances over her shoulder, surveys the path and the route back—no biters in sight. "Okay, it's settled then," she says. "Stay low, and keep quiet . . . we don't want any of these biters on our tail."

They start edging their way back down the hillside toward the riverbed, but all at once Gabe springs to his feet and circles around in front of Lilly, blocking her path with fire in his eyes. "Hold up!" He shoves her back. "We're not going anywhere!"

Austin steps in, getting protective. But Lilly waves everybody back down into crouching positions. "Keep it down, goddamnit!" She turns and looks at Gabe. "What the fuck is *your* problem?"

Gabe burns his gaze into her. "We need to bring back proof."

"Excuse me?"

"Governor's gonna want to see proof this happened."

"Proof?!" She stares at him. "You got four witnesses. What do you want, Gabe—a lock of his hair? C'mon, you want to risk more lives?"

Gabe reaches down to his pant leg. He pulls his Randall knife from a sheath, the blade glistening in the beams of late-afternoon sun. "Do whatever you want, Lilly . . . but I'm not coming back without proof."

Lilly crouches there, dumbstruck, watching Gabe turn and creep down the embankment. She turns to the others. "Goddamnit-to-hell, c'mon . . . we gotta cover him."

By the time they reach the bottom of the wooded path, all available firearms have been drawn, cocked, readied, and aimed. Gabe moves toward the clearing, ducking behind an ancient, gnarled live oak. Lilly crouches down twenty feet behind him, staying low, eyes taking in everything, both her Ruger semiautomatics gripped tightly in her sweaty palms. Austin hovers close behind her, his Glock at his side, while David brings up the rear, scanning the woods behind them for fear of having their escape route cut off.

The silence is excruciating—a ten-ton weight pressing down on them—the only audible sounds now their breathing and their pulses racing in their ears. Lilly sees Gabe bend down and pick up a stone. She aims her Rugers at the distant swarm of walkers milling across the far meadow. So far, none of the creatures have taken notice.

The monster that once belonged to their inner circle—the former football coach who, less than a year ago, shared a New Year's bottle of brandy with Dr. Stevens, Alice, and Lilly—now shuffles directionlessly through the weeds less than twenty-five feet away from Gabe. The creature's opaque-white doll's eyes scan the surrounding trees, his blackened mouth working and chewing involuntarily.

Gabe tosses a small stone across the clearing toward Martinez.

In a frozen tableau of hair-trigger tension, the four humans watch the lone biter become still, cocking its head at the faint sound of the stone clattering across the weeds in front of it. The monster slowly turns toward the noise, and then starts shuffling closer to the clearing.

Gabe pounces.

What happens next occurs with the speed of a nightmare, everything transpiring all at once. Gabe rushes the thing that was once in charge of security in Woodbury, and without hesitation—without even allowing the biter a chance to react—he slashes the eleven-inch blade with all his might at the monster's neck. The knife slices through epidermis, cartilage, arteries, muscles, and cervical vertebrae with the force of a guillotine.

From Lilly's vantage point, it looks as though Gabe has opened up a hydrant of blood. The head detaches and falls, and the body staggers and fountains for a moment before collapsing. Gabe grabs the fallen cranium, and then turns and rushes back toward the path. Unfortunately, the minimal noise generated by the assault—a negligible series of footsteps, grunts, and twigs snapping—proves to be enough of a commotion to rouse the attention of the other walkers. Lilly realizes this one moment before the shooting starts.

She whirls around in time to see Austin and David in the middle of the path with their guns up now, the muzzles flaring brilliant plumes of light—each blast emitting a silenced clap—the rounds chewing through foliage and taking down a half-dozen walkers in quick succession across the southeast corner of the meadow.

Gabe now stands beside her with the dripping head, fumbling for his assault rifle.

In one continuous movement, he gets his free hand around the trigger guard and swings the weapon up and fires off a volley. The short muzzle flares and sends hellfire through the upper bodies of approaching walkers, punching holes through a dozen skulls, sending tissue and bone fragments and a red fog across the foliage, dropping reanimated cadavers of all sizes, genders, and ages into the high grass in gruesome heaps. Gabe's Bushmaster clicks empty.

More creatures stir from their stupors—drawn by the noise of the firefight and the smell of living tissue—and the dynamic changes dramatically out in the meadow. Like a school of fish shifting directions in one great undulating organism, scores of wandering dead turn in drunken choreography and start dragging themselves toward the humans. Lilly stands and begins backing away, mumbling, "There's too many of them, Gabe . . . too many . . . Jesus fucking Christ, *there's too many!*"

Standing beside her, Gabe lets out an angry grunt in response and quickly thumbs the rifle's release, ejecting the clip. He fumbles with the greasy severed head for a moment, swinging his satchel around and stuffing the gruesome artifact into the carrier, and then he yanks another magazine from his belt and slams it into the gun's receiver. He spins and sees another cluster of dead pushing through the foliage on their immediate right—deadly black mouths working like piranhas—and Gabe slaps the bolt release and lets loose another fusillade.

Lilly ducks down into a crouch as Gabe's wild volley zings through the leaves.

The opposite wall of foliage shreds apart as a half-dozen more walkers go down in bursts of blood and tissue. Meanwhile, Austin and David send another half-dozen rounds across the opposite corner of the clearing, putting another three corpses out of their misery in a cloud of blood mist. Lilly keeps backing away, seeing no options, no purpose to the fight, no hope of stanching the swarm. The entire population of the meadow is now converging on them in one great mass of ragged moving corpses.

The guns click empty again, and for one frenzied instant, the other three men glance over their shoulders at Lilly, who freezes. The volume of gunfire and the fury of the counterassault have engulfed the clearing in a haze of cordite and floating particulate, the fog so thick that Lilly can barely see the others as the horde closes in. The only viable course of action is written across her petrified features. There's only one thing left for them to do.

She doesn't even have to say the word.

They run.

Charging headlong through the thick undergrowth, Lilly leads the group, leaping over deadfalls and exposed roots, arms pumping, breath coming in heaving gasps. Once upon a time, she was a track star at Marietta High School—her specialty was the five-thousand-meter run, which she could complete in just under nineteen minutes—and now she falls into that natural pace—not a sprint, not a wild-ass dead run, but more of a smooth churning gait that just feels right to her body. The fear drives all thoughts of her pregnancy from her mind, every muscle in her midsection taut with nerves now, masking any potential twinge of abdominal pain. The columns of black oak strobe past her as she follows the riverbed. Despite her delicate condition, she manages to race along that winding path with both guns still gripped in her cold, numb hands.

Gabe trots along right behind her, his bullish legs churning like an NFL linebacker grudgingly returning to the huddle, with Austin close on his heels, breathing hard. David is the slowest—a lifelong smoker—and he struggles to keep up. At one point, he shoots a glance over his shoulder—the walkers receding into the morass of trees behind him—and the awkward move almost topples him . . . but he manages to stay on his feet.

They cross a quarter mile of forest trail in less than three minutes.

At length, Lilly slows down, wheezing to catch her breath, marveling at the ease with which a healthy human can outrun a cadre of dead. If agitated, a biter can get the jump on a person, but over long distances, the creatures have no chance, and long distances are Lilly's specialty.

Gazing over her shoulder, she sees that the walkers have fallen so far behind them that they're now out of sight, upwind, and no longer an immediate threat. Lilly gets her breath back as she approaches the fallen chopper.

Nobody says anything as they file past the wreckage. What is there to say? Martinez is dead—his mission a failure—his severed head now twitching and ticking in Gabe's knapsack like a tiny engine dieseling. Nobody says much as they find their way back through the swampy woods adjacent to the highway. When they reach the truck, Gus is standing outside it with his binoculars in his hands.

"What gives?" he asks Lilly, who throws her backpack in the rear cargo hold. "You find him?"

Gabe speaks up. "We found him all right." He climbs into the cab. "Let's get the fuck outta here."

"What about Martinez?" Gus says as he climbs behind the wheel. The rear of the truck creaks as the others, still out of breath, struggle on board. Gus looks at Gabe. "What happened? What's wrong with everybody?"

Gabe positions the greasy knapsack on the floor of the cab between his legs. "Just get us out of this fucking place, Gus, will ya?"

Gus puts the vehicle in gear and pulls back onto the highway.

On their way back to Woodbury, Lilly sits off to herself in the rear of the cargo hold, staring out the gap of flapping canvas at the passing landscape, ruminating silently, stewing in her thoughts. Austin tries to get her talking a few times, but she just shakes her head, unable to hide the revulsion on her face, and keeps gazing mutely out at the late-afternoon sunlight slanting through the blur of roadside trees.

She is disgusted at the prospect of returning with the alarming contents of Gabe's pack. She thought Gabe was saner than this . . . but she knows she has to let it go. For the sake of Woodbury, she has to swallow her feelings. After all, if Martinez had died within the confines of the town, somebody—probably Lilly herself—would have likely been forced to chop up his carcass to feed to the arena biters anyway. So why the ambivalence?

Cognitive dissonance.

Lilly remembers a shrink in Marietta once telling her about this obscure psychotherapeutic term—a three-dollar phrase for the games a person's mind plays on itself when faced with two or more conflicting ideas. In simpler times, Lilly struggled with her antithetical feelings of pride and self-loathing, but that was back when she had the luxury to contemplate her navel and whine to a therapist about the trivial annoyances of her cushy daily life. These days, it's hard to argue fine points of morality, ethics, or right and wrong. In this new society, it's all about getting to the next fucking day. Period. That's why Lilly has nothing to add at the moment, and she just keeps staring out at the flickering sunlight—every few moments flinching at another prenatal cramp.

The abdominal pangs have been coming more frequently lately. Lilly has lost track of the triggers—if there are any—but God knows the stress of recent days could very well be bringing on the pain. She worries constantly now about her diet, her sleep, her general health. But how the hell is she supposed to stay on the straight and narrow in this crazy environment? Austin has started planning side runs to find healthy food somewhere. Ramen noodles and Kool-Aid just won't cut it now. Lilly needs real nourishment, and she needs it consistently.

Once they get back to town, and the group goes its separate

ways, Lilly keeps to herself. She doesn't say much to Austin that evening, despite the fact that Austin, as usual, seems worried about her. Word has spread around town that the Governor is planning to make an appearance at the racetrack that night. Austin has to beg Lilly to go with him. He has a feeling that they should both be present—along with each and every resident—because there's no telling what the man might say.

Austin believes that they may be facing a turning point in the evolution of their community, a milestone the likes of which none of them have ever encountered—a truly pivotal moment. But neither Austin nor Lilly—nor *anybody* in Woodbury, for that matter— has any idea how pivotal this moment will turn out to be.

SEVEN

At precisely 9:01 eastern standard time that night—the evening of May 11—in the second year of what some of the more religious folks in Woodbury are now calling the Great Tribulation—the arc lamp high above the south end of the speedway snaps on, shining its magnesium-hot glare down on the racetrack, turning the dusty infield—as well as the aging, weather-beaten oval of a track—a surreal shade of silver. The din of voices coming from the center stack of bleachers immediately dies down to the hushed murmurs and nervous muttering of a congregation preparing to offer supplication and alms to a stern cleric. No whoops and hollers, no cheering—in fact, none of the customary rowdiness that accompanies a typical night at the fights in Woodbury—now there is only the low drone of expectant whispers.

Due to a short in the generator's circuits, or perhaps an imperfection in the spotlight's xenon filament, the radiant beam that shines down on the arena begins to flicker. Other arc lights bang to life, also flickering intermittently. The effect has the dreamlike, nerve-jangling quality of a film projector that is out of registration, the resulting flashes creating slow-motion nitrate ghosts of dust devils and litter swirling across the abandoned track and empty walker pens on the night breezes.

Something epochal is about to happen, and each and every last one of the fifty or so spectators, which constitutes about 80 percent of the town's population—Woodbury is now approaching sixty souls—fidgets in a state of jittery awe. Word has spread to every quarter that the evening's festivities will feature a special address from the beleaguered Governor, and nobody wants to miss it. Some entered the arena that night with high hopes for the proverbial shot in the arm, a dose of reassurance from the man who gets things done and keeps the wheels greased and watches their backs. But as the minutes tick toward the appointed hour, the mood has spontaneously darkened. It's as though the collective dread of living during the Great Tribulation has become a microbe itself, infectious as tuberculosis, contractible through the air, through the furtive glances of the downtrodden.

After a few more minutes—it is now 9:05—the loud crackle of the public address system reverberates across the amphitheater. *"GOOD PEOPLE OF WOODBURY,"* echoes the whiskey-cured pipes of Rudy Warburton, the good old boy from Savannah who has turned his expertise in tuck-pointing into the building of barricades. His words have the stilted quality of a script that was just handed to him—probably by the Governor himself. *"LET'S WARMLY WELCOME BACK OUR LEADER, OUR GUIDING LIGHT . . . THE GOVERNOR!"*

For a moment, nothing happens other than a tepid round of applause and a few halfhearted cheers ringing out from the stands.

Way off in the corner, in the first row, near the cyclone fence barrier, sitting next to Austin, Lilly Caul watches and waits and bites her fingernails. She has a blanket draped over the shoulders of her denim jacket, and she keeps her gaze on the far portal, the Governor's preferred mode of egress on and off the field.

As the awkward pause lengthens, and the collective murmuring kicks in again, Lilly chews her cuticles. She had managed to stop biting her nails a few weeks ago—oddly right around the time she learned she was pregnant—but now the habit has returned with a vengeance. Her fingertips are already looking atrocious, stubby and flaked with tiny fissures. She sits on her hands. She takes a deep breath to ward off another twinge of cramps, a tendril of auburn hair blowing down across her eyes.

Austin turns to her, reaching up and brushing the hair from her eyes. "You okay?" he asks.

"Just ducky," she replies with a wry little smile. They have talked a lot about her morning sickness, her first-trimester woes, the cramps and the soreness. But their unspoken fears lie at the base of everything they talk about now. Are these symptoms normal? Is she in jeopardy of losing the baby? How is she going to get the nutrition and prenatal care she needs? Is Bob capable of caring for her? And the granddaddy of all their concerns: Is the old army medic up to delivering a baby when the time comes? "I just wish he would come out already," she mutters, giving a little tip of the head toward the shadowy vestibule on the north end of the arena. "The suspense is killing these people."

Almost on cue, as if her words have conjured the man himself, the crowd goes silent—and the silence is as unsettling as a fuse being lit—as a gaunt figure appears in the mouth of the portal.

All heads turn toward the north, and scores of anxious faces gape in complete consternation as the man of the hour slowly ambles toward the center of the infield. He wears his trademark hunting vest, camo pants, and jackboots, but he moves gingerly, with the careful tenterhooks of a stroke victim, one step at a time. Rudy, the ersatz announcer, walks beside the Governor with a small grease-spotted cardboard box and a wireless microphone. The thing that transfixes the audience is not the black leather eye patch. Nor is it the profusion of scars and fading wounds visible even at a great distance across the Governor's exposed flesh. The thing that bothers everybody is the missing arm.

Philip Blake pauses in front of them, grabbing the hand mike from Rudy, thumbing the On switch, and looking at the crowd. His face looks as pale as porcelain in the faltering silver arc light, the flicker effect making him look spectral and nightmarish—a character in a forgotten silent film moving in jump cuts.

His voice crackles through high loudspeakers as Rudy trots off the field: *"I APOLOGIZE FOR BEING UNAVAILABLE TO YOU ALL RECENTLY."* He pauses and surveys the silent faces. *"I KNOW SOME COMMUNITY MATTERS HAVE ARISEN THAT I'VE BEEN UNABLE TO HANDLE . . . AND FOR THAT I APOLOGIZE."*

No reaction emanates from the crowd other than a few throats clearing. From her front-row position on the north corner of the stands, Lilly feels a jolt of apprehension. The Governor's condition somehow looks graver in this terrible flickering light.

"THE GAMES WILL BE UP AND RUNNING AGAIN SOON," he goes on, undaunted by the eerie silence and the tension so thick it seems to weigh down on the stadium like a fog. *"BUT AS YOU'VE PROBABLY NOTICED BY LOOKING AT ME—I'VE HAD OTHER, MORE PRESSING MATTERS TO DEAL WITH."*

Another pause here, as the Governor gazes across the rows of somber-faced residents.

Lilly shivers—despite the humid night air, which smells of burning rubber—an inexplicable wave of dread washing over her. *I hope he can pull this one out; we need him back, we need leadership, we need him to be the Governor.* Holding her collar tight with one hand, she feels conflicting emotions crashing within her. She feels sympathy for the man, shame, smoldering anger for the motherfuckers who did this, and swimming underneath the surface of it all— incessant, primal—a debilitating wave of doubt.

"AS YOU KNOW, IT'S BEEN A LONG TIME SINCE WE'VE HAD NEW PEOPLE ARRIVE IN TOWN." He takes a deep breath as though girding himself against a surge of pain. *"SO . . . RECENTLY, WHEN A SMALL BAND OF SURVIVORS SHOWED UP, I WAS THRILLED. I FIGURED THEY WERE LIKE US . . . HAPPY TO BE ALIVE . . . THANKFUL TO SEE OTHER SURVIVORS . . . BUT THAT WAS NOT THE CASE."* In the pause that follows, his words echo up into the sky and slap back at the crowd against the far store-fronts. *"THERE IS EVIL IN THIS WORLD . . . AND NOT ALL OF IT IS IN THE FORM OF THOSE UNDEAD MONSTERS CLAWING AT OUR FENCES."*

Just for an instant, he glances down at the cardboard box next to him. Lilly wonders what's in the thing—a visual aid of some sort, perhaps—and the feeling it gives her isn't exactly comforting. She wonders if anybody else in the stands is as bothered by that damp, moldering, blood-spotted box as she. Does it occur to anybody that whatever is in that box may change the course of their destinies?

"AT FIRST I HAD NO IDEA WHAT THEY WERE CAPABLE OF," Philip Blake continues, gazing back up at the gallery. *"I TRUSTED THEM—IT WAS A GRAVE MISTAKE. THEY NEEDED SUPPLIES, SOME THINGS WE SEEMED TO HAVE PLENTY OF. THEY LIVE IN A NEARBY PRISON. THEY TOOK OUR HEAD OF SECURITY— MARTINEZ—BACK WITH THEM. I GUESS THERE WAS TALK OF COMBINING THE CAMPS—ONE GROUP MOVING TO THE SAFEST PLACE TO LIVE."*

Now he kneels down by the box, and his voice goes low and thick with contempt. The microphone picks up every nuance, every smack of his lips, every click and crackle in the back of his throat.

"SOME OF THEM STAYED BEHIND—AND ONE NIGHT WHILE MY GUARD WAS DOWN, THEY JUMPED ME AND TOR- TURED ME—MUTILATED ME—AND THEN LEFT ME FOR DEAD."

From the corner of the stands, Lilly listens closely, her stomach going cold. She detects a slight embellishment of the truth. "They" jumped him? "They" tortured him? It was a woman with a katana sword, right? What is he up to? The suspicion starts to gnaw at Lilly as the man out in the dusty, flickering pantomime of light continues, his voice getting lower and thicker by the minute.

"THEY ESCAPED," he goes on, kneeling by that mysterious box as though a paper clown is about to pop out. *"BUT YOU ALL NEED TO KNOW THIS."* He pauses and scans the crowd as though taking their measure. *"ALONG THE WAY THEY KILLED DR. STE- VENS. THESE PEOPLE ARE RUTHLESS, INHUMAN SAVAGES."*

He pauses again, as though the exertion of his rage has already exhausted him.

Lilly watches the man kneeling in the flickering pool of phosphorous light. Something is very, very wrong about this. How does he know they killed Dr. Stevens? He was in a coma at the time, and all the witnesses are long gone. How does he know Stevens didn't simply stumble into a nest of biters? Lilly clenches her fists.

"I FEARED FOR MARTINEZ'S LIFE," the man goes on. "NOT KNOWING IF THEY'D TAKEN HIM PRISONER OR WORSE. BEFORE WE COULD SEND OUT A SEARCH PARTY, SOMETHING WAS LEFT AT THE MAIN GATE OVERNIGHT." He flips open the flaps on the top of the box. He pulls out a dark, glistening object about the size of a deflated basketball.

"THEY LEFT THIS!"

He stands and displays the object for the perusal of all in attendance.

Despite the collective inhaling of breaths, faint gasps, and averting of gazes among some of the spectators, a strange transference occurs in the audience. The sight of a severed head when grasped by the hair and allowed to dangle in space provokes an innate reaction in humans formed not only by natural revulsion but also by hundreds of thousands of years of genetic programming.

Off to the side of the bleachers, her hands folded in her lap, Lilly just looks down and shakes her head. She expected something like this. All the lying has taken her by surprise, though, and the sight of the exsanguinated head of Caesar Martinez provokes more repulsion than she would have expected. She glimpsed it once or twice in the woods during their tempestuous retreat from the meadow, but *this*—this ghastly thing suspended by the hair in the Governor's hand—looks *different* somehow in the context of the flickering arc light. A human head detached from its moorings registers to the mind in stages, first as artificial and then almost comically macabre—the pale rubbery face of the once handsome Latino now a mere *simulacrum* of a face—a fleshy Halloween effigy with a look of blank hunger frozen on its features.

Then the true horror quickly makes itself known, and the reality of the spectacle sets in.

For a brief instant, as the Governor silently holds the object for all to absorb, the head turns lazily on its pendulum of hair. To Lilly, the movement looks languid and dreamy in the flashing light. Tendrils of bloody tendons and nerves dangle from its ragged bottom like roots. Black fluid drips from its gaping mouth, and if it weren't for the milky film over the eyes it would be hard to tell that Martinez had already turned at the point of decapitation. A tattered bandanna still clings to the skull, matted and soaked with blood.

The people in the back rows, gazing down upon the abomination at a distance of more than twenty-five yards, can't see that the bloodless face is still twitching with the hectic rigor mortis of the undead—the tics and shudders, the rusty hinges of the jaw still pulsing—as it will for eternity until the thing is incinerated or the brain is destroyed. Lilly is among the few close enough to see this. She recognizes the dreadful signs of eternal damnation. "Jesus Christ," she utters to no one in particular, barely sensing Austin's presence next to her or the gentle reassurance of his hand on her arm.

The man out in the flickering infield comments: "I KNEW NONE OF YOU WOULD WANT TO SEE THIS, AND I APOLOGIZE FOR SHOCKING YOU. I JUST WANT TO MAKE YOU ALL COMPLETELY AWARE OF THE KIND OF PEOPLE WE'RE DEALING WITH HERE"—another dramatic pause from the Governor—"MONSTERS!"

Lilly swallows her disgust. Shooting a quick glance over her shoulder, she sees the insidious transaction rippling through the crowd. Some of the men present clench their fists, their expressions visibly changing from shock to anger, their eyes narrowing with rage. Some of the women clutch their children tighter, turning their faces inward against their breasts, averting young gazes away from the horror on the infield. Others grit their teeth in a pique of hatred and bloodlust. Lilly is mortified by the manipulation under way, the mob mentality emerging in the throng.

The voice from the loudspeakers continues: *"THESE SAVAGES KNOW WHERE WE LIVE! THEY KNOW WHAT WE HAVE! THEY KNOW OUR STRENGTHS AND THEY KNOW OUR WEAK-NESSES!"* He scans the anguished faces. *"I SAY WE STRIKE AT THEM BEFORE THEY HAVE A CHANCE TO COME AT US!"*

Now Lilly jerks at the unexpected chorus of shouts and howls from the stands behind her. It's not only men. The voices represent all ages, genders, and sensibilities—sending up a dark hallelujah of cries into the sputtering silver radiance of the sky. Some of the onlookers pump their fists. Others bellow garbled cries of rage that sound almost feral. The Governor feeds off it. Still holding the head like some deranged Shakespearean character in a play, moving in the surreal slow motion of the flickering lamps, he is pouring on the call to action as he speaks into the mike.

"I REFUSE TO STAND DOWN AND ALLOW THEM TO DE-STROY US—NOT AFTER EVERYTHING WE'VE LOST—NOT AFTER EVERYTHING WE'VE SACRIFICED!"

Some of the spectators begin to holler encouragement as though in a religious call-and-response, which makes Lilly shudder with dread and coaxes another reassuring pat of the arm from Austin, who continually whispers to her now, "It's okay . . . it'll be okay . . . it's okay, Lilly. . . ." Behind them, one man booms, "FUCK YEAH!" Another one yells, "DAMN STRAIGHT!" And the voices rise and swell as the Governor drowns the noise with his amplified growl.

"WE'VE WORKED TOO HARD TO BUILD WHAT WE HAVE HERE—AND I'LL BE GODDAMNED IF I'M GOING TO LET ANY-ONE TAKE IT AWAY FROM ME!"

The crowd roars, and Lilly has had enough. She rises to her feet and gives Austin a look. Nodding, Austin gets up and follows her out of the bleachers and around the corner of the stands.

"I'M GLAD TO SEE YOU FEEL THE SAME WAY," the Governor is telling the crowd now, his tone calming, his voice becoming almost hypnotic. *"FIRST WE NEED TO FIND THEM. I KNOW MOST OF THE PEOPLE WHO LIVED IN THIS AREA MIGRATED TO*

ATLANTA WHEN THE GOVERNMENT ORDERED US ALL INTO THE CITIES . . . BUT THERE HAS TO BE SOMEONE HERE WHO HAS AT LEAST A PASSING FAMILIARITY WITH THE AREA. IF YOU DO—PLEASE LET ME KNOW."

On their way out of the arena, marching through the noxious darkness of a litter-strewn exit tunnel, Lilly hears the amplified voice like a ghostly revenant echoing and reverberating through the passageway.

"THE PRISON THEY LIVE IN COULD BE FIVE MILES AWAY OR IT COULD BE FIFTEEN . . . AND WE'RE NOT EVEN SURE OF WHICH DIRECTION IT'S IN. THIS IS NOT GOING TO BE EASY."

Lilly and Austin emerge from the tunnel and walk away from the edifice, the sound of the crackling voice fading in their ears.

"BUT IT WILL GET DONE—THEY WILL BE PUNISHED—OF THAT YOU CAN BE SURE."

Lilly gets very little sleep that night. She writhes in a tangle of bedsheets next to Austin, feeling heavy and lethargic and nauseous. She's been taking prenatal vitamins for the last week and drinking as much water as possible, and her bladder has been on high alert. At least half a dozen times through the night, she gets up and goes to the bathroom, and while sitting on the toilet she hears the eerie, unsettling, distant voices of the dead drifting on the winds out in the vast fields of scabrous pastureland west of town. The Governor had correctly noted that the biters weren't the true source of evil in this new world, and he was right. But now Lilly stews in a jumble of contrary emotions and festering doubt. She wants to believe in the Governor—she has to—but she can't ignore the fears kindling in her. Her skin tingles and rashes with goose bumps as she wanders her apartment, getting in and out of bed, trying not to awaken Austin.

By the time the gray light of dawn has pushed the shadows away, she has formulated a course of action. She will talk to the man—try to reason with him—he'll listen to her if she approaches it the right way. After all, they all want the same thing: to keep Woodbury safe. But stirring up the people this way—all this gruesome saber rattling—is insane. Lilly has to talk some sense into the man. He'll listen to her. She has to try.

She waits until midmorning—suffering through a tense breakfast with Austin—before setting out to find the Governor. Austin wants to go with her, but for some reason, she wants to do this by herself.

She tries his apartment building first but finds no one home. She goes to the infirmary and asks Bob if he's seen the man, but Bob has no idea where Philip is at the moment. She wanders the streets for a while until she hears the sound of gunfire coming from the fences out behind the racetrack. She follows the sound.

The day has already heated up, the pale sky heavy with humidity. The high sun bakes the cracked asphalt parking lots, and the air smells of tar and manure. Lilly has already sweated through her sleeveless Georgia Tech T-shirt and ripped denim shorts, and the cramps have returned. She has no appetite, and she can't tell which is playing havoc with her system more—the pregnancy or the fear.

On the south side of the arena, she finds Gabe and Bruce standing near a gate, smoking cigarettes, their rifles slung over their shoulders paramilitary-style. The intermittent bark of small-caliber gunfire comes from behind them, from somewhere along the big cyclone fence barricade separating the town from the walker-infested outskirts.

"Is Philip around?" Lilly asks Gabe as she approaches the two bodyguards.

"Whaddaya want?" Bruce Cooper speaks up before Gabe has a chance to say anything. "He's busy right now."

"Hey, lighten up," Gabe says to the big, barrel-chested black man in sweat-damp camo fatigues. "She's on our side." Gabe turns to Lilly. "He's down at the fence doing a little target practice, Lilly. Whaddaya need?"

"Just wanted to talk to him for a second," she says. "Any luck with the search for the prison?"

Gabe shrugs. "We got guys looking up and down Macauster Lane but nothing yet. There something I can help you with?"

Lilly sighs. "Just thought I might have a little chat with the Governor, no big deal . . . just had a few ideas."

Gabe and Bruce share a fleeting glance. "I don't know. He said he didn't want to be—"

Right then, the sound of a gravelly voice rings out from around the corner. "It's okay—let her come on down!"

They let Lilly pass, and she strides through the gate and down a narrow sidewalk, past rows of empty handicapped parking places, until she sees a gaunt, one-armed man in an olive drab army surplus jacket standing in the middle distance near a chain-link barricade.

"An amazing organ, the human brain," he says without looking at her. He stands next to a wheelbarrow brimming with weapons—guns of all size and caliber—and it quickly becomes obvious that he's been shooting at walkers on the other side of the fence as though trying his hand at a grotesque shooting gallery. A dozen or so ragged bodies lie on the ground outside the chain-link barrier, the air almost blue with gun smoke. "It's like a computer that can reboot itself," he mumbles, selecting a small 9mm pistol from the wheelbarrow with his left hand, raising the gun, thumbing the hammer, and aiming it. "Yet so goddamn fragile . . . it can crash at any moment."

He fires at the cluster of walkers on the other side of the fence.

"FUCK!" The bullet grazes the skull of a female in a tattered, bloodstained sundress. The female staggers and stays upright and keeps banging against the fence. The Governor spits angrily. "Ain't worth shit left-handed!" He fires again and again, until the fourth blast shatters the female's skull in a fountain of brain matter that sends her sliding down the fence in a greasy leech trail of gore. "This ain't gonna be easy," Philip grumbles. "Relearning every goddamn thing in the book." He glances at Lilly. "You come to spank me a little bit?"

Lilly looks at him. "Excuse me?"

"I could tell you weren't exactly thrilled with my little presentation."

"I never said—"

"I could tell by your body language, the expression on your face . . . you didn't seem all that crazy about my oratory skills."

The way he says this in his Georgia twang—putting exaggerated enunciation on the word "orrrr-a-tory"—puts her hackles up. Is he toying with her? Is he challenging her? She licks her lips and carefully chooses her words. "Okay, look . . . I'm sure you know what you're doing. I'm not trying to tell you how to run this town. It's just that . . . there were children in that audience."

"And you think I crossed the line when I showed them what was left of Martinez."

Lilly takes a deep breath. "All right, yes . . . to be honest with you . . . yeah . . . I thought it was a bit much."

He puts the 9 mm back in the wheelbarrow and selects a nickel-plated .357. He checks the cylinder and lines up another shot. "There's a war coming, Lilly," he says softly, drawing a bead on another walker out in the shade of an ancient, twisted live oak. "And I promise you one thing." His left arm is as steady as a steel girder now. "If these people are not ready to defend our town at all costs, we will lose . . . *everything*." His left index finger caresses the trigger pad. He's getting the hang of it now. "Everything you love . . . everything that is dear to you, Lilly. You will—I guarantee it— *lose it*."

He closes his right eye and peers down the barrel with his left and fires.

Lilly doesn't jerk at the noise—not even the slightest flinch, despite the volume of the .357's report—but instead just stands there staring at the man, thinking, feeling the cold sensation of dread turning into certainty within her. The man has a point.

On the other side of the fence, a large male biter folds to the ground in a baptism of blood and fluids. Lilly bites down hard. She senses the tiny ember of life within her, struggling, a seedling starving for sunlight.

At last Lilly says very softly, "You're right. I'm with you—we all are—no matter what happens. We're ready. No matter how bad it gets."

That afternoon, the cramps worsen until Lilly can't even stand up straight anymore. She lies in a fetal position on the futon in her bedroom with packing blankets over the windows to block out the harsh light of the spring sun. She spikes a mild fever—a hundred and one by dinnertime—and she starts seeing streaks of light across her field of vision like sunspots, flaring brightly with each stabbing pain in her midsection and dull throb above the bridge of her nose.

By six o'clock the chills have begun quaking through her, making her shiver convulsively under the ratty thermal blanket that Austin has brought over from his place. She feels as though she's about to vomit but can't quite bring anything up. She's miserable.

Eventually she manages to climb out of bed to go to the bathroom. Her lower back twinges painfully, stiffly, as she shuffles barefoot across her hardwood floors, staggering into the john and closing herself into the reeking chamber of cracked tile and ancient linoleum flooring. She slumps down on the toilet and tries to pee but can't even do that.

Austin has been forcing fluids into her, trying to guard against dehydration, but Lilly's system is so out of whack she can't bear to drink more than a few ounces of water at a time. Now she sits in the darkness of the bathroom and tries to breathe through the cramps, which send hot tremors of agony up her bowels and through her guts. She feels weak. Wrung out. Limp. Like a piano just fell on her. Is it just the stress? She looks down and blinks.

She sees the blood, as bright as strawberry jam, stippling the crotch of her panties, which now dangle down around her ankles.

Her entire body goes icy cold. She has been diligent about checking her underwear for spotting, and up until now has been clean. She tries to keep calm, tries to breathe deeply, tries to think.

A loud knocking shakes her out of her daze. "Lilly?" Austin's voice comes from outside the door, tinged with alarm. "You okay?"

She leans over and grasps the doorknob, nearly falling off the porcelain stool. She manages to crack the door open and then looks up into Austin's glassy, terrified eyes. "I think maybe we should go see Bob," she utters softly, her voice brittle with fear.

EIGHT

That night, Philip Blake cleans house—metaphorically *and* literally—a man on the cusp of a revolution, a warrior on the precipice of war. He wants his environment to reflect the clean, austere, sterile organization of his brain. No more disembodied voices, no more ambivalence brought on by his symbiotic second self. In the autoclave of his mind—cauterized and cleansed by his ordeal—any vestige of Brian Blake has been burned away, sandblasted from the dark crevices of his thoughts. He is a clockwork mechanism now—calibrated for one thing and one thing only: *vengeance*.

So he begins the process with the rooms of his apartment, the scene of the crime. There are still faded signs of the abomination; he is compelled to clean deeper.

Bruce brings him cleaning supplies from the warehouse, and he spends hours eradicating any remaining evidence of his torture at the hands of that lunatic bitch with the sword. He wipes down the walls of his living room with Dutch cleanser, working awkwardly with his left hand, and he carefully runs a battery-powered Dirt Devil over the matted carpet, which still bears the faded stains of his own blood. He uses a cleaning solvent on the more stubborn stains, scrubbing with a soft brush until the rug begins to shred apart. He straightens the rooms, makes the bed, bags the dirty laundry, mops the hardwood floors with Murphy's Oil Soap, and wipes the mossy grime from the glass panels of his matrix of aquariums, paying little attention to the twitching severed heads within them.

He keeps Penny chained to the eye-bolt in the foyer while he works, every few moments making note of her presence in the other room—the soft burr of her perpetual growling, the dull rattling of her chain as she strains to escape, the faint clack of her piranha-like teeth snapping at the air with blind hunger. As he cleans around her, he finds himself being more and more bothered by that soft clacking noise.

It takes him hours to sanitize the place to his satisfaction. Working with one arm makes some of the tasks, such as opening a garbage bag or pushing a broom around corners, a little tricky. To make matters worse, he keeps seeing corners that he missed, nooks and crannies still bearing signs of his torment—sticky patches of dried blood, a discarded roll of tape, a drill bit still crusted with his tissue under a chair, a fingernail in the nap of the carpet. He cleans well into the night, until he has nearly erased every last remnant of his suffering. He even rearranges the sparse furniture to cover or hide the scars he cannot expunge—the scorch marks from the acetylene torch, the nail holes in the rug from the plywood panel.

At length, he obliterates any visible proof that torture ever occurred here.

Satisfied with the job, he collapses into his recliner in the side room. The soft percolating of the aquariums calms him, the muffled thudding and tapping of the reanimated faces bumping against the inside of the glass almost soothing to him. He stares at the bloated, sodden faces undulating behind their veils of water. He imagines the glorious moment when he takes that dreadlock-wearing bitch apart piece by piece . . . and eventually he drifts off.

He dreams of the old days, and he sees himself at home in Waynesboro with his wife and child—a mythology his brain has now chiseled into itself with the permanence of a stone tablet—and he is happy, truly happy, maybe the only time he felt such happiness in his life. He holds Penny on his lap in the cozy little sunroom off the kitchen in the rear of the clapboard house on Pilson Street, with Sarah Blake curled up on the sofa next to them, her head on Philip's shoulder, as Philip reads a Dr. Seuss book aloud to Penny.

But something intrudes on the scene—a strange tapping noise—a dull, metallic clacking. In the dream, he looks up at the ceiling and sees cracks forming, each tapping noise spreading another hairline fracture in the plaster overhead, a sifting of dust motes filtering down through rays of sunlight. The tapping noise rises and quickens, and he sees more cracks forming, until the ceiling begins to rend apart. He screams as the room collapses in on itself.

The cataclysm wakes him up.

He jerks forward in the chair with a start, his wounds panging with sharp stabs of agony from the hammer blows and gashes and puncture sores that are still tight with sutures under his clothes. He is damp with cold sweat, and his phantom arm throbs. He swallows stomach acid and looks around the room—the dull glow and bubbling of the aquariums bringing him back to reality—and he realizes he still hears the infernal clacking noise.

The sound of Penny's chattering teeth in the other room.

He has to do something about it.

The last stage of his housecleaning.

"Don't you worry, Lilly-girl, I happen to have quite a bit of practice catching babies," Bob Stookey says, blatantly lying to the couple in the magnesium-silver brightness of the underground infirmary. It's the middle of the night and the cavernous room is as silent as a morgue. Bob has rolled a pulse-ox unit over to the bed on which Lilly now lies covered in a sheet, with Austin nearby, fidgeting, chewing his fingernails, and shooting glances back and forth from Lilly's ashen face to Bob's weathered, smiling visage.

"I ain't no O-B-G-Y-N," Bob adds, "but I had to watch over my share of pregnant gals during my stint in the army. You and your baby are gonna be fine . . . shipshape . . . four by four, little lady."

The truth is, Bob had only dealt with a single pregnant woman during his tour in Afghanistan—a translator—a local girl who had been only seventeen when one of the guys from the PX had knocked her up. Bob had kept her condition under wraps until the day she miscarried. It was Bob who had to give the woman the news—although he was convinced back then, and still is today, that she already knew. A woman knows. That's all there is to it . . . *a woman knows.*

"What about the spotting?" Lilly asks. She lies on the same gurney on which the Governor floated in the balance between life and death for so many days. Bob has inserted an IV stick into her arm just above the wrist—the last bag of glucose in the storage pantry—in order to stave off dehydration and keep her stable.

Now Bob tries to maintain the reassuring tone in his voice as he hovers over her. "It ain't that uncommon during the first trimester," he says, not really knowing what he's talking about, turning to wash his hands in the steel sink behind them. The drumming of the water on the basin is excruciatingly loud in the stillness of the infirmary. The room is a pressure cooker of emotion. "I'm sure everything is right as rain," Bob says with his back turned to them.

"Whatever you need, Bob, just let me know," Austin says then. Dressed in his hoodie and ponytail, he looks like a lost child who could break down into sobs at any moment. He puts a hand on Lilly's bare shoulder.

Bob dries his hands on a towel. "Lilly Caul's gonna be a mom . . . I still can't get over it." He turns and comes back over to the bed. He smiles down at her as he slips on surgical gloves. "This is just what we need around this place," he says with false cheer. "Some good news for once." He reaches under the sheet and gently palpates her tummy, trying to remember how to diagnose a miscarriage. "You're gonna be great at it, too." He turns to a tray of instruments, and finds a flat stainless steel probe. "Some people are just cut out for it. Know what I mean? I was never cut out for it—God knows."

Lilly turns her head to the side and closes her eyes, and Bob can tell she's trying not to cry. "It doesn't feel right," she murmurs. "Something's wrong, Bob. I can tell. I can feel it."

Bob looks at Austin. "Son, I'm gonna have to do a pelvic exam on her."

Austin has tears in his eyes. He knows. Bob can see it in the young man's glazed expression. "Whatever you need to do, Bob."

"Honey, I'm gonna have to go in there and have a look-see," he says. "It ain't gonna be too comfortable, and it's a gonna be a little cold."

Her eyes still closed, Lilly barely emits a whisper. "It's okay."

"All right, here we go."

"Dammit—hold still." Philip Blake crouches in the darkness of his foyer, working with the needle-nosed pliers, his left hand gloved and protected with a layer of duct tape. "I know you're not enjoying this, but I hope you understand how much better this will make things."

He probes the black maw of his dead daughter's mouth with the pliers, trying to latch on to her upper incisors. Penny keeps trying to chew on his hand, but he keeps her immobilized with his jackboot on her lower half. Her reek engulfs him as he works, but he ignores it.

"It really is for the good of our relationship," he says, finally latching on to one of her upper teeth with the pincers. "Here it comes!"

He extracts a tooth—the sound like a tiny cork popping—and pulls the bloody pellet free, trailing delicate threads of pulp. Penny rears back for a moment, her demonic features puckering, her wide, milky eyes fixed on some empty void beyond this world.

"Here comes another one," Philip mutters softly, as though speaking to a pet. "I can feel it loosening." He grunts as another tooth pops free. "There. See? This isn't so bad, is it?" He tosses the second tooth into a wastebasket behind him, and then turns back to the girl-thing. "You're almost getting used to the feeling, aren't you?"

She drools a black, oily substance as he removes one tooth after another, her face now going as blank as the dark side of the moon. "Just a few more, and we'll be done," he comments with fake cheer, working on her lower teeth. "Sound good?" He pulls the last few jagged lower teeth with minimum effort, the tiny threads of tissue looping across the front of her filthy sundress.

Thanks to advanced decomposition, the teeth come out easily on their dead roots.

"There," Philip says reassuringly, "all done."

For a brief instant, standing in that silent infirmary at the foot of Lilly's gurney, Bob remembers that one time in Afghanistan when he assisted the field surgeon in the performance of a D&C on the translator—the removal of any remaining fetal or placental tissue after a pregnancy has been lost—and now he searches his memory for the lessons of that day. He gently reaches under the sheet covering Lilly's lower half. He doesn't look at Lilly's face.

She looks away.

Bob begins the exam. He remembers the way a healthy uterus is supposed to feel during the early weeks of a viable pregnancy—according to the field surgeon—versus the way it feels in the aftermath of a miscarriage. It takes only a few seconds for Bob to find the end of the cervix. Lilly lets out an anguished mewling sound that breaks Bob's heart. He palpates the uterus and finds it completely dilated, heavy with blood and slough. This is all he needs to know. He gently pulls back, removing his hand from her.

"Lilly, I want you to remember something," he says then, removing his gloves. "There's no reason—"

"Oh no." She's already softly crying, her head still turned away, her tears soaking the pillow. "I knew it . . . I knew it."

"Oh Jesus." Austin puts his head down on the gurney's side rail. "Oh God."

"What was I thinking? . . ." She softly, silently weeps into the gurney's pillow. "What the fuck was I thinking? . . ."

Bob is crestfallen. "Now, honey, let's not start kicking ourselves in the ass, okay? The good news is, you can try again . . . you're a young gal, you're healthy, you can definitely try again."

Lilly stops crying. "Enough, Bob."

Bob looks down. "I'm sorry, honey."

Austin looks up, wipes his eyes, and gazes at the wall. He lets out a long pained breath. "Fuck."

"Gimme a towel, Bob." Lilly sits up on the gurney. She has a strange expression on her face, impossible to read, but one glance at it and Bob knows to shut the fuck up and get the woman a towel. He grabs a cloth and hands it to her. "Unhook me from this shit," she says flatly, wiping herself off. "I gotta get outta here."

Bob removes the stick, wipes her wrist, and puts a bandage on the site.

She shoves herself off the gurney. For a moment, she looks as if she might fall over. Austin steadies her, gently holding her by the shoulder. She pushes him away and finds her jeans draped over a chair back. "I'm fine." She gets dressed. "I'm perfectly fine."

"Honey . . . take it easy." Bob circles around her as though blocking her path to the door. "You probably oughtta just stay off your feet for a while."

"Get outta my way, Bob," she says with fists clenched now, jaw set with determination.

"Lilly, why don't we—" Austin falls silent when she shoots him a look. The expression on her face—the teeth gritted tightly, the smoldering cinders of rage in her eyes—takes Austin aback.

Bob wants to say something but figures maybe it's better if he just lets her go. He steps aside, and then looks at Austin, gesturing for him to back off. Lilly is already halfway across the room.

The door slams behind her, the residual tension crackling in her slipstream.

For an endless, agonizing moment, Philip Blake kneels before his monstrous offspring in the dusty gloom of that apartment foyer.

Penny looks strangely hobbled by the slipshod dental procedure. She wobbles on her spindly little legs for a moment, moving her blackened lips around rotten, bloody gums, her empty gaze riveted on the man in front of her.

Philip leans down toward the dead girl, his mind filled with false memories of tucking his daughter into bed at night, reading storybooks to her, stroking her lustrous goldenrod curls, and planting kisses on her fragrant little forehead. "All better," he murmurs to the creature chained to the wall. "Now, come here."

He puts his arms around her and gives her a hug. She feels like a brittle husk in his arms, like a tiny scarecrow. He cradles her cold, mottled jawline in his gloved left hand. "Give Daddy a kiss."

He kisses her rancid divot of a mouth, seeking warmth and love, but tasting only the bitter rot of spoiled meat and flyspecked feces. He rears back, an involuntary jerk, repulsed by the string of slimy tissue adhering to his lips. He gasps and frantically wipes away the black drool, his stomach heaving suddenly.

She lurches toward him, eyes narrowing, trying to bite him with her pulpy black gums.

He doubles over, holding her head back with one arm. The nausea within him turns to a column of hot bile rising up his gorge. He vomits on the hardwood floor, the yellow viscous stew of stomach acids spattering across the floorboards. He wretches and convulses until there's nothing left to expel.

Falling back on his knees, he wipes his mouth, hyperventilating. "Oh, honey . . . I'm sorry." He swallows hard and tries to get his bearings back, tries to push back the shame and disgust. "Don't think anything of it." He gets his breath back. He swallows again. "I'm sure . . . with time . . . I'll . . . I'll . . ." He wipes his face. "Please don't let this—"

All at once the bang of somebody knocking loudly on the apartment door interrupts. The Governor sniffs back his revulsion. He blinks at the noise. "Fuck!" He rises on weak knees. "FUCK!"

Over the course of the next thirty seconds—the time it takes Philip
Blake to get himself together, cross the foyer, unsnap the dead bolt,
and throw the door open—he transforms from a trembling, weak,
unrequited father to a diamond-hard leader of men. "Did I or did I
not say I was *not* to be *disturbed*?" he snarls coldly at the shadowy
figure standing in the dim light of the corridor.

Gabe clears his throat instinctively. Clad in an army surplus
jacket cinched at the waist with a gun belt and bandolier, he measures his words. "Sorry, boss—some shit's going down."

"What shit?"

Gabe takes a deep breath. "Okay, there was an explosion. We
think at the National Guard station—huge cloud of smoke going
into the air. Bruce took some men to investigate. They were gone a
few minutes, and then we heard gunfire nearby."

"Nearby?!"

"Yeah, same direction."

The Governor sears his gaze into the man's eyes. "Then why
don't you just grab a car and—FUCK!" He turns back to the apartment. "Never mind!—Forget it!—Follow me!"

They take one of the armored trucks. The Governor rides in the
cab on the passenger side, holding an AR-15 on his lap, as Gabe
drives. Gabe hardly says a word the whole trip out—down Flat
Shoals Road, past miles of walker-riddled forest, up Highway 85,
and down a long farm road toward the smudge of black smoke visible against the night sky—while the Governor silently broods in
the shotgun seat. A pair of Gabe's men, Rudy and Gus, ride outside
the cab, one on each flank, standing on a footrail in the wind, cradling assault rifles.

As they rumble eastward through the night, the Governor feels
his phantom arm twinge with needles of pain at every bump,
every jerk—a bizarre sensation that keeps tugging at his peripheral
vision in the green glowing darkness of the cab, making him think
there's a tingling ghost-arm protruding from his stump—and it

makes him angrier by the minute. He ruminates silently in the rattling dark, thinking about going to war, thinking about twisting off the head of that bitch who attacked him.

The great military leaders of yore, the men Philip has read about in history books—everybody from MacArthur to Robert E. Lee—stayed away from the front, huddled in tents with their commanders, planning, strategizing, looking at maps. Not Philip Blake. He fancies himself as Attila the Hun, or maybe Alexander the Great, roaring into Egypt with revenge on his mind and death dripping off the bloody tip of his sword. His eye patch itches as the adrenaline courses through him. He wears a leather driving glove on his left hand that creaks as he clenches his fist.

They approach a familiar turnoff snaking off the main two-lane. The wind has blown a letter off the tall roadside sign, which now says:

Wal art ✷
Save money. Live better.

In the middle distance, the Governor can see the vast leprous cement of the Walmart parking lot gleaming like a gray ocean in the moonlight. Near the west edge of the lot, a few dark, ragged objects lie on the pavement near a familiar-looking cargo truck. The Governor recognizes the truck—it's from Woodbury's fleet.

"Fuck!" The Governor points. "Over there, Gabe—near the garbage Dumpsters!"

Gabe guns the truck and it booms across the parking lot, raising a cloud of dust into the night sky. The air brakes come on as they approach the battlefield. Gabe skids to a stop thirty feet away with a jerk.

"FUCK!" The Governor shoves his door open and stands on the skid, gazing at the carnage strewn across the lot like discarded rag dolls. "FUCK!"

The Governor hops off the skid and leads the three other men across the lot to the dead bodies. For a moment, nobody says anything. The Governor surveys the scene, makes note of the evidence. The cargo truck still idles, the carbon monoxide and cordite still hanging in the air like a thick blue shroud over the scene.

"Jesus," Gabe utters, looking down at the four bodies lying in pools of blood across the concrete. One of them is headless, the body also missing hands, the severed cranium lying in a puddle of gore fifteen feet away. Another one—the kid named Curtis—lies supine with arms akimbo and dead eyes still open and staring up at the stars. A third one lies dead in a swamp of blood and tissue, his guts blooming out of a large gash in his belly. It doesn't take Sherlock Holmes to deduce that the long, clean cuts—the neatly severed appendages—are the result of a Japanese katana sword.

Gabe walks over to the largest body, a black man still clinging to life but quickly bleeding out, his neck ravaged by multiple high-caliber blasts. His face sticky with his own blood, his eyes showing mostly whites, Bruce Cooper tries to speak with his last breaths.

Nobody can understand him.

The Governor moves over to the fallen man and gazes down at the body with very little emotion other than simmering rage. "His head is still intact," Philip says to Gabe. "He'll probably be turning soon."

Gabe starts to say something in response when the faint sound of Bruce Cooper's baritone voice—now breathless and choked with agony—can be heard under the wind. The Governor kneels and listens closely.

"S-ssaw the bald f-fuck, the k-kid," Bruce utters, his throat filling with blood. "They . . . came b-back . . . they . . ."

"Bruce!" The Governor leans closer. His angry bark lacks any compassion. "BRUCE!"

The big man on the ground has nothing left. His big shaved head—now stippled with blood as black as pitch—begins to loll one last time. His eyes flutter once, and then go still, fixed, lifeless as marbles. The Governor stares at the man for a moment.

Then the Governor looks down at the cement and closes his eyes.

He doesn't see the others bowing their heads with grudging respect for the iron-fisted enforcer who dutifully did the Governor's bidding, who stood by the Governor without question, without recompense, without hesitation. Now Philip Blake fights the anguish seeping into his thoughts like a volatile chemical clouding his resolve. Bruce Cooper is just one man—a single cog in the Woodbury machine—but he secretly meant the world to Philip. Other than Gabe, Bruce was the closest thing to a friend Philip had in this world. Philip confided in Bruce, let him see the aquariums, let him see Penny. Bruce was unconditional in his respect—if not love—for Philip Blake. In fact, as far as Philip can tell, it was Bruce who saved his life, who forced Bob to get his shit together and treat the injuries.

The Governor looks up. He sees Gabe turning away, bowing his head as though offering deference and privacy to his boss in this excruciating moment, the 9mm Glock still holstered on Gabe's hip. There is only one thing left to do—one loose end to be tied up.

The Governor grabs the pistol from Gabe's holster, making Gabe jerk with a start.

Aiming the muzzle down at Bruce's head, he squeezes off a single shot—point-blank—sending a hollow-point slug into Bruce's skull. The discharge makes everybody else jump, everybody except the Governor.

He turns to Gabe. "They were just *here*." The Governor speaks now in a low, thick voice—a voice charged with latent rage and mayhem. "Find their fucking tracks. Find their fucking prison." He fixes his fiery gaze from one good eye into Gabe's eyes and roars suddenly: "FIND IT NOW!!"

Then he walks away toward the armored truck without another word.

For a long time, standing amid the dead bodies scattered like broken mannequins across the desolate, moonlit parking lot, Gabriel Harris is paralyzed with indecision. Watching the Governor storm away, climb behind the wheel of the armored truck, and rumble off into the night leaves Gabe speechless and bewildered. How the hell is he supposed to find this fucking prison on foot, with no supplies, very little ammunition, and just a couple of men? For that matter, how the fuck are they supposed to get back home? Fucking hitchhike? Then, over the space of an instant, Gabe's state of complete and utter vexation changes to pure, unadulterated resolve when he glances back at the remains of Bruce Cooper, his friend, his comrade-in-arms.

The sight of the big man lying in the moonlight—now as ruined and butchered as a flensed piece of meat—reaches down to some inner reserve deep within Gabe. A wave of contrary emotions wells up in him—sorrow, rage, and fear—and he bites down hard on the feelings. He orders the other two men to follow him.

They ransack what's left of the merchandise rotting inside the defunct Walmart. In the shadowy nooks and crannies, under fallen displays and on the floors behind counters, they find a couple of useable backpacks, a flashlight, a pair of binoculars, a box of crackers, a jar of peanut butter, some notebook paper, pens, batteries, and two boxes of .45 caliber slugs.

They stow the supplies into the backpacks and then set out to the east, at first following tire tracks, wending their way down a dusty adjacent access road, and then making a sharp turn to the south. They follow the tracks down dirt roads all night, until the tracks take a turn onto a stretch of blacktop and instantly vanish.

Gabe refuses to give up. He decides they should fan out. He sends Gus to the east and Rudy off to the west, and they make plans to hook back up at the intersection of Highway 80 and 267.

The men go their separate ways, the thin beams of their flashlights receding into the predawn fog. Gabe uses his eleven-inch buck knife to slice through a stretch of thick foliage, cutting a swath straight south as the sky begins to lighten with the first hints of dawn.

An hour later, he runs into a few errant walkers weaving through the trees, drawn to his scent, and he manages to dodge most of them. At one point, a small one—either a child or a midget, its moldering face blackened beyond recognition—darts out of the brush at him. He takes it down with a single knife thrust to the skull. Sweat breaks out on the back of Gabe's thick neck and drips down the small of his back as he picks up his pace, carving a path through the overgrown, neglected farm fields.

By midday, Gabe reaches the junction of two weather-beaten blacktop roads. He sees Rudy and Gus about twenty-five yards to the north, sitting side by side like owls on a split-rail fence, waiting for him, and judging by the sheepish, morose expressions on their faces, it's obvious that they have each come up empty.

"Lemme guess," Gabe says, approaching them from the south. "You didn't find shit."

Gus gives him a shrug. "Passed a bunch of little farm towns, all deserted . . . no prison."

"Same," Rudy grumbles. "Nothin' but wrecked cars and empty buildings. Ran into a few walkers, was able to put them down without making much of a racket."

Gabe lets out a sigh, pulls a handkerchief, and wipes the moisture from the back of his neck. "Gotta keep trying, goddamnit."

Rudy starts to say, "Why don't we try following—"

A sudden clap of gunfire echoes to the west, cutting off his words. It sounds like a small-caliber pistol. The sharp report reverberates across the sky, and Gabe jerks toward the sound, which comes from behind the tree line.

The other two men look up. Then they look at Gabe, who stares out at the rolling hills beyond the fence. For a moment, nobody says anything.

Then Gabe turns to the others and says, "Okay, follow me . . . and stay down. I got a feeling we just hit pay dirt."

NINE

Lilly spends most of that day holed up in her apartment, chewing aspirin, prowling around her living room in her sweatpants and Georgia Tech football jersey, taking inventory of her storehouse of firearms and weaponry. The overcast daylight filters through the blinds, making her skull throb, but she ignores the aches and pains, operating now on the adrenal charge of pure hatred coursing through her like an electric current.

After a sleepless night and a series of tense exchanges with Austin, she is galvanized now, buzzing with contempt for these bastards who barged into Woodbury and made her lose her baby. After nearly two years of living amid the plague, Lilly has developed a unified theory of proper behavior among survivors. You either help one another—if you can—or leave each other the fuck alone. But these intruders have trampled over all decent modes of interaction and ruined everything, and the outrage burns brightly in Lilly. Thankfully, the tenderness in her midsection has faded slightly—along with the shock of all her dreams going up in smoke—which now only serves to make room for the white-hot loathing for these people that blazes within her as she paces the cluttered apartment.

All the crates and boxes and secondhand furniture have been pushed aside, stacked along the walls to make room for the arsenal of small arms, bladed weapons, and excess ammunition spread out across the floor. It hadn't even occurred to her how much of this stuff she had been stockpiling over the months—perhaps out of paranoia, or maybe via some kind of dark intuition—but now she sees it all laid out in orderly rows. Her two .22 caliber Ruger MK IIs lay side by side at the top of the heap like crests on a coat of arms. An extra pair of 10-round magazines are lined up next to the pistols, and a web belt is coiled directly below the mags. Under this is a row of cartons filled with 40-caliber rounds, a machete, a row of assorted suppressors, Austin's Glock on a stock of spare magazines, a Remington .308 bolt-action MSR rifle, three long-blade knives with varying degrees of sharpness, a long-handled pickax, and an odd assortment of holsters, sheaths, and pouches lined up in a neat little row.

Austin's voice rings out from the adjacent kitchen. "Soup's on!" He announces this with as much vigor and cheer as he can muster, but the sadness is apparent in his voice, a constant weight now dragging him down. "Whaddaya say we eat together in the back room?"

"Not hungry," she calls to him.

"Lilly, c'mon . . . don't do this to me," he says, coming into the room wringing his hands on a towel. He wears a shopworn REM T-shirt, his long curls undone and spilling down his back. He looks nervous. "You need your nourishment."

"What for?"

"Lilly, please."

"Look . . . I appreciate the thought." She doesn't even look at him, just keeps studying the arsenal at her feet. "You go ahead and eat—I'm fine."

He licks his lips, thinking, choosing his words carefully. "You do realize that we may never see these people again."

"Oh, we'll see them . . . I promise you . . . we'll see them again."

"What does that mean?"

She stares at the weapons. "It means we're not going to stop until we find them."

"Why? What good is it going to do?"

She looks at him. "Did the IQ level just drop in here to, like, room temperature?"

"Lilly—"

"Have you not been paying attention to anything that's been going on?"

"That's the problem!" He throws the towel on the floor. "I've been with you every step of the way, I've been paying fucking close attention to *everything*." He swallows hard, takes a breath, and then tries to calm down and measure his words. "I can see you're hurting, Lilly, but I'm hurting, too."

Lilly looks back down at the firearms and says very softly, "I know that."

He comes over to her and touches her shoulder. "This is insane."

She doesn't move her gaze from the weapons. "It is what it is."

"And what is that?"

She looks at him. "It's fucking war."

"War? Really? That sounds more like the Governor talking."

"It's us or them, Austin."

Austin lets out an exasperated sigh. "I'm not worried about *them*, Lilly . . . I'm worried about *us*."

She scorches him with her gaze. "You better pull your head out of your ass and start worrying about *them*, or there's not going to *be* an us . . . there's not going to be a Woodbury, there's not going to be fucking *anything*."

Austin looks down, and says nothing.

Lilly starts to say something else when she stops herself. She sees something in Austin's expression change, his eyes welling up, and a single tear tracking down his face. The tear drips off his chin and falls to the floor. All the fight goes out of Lilly, and her guts tighten with sadness. She goes to him and puts her arms around him. He hugs her back, and then she hears Austin's voice in her ear, barely a whisper, all strangled with sorrow. "I feel helpless," he utters breathlessly. "Losing the baby . . . and now . . . I feel like you're pulling away . . . and I can't lose you . . . I can't . . . I just can't."

She holds him and strokes his long hair and murmurs softly in his ear, "You're not going to lose me. You're my man. Do you understand? It's you and me—end of story. You understand?"

"Yes . . ." His voice is barely audible. "I understand . . . thank you . . . thank you."

For a long moment they hold each other in the ashen light of that cluttered living room, saying nothing, just holding each other as though bracing themselves. She can hear Austin's heavy breaths in her ear, can feel his heart beating against her chest.

"I know what it's like to feel helpless," she says at last, looking into his eyes, their faces nearly touching, their breath mingling. "Not long ago I was the poster girl for helplessness. I was a train wreck. But somebody helped me, gave me confidence, taught me how to survive."

Austin holds her tighter, and he whispers, "That's what you've done for me, Lilly."

She plants a soft, tender kiss on his forehead and pulls him into a tighter embrace. God help her, she loves him. She will fight for him, she will fight for their future, she will fight to the death. She cradles the back of his head, stroking his long hair, but all she can think about now is getting into the shit and exterminating each and every one of these fucking monsters who remain a threat.

At dusk that night, the Governor sits by himself in the empty bleachers of the speedway, the wind tossing litter across the deserted infield. The sky, heavy with toxic particulates, streaks with ribbons of gold and fuchsia as the sun dips below the clouds and dust devils swirl across the track on the bluster of the day's end— all of it reflecting Philip Blake's pensive mood.

A great military leader once called this time "the great inhalation before the storm," and Philip feels a similar weight in the air. Sitting in the waning light, he marshals his energy and fantasizes about the glory of battle and the satisfaction of seeing that bitch who crippled him come apart at the seams like a blood-filled piñata. Philip's mind percolates with the dark energy of war like an atomic particle accelerator—humming with rage—turning this magic-hour light into an unholy rite, a sacred invocation.

Then, almost as if conjured by his thoughts, a harbinger appears—a stocky figure in camo pants, boots, and army surplus jacket—materializing in the shadows of the speedway's far portal.

Philip looks up.

Gabe trots across the infield, breathless from running, his portly face filled with urgency, eyes blazing with excitement. He sees Philip. He circles around the end of the stands, hopping over the iron cordons and climbing the bench seats until he approaches the Governor. "They said I'd find you here," he says, hyperventilating, leaning over and putting his hands on his knees.

"Take it easy, Kemosabe," the Governor says. "I hope you got good news for me."

Gabe looks at him and nods. "We found it."

The words seem to hang in the air for a moment, the expression on Philip's face unreadable in the fading blue light. He stares. "Start talking."

According to Gabe, when they heard the shots that day, they crept through the thick woods adjacent to the two-lane until they snuck up on a couple of chicks and some older dude in a clearing doing some target practice. Gabe and his men stayed out of sight, huddling behind the trees, watching from a distance, as the three unidentified folks took down a few biters, and then started dragging one of the bodies back toward a high fence in the distance.

At first, none of it made any sense, but when Gabe and the boys finally followed a path up a hill to get a better view from higher land—and they got a good glimpse of what lay beyond the fence, spreading across the neighboring patchwork of farm fields like a vast housing block that had simply dropped out of space—all the pieces fell together.

The place once known as the Meriwether County Correctional

Facility stretches almost as far as the eye can see across the pastureland on the eastern edge of the county, a zigzagging network of gray-brick postwar buildings situated behind three layers of security fencing. Gabe realized instantly that the reason nobody in Woodbury had thought of this place is probably due to the fact that it had been defunded by the state of Georgia in the crash of '87, and for years it had been off the radar, sitting out here in the rural hinterlands like a ghost ship. The only reason that Gabe's memory was jogged by the sight of the place was the fact that Gabe's cousin, Eddie, a drug dealer from Jacksonville, had been held here in the late '90s pending his appeal. The state had taken to using the place as a glorified waiting room—technically, a jail for convicted felons—running it on a skeleton crew but essentially keeping it stocked and armed and locked and loaded.

For the most part, the property seemed fairly secure to Gabe—but not by any stretch of the imagination *invulnerable*. Inside the perimeter of razor wire and guard towers, the exercise yards and run-down basketball courts lay deserted, cleared long ago of any biters. And although the outer edges of the fences swarmed here and there with stray walkers—clusters of them drawn to the scent of the human inhabitants like bees drawn to honey—the soot-stained buildings looked relatively solid, with good bones, and stacks on the roof pitches pluming puffs of exhaust. Somebody must have gotten the generators and emergency apparatus up and running. The condition of the place suggested the potential for refrigeration, showers, air-conditioning, cafeterias stocked with food and supplies, amenities such as gyms and weight-training rooms and arcades—all of it just begging to be taken.

"They've got the fences," Gabe explains now, standing on a metal bench only inches away from where the Governor sits intently listening. "And they seem to be letting the biters form a perimeter around those fences, maybe by accident—or maybe they're smarter than we thought." Gabe pauses to let this sink in.

"Go on," the Governor says, not taking his eyes off the empty racetrack, thinking it over as the gathering darkness pulls a curtain down on the arena. "I'm listening."

"The thing is," Gabe says, his voice dropping an octave, getting taut and thick with anticipation. "There ain't a whole lot of them, and they can't have *that* many weapons."

The Governor doesn't say anything, just keeps gazing at the hazy shadows that are deepening at the edges of the track, his single visible eye narrowing.

"We watched them for hours, man," Gabe goes on. "We hit them tomorrow and they go down like chumps. I'm telling you . . . they'd barely put up a fight—"

"No."

The word pops like a firecracker in the gloom, and it has the effect of a splash of cold water on Gabe's face. He does a double take. He looks down at the Governor, and he tilts his head with consternation.

The Governor stares at the night for a moment, and then gazes up at Gabe. "We wait."

Anger and dismay flare inside the stocky man. "Goddamnit, Governor! After what they did to Bruce?! We need to take them down now!"

"Excuse me?" The Governor's one good eye holds Gabe in its thrall for a moment, the tiny pinprick of light in the center of his iris reflecting the moon like a fuse that's been lit. "After they escaped, their guard was up, probably for weeks. We couldn't find them." He pauses with the theatricality of a professor giving a lecture. "After Martinez betrayed them—and they butchered him—their guard was up again. Still, nothing from us."

By this point, Gabe has begun to nod slowly, almost to himself, finally getting it.

"Now they've raided our territory, killed some of our men," the Governor goes on with that dark, glittering gaze locked onto Gabe. "They've got to be expecting us to follow them back. We wait. We wait for them to relax again. That way, they don't expect it. They convince themselves they're safe—that we've given up or we can't find them."

Gabe nods.

"That's when we fucking strike," the Governor says. "And if you want to be along for the ride and not a rotting piece of biter food, you'll shut your goddamn mouth and get the fuck outta my sight."

Gabe stands there for a moment, swallowing back the dismay and shame.

"NOW!"

The booming echo of the Governor's voice carries over the empty stands.

The next day, the dynamic in Woodbury changes. Every man, woman, and child can feel it, but few can articulate the tension that looms sharklike beneath the surface of daily life—the way children are kept mostly indoors and quiet and occupied by coloring books or board games, or the way conversations among the adults become muted and hushed and urgent. Any trace of the gallows humor that once peppered the bitch sessions around the coffee urn at the Main Street diner now fade away completely, replaced by a grim sort of purpose to each exchange, each task, each anxious meeting.

Over the next week, Gabe and Lilly huddle with the town's elders and explain what's going on. In private meetings they prepare the heads of families and the strongest of the young adults—those who will be on the front line—for the coming assault on the prison. They delegate duties required to get the town on its war footing, and soon a kind of organic hierarchy emerges. If the Governor is the high command, then Lilly and Gabe become his generals, relaying orders to the rank and file, organizing the ragtag battalion of residents into a ferocious invasion force. Lilly becomes the self-appointed standard-bearer, turning the fear to righteous rage, spreading the word that this will be a just mission, the only way to protect the children of Woodbury.

The racetrack becomes the official command center, with stock-piles of matériel and ordnance gathered in the garages underneath the stadium and under rain tarps across the infield. The Governor's inner sanctum is established high up in the press boxes, with maps of Meriwether County taped up onto the walls and across the surfaces of folding tables. Late at night, the one-armed warrior can be glimpsed pacing the press box, alone, silhouetted by the yellow light of bare bulbs, compulsively studying the twenty-three-mile distance between Woodbury and the prison—plotting the invasion with the intensity of Eisenhower planning the Allied attack on Anzio.

By the end of that week, Lilly has made an exhaustive inventory of the armaments at Woodbury's disposal. They have twenty-seven crates of 7.62 and 5.56 rounds and enough magazines for a small army, as well as enough Kevlar to outfit half the adults. They have three .50 caliber machine guns and scores of rifles, of both the assault and the long-range sniper variety. They have enough fuel to convey at least a dozen vehicles—most of them from the Guard station—across the twenty-three miles of rural roads to the battle-front. They have six mine-resistant armored trucks, a couple of cargo vehicles, a personnel carrier, two Humvees, and a pair of big Buick four-door sedans that will do in a pinch.

Gabe spends the bulk of the second week getting the single Abrams M1 tank—discovered in mothballs at the Guard station—in working order. The armored tank features a remotely operated .50 caliber turret on top and a 105mm cannon with forty-two rounds in the hull. Since the tank's turbine engine runs on diesel, Gabe has to send two separate parties on fuel runs to nearby truck stops for the last drops of diesel available in the county.

By the end of that second week of waiting and girding and preparing, Lilly has completely shed her fears and finds herself sleeping soundly for the first time since the plague began. She has no dreams now, and she awakes every morning replenished, her spine tingling with anticipation for the fight. Even Austin is on board. He has been target shooting regularly and has gotten very handy with the sniper rifle. Lilly feels a strange tie binding her with Austin—not just the shared grief over the miscarriage, but also the galvanizing purpose of their mission, their common hunger for a better future. They have convinced themselves that this is the only way, and the collective resolve has drawn them closer together.

The following Tuesday night, after dusk has settled down on the town—almost three weeks after Gabe's discovery of the prison—Lilly finishes loading the last of the high-capacity ammo magazines that are lined up on long tables in the corridor under the racetrack. She decides to head home . . . and she is just emerging from the west exit, stepping into the darkness of the speedway parking lot, when she hears a shuffling noise behind her—coming from the shadows of the portal—that raises her hackles and causes her to draw her Ruger and whirl around with the muzzle coming up instinctively in the general vicinity of the noise.

A voice out of the darkness: "Young lady walking around a bad neighborhood alone at night." The slender male figure lurking in the shadows smokes a cigarette, the orange firefly of its tip the only thing visible. "It's a recipe for disaster."

"Who's there?" Lilly holds her gun on the silhouette shrouded in the shadows. The husky voice sounds familiar, but she can't be sure. "Identify yourself, please. . . ."

The Governor steps out of the shadows into the pool of yellow security light. "Good to see your reflexes are sound," he says, tossing the cigarette.

"Jesus, you scared the shit outta me." She holsters her gun and feels her neck muscles relaxing. "You shouldn't surprise people around this place, not if you want to keep your head from being shot off."

"Point well taken." He smiles at her, the fingers of his surviving hand stroking his whiskers thoughtfully. He wears his new trademark fashion statement—the makeshift eye patch—along with his customary camo pants and hunting vest, the stump of his right arm swaddled in yellowing bandages. In the scant illumination, his single surviving eye shimmers. "I've been keeping tabs on you, Lilly."

"Oh?"

"You've been whipping these people into shape, and I appreciate it."

"We gotta be ready."

"You got that right." He tilts his good eye toward her, the iris glittering. "Especially since we're gonna be riding just before dawn."

She looks at him. "Tomorrow?"

"Yes, ma'am." He holds her in the thrall of that single eye. "You're the first one to know this . . . didn't want to get everybody all bent outta shape too soon. I want to come in from the east with the rising sun—through the trees—goddamn trucks make a lot of noise, don't want to tip anybody off. Pass the word for me, will ya?"

"Absolutely." She gives him a nod, her guts going cold, her brain swimming with anticipation. "We're ready, Governor. We're with you a hundred and ten percent."

"Yeah? Good." He rubs his chin some more. "How about that hunka-hunka burning love of yours? He finally master that scope?"

"Austin? He's good. He's ready. We're all ready. You want me to drive the lead truck?"

"You take the transport wagon. I'll have Gabe take the lead in the armored rig on the way out. We're gonna take it nice and slow."

"Right."

"The tank is fast—it tops out at fifty-some miles per hour—but we're gonna take it nice and easy."

"Got it." She looks at him. "Where are you gonna ride?"

"On the way out? I'm gonna be in the back of your transport truck with the boys."

"Okay."

"I'll be on the bitch box the whole way, staying in close contact with you and Gabe and Gus and Rudy. But when we get close, I want to pull everybody over, say a few words, get everybody ready to rock."

"Makes sense."

"When we're ready to launch, I'm going to want to be riding on the tank."

"Good." Lilly licks her lips. "Something I've been wondering about, though."

"What's that?"

"What about the people in the prison?"

He looks at her. "What about them?"

She shrugs. "What if they . . . you know . . . *surrender*? Wave the white flag or whatever?"

The Governor gazes out at the night. He pulls another cigarette from his vest and sparks it with his Zippo, a wreath of smoke curling around his head. "We'll cross that bridge when we come to it," he murmurs in a low, smoke-cured drawl. He looks at her. "You sure you're ready?"

"Yeah . . . whaddaya mean? Yes, absolutely. Yes."

"You're feeling okay?"

"Yes. I want to take these bastards down as bad as you. Why do you ask?"

He takes a deep breath, looking at her. "I know about what happened."

"You know about—?"

"With the baby."

"What?" Gooseflesh rashes down her arms and legs, her midsection clenching. "How did you—?"

"Bob told me." He looks down. "I'm sorry you had to go through all that. It's hard on a woman, that kind of thing. That's all I'm saying."

Lilly swallows hard. "I'm ready, Governor. I told you I'm ready and I meant it."

He studies her in the wan, yellow security light. It makes her very uneasy—the way he's looking at her, with a trace of pity in his eyes—almost makes her ashamed. She wants to fight alongside this man now—this imperfect, vicious, coarse, blunt instrument of a man—more than anything else she has ever wanted.

He takes another drag off his smoke. "I need you, girlfriend."

"You got me," she tells him.

"I got plenty of muscle." He burns that Cyclopean gaze into her. "But you're a thinking person, a natural leader. Plus, you're damn handy with a gun. I need you on that front line, Lilly."

She gives him a nod. "I understand."

He takes another drag. "What happened to you . . . it just goes to show what a dangerous world this is with these motherfuckers out there. They need to be taken care of before something worse happens, and we're gonna be the ones to do it. No matter what—no matter what it takes. You follow me?"

She looks at him for a long moment before responding. Her voice comes out cold and flat. "I'll see you in the morning," she says.

And then she turns and walks away with fists clenched at her sides.

The Governor stands in the shadows of that exit portal, watching Lilly Caul walk away into the night. He can tell by the way she's walking that she's ready. She's ready to kill for the cause.

She vanishes around the corner of Main Street, the night breeze blowing litter in her wake.

Philip takes a deep breath, tosses the cigarette, and snubs it out with his boot. He has one last thing to tend to before the next day dawns—one last member of the tribe to square away before the glorious blood can flow.

He walks down the portico toward the street, whistling now, feeling more alive than he's ever felt in his life—his brain scoured clean of all doubt.

The war has begun.

PART 2

Doomsday Clock

The ground under them split apart and the earth
opened its mouth and swallowed them, with their
households and all Korah's men and all their posses-
sions. They went down alive into the grave, with everything they owned; the earth closed over them.

—Numbers 16:23

TEN

Bob Stookey stands wringing his gnarled hands in the airless, fetid-smelling foyer of the Governor's apartment. Woozy from being dragged out of bed at three in the morning, he tries to get his bearings and not stare at the dead child straining against her chain on the wall ten feet away. The thing that was once a little girl wears a tiny blue pinafore dress with flowers on it—the fabric so stained and tattered and soaked with filth now that it looks as though someone fed it through a meat grinder—her pigtails still flagging off her monstrous head like a cruel joke. Her eyes pop wide—a fish with a hook stuck in its mouth—the toothless black lips gumming at the air as she reaches for the closest human.

"I'll be back soon, honey—don't you worry," the Governor says, kneeling in front of her. He smiles at her with the strangest look on his face. If asked to describe the look, Bob would have to say it resembles a death mask, a clown's rictus planted on the face of a corpse. "You won't even miss me, I'll be back so fast. You be good for Uncle Bob, okay? You be a good girl." The Penny-thing moans and gums at the air. The Governor puts his arms around her and gives her a hug. "I know—I love you, too."

Bob looks away, filled with a strange and overwhelming surge of emotions—disgust, sadness, fear, pity—all of them jumbled up in his guts like a ball of flame. He is one of only three human beings whom the Governor has trusted with the knowledge of Penny's existence, and right now Bob isn't so sure he wants to be one of those confidantes. He stares at the carpet and swallows back the nausea.

"Bob?"

The Governor must have seen the sour look on the man's face because he now speaks firmly to him as though gently chastising a child. "You sure you're going to be able to do this? I'm serious—she means a lot to me."

Bob braces himself against the wall and takes a deep breath. "I can watch her just fine, Governor. I'm sober as a judge. I'll keep an eye on her. Don't you worry about a thing."

The Governor lets out a sigh, gazing back at the drooling creature in front of him. "You can let her walk around if you want . . . but I won't judge you if you leave her tied up." The Governor stares at the undulating black lips of the little girl-thing. "She can't bite anymore, but she can still be a handful—and we don't have anything to feed her right now, so she's gonna get a little cranky."

Bob gives a nod from across the foyer. Beads of sweat breaking out on his forehead, his eyes burning, he realizes right then that he's standing about as close to the thing as he ever wants to get.

The Governor looks at Bob. "Anyone dies, though—and I mean *anyone*—you make sure she gets fed. You understand what I'm saying?"

"Yeah." Bob tries not to stare at the thing. "You got it."

The Governor gives the girl-thing one last embrace, a delicate little stringer of bile clinging to his shoulder as he finally pulls away.

A little over an hour later—at 5:14 A.M.—the Governor stands beside Gabe on the north end of the Woodbury town square. A single security lamp canted off an adjacent telephone pole shines a beam of light down at them through tiny clouds of moths fluttering haphazardly in the glare. Both men now wear the heavy Kevlar body armor procured from the Guard station, the chest pieces and vests giving the two of them a fierce, martial gravitas in the shimmering darkness. The predawn chill shows in faint puffs of vapor pluming from their mouths as they survey the twenty-three members of the makeshift militia standing at attention in front of them.

Nearly two dozen men and women laden with ammo bandoliers and gun belts heavy with firearms and extra rounds stand shoulder to shoulder across the curb, facing their leader, awaiting final orders. Behind them, the single-file row of vehicles—all fueled and idling—stretches down half the block, headlamps shining toward the exit gate.

They are about to leave twenty-five of their fellow villagers behind with nary a firearm or a bullet—the sum total of their arsenal now sitting on the flatbeds, in trunks, and piled into cargo holds. The Governor asked the Sterns to stay behind and watch the town, and when Barbara objected—after all, she and David are among the best shooters in Woodbury—the Governor told her he wasn't asking her to do this, he was fucking ordering her to do it.

"We have them in our sights, my friends!" Philip Blake now announces to the brigade, his booming voice echoing across the dark square.

Each and every face present that morning reflects the gravity of the moment. Underneath the brims of baseball caps and headbands, their eyes glint with sullen purpose and thinly veiled fear. Fingers brush nervously against trigger guards and along the stocks of assault rifles. These are not professional soldiers by any means, but Philip can see the cold slap of survival instinct waking them up now, girding them, galvanizing them.

He applies more of the stimulant to the group with his stentorian voice. "These motherfuckers killed Doc Stevens! They murdered Bruce Cooper!" He scans the row of somber faces and finally sees Lilly standing at the far end of the group. Austin stands next to her with his sniper rifle on his shoulder, his head cocked with grave resolve. Her hair pulled back in a tight, businesslike ponytail, Lilly has her hands on her hips, palming the handles of her twin Rugers, her Remington MSR rifle shouldered behind her. For the briefest instant, something about the look in her eyes bothers Philip. Maybe he's imagining it, but she looks as though she's deep in thought—ruminating about something—when she should be humming like a tuning fork with kill-lust. Philip holds her gaze as he booms, "They mutilated me—and it's time for them to pay!!"

Lilly meets his gaze from twenty feet away and holds it for an endless moment.

Then she nods.

The Governor roars: "PILE IN AND LET'S MOVE!!"

At 5:30 A.M. on the nose, in a flurry of revving engines, creaking chassis, and chaotic shouting, the heavily armed convoy finally embarks.

In the middle of the pack, Lilly follows the red taillights in front of her as best she can, both hands riveted to the gigantic steering wheel of the rumbling two-and-a-half-ton M35 cargo truck. She can't see shit. The drought of recent days has left the road out of Woodbury as dusty and granular as a sandbox, and now the procession kicks up a fogbank of haze in the predawn darkness as it thunders out the south gate. Lilly can barely see the truck's fifteen-foot-long rear payload bay through the back window, enclosed by guard railing and filled with passengers.

She feels like a midget in the enormous cab, her foot barely reaching the accelerator pedal on the floor, the air reeking of the flop-sweat of generations of nervous National Guardsmen. Austin sits next to her in the passenger seat, cradling the two-way radio in his lap. Every few moments, the voice of the Governor crackles out of the speaker, admonishing Gabe to keep it under forty miles per hour to keep the formation tight and to make sure he takes 85 South—NOT NORTH GODDAMNIT!!—and to turn his fucking headlights off before he wakes up the entire county!

Years ago, Lilly spent a lot of couch time at a Marietta mental health clinic working on her panic attacks. The shrink was a kindly, middle-aged woman named Dr. Cara Leone, who preferred talk therapy to medication and devoted a lot of time to parsing the reasons for Lilly's racing thoughts. Partly hormonal, partly growing pangs, partly neurochemical, and partly grief over her mother's lost battle with breast cancer, Lilly's anxiety attacks always came upon her in a public place, in a crowd, accompanied by a pandemonium of thoughts tumbling around her brain. She was ugly, she was a loser, she was overweight, she had cancer in her genes, people were staring at her, she was going to faint, she couldn't breathe, she felt the world spinning, she had a brain tumor, she was going to die right here in this grocery store. Happily, she either outgrew these spells or worked her way through them . . . until now.

Following the cargo truck in front of her, its glowing red taillights veiled behind a miasma of exhaust and dust, she feels the stirrings of a panic attack coming on. She hasn't felt these sensations for at least ten years, but, sure enough, she feels them now; she senses her thoughts slipping off their spindle, making her dizzy as the fears slide around her brain, sending gooseflesh across the back of her neck. She stares at those glowing red orbs in front of her. She stares and stares until they become two red-dwarf planets floating in space . . . and she concentrates on her training. She thinks of the lessons Bob taught her from his days in basic training: the zen of the sniper.

The bullet will travel with a curved trajectory. The sniper must compensate for this by aiming higher at longer distances. If the distance to the target is unknown, the shooter can calculate muzzle height by using some sort of landmark close to the target, a utility pole or fence post, and then extrapolating the adjustment for a nearby target. She thinks about this as she drives, stuffing the fear back down her throat through sheer concentration. The headshot is the preferred goal. The average head is six inches wide, and average human shoulders are twenty inches apart, and the average distance from a person's pelvis to the top of their head is forty inches. In front of her, the cargo truck makes a ninety-degree turn onto Millard Drive, and she calmly follows, turning the wheel and gently commandeering the M35 through the dust and down the two-lane.

She feels better. She feels her racing thoughts settling into the cobra-calm of the sniper's mind-set, a state that Bob once rhapsodized about while in his cups. The bullet type will determine the drop rate. The Remington shoots a .308 caliber, 175-grain projectile at 2,685 feet per second. At six hundred yards, a seventeen-degree-of-elevation adjustment would have to be made to hit the target. She feels the convoy speeding up in front of her, the speedometer edging past forty miles per hour. She follows. Austin says something next to her. "Huh?" She shoots a glance over at him, feeling as though she's just awakened from a deep sleep. "Did you say something?"

He looks at her, the tension like a mask over his boyish features. "Everything okay?"

"Everything's fine."

"Good." Austin nods and gazes out the side window at the horizon. Lilly notices the sky has changed color behind the trees, lightening from a deep black to a washed-out gray. Dawn is just around the corner. She grips the wheel tighter and follows the procession down a dirt exit road, the storm cloud of dust kicking up higher. Every few moments, she glances out at the side mirror and sees the Governor standing in back amid the silent men and women squeezed like silverware in a drawer.

He looks like he's crossing the fucking Delaware, she thinks, and over the space of that instant, she experiences a wave of contrary emotions. She's a little embarrassed for him, the way he's standing back there with his rakish eye patch and body armor—his head upturned in defiance, his one good hand holding on to the cab in order to steady himself against the bumps—looking like a wounded Spartan general out for revenge. All of which, she realizes, is true. But another part of her drinks in the sight of the Governor's Stonewall Jackson routine. He is the baddest of the badasses, and she feels confidence coursing through her now, knowing that she's going into battle with this man. Who better to remove this cancer?

Fifteen minutes later, the sun has begun to blaze bright orange behind the palisades, and the road begins to wind up a gentle grade.

The forest on either side of the convoy thickens, the smell of pine and humus and walker droppings wafting through the cab's interior. Another glance out at the side mirror reveals the Governor in the cargo bay in back, peering into the distance, and fumbling, one-handed, with his map, which flutters in the breeze. He grabs the walkie-talkie off his belt. The other passengers, seated in rows on either side of him, lift their rifles and check their chambers, their jaws tensing in anticipation.

The Governor thumbs the Talk button. The sound of his voice crackles in the truck's cab: "We're closing in on the hill that overlooks the prison . . . right, Gabe?"

Gabe's voice sizzles and sputters: "We are, boss—prison's about five hundred yards away, down in the flatlands, on the edge of the county line."

"Okay," the Governor's voice replies. "Here's what we're gonna do. Find a wide spot to pull off, preferably within eyeshot of the place."

"Copy that!"

The morning sun hammers down on the forest, filtering in gossamer ribbons through the boughs, the ghostly cottonwood tufts floating through the beams, giving off an almost primordial air. It is now exactly 6:15 A.M. Gabe finds a narrow clearing to pull off, and the rest of the convoy follows—moving slowly, keeping engine noise as quiet as possible—one after another gently coming to a stop.

Lilly pulls the M35 over behind the cargo truck, shoves the shifter into neutral and yanks on the parking brake.

For a long moment, everybody sits in silence. Lilly can hear her bloodstream pulsing in her ears. Then, one by one, the sound of doors gently clicking open signals the point of no return. Lilly and Austin climb out of the cab, their joints sore from the tension, their stomachs queasy with nerves. Lilly hears rifle bolts clang softly in the cool, blue shadows of the trees. Rounds are fed into chambers. Straps are tightened on ammo harnesses. Kevlar vests are adjusted, sunglasses go on, and everybody stands by the front grilles of their softly idling vehicles.

"Here we are," the Governor announces from his perch on the back of Lilly's cargo truck. The sound of his voice makes everybody go still. He makes a grand gesture toward a break in the trees to the east, a dirt path leading down a gentle rise into the valley. The prison is visible in the heat waves about four hundred yards away. "So close we can smell their evil."

All heads turn toward the conglomeration of stone buildings in the distance, the complex looking like some kind of exotic Bedouin compound plopped down in the middle of nowhere. The low-slung dormitories are tucked behind layers of chain link and razor wire, the guard towers unmanned, empty, and impotent. The place calls out to Lilly—a haunted house, doomed and desecrated by ghosts, its warrens once filled with the dregs of society. It now looks as though it's asleep—a network of dirt roads surrounding the outer perimeter—the only movement at present a mob of walkers, as thick as a subway platform at rush hour, wandering the edges of the fencing. They look so small and dark at this distance, they resemble bugs.

"Try and keep pace with the tank as we close in," the Governor orders from his platform, speaking loudly enough to be heard, but not so loud as to announce their presence to anybody, at least not just yet. "I want to seem like an unrelenting wave on the horizon. We want to intimidate them right away—make them sloppy!"

Lilly pulls her rifle off her shoulder and checks the breach—it's locked and loaded—her spine tingling with anticipation.

"When it begins, when the killing starts," the Governor goes on, surveying with his single eye each and every one of his warriors, "don't let their appearance deceive you. You will see women— children, even—but I assure you, these people are *monsters*—no different than the biters we kill without a second thought!"

Lilly shares a tense glance with Austin, who stands next to her with his fists clenched. He nods at her. His expression is heart- breaking—a once boyish face now aged many years in the harsh light of dawn.

"Life out here," the Governor tells them, "it has changed these people, twisted them into creatures who will kill without mercy, without thought—with no regard for human life. They do not de- serve to live."

Now the Governor climbs over the side rail and hops down to the ground. Lilly watches him, her pulse quickening. She knows exactly where he's going. He strides over to the lead vehicle, his boots crunching in the gravel, his gloved hand creaking as it makes a fist.

Gabe sits behind the wheel of the head truck, leaning out the open window with a puzzled expression. "Everything okay, boss?"

The Governor looks up at him. "Get in line with the others. I want the whole fleet spread across the width of the valley. And send a scout around the back of the place to keep an eye on any of them trying to slip away."

Gabe nods, and then looks at him. "You're not coming?"

The Governor gazes out at the distant prison. "I wouldn't miss this for the world." He gazes back up at Gabe. "I'm riding on the tank."

They come out of the east, with the sun at their backs, raising a dust storm.

As they roar down the grade and across the valley, the Governor rides on the nose of the tank, his gloved hand welded to the turret as though he's mounted on a bucking bronco. The massive treads of the tank, as well as the enormous wheels of all the military vehicles, kick up the drought-wasted earth as they close in, engines singing high opera—an army of Valkyries swooping down upon the damned—the dust cloud so profuse now it practically engulfs the entire fleet.

By the time they approach the outer access road—about fifty yards from the fence—a number of things have changed. All the walkers in the general vicinity, drawn to the noise and clamor, have now crowded in toward the east edge of the prison, the dead numbering a hundred or more—an added layer of protection, either planned or coincidental, for those inside the prison. At the same time, frenzied voices have begun to echo across the cement lots behind the fence—the inhabitants caught off guard and now scrambling for cover.

Adding to the pandemonium is the vast storm front of dust, now as big and thick as a sirocco, completely swallowing the convoy. Blinded by the dust cloud, Lilly slams on the brakes, nearly throwing her entire cargo bay of armed men and women through the cab's rear window. Austin slams against the dash, smacking his forehead on the windshield. Lilly catches her breath and turns to Austin. "You all right?"

"I'm good," he mutters, scrambling to get his gun up and ready.

The dust cloud begins to clear. The harsh morning sun shines down through the nimbus like firelight through gauze, turning everything luminous and dreamlike. Lilly's heart hammers in her chest. Her head throbs with nervous tension. Through the dirt-filmed windshield, she can see the prison's outer fence with its barbed crowns—thousands of feet long—teeming with walking dead.

They swarm and burrow in toward the fence like wasps engulfing a nest—hundreds of them, all shapes and sizes and genders, snarling and drooling, moving as one great organism—driven mad by some innate demonic hunger, whipped into a frenzy by the noise of the convoy, the frantic movement inside the compound, and the smell of human flesh.

Through her side window, in her peripheral vision, Lilly senses movement. The Governor has climbed out onto the tank's prow like a glorious figurehead on the fore beam of a ship, his chest puffed up with adrenaline and hubris. He raises his one gloved hand and points at the throngs of undead. His voice booms with the impact of a cannon shot.

"DESTROY THEM ALL!—NOW!!"

The fusillade erupts all across the pasture—a horizontal tornado ramming into columns of dead flesh, mesmerizing Lilly, paralyzing her in ear-splitting wonder. Walkers begin erupting in gouts of blood and rotting tissue. Heads explode in choreographed, sequential explosions as the .50 calibers fire up—full auto—skulls popping like great strings of lightbulbs bursting and splattering the fence. Ragged bodies spin and pirouette in the dust. Spent shells spew into the air behind the vehicles with the profusion of fountains. The fence undulates and rattles with the mass slaughter, bodies piling up against the chain link. Lilly doesn't even get a chance to lean out her window and fire a single shot. The massive onslaught of gunfire lasts only a few minutes—purely for show now—but in that time, it rips through the dead with the strength of a tsunami, a grisly red tide of destruction, shredding flesh and tearing limbs from their sockets and uncorking the tops of skulls and turning monstrous faces to red pulp. The noise is tremendous. Lilly's ears ring, and she puts her hands over them, flinching, as the very air around her thumps and vibrates. The cordite forms a blue cloud over the east edge of the prison until most of the walkers have gone down.

As the last few corpses are slaughtered, much of the gunfire dwindles, until Lilly can just barely hear over the ringing of her ears the frantic voices of human beings inside the prison barricades hollering at each other—"GET DOWN!"—"STOP!"—"LORI!"—"GET DOWN, GODDAMNIT!"—"ANDREA, STOP!"—but

Lilly can't see much of anything behind the veils of dust and gun smoke being whipped up by the display of force.

At length, as the last few large-caliber blasts crackle in the fog-bound sunlight, Lilly hears the sound of the Governor's voice—now amplified by a bullhorn—piercing the intermittent popping of small arms fire.

"—CEASE FIRE!—"

The last of the shooters draw down, and all at once an eerie silence grips the landscape. Lilly stares through the dusty windshield at the tattered, mutilated, smoking bodies drifted against the fence. For one horrible instant, the sight of them registers in Lilly's brain as a memory of atrocity photos she saw once from World War II—the bodies of prison camp victims piled by bulldozers into snow-dusted ditches of mass graves—and the feeling it gives her makes her blink and shake her head and rub her eyes as she tries to drive the unbidden thoughts from her mind.

The sound of a gravelly, smoky voice amplified by a bullhorn interrupts her stupor. *"TO ANYONE INSIDE LEFT ALIVE—THIS IS YOUR LAST CHANCE TO MAKE IT OUT OF THIS WITH YOUR LIVES."* Standing on the front bulwark of the Abrams tank, the Governor aims the megaphone at the vast, deserted yards inside the fence—his voice echoing off the inner walls of cellblocks and administrative buildings. *"I WILL NOT MAKE A SECOND OFFER."*

Lilly silently climbs out of the cab, Austin emerging from the other side.

They both crouch down behind the truck's massive front wheels with their guns ready to go. They peer around the edges of the doors at the prison in the middle distance, and all the deserted basketball courts and parking lots and exercise yards. Nothing moves within the confines of the fences, only a few shadows flitting and flickering here and there across gaps between buildings.

"YOU HAVE KILLED AND MAIMED US—AND NOW YOU HIDE BEHIND YOUR FENCES—BUT YOUR TIME IS OVER!"

This last word is pronounced with such venomous zeal that it seems to echo and penetrate the walls of the prison with the insidious half-life of an infectious disease. *"WE WILL SHOW YOU MERCY . . . BUT ONLY UNDER ONE CONDITION."*

Lilly glances over her shoulder at the Governor, standing on the tank with the bullhorn. Even from this distance—twenty-five, maybe thirty feet away—she can see his one visible eye blazing like a burning ember. The sound of his amplified voice is like a tin can being torn apart.

"OPEN THE INNERMOST GATE . . . GATHER UP ALL YOUR WEAPONS, ALL GUNS, ALL AMMO, ANY KNIVES, WHATEVER YOU HAVE—THE RIOT GEAR, EVERYTHING—AND PILE IT UP IN FRONT OF THE INNERMOST GATE. THEN I WANT YOU TO CLOSE THE GATE, LOCK IT, AND WAIT WHILE WE CLEAR AWAY THE BITERS."

The Governor pauses and listens to the silence, the stillness broken only by the fading echoes of his voice and the sound of engines softly idling all around him.

"WE DON'T HAVE TO KILL EACH OTHER . . . THERE'S STILL A CHANCE WE CAN WORK TOGETHER."

More silence.

From her position behind the M35's wheel, Lilly can see more walkers coming from the north, shambling around the corner of the fence toward their fallen brethren. She surveys the vast exercise yard inside the fence, the weeds fringing cracks across the sun-bleached pavement, the stray wads of trash rolling in the breeze. She squints. She can barely make out a few dark objects lying here and there that, at first glance, look like discarded bundles of trash or clothing shifting in the wind. But the more she stares, the more she becomes convinced that they're humans crawling on their bellies for cover.

"DO AS I ASK AND OPEN THE GATES." To Lilly's ear, the Governor's voice sounds almost reasonable—rational, even—like a teacher explaining to his students with great regret the protocols

of detention. He says into the megaphone, *"THIS IS YOUR LAST CHANCE."*

The Governor lowers the bullhorn and calmly waits for a response.

Lilly crouches silently behind her door with the Remington rifle now gripped tightly in both hands, one sweaty finger on the trigger pad, and the pause that ensues—lasting only a few minutes—seems to go on for an eternity. The sun beats down on her neck. Sweat trickles down her back. Her stomach somersaults. She smells the faint stench of walkers on the wind and it makes her nauseous. She can hear Austin's breathing on the other side of the cab, and she can see his shadow. He stares at the ground with his rifle cradled in his arms.

All at once, a series of cramps twists Lilly's gut, sending sharp daggers of pain through her midsection and seizing her up against the truck's fender. It feels like a circular saw tearing her in half, and she doubles over in agony. She tries to breathe. She feels the menstrual pad between her legs stinging and getting heavy, the flow of blood practically hemorrhaging inside her.

She's been using tampons as well as pads since the miscarriage, and the flow has been off and on, but now the bleeding returns with a vengeance—either due to the stress or the aftermath of the exam or *both*—and it's starting to drive her crazy. She tries to focus on the distant yards of the prison and ignore the cramps, but it's pretty much a losing battle now. The pain throbs and twinges within her, and she starts associating the misery inside her with the evil bastards inside this prison. She knows it's a stretch, but she can't help thinking . . . *This is their fucking fault, this pain, this misery, this fire raging inside me; it's all because of them.* Lilly hears the low murmur of the Governor's voice then, and it sends a fine layer of chills down her spine.

From his perch on the tank, he mutters, "Motherfuckers . . . can't make it easy."

By this point, at least a dozen more walkers are lumbering toward the convoy, a few coming around the corners of the fence from the south and the west, and the Governor lets out an exasperated sigh. At last, he raises the bullhorn. *"RESUME FIRING!"*

Barrels go up, bolts snapping shells into breaches, but before anybody gets a chance to fire another shot, the sound of a single high-powered rifle pops loudly in the still, blue sky high above one of the guard towers.

The blast strikes the Governor's right shoulder just above the pectoral.

ELEVEN

A bullet fired from a military-grade sniper rifle leaves the muzzle at velocities of up to thirty-five hundred feet per second. Most rounds traveling at this speed—in this case, a .308 caliber Winchester zipper from the prison's armory—can easily penetrate Kevlar body armor and do mortal damage to a target. But the distance between the guard tower (at the southeast corner of the property) and the tank (parked nearly a hundred yards east of the outer fence) causes enough friction from air resistance to slow the bullet down considerably.

By the time the zipper reaches the Governor's shoulder armor, it's traveling at just under two thousand fps, and it merely punches a deep pucker in the Kevlar that feels to the Governor as though he's just absorbed a roundhouse from Mike Tyson. The shock of the impact sends him careening backward off the edge of the tank.

He lands hard in the weeds, the breath knocked from his lungs.

The rest of the attack force bristles suddenly, each and every gunner looking up from their sights. The group paralysis lasts only a split second—even Lilly has frozen in her crouch behind the cab door, gaping at the fallen man—until the Governor gasps and rolls over, filling his lungs, blinking back the shock. He takes deep, wheezing breaths, getting his bearings back. He levers himself up to his feet, taking cover behind the iron bulwark of the tank.

"Shit!" he hisses through gritted teeth, looking around, trying to gauge the direction from which the bullet came.

Lilly gazes up at the southeast corner of the prison yard, the guard tower gleaming in the harsh rays of the rising sun. The wooden structure tapers near the top, crowned by a small shed surrounded by a catwalk. From this distance, it's nearly impossible to discern if anybody's up there, but Lilly is fairly certain that she sees a dark figure lying belly-down on the floor of the catwalk.

Lilly is about to say something about it when another flash— like the glint of a sunspot on a mirror—flares off the corner of the tower, the booming report following a nanosecond later.

Thirty feet away from Lilly, just off her left flank, one of the Woodbury gunmen—a young man with a goatee and unruly blond hair who goes by the nickname Arlo—convulses suddenly in a cloud of blood mist. The .308 caliber slug rips a pathway through his neck, spewing tissue through the exit wound and sending him backward with a lurch.

His Kalashnikov rifle goes flying as he bangs into the young man standing behind him before collapsing into the weeds. The other gunman lets out a yelp, blood spattering his face, and he immediately goes down on the ground. Thunderstruck, panicking, he crawls on his belly toward the undercarriage of Lilly's truck.

The Governor sees what Lilly has already seen. "THE TOWER!" He points at the southeast corner of the lot. "THEY'RE IN THE DAMN TOWER!"

Another strobe of silver light against the sun flickers right before the third blast rings out. Another Woodbury man—this one twenty feet off the Governor's right flank—jerks backward with the impact of a direct headshot. A piece of his skull is propelled through the air on a fountain of blood as he tumbles backward into the tall grass.

By this point, the entire invasion force is scrambling for cover, frantic voices blurting out inarticulate cries, many of the militia members lunging toward their machine-gun turrets and taking cover behind the quarter panels of vehicles and open doors of truck cabs.

"THERE!" The Governor points at the tower. "THE ONE ON THE LEFT!!"

Lilly aims her Remington through the window opening of the cab door and draws a bead on the sun-drenched tower. Through her scope, Lilly sees a figure lying prone on the floor of the catwalk, a long-barreled weapon aimed down at the lot. Lilly sucks in a breath. It's a woman. Lilly can tell by the ponytail flagging in the wind and the slender body. For some reason, this revelation fills Lilly with rage, the likes of which she has never felt. But before she has a chance to squeeze off a single shot, a volley of thunder erupts on either side of the truck.

The air lights up as the entire brigade unleashes holy hell on that tower—the barking reports of high-powered rifles syncopated with the rattling, roaring .50 cal machine guns and assault rifles on full auto. Lilly cringes at the noise and heat, her ears already ringing unmercifully as she tries to get a few controlled shots off herself. Another surge of cramps steals her breath, throws off her aim, and kindles her agony into a brushfire of rage. She ignores the pain, holds her breath, makes the adjustment to her point of aim for the drop rate—aiming just a few inches high on the target— and then fires. Her rifle booms, the recoil punching her in the shoulder, the spit of cordite on the side of her face like hot grease.

Way up at the top of the guard tower, the edge of the catwalk comes apart in a daisy-chain of tiny explosions, sending a chain of dust puffs into the air, pulverizing the wooden supports, pinging and sparking off the metal railing, and riddling the area around the dark figure with smoking bullet holes.

It's hard to tell the extent of the physical damage they're doing to the sniper, but by the looks of the erupting wood shards and shattering glass, it would be a miracle if anybody survived the barrage—which goes on for at least a minute and a half—during which time Lilly goes through nine more rounds, pausing once to eject a spent cartridge and reload. At last she sees through the scope a splash of blood stippling the inner wall of the guard tower.

The gunfire ceases for a moment. In the lull, the guard tower remains still. Someone has apparently scored a headshot, very likely a mortal wound for this murderous bitch, but in all the chaos, it's impossible to parse who actually did it. Lilly lowers her muzzle and notices two young gunmen on her left, each crouching down by the tailgate of a cargo truck, giving each other high fives.

Lilly hears the Governor's voice: "Well?! You want a fucking medal?"

Glancing over her shoulder, she sees the one-armed man pushing his way in behind the two young gunmen. "Stop jerking each other off and get these bodies in bags!" He gestures toward their first casualties, the victims of the lady sniper—their human remains lying in heaps in the tall grass—their heads soaking in puddles of gore. "And kill the rest of these biters," he says, indicating the few straggling reanimated dead that are now trundling around the corners of the fence, moving through the blue haze of gun smoke. "Before they find their way over here and start chewing on our fucking asses!"

Lilly lets the others finish off the remaining few walkers skulking along the fence. Instead, she crouches down behind the open door of the M35 and lowers her Remington and waits for the salvo to run its course. The sun beats down on her. Just for an instant, she thinks about the young men who were cut down only moments ago by the sniper in the guard tower. Lilly had a passing acquaintance with the first one, Arlo, but never even knew the second one's name. Her mind swims with contrary emotions—sorrow for the fallen men, searing rage for these animals in this prison. She wants to burn this entire encampment down, nuke it, blast it off the face of the earth—but something deep down inside her, a kernel of doubt, now sits in the pit of her stomach like a cancerous tumor. Is this the best way? The only way? She can see Austin through the open cab, crouched behind the open passenger door, firing every few seconds as though on a shooting range. He appears calm and centered, but she can see the madness in his expression. Is Lilly now as insane as he? She sees something else blur in her peripheral vision, and she twists around just in time to see Gabe running behind the trucks.

The big, sweaty behemoth looks worried, panicked, as he approaches the tank, behind which Philip now stands looking exceedingly imperious and impatient, his one surviving hand clenched into a fist. The two men get into a shouting match. Drowned by the crackle of gunfire, Lilly can't tell what they're saying to each other, but it has something to do with "costing us too much ammo" and "these people are terrible shots" and "why don't we just drive it through the fence? . . ."

Finally, the Governor turns to the front line of amateur warriors and bellows at the top of his lungs, "Stop!—STOP!—CEASE FIRE!!"

The excruciating din comes to an abrupt halt. Silence crashes down on the meadow. In Lilly's ringing ears, the echo of the .50 caliber turrets blends with the white noise in her brain. She peers over the top of her door and sees quite a few walkers still standing by the fence—at least a dozen or more of them—mangled and scourged with bullet holes but heads still intact, still shuffling through the dirt—cockroaches impervious to the spray of exterminators.

Lilly hears the Governor's voice to her left. "Jared! Fire up the tank!"

Lilly swallows her nerves and manages to rise on sore legs. She picks up her rifle and creeps around the back of the M35. She finds Austin diligently reloading his Garand rifle, sliding the rounds into the breach with trembling, sweat-slick fingers. Tendrils of his hair have come loose from his ponytail and hang in his face, some of the curls matted to his sweat-damp forehead. "You okay?" she asks, coming up behind him and putting a hand on his shoulder.

He jumps. "Yeah—I mean—yeah, I'm fine. I'm good. Why do you ask?"

"Just wanted to make sure."

"What about you?"

"Fit as a fiddle, ready to rock." She gazes over at the plume of exhaust suddenly issuing out of the tank, the turbine engine growling. "What the hell are they doing?"

Austin watches the tank begin to lurch toward the fence, and he stares, momentarily rapt by the strange contraption rumbling like a corsair toward the shuffling cluster of upright cadavers.

Moments later, the Abrams M1 plunges into the disorderly regiment of walkers milling along the fence. A dozen or more of the undead are pulled under the iron treads, the sound of their flesh and bones being ground to pulp like the hacksaw groan of a gigantic trash compactor. Lilly looks away. Nausea threatens to bring up her breakfast. The tank makes an abrupt ninety-degree turn in the greasy swamp of human carnage, and then starts chugging along parallel to the fence, bowling over walker after walker with the gruesome efficiency of a harvester gobbling stalks of wheat. Skulls are smashed, and organs pop like blood-filled blisters, and the collective hemorrhaging of literally hundreds of putrid bodies begins to send up a virtual fogbank of reeking, foul, hideous stench.

By this point, the Governor's troops—most of them now hiding behind the cover of vehicles, their weapons at the ready—have become highly aware of movement inside the fences, along the shadows of passageways, in the gaps between distant cellblocks, and amid the dark alcoves on the edges of the yards. With the herd of biters being cleared now, the prison grounds are more exposed, more visible to the invaders. Figures dart here and there, running for cover or crawling on their bellies toward safety inside the nearest edifice. Lilly sees an older man wearing a floppy hat frantically crawling across the exercise area for cover. But it isn't until the tank reaches the terminus point of the east fence and comes to a noisy stop, that Lilly realizes there are still dozens of walkers—maybe thirty or more—lurking beyond the outer corners of the property, stepping over the grisly remains of their fellow creatures.

The tank sits idling at the end of the fence for a moment as the

Governor comes around behind one of the trucks, his eye bright and shiny with rage. He walks past Lilly's cargo truck, pauses, and surveys the fence line, which is littered with rotting remains now. Gabe joins him, and Lilly listens to their conversation.

"I got an idea," Gabe says to Philip. "The sight of the tank ain't enough to scare them out—but what if we tried to fire that fucking cannon at them? That could get their attention, right?"

The Governor doesn't even look at the man, just continues staring at the fences, stroking his whiskered chin and thinking. The tank rumbles back to the front gates, swinging awkwardly back around into its original position. The Governor watches it skeptically. "It took Jared five months to learn how to drive that fucking thing, but he never got around to figuring out how to load and shoot it. The truth is, it's more or less just for *show*."

Now the Governor glances at Gabe, and a glint of something disturbing—Gabe can't identify exactly what it is—kindles in Philip's eye. "The thing is, it's really just there to thin the herd to a manageable level for the Pied Piper."

Gabe looks at him. "The what?"

It begins with an engine revving behind the cargo trucks, and a blur of movement as one of the smaller vehicles—a gray, rust-speckled Chevy S-10—backs up toward the fence. Lilly and Austin stay behind their truck's doors as the dynamic of the battlefield suddenly changes. They see two Woodbury men in body armor sitting on the pickup's rear gate, waving their hands and hollering inarticulate taunts at the reanimated corpses still milling about the fences. This gets the attention of most—if not all—of the monsters.

The truck slowly pulls away, and the walkers begin lumbering instinctively after it.

While all this is going on, the Governor decides the area is clear enough, and it's time to fucking end this, so he gives the order to shoot them all. Fucking shoot them all. Now. NOW!—

—*SHOOT TO FUCKING KILL!*

___

Inside the barriers, the settlers dive for cover as the air around them ignites, some of the weaker ones covering their heads and staying on the ground, others crawling madly for safety, some of the older ones trying to help the younger ones. The tremendous barrage from the east, from every corner of the pasture, sends tiny explosive dust puffs across the cracked macadam, crisscrossing the lots, sparking off Dumpsters and basketball backboards and gutters and downspouts and vent fans and air-conditioning compressors. Howling voices reach Lilly's ears as she picks out moving targets and holds her breath and fires pinpoint blasts. "DOWN!" yells one figure, wrestling a woman to the concrete. "EVERYBODY DOWN!" shouts another, tackling another woman trying to flee the assault. The grounds become a blur of chaotic movement. Few of the figures—if any—appear to be armed. This bothers Lilly, to the point of making her pause and lift the scope from her eye. For a moment, she just watches as an older man—shirtless, portly, bearded, with long, wild hair—makes a mad dash for a doorway. A sudden burst riddles his shoulder with bloody bullet holes, tearing chunks from his hairy arms and belly. The old codger careens to the ground in a scarlet spray, and Lilly lets out a tense breath.

She sees another fleeing figure—for a brief instant, she recognizes the man.

She adjusts her scope, and in the telescopic field she sees the square-jawed man named Rick Grimes—the son of a bitch who led the escape from Woodbury, the leader of these animals, the one who tangled with the Governor and probably killed Martinez and God only knows what else—now grabbing a woman and shouting at her. "GOTTA GET INSIDE!—NO PLACE FOR COVER OUT HERE!—YOU HEAR ME?!!" He drags the woman toward the closest building—twenty yards between him and the building—a hundred and fifty between him and Lilly.

The litany of Bob's sniper school steadies her, calms her down—*breathe in, acquire the target, figure the distance, adjust your point of aim*—and now she has the man named Rick centered in the scope. She slowly releases her breath. She begins to squeeze the trigger . . . but stops herself. Wait. Something flicks brightly, deep in the folds of her brain, something she can't identify, something inchoate and almost electrical—like a synapse misfiring—causing a series of flashes in her mind's eye, the images too fast to register.

She jerks at the sound of the Governor's voice, coming from behind the tank, twenty feet away: "We've got them pinned down now! Only a matter of time before they—!"

The metallic ping of a ricochet zinging off the apex of the tank's steel turret cuts off his words. He ducks. He looks across the prison grounds at the northeast guard tower on the opposite end of the property. The others whirl around, and all at once everybody sees the glint of another gun barrel up there against the sun—a second sniper. The Governor crouches behind the tank. He grabs the walkie off his belt, thumbs the switch, and issues a snarling, enraged order: "Take that fucker out!"

A pair of .50 caliber machine guns on the rooftops of adjacent cargo trucks swing to the north, and Lilly grits her teeth as the clattering roar of full-auto gunfire sends a world of hurt up at the tower. The high windows erupt against the pale blue sky. Waves of broken glass convulse into the air, a chorus of atonal crashes, sparkling tendrils issuing in all directions.

In her peripheral vision, from her position low on the ground, Lilly senses more movement inside the prison barricades. Many of those pinned down now take advantage of the distraction and make mad dashes for the cellblock entrances. The Governor sees this as well. He turns and shouts at the gunman: "HEY!" He points at the prison yards. "They're making a break for the goddamn buildings!" He points at the tower. "We only need a few of you to be shooting up there to kill that prick! C'mon, goddamnit—use your heads!!"

A number of shooters now turn and spray the yards indiscriminately. Across the grounds, those who are fleeing once again dive for cover in the hail of gunfire. Lilly looks through her scope and sees several souls now scrambling for weapons. She sees a teenage girl with short black hair crawling toward a rifle, and she sees a big African American man digging in a satchel, and she sees the dreadlock-wearing woman—*Michonne*—snatching a small black pistol off a man's belt that looks from this distance like a 9 mil. Dreadlock-lady spins and starts shooting. Her actions embolden another man to fire, and another, and another.

"FIND COVER!" The Governor's voice raises up an octave. "EVERYBODY—FIND COVER NOW!"

Within moments, more members of the Woodbury militia begin to fall.

Johnny Aldridge was a forty-year-old drifter who ended up on Martinez's crew, a gentle soul who could name every member of every heavy metal band who ever toured the South in the 1990s. Now he lies in the high grass next to Lilly, close enough for her to smell stale cigarette smoke on him, the man's glassy eyes propped open in death, his Adam's apple pulsing its death throes in a rhythmic gushing of arterial blood. Lilly looks away and closes her eyes. Cauterizing horror and anguish course down her spine.

She turns to Austin, who lies on his belly in the grass next to her. He swallows hard and doesn't say anything, but the look on his face says it all. His eyes simmer with terror. She starts to say something when she hears the firestorm from the prison yard fading slightly, the last crackle of gunfire echoing up into the morning sky. Are they reloading? Have they managed to make it back to the buildings? Then she hears the Governor's voice again, drenched in madness and fury: "FALL BACK! FALL BACK, GODDAMNIT!"

Lilly hears the harsh noise of gears grinding all around her, engines revving, exhaust pipes backfiring. The Governor's voice is nearly drowned by the collective clamor of all the vehicles firing back up. "We need to regroup, goddamnit—need to get our shit together!"

Climbing out of her hiding place, she cautiously struggles back into the cab, keeping her head down, pushing open the passenger door for Austin. He climbs back into the shotgun seat, head down, breathing hard, flinching at the intermittent pop of handguns still firing through the fences. Out of the corner of her eye, Lilly sees Gabe hurrying around the back of the tank.

The portly man, still huffing and puffing, crouches next to the Governor. "Whaddaya think?"

"This isn't working," the Governor says, speaking more to himself than to Gabe. Clenching his one gloved hand so tightly it creaks, he bites down on the words, hissing psychotically, "THIS FUCKING ISN'T *WORKING!*"

Gabe starts to reply when the Governor rears back and punches Gabe in the jaw, hitting him so hard that the impact whiplashes his head back and busts his lip open. Stringers of bloody drool fling off Gabe's mouth, and Gabe flinches against the tank's hull with a start, blinking, pressing his hand down on his lip. He stares at the Governor with fire in his eyes. "WHAT THE HELL?!"

The Governor fixes his blazing eyes on the stocky man. "Just get in the fucking truck."

Lilly watches all this from twenty-five feet away, from inside the M35's cab, and she only hears about 80 percent of it, but she's seen enough. Her stomach has gone cold, her throat filling with acid. She shoots a glance at Austin, who says nothing. She revs up the engine and puts the truck into gear, grinding the shift lever into reverse. But just for that split instant, before backing away, she glances at the prison yard.

Through the layers of ancient cyclone fencing, she sees a solitary figure lying on the edge of the exercise yard, soaking in a spreading pool of blood. Clad in a prison jumpsuit, male, late thirties maybe, sandy hair, grizzled, rugged looking, a stump where his right arm should be, he slowly tries to drag himself back toward the buildings, but he's been mortally wounded—a gut shot—and all he can do is crawl, inch by inch, leaving a leech trail of blood. Even from this distance, Lilly can tell it's the man named Rick, and from the looks of his wounds, his chances of survival are min-imal at best.

She turns away as the convoy of vehicles begins to withdraw, one by one, the trucks doing U-turns and rumbling away toward the eastern horizon. Lilly follows the tank on its retreat, plunging into the fogbank of dust being kicked up by all the massive wheels, feeling nothing for the man named Rick . . . neither sympathy nor satisfaction . . . only emptiness.

TWELVE

"I feel like we should say something," Austin ventures an hour later, speaking in a hoarse, exhausted voice, standing on the bank of a dry riverbed, three miles east of the prison, shivering, gazing down at a mass grave. Down in the trench, the bodies lie on top of each other, arms and legs akimbo, bloodstains turning black in the dusky light. The stagnant air swims with gnats and particulate floating through the beams of sunlight canting through the pines.

"I don't know . . . yeah, probably we should." Lilly stands next to him, chewing her fingernails, tendrils of her auburn hair that have come loose from her ponytail hanging down across her sullen face. Her guns are holstered on her hips, and her elbows are scuffed and bloody. Her lower back throbs with pain, her joints twinge with the dull ache of exhaustion, and daggers slice through her gut—the latest wave of cramps taking their toll on her. She sniffs back the agony and stares at the casualties.

Lilly knew all of these men—if not by name, certainly by sight—now stacked like cordwood down in the ditch to avoid adding to the walker population or having one of them end up as lunch for the swarm. These men who passed Lilly on the street in Woodbury from time to time, said hello, tipped their Caterpillar caps at her, winked at her a few times—they weren't perfect by any means but they were decent, simple men. Some of them—Arlo and Johnny, for example—were sweethearts who shared their rations with Lilly on more than one occasion. Now Lilly feels a vacuum in her soul as she gazes down at them. Darkness presses in on her organs and chokes her as she tries to muster up a eulogy.

"Johnny, Arlo . . . Ronnie, Alex, and Jake . . . Evan and . . . um." She can't remember the last young man's name. She looks helplessly at Austin.

His eyes shimmer with sadness. "Andy."

Lilly nods. "Andy . . . right." She bows her head and tries not to look at the bloodless forms piled in a grisly heap down in the leaves. As her Grandma Pearl would say, *"They are just the shells left on the beach . . . their spirits have flown, dear."* Lilly finds herself wishing she believed in God. How could anybody believe in a loving deity in times like these? But it would be nice. Lilly swallows back the bitter anguish and softly says, "Each and every one of you gave your lives for a higher purpose . . . to protect your community . . . you gave your all." Her voice weakens slightly, the weight of exhaustion dragging on her body. "Here's hoping you're in a better place now. May you all rest in peace."

A long moment of silence follows, broken only by the distant, lonely call of a heron. Lilly senses the presence of others standing downstream, and she gazes to the south.

About fifty yards away lurks a dark figure standing on the edge of the trees—eye patch, missing arm, coal-black body armor—grimacing as he stares into the trees across the creek bed. Gabe stands next to him, not saying a word as he screws a silencer onto the muzzle of a stainless steel short-barrel .357 revolver. Two other men stand at a respectful distance downstream with shovels. The sixteen other surviving members of the makeshift militia—a dozen men and four women—can be seen through the trees, attending to the wounded and skulking around the circle of vehicles parked in a dusty clearing, the machine gunners keeping watch. Nobody seems too interested in graveside memorials right now.

Gabe hands the gun to the Governor, who gives him a terse nod. Then Philip Blake turns and strides along the embankment toward

Lilly. "You finished?" he asks as he approaches with a dour look on his face.

Lilly nods. "Yeah . . . go ahead."

The Governor steps in front of her, looming over the mass grave. "My uncle Bud fought in World War Two in the Pacific." Philip doesn't even look up as he speaks. He thumbs the hammer on the .45 and stoically fires the first round into the blood-caked cranium of Arlo Simmons.

Lilly barely reacts to the dry snap of the silencer—her nerves deadened now. The Governor aims at the skull of another victim and fires again into the open grave. This time Lilly flinches slightly at the horrible snapping noise of the bullet punching through bone.

The Governor glances over his shoulder at the others gathered across the clearing. "I want everybody to hear this! Come on over!"

Slowly, reluctantly, the others put down their canteens, ammo mags, and first-aid kits, snub out their cigarettes, and make their way across the clearing to the edge of the trees. The sun is dipping behind the western horizon and the deepening shadows add to the tension.

"My uncle Bud lost his life on the USS *Sonoma*, October of 1944," Philip says in a cold, flat voice as he aims at another skull and fires a slug into dead tissue. Lilly jumps. Now the Governor speaks loudly enough for the whole group to hear. "Ship got hit by the Jap kamikazes . . . sunk . . . destroyed by savages with no respect for the conventions of warfare or life in general." He fires again and again into the cairn of bodies, demolishing skull after skull. He pauses and turns to the onlookers, their ashen faces peering out through breaks in the foliage. "That's what we're dealing with here, and I don't want any of you to ever forget it."

He pauses to let this register, and then he glances over his shoulder and gives a nod to the pair of men with the shovels. "Go ahead, boys, cover 'em up now." He looks at the others. "These men did not die in vain."

The two men with the shovels approach and begin covering the bodies with loose dirt from the riverbank. The Governor watches.

He takes deep breaths, and his expression goes through a series of transformations. Lilly sees it out of the corner of her eye but doesn't stare.

"These people we're fighting," he goes on, "they're worse than the fucking biters . . . they're pure evil . . . they're monsters with no regard for the lives of their children or elderly or anybody. You've seen them in action. You've all seen how they will shoot any one of you in the back of the head and not blink an eye. They'll take everything from you and do the two-step on your fucking corpses."

Philip Blake's face subtly rearranges itself then in the gloomy, fading daylight . . . from an expression of simmering anger to something stranger and more delusional—a vainglorious tilt of the head, an ember of righteous rage burning in his one visible eye that makes Lilly nervous. He looks at his ragtag battalion.

"But I got news for these savages," he says as the men behind him complete their shoveling and stand back from the mound of earth with heads bowed.

The tone of Philip's voice changes, deepens and softens, like a preacher moving from the fire and brimstone to the psalms.

"They can attack us all they want . . . they can mutilate me . . . they can spit on our graves . . . but we will keep coming at them because we're on a holy crusade here, people . . . not only to protect our community from these monsters . . . but also to rid the world of this evil." He looks from face to face, taking his sweet time as he scrutinizes every last member of his private army. "We're going to redouble our efforts. We're going to fight fire with fire. It ain't gonna be easy. We're gonna have to give it everything we got."

He looks at a middle-aged man in a Braves cap and denim shirt standing nearby with his hands on the stocks of his twin Colt .45s. "Raymond, I want you to pick a couple men and scout the perimeter tonight. Look for weak spots in their compound, any suspicious movement—I want to know what they're up to in that roach motel they're hiding out in." He looks at another man—a bearded biker in leathers with a pump-action 20-gauge. "Earl, I want you and three others standing watch on all sides while we're regrouping.

You see anything that doesn't look right, you blow it away. You understand?"

The bearded behemoth gives a nod, and then hurries off to choose his crew.

The Governor turns to Lilly and lowers his voice. "I'm gonna need you and Gorgeous George here to help do an inventory, figure out what kind of ammo situation we're looking at. I want to hit back hard, but I want to make sure we got the wherewithal, all right?"

Lilly nods. "No problem . . . we're on it."

The Governor looks around, gazes up at the sky. "Gonna be dark soon."

Lilly looks at him. "What are you thinking?"

He looks at the grave. "I'll let you know." And then he turns and walks off.

Nobody in the beleaguered Woodbury militia sees the two figures three miles to the east, darting out of the unmarked rear exit of Cellblock D and hurrying across the back lot of the prison, slipping off the premises through a temporary gate in the northwest corner of the fences.

Nobody in the Governor's scouting party sees the dark silhouettes of a man and woman running side by side through the tall grass and into the thicket of trees along the western horizon. It's not yet full-on darkness, and the golden dusk is turning the surrounding meadow into a gauzy, softly lit knoll. Shadows of live oaks and exhaust chimneys from the prison buildings stretch and elongate into surreal, ghostly patterns as the two fleeing figures pass unnoticed—their weapons sheathed and strapped and secured to their backs—into the tree line at precisely 6:17 P.M. eastern standard time.

At this point, Raymond Hilliard's scouting party hasn't lit out yet—they're still discussing what weapons to bring along, how much ammo, and what supplies they might need. Meanwhile, the men on the steel bonnets of truck cabs, keeping an eye on the periphery of the Governor's camp, are positioned far too low to see over the surrounding pines. If they were indeed elevated above the treetops, they might see the subtle peristalsis of twitching foliage, the twig-snapping and jiggling limbs marking the course of the two stealthy invaders as they weave their way through the deeper woods toward the militia's temporary encampment.

At that moment, on the edge of the clearing along the riverbed, outside the circle of trucks, three men and one woman huddle in the gathering shadows, checking their weapons and taking stock of their ammunition.

"Leave that shit here," Raymond Hilliard orders the oldest man in the scouting party.

"What—*this*?" James Lee Steagal, a rangy old farmworker from Valdosta with thinning hair and hound-dog eyes, indicates his little stainless steel flask, from which he has just taken a slug of cheap whiskey.

"No, ya moron—the goddamn backpack," Raymond says, pointing at the heavy rucksack on the farmworker's back. Raymond Hilliard is a former football coach with a Class C college team out of north Atlanta—a tall, sinewy, grizzled good old boy—with a Falcons cap pulled down low on his forehead over dark, cunning eyes. He carries an AR-15 with a high-capacity clip. "We're traveling light, just bringing enough to defend ourselves."

The woman steps forward. "Is my Tec-9 gonna be enough, Ray?" Gloria Pyne is a small, compact, ruddy-skinned woman—tough around the eyes—with deep crow's-feet that belie her age and a thick thatch of red hair tucked under a visor that says I'M WITH STUPID.

"Yeah, just bring an extra mag or two." Raymond turns to the other men standing behind Gloria—both of them younger, dressed in the tattered hip-hop regalia of urban youth—baggy shorts, high-top Jordans, mesh shirts, tats. They both look sheepish and a little scared, despite the fact they each pack an AK-47 with a high-capacity mag. "You two bring up the rear flanks, keep an eye on our backside."

One kid looks at the other kid, clearing his throat nervously, muttering under his breath. "I ain't staring at nobody's backside, least of all Gloria's."

"Shut your mouth!"

The baritone growl comes from behind one of the vehicles, the shadow of a portly figure marching toward them. Gabe comes around the rear of a cargo truck with his MIG shouldered and a surly look on his face. His eyes blaze with tension. He storms up to the two younger men and hisses at them through gritted teeth, his thick neck beaded with perspiration, his black turtleneck damp with sweat spots: "Stop fucking around and get this show on the road!"

Raymond thumbs the safety off his assault rifle and gives the group a nod. "All right, let's move out."

They get less than five hundred yards from the clearing—moving single file through the deep woods, Raymond on point, Gabe coming along to keep watch on the proceedings, the others following closely behind—when Jim Steagal realizes he has to pee.

For the last few years, Jim's prostate has been acting up. He forgot to relieve himself before they left camp, and now the combination of his weak bladder and the many sips of whiskey he's been tippling all night make the trudge through the silent, shadowbound forest very uncomfortable. But he doesn't say anything at first. He just follows closely behind Gabe, twitching at every faint noise and chirring cricket that floods the dark woods with a low droning symphony of night sounds. Darkness has pressed in, and the air sparkles with fireflies and the occasional moth that ticks across their path. They can smell walker stink, but not in a profusion that worries them. The biters seem to be flocking toward the activity in the prison, which is keeping the adjacent woodlands blessedly clear of the dead. Jim grits his teeth at the urgent fullness of his bladder as they start down a winding path.

They reach a clearing—a mossy ravine about the size of a tennis court—the moonlight now as bright as a reading lamp. Raymond pauses. *"PPSSSSST!"* He turns to the others, and with hand gestures orders everybody down. His whisper is barely loud enough to be heard above the crickets. "Everybody just cool your heels for a second."

Gabe comes over to him, and the two men crouch on the edge of the clearing. "What's the problem?"

"I heard something."

"What was it?"

Raymond gazes out across the clearing, toward the opposite line of trees. "I don't know, maybe nothing." He looks at Gabe. "We're close to the prison, ain't we?"

"Yeah, so?"

"Maybe we ought to find higher ground and take a look at what's cooking down there."

Gabe nods. "Okay . . . let's double back and take that other trail up to the ridge."

"I'm right behind you."

The two men rise to their feet and are about to head back the way they came, when Jim Steagal comes up to them. "Guys, you go ahead. I'll catch up with you."

Gabe and Raymond look at each other. Gabe says, "What the fuck is the problem?"

"Nature calls, boys—gotta take a whiz."

Gabe lets out an exasperated sigh. "Just be quick about it, and get your ass back in line."

Jim gives them a nod and heads to the other side of the clearing.

Gabe and Raymond lead the others back up the trail and wait at the top of the ridge for the older man to finish his business. Jim goes over to a log, shoulders his rifle with its leather strap, and unzips. The urine stream arcs out over the hard-packed earth and makes a loud spattering noise as he empties his bladder.

He exhales with relief. Then he hears a noise off to his left, a twig snapping perhaps, or maybe he's just imagining it. The woods tick and breathe. His piss puddle spreads across the cracked earth.

Movement in his peripheral vision gets his attention as he continues peeing. He glances to his left. He sees a shadow burst out of the woods—accompanied by the sound of body armor rattling—and he lets out an involuntary noise from deep within his lungs: "W-WHU—?!"

The woman comes at him with a gleaming katana sword, a blur of black Kevlar and dreadlocks flowing off her head, her slender, sculpted ebony face partially obscured by a riot helmet.

It all happens so quickly the piss stream continues unabated as she expertly swings the blade. The last thing Jim Steagal sees is the gleam of the blade's beveled edge in his eyes.

The sword slices through his face between the earlobe and jaw-line with the sick crunching sound of a celery stalk snapping.

The top of his skull jettisons and tumbles to the ground. Blood fountains out of the concavity left behind, while his eyes continue sending imagery to his brain. For a split second, as the severed head hurls through the air, the optical nerves register the wobbling body left behind, still peeing, the involuntary urine stream continuing to fountain in a high arc. Then, what's left of Jim Steagal collapses to the hard mud in a heap of blood and piss—and the rest of the events in that clearing go unheard and unseen by the dead man.

"Quickly, Tyreese!" The woman in dreadlocks whirls toward the fallen man. "Help me with the body!"

At that moment, up on the ridge, behind a netting of over-growth, the face of Raymond Hilliard appears—peering through a break in the foliage—and his eyes bug. "OH—FUCK!"

Then things begin transpiring very quickly—almost too quickly for the naked eye to take in—as Raymond lurches down the trail toward the clearing with his AR-15 locked and loaded and coming up quick. Another blur of blue-black Kevlar appears out of no-where and charges across the clearing toward the oncoming gun-man. This enormous African American man—his shoulders as solid as bridge trestles—performs a flying tackle on Raymond Hilliard.

Raymond's assault rifle discharges on impact—shattering the night air with a booming report—the blast going high into the treetops, shredding leaves and sending a flock of bats into the dark heavens. Raymond sprawls to the ground, the armored black man landing on top of him. Hitting his head on a rock, Raymond plunges into momentary unconsciousness.

Almost simultaneously, the woman named Michonne, standing twenty feet away on the opposite side of the clearing, sees the other members of the scouting party roaring toward the scene with guns coming up and muzzles starting to flare magnesium-white in the darkness.

"Oh shit," she mutters, ducking down, as bullets whiz all around her.

Charging toward the clearing, Gabe sees Raymond writhing on the ground fifteen feet away, momentarily senseless, blinking at the sky, and the other man—the gigantic African American—struggling back to his feet. He stands at least six-four, and has almost 275 pounds on him—very few of those pounds fat—and it strikes Gabe that this guy is moving very quickly and nimbly for such a huge man.

The big man lurches back across the clearing and grabs the woman's hand and tries to pull her away. "RUN!" he cries. "C'MON!"

"NO!" She wriggles out of his grasp. Gabe spins toward the blur of dreadlocks and fires—the bullet nicking off her shoulder armor, a firecracker in the dark, and she darts behind a tree. The huge man dives to the ground. In the flickering darkness, the woman's voice cuts through the noise of gunfire. "We do this now, Tyreese! Or not at all!"

By this point, Gabe has taken cover behind deadfall logs across the clearing—along with the other members of the scouting party—and he squeezes off another pair of blasts that coax more shots from his team . . . until everybody is firing at will.

The arrhythmic crackling reports fill the air with silver lightning, tearing the foliage apart. Gabe uses a .357 Magnum revolver with a laser sight—the luminous red thread dancing across the clearing as he tries to lock onto the moving silhouettes—and his first three blasts kick up spits of dirt inches away from where the big black man lies on his belly, chunks of bark blowing off a tree trunk above him.

"FUCK!" the man named Tyreese grunts through clenched teeth, covering his head.

"Hey!" The sound of Michonne's voice in the nearby shadows gets the big man's attention. "Here!—Tyreese!—This way!" She gets her hand around the edge of his armored shoulder plate and yanks hard.

Tyreese careens backward, out of control, sliding on his ass down a small embankment formed by a trench or a burrow dug under the massive deadwood logs by possums or raccoons or God knows what. Gabe blinks and swings the gun downward as the giant slips away into the void of blackness, right behind the woman.

Like magic.

Both of them . . . vanishing into the dark.

"WHAT THE FUCK?!" Moments later, Gabe stands on the edge of the clearing with Gloria Pyne and the two younger men in their baggy shorts and silk jackets—each of them holding hot steel, muzzles smoking—their eyes wide and alert as they survey the deserted area. The stillness of night presses down on them—the crickets like a jet engine roaring in their ears—the moonlight shining off their tense faces.

"How the fuck did they—?" Gloria starts to pose the obvious question when the sound of Gabe's bellow cuts her off.

"FIND THEM!" Veins pulsing at his temples, his thick neck and shoulders as tense as girders, Gabriel Harris ejects a spent casings into the dirt, and then grabs a speed-loader off his belt and slams another six rounds of hollow points into the Magnum. But before the others get a chance to even turn around and start their search, a noise from the other side of the clearing stiffens everybody's spine. They all go still, their hackles up, the two young men—Eric and Daniel—staring at each other. It could be anything—the wind, animals. Those bastards that just attacked them could be a mile away from here by now.

Another noise—a plunking sound in the dark, almost like the snap of a switch, or a stick breaking—draws the attention of everybody to the west edge of the clearing. All their barrels go up, a collective inhalation of breaths, fingers on triggers. Gabe's flesh crawls as he double-hands the Magnum, his beefy, ham hock arms locked in the shooting position, front sight aimed on the dense, primordial dark across the tree line. Nobody says a word for the longest time as they wait, and wait, and wait for something to move behind the dark veil of foliage, but nothing moves. They wait for another snapping noise, but silence grips the clearing. Gabe can hear his heart pulsing in his ears.

After another endless second or two, Gabe silently motions with hand gestures for Eric, the youngest of the two hip-hoppers, to go wide to the left, and the other, Daniel, to go wide to the right. With quick nods, the two young gunmen fan out slowly across the clearing, stepping softly over the hard-pack, moving as silently as possible. Gabe gestures to Gloria to stay quiet and follow him. Inching slowly toward the wall of black oak and wild brush—now as dark as black velvet curtains before them—Gabe aims the .357 as he goes, Gloria doing the same with her Tec-9, two-handing it, the tension narrowing their eyes and furrowing their brows. The woods remain silent as Gabe approaches the wall of undergrowth. Now he's thinking it could be walkers in there, lurking, getting ready to pounce. It could be—

All at once, without warning, the sound of a woman's voice bellowing at the top of her lungs pierces the silence from behind them—

"NOW!!"

—and Gabe has just enough time to spin around when two figures pounce from opposite corners of the clearing. And in that frenzied instant before a single gun discharges, Gabe's mind races with a jumble of panic-stricken realizations—even as he swings the .357 up and starts to squeeze off the first shot—the variables flashing in his brain like sunspots in the darkness: *They were tossing fucking pebbles or something across the clearing, the oldest goddamn trick in the book, and we fell for it*—and now something glimmers like a streak of light in the darkness in front of Gabe's face before he fires—watch out—WATCH OUT!

The katana sword gripped in the black woman's hands whispers past Gabe's face—coming within a centimeter and a half of his throat—and it's only because of Gabe's involuntary reaction of rearing back and accidentally firing the Magnum up into the air that he's lucky enough to keep his head attached to his neck. He lets out an involuntary cry, and that's when the clearing suddenly ignites.

For a moment, the mass chaos that ensues—the strobelike effect of all the muzzle flashes, the collective tumult of gunfire and yelling and flashing steel and bullets whizzing and two armor-clad ambushers diving out of the line of fire in different directions—turns the narrow clearing into bedlam.

THIRTEEN

The skirmish lasts for mere seconds, not even a full minute, but when the dust clears—the last gunshots echoing and fading over the far hollows of the forest—one of the younger scouts—Eric—lies on the ground, dead, his neck opened by the katana blade. One of the two assailants also lies facedown on the cold ground, wounded. The other has vanished, her katana sword lying in the weeds.

Gabe hyperventilates as he quickly scans the tree line around the edges of the clearing. "WHERE THE FUCK DID SHE GO?!!"

He hears a noise, and he realizes that in all the excitement the woman has slipped their grasp, careening down an adjacent embankment into the deeper woods. He lurches over to the edge of the slope and sees a shadowy figure down in the darkness to the east, now struggling to escape through thickets of deadfall and undergrowth. He can hear her heavy breathing and panting as she flees.

"STAY HERE!" Gabe roars at the others, pointing at the big black man on the ground. "KEEP HIM ALIVE!"

The man named Tyreese lets out an involuntary moan. One of Gabe's rounds has penetrated the armor of the giant's right thigh, passing through the fleshy part of his leg and disabling him. Now Daniel and Raymond hold the man down, shoving their muzzles against the nape of his thick neck, pressing their knees into the small of his back.

Gabe slams another speed-loader into his .357 and lurches down the embankment.

The darkness and chill air of the forest engulf Gabe as he hurtles headlong through the trees, two-handing the Magnum, flipping on the FastFire tactical light. The red dot dances on the leaves ahead of him. The woman has a head start, but the woods are so thick to the east, Gabe gains on her quickly, his girth bulldozing through the foliage. He can see her shadow maybe fifty yards ahead of him now, darting toward another clearing. She reaches the clearing and bursts out of the trees in one great paroxysm of churning arms and pumping legs—her stride gazelle-like as she races for the far barrens.

Gabe reaches the clearing and realizes he'll never catch up to her—not in a full-on footrace across open land—so he cobbles to a stop on the soft ground and drops to one knee. He aims the laser sight at the fleeing bitch—now a blur of black Kevlar receding into the distance.

The slender thread of crimson light arcs out across the darkness and teases around her heels.

Gabe fires off half a dozen successive blasts, each booming report echoing up into the starry heavens, the recoil making his arms shudder. Through the scope, he can see the near misses—one goes high, a few puff off the dirt at her feet, and the rest go wide. She keeps running until he can't see her anymore.

"FUCK!—FUCK!—FUCK-FUCK-FUCK!" Gabe spits angrily into the dirt and lets out an inarticulate growl of rage. The woman is long gone now—a swirl of night wind tossing leaves across the deserted meadow in her wake.

A noise to Gabe's immediate left draws his attention to a new shadow moving out of the trees.

The stray walker lumbers into the moonlight, drawn to the commotion—a male in ragged bib overalls and a long, wrinkled face the color of earthworms—the dead arms reaching for Gabe, the rotting dentures snapping like castanets. Gabe calmly reaches down to his boot and draws an eleven-inch Randall knife. "Bite this, motherfucker!"

Gabe drives the knife blade up through the biter's jaw and into the sinus cavity. The creature sags immediately, the luminous fight in the thing's yellow eyes going out like pilot lights. Gabe lets go of the hilt and the thing collapses in a heap, the Randall knife still sticking out of the creature's double chins.

For a moment, Gabe just stares at the rotten remains lying in the tall grass at his feet. The sight of it gives him an idea. He gazes back out at the far reaches of the meadow, surveying the dark trees into which the woman has just vanished. Inspiration strikes.

"Fuck her," he says to himself as he pulls his knife out of the walker. He has her sword. He knows what he's going to do. He turns and starts back toward the others, formulating his story.

The Governor stands in the circle of vehicles—a single Coleman camp lantern glowing on a stump providing the only illumination in the dusty clearing at the top of the ridge, throwing a dim circle of pale yellow light on the other members of the militia tending to their wounds and taking stock of their supplies—when the sound of footsteps interrupts his thoughts.

"What the fuck?" he mutters as he turns and sees the group of battle-weary figures trudging out of the woods directly behind him. Many heads turn—nerves are frayed from an increase in walker activity in the area—and many breathe a sigh of relief at the sight of humans.

A stout man built like a Mack truck leads the ragtag brigade. Behind Gabe, two members of the scouting party—Raymond and Daniel—drag a fourth man, clad in black body armor and apparently wounded, between them. The ailing prisoner—the woman called him Tyreese—drips blood from his lolling face and barely shuffles along with his huge arms over the shoulders of the two other men. Gloria Pyne brings up the rear, carrying an armful of rifles and weapons.

"Yeah—we found him in the woods," Gabe reports as he walks up to the Governor. "He and the woman attacked us. They killed Eric and Jim."

The Governor's expression hardens in the gloomy light of the lantern. "The woman? You talking about the hell-bitch that tortured me?"

Gabe gives him a nod. "Yep—the very same. We followed them into the woods. They put up a fight, but they couldn't hold us off for long."

The other men drag the big black man around the stump and hold him up for the Governor's inspection. Barely conscious, his visor gone, his face starting to swell from the beating, Tyreese tries to raise his head but it's a losing battle. He lets out a pained breath through clenched teeth.

"Thought you might like a chance to sit down with this one," Gabe ventures, jerking a thumb at Tyreese, "maybe have a little chat with him?"

The Governor stares at the wounded giant. "The girl, Gabe. What happened with the girl?"

"She broke away from us—took off for the woods—so I did you a favor."

The Governor cocks his head. "A favor? What the fuck are you talking about?"

Gabe gives the Governor a look. Neither a smile nor a grimace, the expression on the stocky man's face is hard to read. Finally he says, "I ran her down and blew her fucking brains out."

A brief instant of silence follows, during which time Philip Blake braces himself against an unexpected storm of contradictory emotions smashing down on him—relief, anger, morbid curiosity, disappointment, and more than anything else, *suspicion*. "You shot her in the head?" he asks at last. "You killed her?"

"Yeah." Gabe looks into the Governor's eyes—a prodigal son returning with the elixir—and the pause stretches. "She's fucking dead, boss."

The Governor thinks about it some more. "You saw her die?" He wants to know every detail, wants to know the look on her face in her last moments—wants to know that she suffered. Instead of asking about all these things, he simply says, "You witnessed it?"

Gabe turns and looks over his shoulder. "Gloria!" The woman in the I'M WITH STUPID visor comes forward, fumbling with her cache of weapons. Gabe explains: "The bitch ran away. She got pretty far. I saw her run. I shot her. I saw her fall down. I saw her stop moving." Gabe licks his lips, measuring his words carefully. "I'm sure it wasn't as slow and painful as you would have liked—but she's dead, boss." Gloria hands him something wrapped in a chamois-like cloth. "But before she got away from us—"

Gabe takes the object, carefully unwraps it, and reveals it to the Governor.

"—we took this." Gabe holds it up so that it gleams dully in the jaundice-yellow light. "Figured you would want a trophy."

Gabe brandishes the katana sword with a flourish, holding it over his head at a parallel angle to the ground, looking somewhat foolish to the Governor. Gaping at the thing, taking in all the implications, he breathes in a long breath. Then all at once he snatches the thing away from Gabe, and the rest of the scouts step back with a jerk. Gabe goes stone-still, staring at the Governor.

Latent violence glitters in Philip's gaze as he squares his shoulders, raising the gleaming blade over his head. For a moment, Gabe's spine goes cold with terror. Then, with a decisive one-handed swing, Philip slams the tip of the sword down into the center of a tree stump, making a loud *thwack!*

Another horrible moment of silence transpires as the sword sticks rigidly out of the rotten timber like a flag planted on a summit.

"Bring him over to my private office," the Governor finally says, gesturing at the wounded man in body armor. "We'll have a little talk."

"We're on the same side, you and me," the Governor says to the huge man sitting on the bench in the rear of the cargo vehicle. The airless enclosure reeks of sweat and the coppery stench of blood. A single flyspecked dome light shines down on the steel tread-plate floor as the Governor paces, his boots ringing on the iron. "You realize that, don't ya?"

The black man slumps against the wall in his battered black Kevlar, his hands bound behind his back, his swollen face drooping forward and from side to side. He spits bloody saliva on the floor and manages to look up, his grizzled ebony visage screwed up with pain and rage. "Really?—What side is that?"

"The side of *survival*, homie!" The Governor flings his words at the man, trying to get a rise out of him, trying to provoke him. "We're all in the same boat—fighting for our lives—am I wrong, homes?"

The black man swallows and looks into the Governor's eyes, replying in a very low, taut voice, as though on the verge of a scream. "The name's Tyreese."

"Tyreese! *Ty-rreeeeeese* . . . I like that." The Governor paces. "Okay, Tyreese, let me ask you a question. And be honest."

The black man spits again. "Whatever . . . I got nothing to hide."

"We could torture the shit outta you, make your last moments a living hell, all that good stuff, but c'mon . . . do we really need to go through that dance again? I hurt you real bad, take you to the point of passing out, but not quite, and when you refuse to talk, I break you, flay the skin off you or something, blah-blah-blah . . . do we really need to go through that ridiculous shit again?"

The big man looks up and fixes his gaze on the Governor and says, "Have at it."

The Governor slaps him. Hard. A sharp, forceful backhand slap from his gloved left hand—violent and abrupt enough to slam the back of the man's skull against the wall behind him—making Tyreese gasp and blink as though snorting smelling salts. "Wake up, man!" The Governor maintains a cheerful, helpful, benevolent tone. "You're not thinking this through—I'm just sayin'!"

Tyreese takes heaving breaths, trying to control his rage and blink away the pain. His enormous shoulders tremble under the battered armor. "Fuck you."

"Tyreese, c'mon." Now the Governor sounds disappointed, crestfallen. "Don't make this one of those annoying situations where I gotta hurt you real bad—worse than you've ever been hurt. A few simple questions is all."

Tyreese sniffs away the pain. "What do you want to know?"

"Weak spots in the prison, for instance."

Tyreese chuckles then, a wry, weary, amused chuckle that lasts for several moments. Then he looks up. "There ain't no weak spots—it's a fucking prison, Sherlock!"

"How about you tell me how many people you got up in there? What kind of arsenal you got, ammunition, supplies, what kind of power you runnin'?"

The black man looks at him. "How about you eat shit and die?"

The Governor stares at the man for a moment, then winds up to hit him again—this time with a balled-up fist—but right before he swings, the sound of knocking interrupts. Somebody is tapping on the doorframe outside the truck's tarp-covered rear hatch.

"Governor?"

It's Lilly's voice, and the sound of it sends a warning alarm like icy water trickling down the Governor's spine. He chews on the inside of his cheek for a brief instant before answering, thinking it over. Maybe this is a good thing—maybe she should see this—see the brutality in the man's dark eyes, see who they're fighting. "Come in here, Lilly," Philip says at last. "You can be a witness."

The tarp folds inward, and Lilly Caul climbs up into the enclosure. She wears a tattered denim jacket, her hair pulled back from her suntanned face, which is shiny with sweat and bright with nervous tension. She keeps her distance, watching from the rear.

The big man on the bench glances up at her, breathing hard,

trying to control his emotions. He looks as though he's on the verge of exploding.

The Governor sees that the man is about to lose it, and leans down close to him, staring into his eyes. Tyreese looks up at him. The Governor smiles and speaks softly, as if to a child: "Lilly, meet Tyreese. Nice enough fella, good head on his shoulders. I was just trying to talk some sense into him, seeing if there was a way he could talk to this Rick fella, get him to wise up and surrender, so we could all avoid more bloodshed and—"

The big man lunges suddenly—putting all of his 275 pounds into the move—slamming his forehead into the Governor's face. The head-butt, instantaneous and brutal, sounds like a board snapping, taking the Governor completely by surprise, knocking him momentarily insensate and sending him flinging backward against the wall. He slams into the struts with a gasp and then topples to the floor.

Lilly draws her Ruger and aims it at the big man. "GET BACK!" She thumbs the safety off. "GET BACK, GODDAMNIT—NOW! *SIT DOWN!!*"

Tyreese sits back down, his wrists still bound, and he exhales angrily, his face twitching with rage. His thigh drips blood from the gunshot wound, but he barely seems to notice it. A former NFL linebacker, as well as a bouncer for some of the toughest bars in Atlanta, he looks like he could snap Lilly in two. His grizzled face remains stoic as he spits blood from a split lip, looking down and shaking his head. He mumbles something inaudible.

Lilly goes over to the Governor, kneels, and helps him sit up. "You okay?"

The Governor blinks and tries to get his bearings, tries to draw breath into his lungs. His forehead is bleeding, and he coughs convulsively, but the pain braces him, galvanizes him, energizes him. "See?—See what I'm talking about?" he utters thickly. "You can't reason with these people . . . you can't . . . *bargain* with them . . . they're fucking animals."

Across the enclosure, the big man mutters something else, his head down.

Lilly and the Governor look up. Tyreese speaks under his breath as though talking to himself, "And the nations were angry . . ."

"What was that, asshole?" the Governor snarls at him. "You want to share it with the rest of the class?"

Tyreese looks up at them, his dark face filling with sullen, baleful hate. "And the nations were angry, and thy wrath is come, and it shall be the time of the dead, that they should be judged, and to them that fear my name, small and great, thou shouldest destroy them which destroy the earth . . . and there will be war in heaven." He pauses and looks at them. "It's from Revelation . . . not that you would know shit about the Bible. It's what's happening. You can't turn back the tide; you've opened the door. Kiss your asses goodbye. You'll die by your own fucking swords and you don't even—"

"SHUT UP!" Lilly springs to her feet, lunges toward Tyreese, and presses the Ruger's muzzle against his forehead. "JUST SHUT THE FUCK UP!"

The Governor lifts himself to his feet, moving in between Lilly and Tyreese. "Okay, let's dial it down now. Back off, Lilly. I got this." He gently ushers Lilly away from the prisoner toward the rear hatch. "It's okay. I got this. I'll take care of it."

Lilly, breathing hard, stands in the hatchway, re-engaging the safety and shoving the gun back into its sheath on her hip. "I'm sorry."

"Don't worry about it," the Governor says, giving her a reassuring pat on the arm. He wipes the blood from his forehead. "I'll handle this. You go and try and get some sleep."

Lilly looks at him. "You sure you're okay?"

"I'm good. I got this. Don't worry."

After a long pause, she glances back at the prisoner, who now sits staring at the floor. She lets out a pained sigh and makes her exit.

The Governor turns and looks at Tyreese. Very softly, under his breath, Philip Blake murmurs, "I got this." He goes over to the bench facing the prisoner on the opposite side of the enclosure. Under the bench, in the cobwebs and litter, Philip finds a baseball bat lying next to a pile of rags. "I got this," he says in barely a whisper as he picks up the bat, then goes over to the rear hatch and pulls down the metal door. The door clangs shut, giving them privacy. The Governor turns to the prisoner.

Philip smiles at the man. "I got this."

Very few surviving members of the Woodbury militia get any sleep that night—least of all Gabe. Tossing and turning on a hard pallet in the back of his cargo truck, his rotund, barrel-shaped belly wedged between the wall and a row of supply crates, he tries to clear his mind, but his brain revs and chugs and circles back around to his lies. How many times has he lied since the plague broke out? He's lost track. But this latest lie could truly bite him on the ass—the bitch with the hair braids is still out there. What will the Governor do when he finds out? Gabe wonders if he should bail out of this whole fracas with the prison people. He tosses and turns some more. The drone of crickets and frogs and loons outside the truck rises and swells in the dark until it sounds positively thunderous to Gabe, like a rainstorm, and he puts his hands over his ears and tries to drive the thoughts away. His stomach burns and seethes with nervous indigestion. He's been having upper GI problems for months now—a combination of the shitty diet he's been on and the constant stress—and now he feels stickpins stabbing him in the guts, piercing his innards. He tries to breathe evenly, deeply, and eventually the breathing exercise sends him into a half-comatose doze in which he dreams snippets of night terrors such as the black lady with the dreadlocks sneaking up on him and driving her katana sword into his abdomen just above the belly button and then swizzling it around as though trying to open a doorway in his guts, and he tries to scream in the dream but nothing but silent air will come out of him, and he wakes up right around dawn with a gasp.

Somebody is knocking on the rear hatch, and Gabe blinks at the pale light filtering through the tarp, and the sound of a deep, smoky baritone voice. "Hey! Gabe, get your fat ass up. I need you right now!"

The Governor appears in the back hatch of the cargo truck as Gabe is struggling off the pallet, clutching for his wadded turtleneck shirt, and starting to get dressed. "I'm up, boss. Whaddaya need?"

"I'll tell you on the way. Grab your AR-15 and give me a hand with the big dude."

Gabe follows the Governor across the clearing to a transport truck. Inside the passenger hold, the man named Tyreese is barely alive, curled into a fetal position on the floor of the payload bay, his body armor gone, his wrists still bound by rope and wire, his flesh battered and scourged by the Governor's constant assault throughout the night with the baseball bat. Now the man barely draws a breath, both his eyes swollen shut, his lips cracked and bleeding, mouthing silent litanies, prayers, apocalyptic Bible quotes that nobody can hear.

The Governor and Gabe lift the man onto a bench—not an easy task, considering the 275 pounds of nearly dead weight—then they tie his wrists to the wall. The Governor covers the man with a tarp and mutters, "We'll unwrap the present when we get there."

Gabe looks at Philip. "Get where?"

Philip lets out a sigh. "You are one stupid motherfucker, Gabe."

They hop out of the rear hatch and go around to the cab, Gabe climbing behind the wheel, Philip taking the passenger seat. Philip orders Gabe to take it nice and slow—no headlights—and they pull out of the clearing unnoticed by everyone but Lilly.

She appears in their path in the predawn glow like a ghost, waving them to a stop.

Gabe pulls up to her and rolls down his window. "What do you want, Lilly?"

"What are you doing? Where the hell are you going?" Lilly peers into the cab and sees the Governor. "Let me come with you. I'll get my guns, just give me a second."

"No!" From the passenger seat, the Governor leans forward and makes eye contact with her. "You stay here and keep an eye on things. We're going to go and try and negotiate with them, use the big boy as leverage."

Lilly nods slowly, reluctantly. "Okay, but be careful, you're gonna be outnumbered."

"You let us worry about that." The Governor gives her a wink. "You hold down the fort."

They take off in a cloud of dust as Lilly watches from the shadows.

She realizes right then—for some reason, with mounting dread—that Michonne's sword was leaning against the Governor's hip as they drove off.

They arrive at the prison at 6:53 A.M., according to the clock on the truck's dash, barreling through a cluster of walkers wandering the tall grass east of the grounds. The truck's grille smashes through groups of reanimated cadavers with a series of watery thuds and brittle bones cracking beneath the massive wheels. On Philip's orders, Gabe blows the air horn once, waking anybody who might still be slumbering inside the gray stone cellblocks behind the razor wire. Gabe pulls up close to the east fence and then makes a huge U-turn. He rolls his window down and grabs the .38 Special lodged under the dash, firing out the side of the truck at a few stray biters. Heads snap back in mists of blood and brain tissue—at least a half-dozen more going down in sequence like bowling pins.

"Now back it up to the fence," the Governor orders, peering out his side mirror.

Gabe slams on the brakes, then wrestles the stick into reverse and makes a big show of revving the engine and backing toward the chain link as if they have a pizza to deliver. A blur of movement catches the corner of Gabe's eye in his mirror as he navigates the truck closer and closer to the fence—the inhabitants of the prison dashing across gaps between the buildings, waking each other up, scurrying for their weapons. Over the noise of the diesel engine, Gabe can hear the faint shouts of alarm.

The truck clatters to a stop less than ten feet from the outer fence.

"Let's do this," the Governor murmurs as he kicks open his door and climbs out.

The two men calmly step off the running boards, and then stride around to the rear of the truck. The katana sword, tucked into its scabbard, bounces off the Governor's hip as he reaches up and pulls open the hatch. Gabe feels the eyes of both walkers and humans on the back of their necks. Before climbing up into the cargo bay, the Governor mutters under his breath, "Keep the fucking biters off us long enough for me to finish, okay?"

"Will do," Gabe says, and slams a magazine into the AR's receiving port. He thumbs the safety as the Governor climbs up into the cargo enclosure.

The tarp comes off the dazed black man with the abruptness of a Band-Aid being torn off a wound. Tyreese still breathes shallow breaths, his eyes swollen to slits. He tries to see, and makes a feeble attempt to move, but the pain keeps him docile. He makes a choking noise deep in his throat as the Governor yanks him to his feet.

"It's showtime, homes," Philip whispers, with the tenderness one might proffer to a sick animal on the way to the veterinarian.

FOURTEEN

Inside the barricade of razor wire and tall cyclone fencing, many shadowy figures suddenly stop in their tracks, many pairs of eyes fixing themselves on the unexpected sight of their comrade being displayed in the back of a truck, in full view of the prison. The Governor has positioned the dazed black man on the edge of the truck's rear hatch, on his knees, facing the prison complex, head drooping, the strange tableau almost reminiscent of some obscure Asian death-cleansing ritual. The rear hatch and the truck's cargo area have momentarily become a theatrical stage. The big man's wrists are still bound, his head drooping as though it weighs a ton. The silence spreads across the grounds like a black tide. The wind tosses the Governor's hair across his eye patch as he dramatically draws the gleaming sword from its sheath.

"BEFORE ANYONE GETS TRIGGER HAPPY," he calls out to those inside the ramparts, holding the sword over the hunched figure of Tyreese, "KNOW THAT I'VE GOT THE WOMAN, TOO!" He takes in the stillness, the silence. "MY FAT FRIEND AND I DON'T GET BACK TO OUR CAMP IN ONE PIECE, SHE DIES!"

He pauses for a moment to allow this prefatory matter to settle in.

"SO NO SUDDEN MOVES—OKAY?"

Again he pauses, hearing his voice echo across the warrens of passageways and cellblocks. He interprets the overwhelming silence as cooperation and nods.

"FROM THAT I THINK YOU CAN SEE WHERE THIS IS GO-
ING. OPEN THE GATES. GET IN THIS TRUCK AND COME
BACK WITH US—OR I DO SOMETHING HORRIBLE TO YOUR
FRIEND."

The Governor lets this sink in and then starts to say something
else when a sharp movement inches away from him yanks his attention down to the prisoner. Tyreese jerks his head up with great
effort and peers through swollen eyes out the rear hatch at the
prison grounds.

"D-don't let him in!" The voice that comes out of him is strangled with pain, garbled by blood in the back of his throat. "Don't—"

Philip smashes the blunt end of the sword down on the back of
the man's skull, hard enough to make a cracking sound and drive
the man to the corrugated iron floor. Tyreese lets out a half grunt,
half moan.

"Shut up!" Philip gazes down at the man as though looking at
garbage. "Shut your fucking mouth!" Then he looks back up at the
barren, silent prison grounds. "SO WHAT'S IT GOING TO BE,
PEOPLE?"

He waits for a moment, the sound of Tyreese's ragged breathing
the only audible sound.

"YOU HAVE ONE MINUTE TO DECIDE!"

An endless minute passes, and over the course of that time, the
Governor realizes he's being watched from every quarter of the
property—a small cluster of figures huddling behind one of
the guard towers, another group lurking inside a dark alcove of the
main cellblock, a few scattered at opposite ends of the yards—all
eyes fixed on him. Some of the people aim weapons, while others
frantically whisper and argue. But in very short order, the verdict
becomes clear to Philip—he knows what he has to do.

"SO THAT'S IT, THEN?" He feels a tingling sensation at the
base of his spine—that familiar clarion ringing in his brain, a
red shade coming down over his solitary eye. His skin prickles,
and his mind goes still—the great silent cobra-calm before the
strike.

The first blow comes down decisively yet slightly impeded by the uncoordinated tendons of Philip's left arm—he has to awkwardly twist his body to get a good angle—and the blade buries itself a mere inch and a half into the man's neck. Tyreese lets out a strangled hiss. His entire body hunches suddenly as if electrocuted.

"Fuck!" the Governor grumbles under his breath as the blood sluices around the beveled edge of the katana sword, the blade caught in the cords and cartilage of the big man's nape. The faint gasps and moaning sounds coming from within the confines of the prison barely register in Philip's ears. He puts a boot on the man's shoulders and yanks the blade free with a watery smacking noise.

All the fight instantly drains out of the big man as though someone flipped a switch, the shock paralyzing him, keeping him pinned to the floor of the cargo bay, his head shuddering as major arteries disconnect from their moorings.

Tyreese sags lower, but somehow—in his involuntary stiffening, his nervous system shutting down—he manages to remain on his elbows and knees, his face pressed to the cold floor now, his arms and haunches trembling in their death throes, his lungs heaving as he drowns in the tremendous hemorrhage soaking the rusty platform beneath him.

The Governor raises the sword for a second blow, and this time, he brings it down harder. The blade sinks halfway through the man's thick neck—blood gushing now with the force of a geyser, arcing up through the air, sluicing down until it floods the entire cargo hold—and this time the Governor can hear the startled gasps from inside the fences. He yanks the blade back.

Tyreese collapses. His head lolling, barely connected now, he lands at an awkward angle, his lifeless face pressed against the blood-sodden iron floor, the gaping maw of his neck now displaying the coils and strands of his circulatory system as it pulses futilely. Other than a few postmortem twitches and tics of the big man's musculature, he lies still, gone, his spirit flown.

With a flourish, the Governor delivers the final blow—the massive force causing catastrophic damage to the enormous man's neck—sending a font of blood spurting up. The blowback spatters the Governor as the head finally detaches. The expression frozen on the unmoored face is almost tranquil as the head wobbles free, its eyes frozen shut with a strange look of deliverance. The head rolls a few centimeters from its former spindle, which now releases a torrent of blood like a baptismal font flowing over the edge of the rear gate.

Winded from all the exertion, taking in huge breaths, huffing and wheezing, the Governor steps back from the horrible spectacle, the sword still gripped in his left hand. Even at this distance, he can hear the traumatized mutterings coming from inside the prison. It sounds like white noise on the wind—the sound of revulsion mixed with despair—and it fuels Philip's rage.

He kicks the loose cranium off the ledge of the rear gate, and the severed head goes bouncing off into the tall grass, rolling nearly twenty yards before coming to a stop facedown. Philip shoves the blood-drenched remains of Tyreese's body off the rear as well, the massive form flopping to the earth with a wet, hollow thud.

By this point, Gabe has moved back toward the truck's cab, his watchful eyes on the dozens of walkers shambling this way from the north and the west, drawn to all the hubbub. He opens the driver's-side door as Philip hops off the blood-slick rear ledge and circles around the truck.

"We'll leave his body for the biters," Philip mutters as he walks calmly toward the cab. He doesn't hurry; he doesn't show any fear. He approaches Gabe and says, "Let's roll before the biters get too close or one of these shell-shocked fucks decides to—"

The dry, harsh clap of a high-powered rifle cuts off his voice, and the Governor instinctively ducks down as the first shot rings off the front fender, dimpling the steel and sending a rosette of sparks into the air.

"FUCK!—*FUCK!*" The Governor stays down on the ground

as more shots are fired—another three high-caliber rounds—
puncturing the quarter panel and raising puffs along the ground
mere centimeters from Philip's head. He crawls around the front
of the truck as Gabe slams the driver's-side door and fires up the
engine.

"DRIVE, GODDAMNIT—DRIVE!!" the Governor booms after
climbing in the shotgun side. The truck lurches, and a cloud of
dust swirls after it as Gabe slams the pedal to the floor and makes
a beeline for the main road a quarter mile away. Within seconds
they have crossed the adjacent pasture and screeched back onto
the south road—

—vanishing into the early morning heat rays as abruptly as they
arrived.

Two figures stand sentry at the threshold of the dusty clearing as
Gabe pulls the truck back up the winding access road leading to
the temporary camp. Raymond Hilliard and Lilly Caul stand on
opposite sides of the road, hands on their hips, the sun blazing
down on the circle of military vehicles behind them. They each
look worried.

Gabe drives past them, pulls the cargo truck across the clearing,
and parks next to the tank. He turns off the engine with a sigh of
relief.

The Governor has already climbed out his side and sees the two
sentries approaching.

"Well?" Raymond Hilliard speaks first, taking off his Falcons cap
and wiping the sweat from his bald pate. "Uh . . . how did it go?"

"How did it *go*?" the Governor says, not even breaking stride,
walking angrily past the man. The katana scabbard bounces on his
hip as he walks. "It didn't go well, that's how! IT DIDN'T FUCK-
ING *WORK*!"

Raymond watches the man head back toward the temporary
tent set up on the edge of the clearing for supplies. Lilly hurries
after him.

"What happened?" she asks, catching up with Philip and gently grabbing his left arm.

He pauses and burns his gaze into her, Gabe standing behind him, looking sheepish and guilty. "We tried to get them to open the gates—trade their man for access inside. We even threatened the man's life." The Governor holds Lilly's stare, his single, dark, glittering eye radiating madness at her. "These crazy, evil sons of bitches shot their own man!" Behind Philip, Gabe lowers his head, stares awkwardly at the ground. "We had a bit of leverage and so they shot their own guy in the fucking head!"

Lilly gapes, mumbling. "Why the fuck—?"

"They killed him so we couldn't use him against them!" The Governor stares at her. "You follow me? You understand what we're dealing with here?"

By this point, others have gathered behind Lilly to listen to the news—eleven weekend warriors standing slack-jawed and stunned, their eyes telling the story. This is more than they bargained for. This is closer to the bone than any of them have ever ventured. Gloria Pyne looks down and kicks the dirt, turning things over in her mind. Raymond Hilliard pushes his way between Gus and Gabe and says to the Governor, "So . . . what do we do now?"

The Governor slowly turns—aiming his one good eye at the man like a beacon—and says very softly, very coldly, "What do we do?"

Raymond Hilliard gives a terse little nod, the nod of a lost child.

The Governor snarls, "We fucking kill every last one of them—
THAT'S WHAT WE FUCKING DO!"

Lilly clenches her fists at the unexpected cymbal crash of the Governor's voice—the clenching is involuntary at this point—her gaze riveted to Philip Blake. He backs away from Lilly and turns to the group. He looks down at the katana sword gripped in his hand as if he's forgotten it's there. He speaks in a dry, flat monotone as he stares at the sword's fine craftsmanship. "No more waiting—no more stalling. It's time to finish this." He sniffs suddenly, blinking as though from an electric shock. A rustling noise comes from behind him, Gabe mumbling something under his breath, but he barely notices it. "WE MOVE *NOW*!"

The others stand paralyzed for a moment, like totems in the morning light, which dapples the ground around them with fiery yellow pools. They stare and stare, their mouths agape, some of them swallowing hard or reaching for their guns. The Governor swishes the sword through the air.

"NOW!" He stares at them. "Get in your cars—load your fucking guns and let's move! We're taking these monsters down—ridding the world of their evil, right here—RIGHT NOW!" He looks at their pallid, ashen expressions. "What the fuck is wrong with you people—you heard me—get your shit together and let's move!"

Nobody budges. The Governor hears a quick inhalation of air coming from Gabe, and he turns and looks at the stocky, thick-necked man in the turtleneck. "What the hell is your problem?"

"I—Uh—!" Gabe struggles to say something, gazing off at the shadows behind a nearby cargo truck, the same shadows from which a dark figure has just lunged, taking everybody by surprise.

The Governor sees Gabe's eyes shifting toward the area around the cargo truck behind them, but before Philip even has a chance to turn around, he feels the unmistakable kiss of cold, blue steel against the back of his neck just above his upper vertebrae.

Philip remains still, the barrel of a high-powered rifle pressing hard against his neck cords. He lets out a puff of air and a single, strangled word: "*Fuck.*"

Gabe is the closest to the assailant, and he licks his lips cautiously before saying anything—a player in a deadly game of chess, the starter clock now beginning to tick—his hand on the butt of his spare semiautomatic wedged between his belt and his hip. "Okay, you're not stupid," he says very softly to the invader standing behind Philip. "You gotta know, if you *do* kill him, you're gonna be going down next."

"Yes . . . I'm aware of that," the familiar voice replies inches away from Philip's left ear. It's a woman's voice, calm and measured as a telephone operator. The sound of it stiffens the Governor's spine. Very slowly, very subtly, the onlookers standing around the clearing begin to reach down for their pistols, or carefully thumb the safeties off their assault rifles.

"Okay, do the math," Gabe says to the woman with as much sincerity and reason as he can muster. "You see how many of us there are, and basically you're surrounded, so . . . you know . . . it's kinda academic."

"You really think I care?" she says. She wears her body armor secured around her slender form and has a samurai-style headband wrapped tight around her cascading dreadlocks. She holds an AK-47 on the Governor, a weapon capable of firing 100 rounds of 7.62 mm hellfire per minute. "You think I haven't planned for that?" She lets out an amused grunt. Philip hasn't moved one millimeter since the conversation began. The woman says, "*You're* the stupid one."

"Really?" Gabe smiles, drawing his .45 in one easy movement. "That a fact?"

"Gabe—don't." The Governor's single eye gazes with fiery intensity at the barrel of Gabe's semiauto coming up in the air. "Gabe!"

"You got a death wish, lady?" Gabe aims the gun at the general vicinity of the Governor's head. "Fine . . . I'll grant you that wish!"

"GABE!!"

The booming report of the .45 shatters the still air at the precise moment Michonne's rifle roars, making her jerk from the recoil one nanosecond before Gabe's metal-jacketed hollow point bullet strikes her shoulder piece, chewing a divot in the Kevlar and sending a chunk flying. The Governor has already convulsed forward and gets grazed in the lower mandible just under his wounded ear.

The noise drives everybody in the area down to their bellies or behind the nearest cover as the tense tableau explodes apart in a blur of lightning-quick movements—actions and reactions, one tumbling into another—the slap-back reports echoing and rising in the sky. The Governor instantly ends up on the ground, the wind knocked out of him, his bloody drool flinging across the earth, the sword flying out of his hand. Michonne moves with the feral grace of a panther as she dives for the sword, the other combatants getting their bearings now. Lilly comes up behind the front quarter panel of the cargo truck with her Ruger gripped in both hands—the Weaver position that Bob taught her, the Israeli-commando tactics almost second nature to her now—and she scans for the dark figure in her front sight. Gabe, on the ground now, fires wildly at the blur of motion while he simultaneously crawls toward the fallen Governor—emptying the .45's entire clip—unable to hit anything but the heels of Michonne's jackboots. By this point, Michonne has gotten her gloved hands around the finely tooled handle of the ninja sword and is spinning sideways toward Raymond Hilliard, who is backing away with his AR-15 jerking sideways and up and down, seeking a target. In one fluid movement, Michonne spins and slashes, opening a gap in Raymond's midsection with silent efficiency.

A tide of blood spumes down Raymond's lap as he cries out and drops his gun and tumbles backward to the ground, and now several things transpire with the flickering, dreamlike speed of a nightmare in the harsh rays of sunlight stabbing through the trees.

The other militia members have scattered for cover, alarmed by the advent of that gleaming, deadly sword, while Gabe has climbed on top of the fallen Governor to provide a human shield. Meanwhile, Michonne has spun behind the trunk of an ancient live oak with her assault rifle raised and ready now, and she opens up on the stragglers.

With one hand, she sprays armor-piercing shells across the cracked earth of the clearing, raising chunks of turf, puckering the steel of adjacent trucks, sparks pinging and blooming off fenders, sending bark chips flying, and generally gobbling the clearing in a maelstrom of fire and hot lead. The Governor, pinned to the ground beneath the portly Gabe, slams his eye shut as dust and sparks spit all around him.

And then—just like a switch has been thrown—the assailant is gone.

The silence that abruptly follows the barrage takes everyone by surprise. The fusillade has ceased as suddenly as it began, and for several moments, the Governor lies with his face in the dirt, the cold sting from his wounded jaw spreading down his spine. "Get the fuck off me," he hisses at last, wriggling under the massive lump of his bodyguard. "The girl, goddamnit—THE GIRL!"

Gabe rolls off Philip, struggles to his feet, and quickly scans the perimeter—simultaneously ejecting the spent clip from his .45, chucking in a fresh mag, and releasing the slide. He lowers the gun. "Shit." He looks in all directions and sees that the girl has vanished. "Shit—shit—shit!"

The Governor climbs to his feet, holding his gloved hand over the deep gash along his jawline, the blood seeping through his fingers. He looks around the clearing. In the blue haze of cordite, he sees Raymond lying in a spreading pool of blood, the others cautiously coming out of their hiding places, frazzled, angry, and scared. Lilly steps out from behind a vehicle, her gaze riveted on the Governor.

Without even a glance at her Ruger, she dumps the empty mag on the ground—her furrowed expression fixed on Philip. She breathes heavily, her lips trembling with rage, her eyes blazing with anger. She looks as though she would follow Philip into hell now.

Philip turns to Gabe, who's still surveying the periphery as though Michonne might materialize out of thin air at any moment. Then Gabe notices the Governor staring at him with baleful intensity. Gabe swallows hard. "Boss, I—"

"That what it was like?" Philip interrupts in a low, thick growl, his voice dripping with contempt, his gloved hand still pressed to his jaw, barely stanching the bleeding gash. "Last time you 'blew her fucking brains out'—was it just like that?"

"Boss—" Gabe starts to explain but stops himself when he sees the Governor raising a bloody gloved hand.

"I don't want to hear it." Philip jerks his thumb at the others. "Get them ready to roll—we're gonna end this thing now—RIGHT FUCKING NOW!!"

With Austin at her side, Lilly orders every last crate of ammunition opened and loaded into weapons, every last ounce of fuel poured into tanks, every ammo clip filled, every available piece of body armor put on and secured. She has Gus tend to the Governor's wound, using the dissolving sutures in the first-aid kit to do a quick field stitch. She checks all the radios, checks all the vehicles, all the tires, all the engines, all the batteries, all the fluids, all the gun turrets, the scopes, the binoculars, the helmets, the visors, and the incidental supplies. Her pulse quickens as she nears completion of the last few preparations, the gravity of the situation quickly taking hold of her. It feels different this time.

Hate is a microbe that passes from one host to another, and it has passed fully from the Governor to Lilly. She hates these people now like never before—enough to launch a slaughter, enough to wipe them off the face of the earth. She hates them for what they have done to her town, her future, her hope for a better life. She hates them for their brutality. She hates them for what they have taken from her. Lilly's life is meaningless now in the Grand Scheme of Things. Nothing has meaning anymore but her hate. Lilly has gone completely inward to the other side, completely self-contained and ready to kill . . . ready to burn these motherfuckers to the ground.

At one point, Austin notices her unfamiliar aura as she loads extra magazines into the truck's cab for easy access. She has two sniper rifles tucked behind her seat.

"Hey, you okay?" he asks, giving her a tender pat on the shoulder. "What's with the humming?"

She pauses, looking at him. "Humming?"

"You were humming to yourself—didn't recognize the song—but it struck me as kinda weird."

She wipes her face. All around the clearing, engines are firing up, gouts of exhaust spewing from tailpipes. Doors slam, gunners climb into place on the backs of turrets, and the Governor stands on his beloved tank, watching it all, looking stiff and pale, blanched of all humanity, like a golem rising from the mud. It takes Lilly's breath away. She wants to see him tear limbs off these people, chew their jugulars out with his teeth, burn the prison to ashes and then bury the ashes and seed the ground with fucking salt. "Get in, pretty boy," Lilly says at last, climbing behind the wheel. "We got a fucking job to do."

They pull out of camp at just before noon, the sun high and pale in the sky.

Austin doesn't say much en route, just sits in the passenger seat, cradling his Garand in his lap, every once in a while glancing out at the side mirror to check on the four soldiers riding in the back. Lilly drives in silence, feeling a strange sort of calm. In every transaction, the person willing to lose everything has the advantage—Lilly has nothing else to live for but her hate—and this strength makes her flesh tingle as the convoy climbs the winding access road toward the eastern horizon. She slams the shift lever into the lower gears and hums a tuneless tune, more of a tic than an actual melody. She glances across the cab at Austin, and all at once something flutters in her gut, a jolt of unease nagging at the back of her mind, pinching her midsection and shattering her confidence.

His head down, his hair hanging in his face, Austin Ballard has never looked younger or more vulnerable to Lilly than he does at this moment, and it wakes her up, breaks through her stupor, and sends an unexpected wave of dread coursing through her. His life is on the line as well, and the realization crashes down on her—*he's not ready for this, he's not equipped*—and this revelation leads to another unexpected bombshell. At first, she sees it out of the corner of her eye, and she's not sure anybody else in the regiment of vehicles notices it.

Just as the procession of vehicles crests the top of the ridge east of the prison and the wide, scabrous slope of pastureland bordering the property comes into view through the trees—in the middle distance a few dozen dead straggling across the meadow in the front of the prison—Lilly sees faint signs of movement on either side of the dirt road, way back in the shadows of the woods, blending in with the dark columns of pines, milling through the gloom with the hectic purpose of ants in an ant farm.

Scores and scores of walkers, maybe hundreds of them, have converged on the area—drawn over the last thirty-six hours to the commotion of the skirmishes—their number now multiplying like amoebas growing in the vast petri dish of the forest. Lilly knows what this means. She's tangled with herds of undead before. Autumn of last year, during the ill-advised coup d'état attempt on Woodbury, a herd had engulfed Lilly's band of conspirators in the woods like a tidal wave, nearly overturning their van and devouring everything within miles. Lilly knows all too well how unpredictable and dangerous herds can be, especially if they coalesce into a slow-motion stampede. In their legion of stubborn, clumsy, shuffling bodies, they can mow down the sturdiest barricade, turn settlements to rubble, and break through the fences of any prison.

In that one horrible instant, as the convoy crosses over the ridge and vehicle by vehicle starts down the slope, Lilly's brain registers a dark truth. She realizes at last the difference between this assault and the last.

Now both sides are fucked.

FIFTEEN

The people in the prison are prepared this time. The convoy barely gets halfway across the pasture before the yards light up with heavy fire, taking the invasion force by surprise. Air breaks hiss. Windshields shatter. Ricochets shriek off iron and steel. Trucks skid on the damp turf. Drivers and passengers alike duck down for cover, some of them diving off flatbeds and belly-crawling under the chassis of the massive transports. Lilly slams on her brakes and brings the truck to a shuddering stop and screams for Austin to get out in case the fuel tanks go up in the barrage. She kicks the door open, lurching out of the cab and hitting the ground, a series of divots exploding in the dirt around her. She can't see anything. Austin has vanished out the other side of the cab. Over the din of the gunfire, Lilly can barely hear the Governor's ranting and raving somewhere in the gathering haze of gun smoke and dust, but she can't locate his position. She tries to fumble with her rifle, and maybe return fire—some of the militia members are making feeble attempts to answer the salvo—but Lilly's hands won't obey the signals her brain is sending to them. The people in the prison have taken positions behind parked vehicles, on their stomachs, firing from underneath the cars, causing mass chaos now, taking down more and more of Woodbury's beleaguered militia. Lilly hears Gabe's baritone voice barking frantically, hollering above the noise, arguing with the Governor, demanding to know why these insane tactics are going to work this time. Lilly covers her head as the turf continues to get chewed up around her, puffing up clods from the relentless bombardment. She tries to take deep breaths and focus on her weapon and her rage and her meager training, but something else is intruding on her thoughts. Out of the corner of her eyes, she sees the edges of the battlefield filling up with ragged, stumbling figures, and her chest freezes with the realization: There's countless more of them now, coming from every direction, descending upon the meadow like a moving plague.

Lilly manages to crawl under the M35. She sees Austin's feet shuffling next to the cab—he's struggling to rise up and return fire— and she calls out above the noise for him to get the fuck down and get under the fucking truck for fuck's sake.

Walkers have surrounded them, most of them managing to shamble between the gunshots or turn away from the bullet-riddled fences and lumber toward the invaders. Lilly starts firing at walker feet, knocking them down and then systematically sending slugs into their crania. Skulls pop out like fuses overloading, sending blood stringers across the grass and onto Lilly's arms and legs, but she keeps firing. The ragged figures continue dragging themselves toward the invaders, and Lilly keeps blasting away, until her clip clicks dry and a cloud of blue haze builds around her truck. Her heart drumming in her chest, Lilly suddenly feels a vise tighten around her ankle. She lets out a yelp of shock, and she looks down at her lower half.

A large male walker in a funeral suit has crawled under the truck and has her leg in his blackened, gnarled hands, his rotting mouth opening—the mossy green teeth inches away from the exposed flesh of her slender shin between the top of her boot and the cuffed leg of her jeans—and the sight of it paralyzes her for a moment. She swings the barrel of the Ruger down at the thing's skull and pulls the trigger—forgetting that the gun needs a fresh mag, the feeder slide gaping open—and now nothing but a click issues from the empty gun.

Lilly screams and kicks and scrambles for the magazine in her belt when a third figure fills the narrow space under the M35—just a dark blur at first—and then the gleaming blue steel of Austin's Glock.

A flare of a spark and the flat blast puts the male biter down in a gushing stream of oily fluid from its freshly breached skull, spreading across the matted grass under the truck, the stench of the dead now engulfing Lilly as she lets out a pained, shocked sigh of relief. Austin crawls over to her.

"You okay, did he get you, did he nick you?—You all right?!" Austin babbles, putting his arm around her, tenderly wiping away the damp tendrils of hair loosened from her ponytail.

Lilly manages a nod, swallowing back the coppery taste of acid in her throat. The noise of another volley from all around them makes it impossible to be heard. She twists back around and reaches for her rifle, crawling out from underneath the truck.

The air has gotten so thick with cordite and crisscrossing gunfire, it looks as though night has rolled in, and it chokes the breath out of Lilly, numbing her senses, making her eyes water. She positions herself against the cab. She tries to get her bearings back, slamming another clip into the Ruger pistol, shoving it into her belt, and then swinging the Remington around into shooting position. Austin huddles behind her, aiming the Garand at the sparking, flaring gunfire coming from inside the fences.

Lilly is lifting the scope to her eye when all at once she sees a tiny object floating up through space above the razor-wire fence tops and everything slows down.

A momentary lull in the firefight ensues unexpectedly, and the fast-forward motion of the skirmish slams on its brakes. In her mind's eye, Lilly sees the projectile arcing over their heads in extreme slow motion until it lands on the ground in front of a big Buick sedan, bouncing once and clattering under the car's dented front grillwork.

The explosion that follows rocks the earth and sucks the air pressure out of the landscape, turning the pasture—just for an instant—into the surface of the sun.

The grenade propels the two-thousand-pound vehicle into the air, tearing shrapnel from its front half and sending every man and woman within a fifty-yard radius falling to their feet. The boom shatters eardrums and rattles the trees and throws the Governor and Gabe into different directions, each man sprawling to the ground and rolling.

The Governor slams into the undercarriage of the tank, his breath squeezed from his lungs as he catches a bleary glimpse from his one working eye of the projectile-spray blooming in the sun— razor-sharp particles of the Buick's front end—ripping through the closest, unsuspecting combatants. Jagged pieces of metal punch through portly old Charlie Banes, tearing a chunk out of his chest, lifting him four feet off the ground and sending him hurling backward, arms pinwheeling, the gush of lifeblood enrobing him in liquid scarlet as he lands in the weeds, his heart shutting down and his life draining out of him before he even stops rolling.

At the same exact moment, on the other side of the lot, a constellation of shards like tiny missiles have passed through Rudy Warburton's upper body, causing him to momentarily jitterbug in a gruesome death dance, his gun flying off, his deep, whiskey-cured voice—the same ringside announcer's voice that proudly introduced the Governor to crowds at the racetrack arena—now bellowing a death wail that sets the Governor's teeth on edge.

"F-FUCK!" The Governor rolls out from under the tank, gasping for breath and seeing double through his lone eye. He tries to focus on the ground. His eye patch has come askew. Blades of crabgrass are in his hair, the stench of burning fuel in his nostrils. His body screams with pain. His bandaged face feels wet and hot, his phantom arm twisting and clawing at the air on its ghostly stump. "F-FFF-FUCK!—F-FFFF-FUCK!!"

He rises to his hands and knees, his ears ringing, his brain blazing with rage. He barely hears the return fire screaming over his head. Most of the surviving militia have ducked behind cover and have started firing wildly at the guard towers and the nooks across the prison grounds. The air ignites with tracers and ricochets. A total of six men lie in heaps around the blackened, scorched earth cratered by the grenade blast.

Charlie is gone. Rudy, Teddy Grainger, Bart, Daniel, and even big Don Horgan, the wrestler—all gone—mutilated to shreds by either gunfire or the deadly shrapnel.

The Governor sees Gabe on his back about thirty feet away, next to the flatbed, his head drooping, the concussion blast knocking him silly. Magnesium-hot rage courses through Philip as he struggles to his feet, wincing painfully as .50 cal bursts zing over his head. On top of a nearby flatbed truck cab, the machine gunner, Ben Buchholz, sprays the prison grounds furiously, without strategy or purpose. A quick glance at the southeast guard tower reveals puffs of white flame as a lone sniper rains pinpoint shots down on the convoy, the bullets ringing off fenders, shattering windshields, and nipping at the heels of surviving militiamen.

"GABE!"

The Governor's voice sounds muffled and garbled to his own damaged ears. He manages to dart across the gap between the tank and the flatbed. By this point, Gabe is hauling himself back to his feet, blinking away the shock and pain. The Governor reaches the fat man and grabs the nape of his turtleneck as though lifting a runt from a litter. "GET THE FUCK OVER HERE!"

Philip drags Gabe across the wasted ground to the rear of the Abrams.

"C'MERE!" The Governor slams the portly Gabriel Harris against the back of the tank, knocking the wind out of Gabe's lungs as more high-velocity blasts ping and spark off the armored Abrams.

"Wh-what the—!!" Gabe convulses with agony, jerking at the buzz-saw grind of the .50 cal twenty yards away. Bullets blaze around them for a moment, distracting them, making each of them duck and twitch with nervous tension, giving each man a weird sort of tunnel vision.

Neither man sees the giant, battered, road-worn Winnebago

camper roaring out of the trees directly to the west, skirting the edges of the battlefront in a fogbank of dust. In fact, at first, *nobody* in the attack force notices the new addition to the war zone.

"We have *got* to rethink this fucking thing," Gabe proclaims a few seconds later in a strangled, exhausted voice, standing with the Governor behind the armored tank while bullets whiz over their heads like wasps. Burning his gaze into the Governor's solitary eye, speaking loudly enough to be heard above the noise of intermittent gunfire, Gabe deploys a tone of voice he has never used with the Governor—a tone dripping with recrimination and anger. "Our people are scared shitless! They're getting the shit beat out of them—dropping like flies—you gotta do something, man, you gotta fucking take charge!"

The Governor's left hand thrusts out and grabs Gabe by the throat, slamming the heavyset man against the riveted hull of the Abrams. "Shut your fucking mouth, Gabe! We're not gonna pussy out this time—we're taking this place down—it's now or never!!"

In that tense millisecond of a pause, Gabe stares wide-eyed at his boss—his mentor, his father figure—and a spark of shame kindles in Gabe's gaze. Neither man is aware of the Winnebago circling around the far western edge of the battlefield, far enough back to go unseen by most of the combatants—even those within the confines of the prison. The camper skids to a stop in a whirlwind of dust, and a figure appears like a specter on the roof, a solitary woman holding a sniper rifle.

"Okay, okay, I'm s-sorry, sorry," Gabe babbles, both his gloved hands on the Governor's wrist, trying to wrench it off the ample girth of his bullish neck. Philip releases his grip. Gabe hyperventilates as he goes on raving over the noise of the firefight. "I'm just saying, we're getting beat up and we need a plan! We can't just keep hammering away at these cocksuckers without a—"

"SHUT THE FUCK UP!"

Philip Blake trains his blazing eye on the burly man and hears voices in his head bubbling up from the dark catacombs of his brain—*Philip's dead, gone, Philip is dead and buried, he's dust*—and Philip flinches suddenly at the unexpected banshee shrieking in his head—*Shut up, shut up!* Guns roar behind him, the crackle making him twitch, distracting him from the sight of the lone sniper standing on the roof of a rust-pocked camper hundreds of yards away, ghostly in the mirage of heat rays on the edge of the forest.

"Listen, listen to me, you chicken-shit fat body—we're not gonna fucking pull back again!" Philip manages to bellow in a strangled voice, shoving Gabe across the slimy iron bulwark of the tank. "You understand?! You got that?! We're gonna end this thing NOW!— NOW!!"

Gabe backs away, rubbing his neck, blinking back tears of dread, looking suddenly like a little boy who would say or do anything to appease his abusive father, who would lie and steal and kill and rape and pillage, *anything* to please his angry parent and squelch the taunts of schoolkids who once called him a big tub-o-lard.

The single shot that rings out from the west, a large-caliber bullet fired with the precision of a beesting from the roof of a mobile home 350 yards away, hits the exposed part of Gabriel Harris's skull.

The Governor jerks back as Gabe's head erupts, washing the tank with a splash of gelatinous pink brain matter, forming a giant fuchsia blot on the iron. The Governor's breath freezes in his lungs as Gabe teeters on wobbly legs for a moment, his glassy eyes fixed on Philip, a death stare reminiscent of a computer crashing, locked onto Philip's face, endlessly looking for a parent's approval that will never come. And then the big man collapses as if swooning.

He hits the earth with a thud that wakes Philip up with the force of a cold slap.

"MOTHERFUCK!"

Philip Blake lurches behind the tank and peers around the other side.

"FUCK!—FUCK!—FUCK!—FUCK!!" In quick stages, he sees the distant Winnebago and glimpses the female figure standing boldly on the roof like some mythical creature, some Valkyrie swooping down from the heavens to aid and assist the inhabitants of the prison, and finally he notices the pickup truck parked fifty feet off his left flank in the weeds. He sees Gus crouched behind the rear gate, firing an AR-15 at will, cursing and firing and cursing.

"GUS!" Philip roars. "GET IN YOUR TRUCK AND DRIVE IT UP THAT WOMAN'S ASS—RIGHT NOW!!"

It takes only a moment for Gus to see what the Governor is talking about. With a terse nod, Gus gets moving, staying low and duckwalking around the other side of the Chevy S-10 to the cab. He climbs behind the wheel, the windshield already cracked into a million diamond-bright shards of broken glass from all the gunfire.

The tailpipe coughs vapor as Gus slams it into drive and blasts off toward the camper.

The Governor goes over to Gabe's body and untangles the Bushmaster rifle from the dead man's shoulder, and by the time Philip has straightened back up and taken stock of the battlefront, things have begun to go from bad to worse.

From behind the tail gate of the M35, Lilly Caul watches the chain of events unravel and implode like a nuclear reaction, her lungs heaving for air, her heart banging as loudly as a timpani drum against her rib cage. She grips her Remington with sweat-sticky hands and jerks at the concussive blast of metal on metal thundering on the horizon to the west. She peers around the edge of the hatch just in time to see Gus ramming his pickup into the Winnebago, nearly breaking the massive camper in two.

The impact sends particles of broken glass and shards of trim and metal fittings into the air and throws the sniper—a fair-haired woman in a ponytail and prison dungarees—cartwheeling off the roof and into the weeds on the edge of the woods. It's hard to tell at this distance, but it looks as though Gus has been hit—his door springing open on impact, his squat body flopping out of the cab, a swirl of black smoke obscuring the crash site.

Lilly hears a strangled, maniacal laugh and glances to her left and sees the Governor crouched behind the tank watching Gus's pickup and what's left of the Winnebago go up in a mushroom cloud of smoke and flame. "TAKE THAT, BITCH—YOU FUCK WITH US!—YEAH, THAT'S RIGHT!" He sounds to Lilly like he's finally slipped his tether.

"Jesus . . . Jesus . . . this is insane!" Lilly ducks behind the hatch and jumps at a booming series of blasts that nearly pop her eardrums, the gunfire coming from inches away. She wrenches around and sees Austin, crouched behind the opposite end of the hatch, firing his Garand at the guard tower, the .308 shells booming and ringing. He's yelling something. Lilly tries to get his attention. "Austin!—AUSTIN!"

"—fuckers are picking us off like flies!" He shoots some more, glancing at Lilly, shooting, then glancing at her again with eyes blazing. "C'mon!—Lilly, what's wrong?!—Whaddaya doing?!"

"Save your ammo, pretty boy!"

"Whaddaya talking about?!"

"You're gonna—!"

Lilly starts to explain that they have a finite amount of rounds and they need to get better positions and these bastards could lob another grenade at any second when the sound of the Governor's voice rings out above the gunfire. She twists back around and sees him limping across the battlefield, his face filled with psychotic glee.

"Only a matter of time now!" He walks toward a pair of shooters huddled behind a pile of fallen supply crates, firing blindly at the towers. "We got 'em pinned down! Motherfuckers can't last!"

One of the shooters behind the crates—an older man with thinning hair and yellow aviator sunglasses—looks up from his scope when a round hits him in the left eye.

The blast shatters the aviator lens and bursts out the back of his skull. He convulses backward, his rifle flying out of his hands—his brain matter spraying the weeds behind him—as he collapses less than ten feet from where the Governor is shuffling along.

"We got them right where we want them!" Philip strides along behind the row of vehicles and shooters like a black-clad General MacArthur. "Don't let them take a fucking breath! Keep the pressure on!"

"Hey—Governor!" Lilly tries to get his attention from behind the M35. "HEY!"

Another hail of bullets streaks down from the tower—the Governor doesn't even flinch, the blasts puffing at his feet—and all at once another militia member goes down in a burst of blood mist from the back of his skull, the man's Caterpillar cap flying off as he drops to the ground.

"GOVERNOR!!" Lilly screams at the man. "THEY'RE KILLING US!—WE CAN'T DO THIS!"

Some of the men are backing away from the line of fire now, searching for cover, running this way and that, diving under truck chassis.

"The fuck are you *doing*?!" the Governor booms at the retreating troops. "WE CAN'T GIVE UP NOW!! WE CAN'T LET THEM WIN!!"

Another volley of sniper fire drives Lilly back to the ground behind the M35—Austin on his belly inches away from her—gouts of turf kicking up with each blast, dirt spitting in their faces. Dizziness washes over Lilly and threatens to steal her eyesight, her ears ringing so badly now the gunfire sounds as if it's underwater—PLING! PLING!—PLINK-PLINK-PLINK!!—and she hears the Governor bellowing something and tries to see through the growing haze of dust and gun smoke engulfing the meadow.

"FUCK IT!" The Governor marches toward the tank like a wooden soldier, his single arm flexing stiffly, his solitary gloved hand balled into a tight fist. "FUCK IT!—FUCK IT!!—*FUCK IT!!*—IT'S TIME TO END THIS!!"

He reaches the Abrams and then climbs up the steel side ladder.

In Lilly's compromised vision, as watery and bleary as runny ink, she can barely take in the surreal sight of the Governor pounding on the tank's hatch, as though he has a parcel to deliver to the crew. He howls at Jared to let him in, and the hatch unscrews suddenly, springing open like a jack-in-the-box. The Governor plunges down into the darkness of the enclosure, the hatch slamming shut just as his booming cry reaches Lilly's ringing ears: "—JUST DRIVE!"

A plume of dense smoke suddenly spews from the back of the tank as the treads engage. The engine roars, and the beast begins to move.

Lilly freezes on the ground, gaping at the bizarre sight of the armored monolith rolling toward the fence. Her irises dilate involuntarily, her breath stalling in her throat, as she sees the course of the battle suddenly take an unexpected turn.

The tank rattles toward the chain-link barrier, mowing over the last few walkers that still stand in its way, the massive treads pulverizing rotten bones and flesh. The front of the tank slams into the fence, the chain link and concertina wire heaving, the reverberations traveling a city block in each direction. The noise is like a metallic rainstorm.

The outer fence gives way in a paroxysm of steel ripping apart.

The Abrams grinds over the first barrier with the ease of a giant trash compactor, smoke billowing from its turbine, treads smashing the chain link into spaghetti. A hundred yards of cyclone fence in each direction collapses as the beast crosses the gap to the next fence. The second barrier goes down as easily as the first.

While all this is transpiring, Lilly observes the eerie cease-fire inside the prison grounds. The only sounds now—barely audible above the creaking, complaining, ringing chain-link fences—are footsteps running in all directions, as the folks inside scatter for cover.

In a dust cloud of haze and crisscrossing sniper fire pinging off the tank's iron carapace, the Abrams devours the last barrier—the innermost fence—as sparks snap and crackle in the air. Most of the walkers in the general vicinity have been vanquished either in the cross fire or beneath the treads of the tank.

Now the ricochets echo eerily across the passageways between cellblocks.

Soon, even the towers go silent and still as the armored monolith comes to rest twenty feet inside the gate, trailing shreds of metal linkage in its treads like particles of food stuck in the teeth of a ravenous monster. The engine revs for a moment, almost like an overture to the next movement of this terrible symphony. Exhaust huffs from the ass-end of the tank. The pause that follows—the duration of which is mere seconds—seems to Lilly to last for hours.

"Lilly?! You all right?! Talk to me!" Austin's voice, barely audible to Lilly, cuts through the white noise of her racing thoughts. She turns and sees him huddled next to her behind the M35's rear gate, his M1 Garand gripped white-knuckle tight. "Whaddaya think?" he asks her with fear shimmering in his eyes. "What now?"

She starts to mumble something in response when the sound of another voice cuts through her daze.

"C'mon, we got them outnumbered!" It comes from behind her. She twists around and sees the remaining members of the militia coming out from behind the vehicles with their guns raised and ready. Tom Blanchford, a big mechanic from Macon, has his back pressed against the side of his flatbed. "C'mon!—Let's put these evil bastards out of their misery once and for all!—COME ON!!"

One by one, creeping low and quick, weaving between the vehicles, the surviving men and women of the Woodbury militia make their way across the battlefield, over the smashed remnants of mangled chain link, and into the prison.

"Let's do this," Austin says, rising to his feet, and then reaching down to help Lilly up.

For the briefest instant, she pauses. She stares at Austin's hand.

She feels the pulse of acid throbbing in her spine, down her arms and legs, tasting of copper and blood in her mouth.

Then, in a hoarse, faint whisper, she says, "Yeah, let's finish it."

She takes his hand, springs to her feet, swings the Remington around into shooting position, gives a quick nod, and charges into the fray.

SIXTEEN

Inside the prison yard, in a fogbank of dust, the tank's top hatch bursts open and a dark, cadaverous, blood-caked face surfaces like a shark emerging from the oceanic darkness. "OPEN FIRE!—KILL THEM ALL!!—WE GOT THEM PINNED DOWN!!"

On either side of the tank, a total of seven members of the Woodbury militia fan out in different directions, most of them leading with the barrels of their assault rifles, shooting at anything that moves. The exercise yard crawls with chaos for a moment. The prison's inhabitants flee for cover, retreating into the convolutions of the buildings—cockroaches vanishing into cracks.

Bursts of automatic gunfire crackle and echo back and forth. Movement blurs. The Governor shouts orders from the tank's hatch that get drowned in the noise. Gunners on either side dart behind the corners of buildings or under shadowy overhangs, searching for cover and purchase in the onslaught. One of the Governor's men takes the initiative to climb the southeast guard tower, his buck knife clenched between his teeth, his M4 strapped to his shoulder.

The tide of the battle has turned, the denizens of the prison now scattering for cover and the most expedient ways to escape.

Lilly and Austin follow the last contingent over the fallen fence and into the prison yard, their heavy boot-steps making the chain link jangle. They move quickly with their guns cocked and ready, hot on the heels of two other men, the sun in their eyes. Lilly has a pistol in each hand, her Remington strapped and bouncing on her shoulder. Austin hyperventilates as he runs, a combination of fear, exhaustion, and rage.

The passage of time seems to slow, now moving in milky, syrupy impressions, as Lilly and Austin reach the closest building—thirty feet away from the Governor's tank—and slam their backs against the stone wall. Lilly's heart races. Even amid the adrenaline rush of storming the grounds, she feels a surreal kind of claustrophobia inside the massive compound. Three-story cellblocks press down on them from all sides, throwing long shadows on the yards. The air has the acrid smell of overloading circuits and burning rubber. Muffled voices and the sound of running emanate from within the walls.

A moment later, Lilly jerks at a flash of movement between two buildings, raises one of the Rugers, fires a single shot at the blur, and hits nothing but stucco wall. She sees the puff of plaster dust atomizing in the shadows twenty yards away. She glances across the yard at the tank. She sees the Governor climbing out of the iron beast with a Tec-9 pistol gripped in his gloved hand. Then she sees something else in the distance behind the Governor that makes her spine go cold and her throat go as dry as sawdust.

Way out across the adjacent meadow—the earth now scarred and rutted with tire tracks, scorched and cratered from the grenade blast, and littered with the carnage of the undead—Lilly can see the distant forest. Up along the ridge, behind colonnades of ancient oaks and dense curtains of foliage, the woods teem with innumerable ragged figures birthing themselves from the shadows, pushing their way out of the undergrowth—hundreds of them—emerging stiff-legged and ravenous into the daylight. There are so many of them now that they resemble, from this distance, a black tide—a putrefied dark wave the width of a soccer field—slowly unfurling and rolling down the hill toward the noise and confusion of the prison. In that horrible instant, over the course of a single electrical impulse firing in her brain, Lilly makes a spontaneous calculation. Within a matter of minutes—ten, perhaps, maybe fifteen at the most—the prison will be overrun.

The Governor climbs down the tank's steel hull and takes a supervisory position behind the stern of the Abrams. Most of the surviving inhabitants of the prison have now vanished inside cellblocks and outbuildings, but a few of the sturdier souls have remained outdoors, putting up halfhearted resistance, the intermittent crackle of suppressing fire and panicky shouts making Philip Blake twitch and flinch as he points at one of his soldiers.

"HEY! YOU!" The Governor signals to a tall, rangy man with a shaved head who is busily firing his assault rifle at the barred windows of the nearest building, a man Philip has seen on Martinez's crew before, a man whose name Philip never bothered to learn. "C'mere!"

The man ceases firing and trots over to the Governor. "Yessir?"

The Governor speaks with jaws clenched, his wounds tingling, the voices in his head plaguing him now like static crackling on a shortwave radio, distant signals from a ghostly transmission interfering with his thoughts. "There ain't many of them left!" he shouts at the bald man. "I want you to gather a few of your men—are you fucking listening to me?"

A manic nod from the bald man. "Y-yessir—yes."

"I want you to take your men inside—understand?—you're looking for anyone hiding or trying to hold out inside—you follow me?"

"Yessir . . . and you want us to . . . what?"

The Governor snarls at him. "I want you to fucking read them a fucking bedtime story. . . . YOU FUCKING IDIOT, I WANT YOU TO WASTE THEM!"

With a nod, the man with the shaved head whirls and runs off in the direction of the other gunman. The Governor watches him for a moment, twitching, his blood-spattered face prickling hotly, his wounded jaw throbbing and feverish. He shakes off the voice reverberating behind his thoughts and murmurs to himself, "Only a matter of time now . . . so shut the fuck up . . . leave me alone."

He sees a shadow flit between two buildings dead ahead, fifty yards away, a small group of survivors huddled in an alcove, arguing, two men and a woman . . . and he ducks down behind the tank, raising Jared's Tec-9 and taking aim. He gets the woman in his front sight and squeezes off three quick blasts—the recoil nearly dislocating his shoulder—the distant puff of blood mist across the alcove invigorating to him, the sight of the woman dropping to the ground like a blast of smack in his veins.

The Governor nods with satisfaction, but before he can draw another breath, he sees the other two figures—an older man and a younger man, both clad in body armor, maybe father and son— suddenly dart out of the hiding place and make a run for it. They pass out of range quickly, charging toward the motorcade of battered prison vehicles parked along the west side of the grounds. The Governor notices three of his gunmen milling around the base of the guard tower to his left, and he calls out to them. "TAKE THEM BASTARDS DOWN RIGHT NOW!"

Within seconds, the men by the tower open up on the twosome, a barrage of automatic fire bursting like a drumroll—plumes of silver sparks flickering in the daylight—filling the air with ugly noise.

The Governor sees the cross fire engulf the two fleeing men, and a direct headshot knocks the younger man off his feet. The kid in the armor sprawls to the concrete in a swath of blood as dark as crude oil. The older man screeches to a halt and goes back to the younger man.

The gunmen hold their fire now as the older one tries to help the younger one up—it's hard to see exactly what's going on out there in the haze of blue smoke and dust, but it appears to the Governor that the older one is sobbing—a father stroking a dying son— cradling the younger man's ruined skull in his lap, and then letting the wave of agony come out in sobs.

The older man weeps and weeps now on the ground, holding the boy, oblivious to the dangers around him, presumably beyond caring about his own life. The whole thing makes the Governor want to puke.

Philip marches over to the militia members standing sheepishly by the tower, their guns lowered, their stricken gazes locked on the death scene across the yard. "What the fuck is your problem?" the Governor demands as he approaches the first gunman.

"Oh God . . . I . . . Oh God." The man in the Massey Ferguson hat and long sideburns—he goes by the moniker Smitty—once chatted with the Governor at Woodbury's Main Street Tavern about shooting turkeys for Thanksgiving. Now the man's grizzled, wind-chapped face has fallen, his red-rimmed eyes welling with tears. "I just . . . I killed a boy." He fixes his anguished gaze on the Governor. "I just killed that man's boy like he was some kinda sick animal."

The Governor throws a glance across the dusty yard and sees the older man—grizzled, graying temples, late fifties, maybe early sixties—on his knees, slumped over the boy, tears streaming down the geezer's face. From the jut of the man's jaw, his pomaded iron-gray hair, and the wind-burned lines around his eyes, he looks like a laborer or farmer, but with a certain gravitas, which makes the crying all the more incongruous. The sight does nothing for the Governor, makes no impression other than a slight tremor of alarm that nobody's blowing this wrinkled fuck away. The Governor turns back to Smitty and says, "Listen to me, listen, this is important—you listening?"

The man named Smitty wipes his face with the back of his arm. "Y-yessir."

"How many of our people did that so-called 'boy' kill with his fucking rifle? Huh? HOW MANY?!"

Smitty looks down. "Okay . . . I get it."

The Governor puts his gloved hand on the man's shoulder and squeezes. "You should be proud that you killed him!" Then a gentle shove. "C'mon! Get your ass in gear—this isn't over yet!"

"Okay," Smitty says with a terse nod. "Okay." He looks down at his rifle and slams another shell in the breach with a grunt, his voice barely a whisper now. "Whatever."

The Governor has another thought and starts to say something else when a streak of movement off to his left crosses his peripheral vision. He snaps his head toward the nearest building and sees four figures darting out of a side exit. At first, the Governor just points and starts to say, "There!—THERE—HERE COMES—!"

But his words stick in his throat when the identity of two of these figures suddenly registers over the space of a heartbeat.

He recognizes the big, handsome man named Rick—the self-proclaimed leader—limping furiously across the grounds, his tattered prison coveralls now bunched in the midsection with heavy bandages where he was shot. He trundles along with a woman on one flank, a little boy of about nine on the other. Rick helps the woman leap over a pile of wreckage as though she's sick. Plunging through the fogbank of dust, wide-eyed and frantic, they look as if they're making a break for the far gate on the northwest corner of the yards. Following closely on their heels, the fourth figure—a younger woman in a stained white lab coat—carries a lever-action Winchester and already has the weapon raised to her eye.

The Governor recognizes Alice and suddenly cries out to his minions. "TAKE THAT BACKSTABBING BITCH DOWN!"

Thirty yards to the east, under the overhang of Cellblock D, Lilly Caul sees the encounter developing across the wasted grounds, the first bark of automatic fire shattering the temporary lull in the assault, raising hackles on her neck—and she swings her gun up—forgetting, just for a moment, the oncoming horde of undead.

Already the battalion of walking corpses, as densely packed as a stockyard full of cattle, have made their way down the far slopes of the meadow and have begun shuffling and trundling as one great undulating mob of rotting paralytics across the tall grass of the adjacent pasture. They look from this great distance like an invasion force, an army of dead centurions hailing from some hellish necropolis—arms outstretched, banging into each other, heads lolling, eyes like yellow reflectors catching the pale sunlight—coming into clearer and clearer focus as they approach the outer fences. From Lilly's vantage point, their myriad varieties of age, shape, size, gender, and degree of decomposition are all still a blur, but they're getting close enough to smell and hear. The rancid aroma of gaseous decay and incessant choruses of toneless moaning rise on the gentle breezes of the afternoon.

Distracted by the appearance of Rick Grimes, his family, and Alice, her adrenaline spiking with equal parts panic and rage, Lilly has lost track of the terrible onslaught of the dead and now grabs Austin with her free arm. "Look!" She pulls him toward the skirmish across the grounds. "Look who it is! Jesus Christ, Austin—COME ON!"

They dash across the leprous cement of a defunct basketball court, their weapons raised and ready to fire. Dead ahead, about twenty yards away, half a dozen militiamen fire on the fleeing family.

"Go!—Keep going!—RUN!!" Alice cries out at Rick, and then fires off a series of wild shots.

Lilly bounds headlong toward the fracas, her teeth cracking with tension. She sees Alice making a feeble attempt to keep firing long enough to give the Grimes family a chance to flee. But the nurse is quickly overcome. One of the rounds chews through her leg, knocking her feet out from under her, another one grazing her shoulder and sending her to the ground.

Lilly gets close enough to see the Governor marching toward the nurse.

Alice looks up with blood on her face, seeing three separate men approaching her commando-style with muzzles raised, and she spits. "FUCK YOU!"

She fires one last time, hitting one of the men next to the Governor in the gut.

"FUCKING BITCH!" The Governor lunges at her and kicks her rifle from her hands.

Lilly approaches from the opposite direction with her Remington ready to fire, and she aims it down at the fallen nurse. She makes eye contact with Alice, and Alice holds her gaze, and for the briefest moment, the two women stare silently at each other. Lilly can barely recognize the woman who was once her friend and confidante. Alice spits blood at Lilly, and Lilly feels a twinge of rage like a match tip igniting in her guts.

In her peripheral vision, she can see the Grimes family fleeing toward the far gates. A shot rings out—a near miss—sparking off the concrete at Rick's heels.

The one-armed Governor looms over the fallen nurse and jacks the cocking mechanism on his Tec-9 by yanking it down against his belt with a loud metallic click. His teeth are showing. He breathes thickly through his nostrils as Alice closes her eyes and looks away. She's ready to die. The Governor aims the Tec-9 at her face and growls softly at her, ". . . traitor . . ."

The single burst from the Tec-9 makes Lilly jump as the back of Alice's head erupts in a wet red particle bomb across the concrete.

"Take them out," the Governor says softly to Lilly, but Lilly doesn't hear him at first.

"What?" She looks up from the murdered nurse. "What was that?"

The Governor scowls at Lilly. "I said take those motherfuckers out." He points the pistol's muzzle at the fleeing family. "NOW!"

Lilly assumes a shooting stance and squares her shoulders

and sucks in a breath, raising the weapon toward the three figures fleeing in the distance. They are twenty-five yards away from freedom.

Over the course of that next second and a half, before she puts the scope to her eye, Lilly glimpses several things out of the corner of her eye that register like screaming warning alarms in her brain. She sees the other members of the Governor's army whirling toward the devastated cyclone fence, some of them backing away, wide-eyed and jittery. Outside the mangled remnants of chain-link barricade, the tsunami of walking dead rolls toward the prison.

Closing the distance to about fifty yards now, the leading edge of the herd looks like a nightmarish chorus line of encephalitic monsters dressed in ragged civvies—moldering suits, tattered dresses dark with bile, and denim overalls hanging in shreds—their autonomic yellow stares fixed on the fresh meat scurrying across the grounds. The stench engulfs the general area, mingling with the dust devils, forming a fogbank of death scent. The dissonant symphony of mortified vocal cords rises to the level of a psychotic marching band, now throbbing and droning with the off-key music of their insatiable moaning.

Lilly focuses on the task at hand, and puts the scope to her eye.

For a single, frenzied instant she calculates the distance and the drop rate, and all at once she registers the fleeing woman, now running one half step behind Rick Grimes and holding something close to her chest.

Through the cross hairs, the woman's cargo looks like ordnance of some kind—a bomb, a bundle of grenades, a short-barreled automatic weapon wrapped in cloth—so Lilly puts the woman in her sights.

She holds her breath, puts the center hairs on the woman, and quickly, decisively yanks the trigger.

The recoil punches Lilly's shoulder, and one nanosecond later she sees the woman come apart in the scope's telescopic lens.

In the narrow, magnified field of vision it looks like a silent movie death, the woman's back opening up in a bloom of scarlet, her body thrown off stride, the impact of the .308 round tearing through her body as well as her mystery package—sending fragments of bone, tissue, blood mist, and fabric into the air.

The woman sprawls to the ground on top of the bundle, a tiny object flopping out of a blanket, visible now in the scope's tunnel vision. Lilly freezes. The scope adheres to her eye socket as though dipped in liquid nitrogen. She stares at the object.

Lilly's midsection goes cold as she stares and stares at that pink, smooth object visible in the upper right quadrant of the scope.

The distant howl of anguish from the man named Rick reaches Lilly's ears. The man scuttles to a stop, gazing over his shoulder in absolute horror at his fallen wife. He stands paralyzed for a moment, staring at the fatally wounded woman and the object sticking out from under her chest. The boy reaches the fence and turns to see what happened, and the man waves him on. "Don't look back, Carl! JUST KEEP RUNNING!!"

The boy darts toward a flatbed truck parked near the northwest gate, as more shots ring out from some of the other militiamen, but now the man named Rick lunges toward the boy, grabs him. "NO, CARL! WE WON'T MAKE IT TO THE TRUCK—!" The man spins the child in the other direction. "WE'VE GOTTA GO THIS WAY!—KEEP YOUR HEAD DOWN AND, WHATEVER YOU DO, DON'T STOP RUNNING!"

Lilly barely notices the man and boy changing course and heading back along the fence toward the opposite gate, which is now crowded with the first wave of walking dead, the leading edge of the herd shambling over the chain-link wreckage and pouring into the prison with mouths working and dead arms reaching and flailing. They come one by one through the massive gap in the fence, fanning out across the yards in their slow-motion stampede, hungry yellow eyes scanning, but Lilly is beyond caring.

She can't tear her gaze from the scope, or stop staring at the tiny, fleshy object sticking out from under the fallen wife, an object that reveals itself to be an arm.

A baby's arm.

———

At first, the Governor doesn't notice Lilly's catatonic stupor. He's preoccupied with the quickly shifting dangers coming at them—the first wave of corpses now less than fifty yards away, shuffling awkwardly across the cracked cement toward the surviving militia—spreading their stench and noise like a pox on the barren grounds.

The Governor can see Rick Grimes and his boy reach the gap between the two demolished fences and weave through the oncoming horde, the man firing into the heads of the closest creatures, making an opening through which they can escape, creating quite a racket. "Crazy fucks," Philip grumbles to his men. "Don't waste any more bullets—the biters will get them before we can."

Sure enough, Rick and his son's frenzied flight begins to draw the attention of the leading edge of the herd, giving the Governor and his men time to clean up and take possession of the prison.

"What the fuck?" The Governor notices the older man in body armor twenty-five yards away, slumped on his knees next to the body of his son. "Why the fuck is that old bastard still breathing?"

Next to Philip, a gangly former high school math teacher nicknamed Red gives a nervous shrug, fingering the trigger pad of his AR-15, glancing over his shoulder at the herd bearing down on them, then glancing back at the old man in body armor. "Wasn't moving—dropped his gun, looked like he was surrendering."

The Governor walks over to the old man. The buzzing drone of the walkers fills the air. Philip feels as though ants are crawling on his skin. He can see the encroaching horde out of the corner of his one good eye. His phantom arm itches as he trains his Cyclopean gaze down at the sobbing man with gray slicked-back hair.

The old man slowly looks up as though seized up in a bad dream, still struggling to wake up. The two men make eye contact. "Dear God," he mutters softly, almost as if reciting a litany. "Please . . . just kill me."

The Governor puts the muzzle of the Tec-9 against the furrowed brow of the old man. But he doesn't pull the trigger—not at first—he just presses it against the man's forehead for an endless moment, staring, hearing the incessant crackle of radio interference in his head: . . . *dust to dust, dead and gone, he's gone, Philip Blake is gone.*

The blast of the Tec-9 cuts off the voice and sends the old man into the void.

For a moment, Philip Blake stares down at the old man now lying in a fresh pool of deep-crimson blood next to his son, the puddle spreading, forming wings on the cement, like a Rorschach inkblot test, two angels lying in state, one next to the other—martyrs, sacrificial lambs. Philip starts to turn away when he hears another voice, anguished and grief-stricken, coming from somewhere nearby.

He turns and sees that Lilly Caul has moved across the yard, and now stands over the Grimes woman, who lies frozen in death on top of the pale remains of her baby. Austin Ballard stands twenty feet away from her, looking horror-struck and confused, spinning toward the oncoming biters. The herd has progressed across the grounds, closing the distance to about thirty yards or so. The stink and noise have risen to unbearable levels, and now some of the Governor's men have begun firing at the front line, picking off the closest ones—one after another—the escaping fluids painting the weathered cement Day-Glo red and squid-ink black.

"What the fuck is *her* problem?" the Governor says to no one in particular as he strides over to where Lilly stands, slowly shaking her head, her Remington still gripped in one hand, tendrils of glistening auburn hair unmoored from her ponytail and dangling in her face.

The Governor yells at her, "What the fuck is *wrong* with you?—We gotta get our asses inside!—WHAT IS YOUR FUCKING DEAL?!—ANSWER ME!!!"

Very slowly she turns and scorches him with such a contemptu-
ous look that it nearly takes his breath away. She utters something
that he doesn't hear at first, his one-eyed gaze held rapt by her
blazing stare.

"What was that?" he demands of her, his single gloved hand
balling into a fist.

"You monster," she says again, louder this time, through clenched
teeth.

The Governor goes very still, serpentine-still, a boa coiling itself
in the presence of a threat—all this in spite of the looming threat of
the horde filling the general vicinity with the odor of rotten meat
and the sound of broken gears grinding and groaning. Very carefully, enunciating every word, the Governor says, "What. The. Fuck.
Did. You. Just. *Say to me?*"

Austin whirls toward the Governor and raises his gun as though
trying to decide whom to shoot.

"I *said*," Lilly Caul barks at him, her words like darts now, pro-
jectiles aimed at his face, fueled by scalding tears tracking down
her face, "you are a fucking monster! LOOK AT WHAT YOU
MADE ME DO?!" Without tearing her gaze from him, she gestures
down at the murdered woman and baby, the pathetic carnage
joined in the eternal bond of mother clutching child to her bosom.
"JUST FUCKING LOOK!!"

He *does* look now, and he *does* see, and maybe for the first time
since he took control of Woodbury, Georgia—since he became
the Governor—the man who calls himself Philip Blake *does*
sees the consequences of his actions. "F-fuck," he utters to himself,
his voice drowned by the clamor of gunfire staving off the pitiless,
rotting, hellish onslaught now bearing down on them.

"A baby!" Lilly roars at him. "A BABY!" She turns her gun around
and slams the butt into the Governor's face. The pain shoots up the
bridge of his noise, the impact making a wet thud that momentarily blinds him and drives him to the ground. "YOU MADE ME
KILL A FUCKING BABY!"

The Governor flops onto his back and tries to sit up, but his head is ringing like an alarm, the dizziness washing over him and stealing his breath. "W-what are you—?"

Lilly Caul turns the barrel of her Remington around and lunges at him. She rams the blue-steel muzzle into his mouth hard enough to crack two of his front teeth. The barrel lodges itself so deep in his throat that it forces a strangled gag out of him.

Lilly's finger starts to tighten on the trigger. Philip Blake's single eye finds her eyes.

The entire world seems to stop—time standing still—as if hell has at last frozen over.

PART 3

The Fall

The call of death is a call of love.
—Hermann Hesse

SEVENTEEN

"LILLY, *DON'T*!!" The voice blurts out of the closest militia member—Hap Abernathy, the retired bus driver, in his soiled Atlanta Braves cap and gray eyes, now bugging as big as silver dollars—as the other men press in toward the horrible tableau. Some of them involuntarily raise their hands. Others aim their guns at Lilly's head. She barely notices her fellow combatants as she stares down intensely at the kneeling Governor, the barrel of her Remington still thrust into the man's mouth.

Why isn't she firing? Inside her brain, a clock ticks . . . impassive, cold, cruel, undeniable . . . counting off the moments until she finally decides to yank the trigger the rest of the way and bring this terrible era to a conclusion. But she doesn't pull the lever. She just stares . . . into the face of the poster boy for all that is base and feral and brutal in the human animal.

What Lilly doesn't realize, though—at that moment—is that the gunmen have momentarily lost track of the oncoming horde. The first walkers—now shuffling a few paces ahead of the herd—have closed the distance across the weather-beaten grounds to about twenty-five yards. Now they lock their glassy doll eyes on the humans and trundle awkwardly toward the sweet scent of living tissue, their dead arms rising, their fingers curled into talons and innately reaching, clawing the air, eager to rip into the living.

"Lilly, listen to me," Austin Ballard says as he pushes his way through the other gunmen, pressing in next to her, speaking softly yet urgently into her ear. "You don't have to do this . . . listen to me . . . there are other ways to handle this . . . you don't need to do this."

A single tear traces down from the corner of Lilly's eye and drips off the edge of her jawline. "A baby, Austin . . . it was a baby."

Austin fights his own tears. "I know, sweetie, but listen, listen to me. This is not the way to—"

He doesn't get a chance to finish his thought because a long shadow suddenly blots out the sun. His Glock still gripped in his right hand, Austin jerks around a split second before the first slimy, molting, clawlike fingers take a swipe at him with feral bloodlust.

Lilly twists around and screams. Austin jerks back and squeezes off four quick blasts—number one going high, numbers two and three going into the head of the closest biter, number four hitting a second one in the jugular. The first biter convulses, a flood of brain fluid and blood showering down over its body before it collapses to the pavement. The second biter rears back, its neck gushing, but it doesn't go down. It merely backs into its brethren, stupidly knocking over a couple of smaller creatures.

Meanwhile, the rest of the militiamen scatter, furiously blasting away at the army of reanimated corpses engulfing the area. The dusty haze flickers with gunfire, sparking ricochets, and plumes of muzzle flares percolating out of the assault rifles on full auto. Some of the men make mad dashes for the closest ingress—a door partially visible in the shadows of a nearby alcove—while others fire frantically into the heart of the encroaching herd, sending fragments of rotten flesh flying off in all directions.

Lilly turns back to the Governor at the exact moment he makes his move.

Grabbing the barrel of the Remington, Philip slams the butt of the rifle as hard as he can into Lilly's face. The stock hits her chin, the impact splitting her lower lip, chipping a tooth, sending Roman candles of stars across her field of vision, and knocking her momentarily senseless. She jolts back with a start. The gun slips from her hands and clatters to the pavement as the Governor springs to his feet.

A biter lunges at Lilly, and she smashes a boot into its midsection at the last possible moment. The dead teenager in gouged black leather doubles over and staggers backward but doesn't go down. Lilly manages to dart away, and while she runs, she reaches around to the back of her belt and grabs her .22, despite her double vision and throbbing, wet, bleeding lip.

"LILLY, THIS WAY!" Austin stands twenty feet north of her now, firing into another wave of biters coming from the opposite direction. He frantically indicates the alcove about thirty-five feet away.

Lilly hesitates. She glances over her shoulder. She sees the Governor whirling around with the Remington rifle in his hands. He blows away a female biter at point-blank range, practically vaporizing the crone's gray head in an eruption of moldering scalp and particles of rotting brain tissue. The blowback sprays across his face and makes him flinch and stagger backward, coughing and spitting.

A scream rings out in the opposite direction, and Lilly spins around in time to see a Woodbury man—a squat, heavyset pipe-fitter from Augusta named Clint Mansell—succumb to the black teeth of a huge male walker. The corpse latches onto the portly man's neck, burrowing into the hemorrhaging nerve bundle underneath the fat, while another biter pounces on the man's back. Clint Mansell's watery, choked death cry as he goes down gets the rest of the men moving.

"THERE'S TOO MANY OF THEM!" cries one of the older men as he backs toward the alcove, firing bursts from his AK at the gathering horde.

Lilly gets off a series of controlled blasts at a cluster of biters that are closing in on her. Each shot slams through a rotten cranium, sending plumes of black matter out the back of every skull, when she hears the psychotic jabber of the Governor behind her.

"DON'T PANIC! THEY CAN'T—THEY CAN'T OUTRUN—
WHERE THE FUCK IS—? SHUT UP! LISTEN TO ME, WE
CAN—WE CAN—SHUT THE FUCK UP!!—WE CAN—GET IN-
SIDE THE—CLEAR OUT THE—WE CAN REBUILD THE—WE'VE
GOTTA STICK TOGETHER, PEOPLE—FUCK! FUCK!—WE CAN
MAKE THIS WORK—!!"

All at once, Lilly feels a tingling sensation at the base of her
spine and a strange kind of stillness coursing over her, the noise
and chaos fading in her ears to a low drone. She ejects the spent
magazine from the Ruger, draws another one from her belt, slams
it into the hilt, and racks the slide. Then she turns toward the Governor, who is gibbering at the voices in his head, his back turned
to her.

She has about sixty seconds before the next cluster of biters
reaches her.

She blocks out everything, the pain, the sound of Austin's voice
calling out to her, the fear, the pandemonium—everything.

Thirty seconds now before the Governor spins around and sees
her.

She aims the Ruger at the back of his head and she sucks in a
breath.

Fifteen seconds.

She aims.

Ten seconds.

She fires.

Considering the fact that the .22 caliber long-rifle 40-grain round
strikes the Governor in the back of his head—plowing through his
brain and exiting out his eye socket—he feels surprisingly little
pain. His one good eyeball jettisons into the air on the wake of a
bloody thread, and the cold wind slams through the trough in his
head.

For one horrible instant, like a brain surgery patient remaining
lucid and semiconscious during his procedure, he remains up-

right, standing on faltering knees, his back to his assailant, only semi-aware of his mortality rushing toward him with the unstoppable inertia and brilliant white light of a freight train.

A mere fraction of a second passes before his frontal lobe and the rest of his brain shut down and stop sending involuntary signals to his central nervous system, but it's enough time for his condition to register to the deepest chasms of his brain, the bad news spreading throughout his cerebral lobes and hemispheres, his memory centers, and the mysterious fissures and convolutions of his secret disorder. The voice in his head returns with renewed strength, giving him even *worse* news that will carry him into oblivion: Philip Blake has been gone for nearly a year. Philip Blake is dust. Gone. The Governor's reign has been a sham . . . a lie.

"NNNGGHHUH—!!" A garbled yowl comes out of the Governor as he blindly staggers for a brief instant, trying to argue one last time with the voice in his head, his body now as heavy as an elephant, a dying elephant gripped in the paralysis of its own dead weight.

The oncoming swarm of biters closes in, their talonlike fingers reaching en masse for the Governor's warm, nourishing flesh. Their cumulative jet-engine drone of rancid breath and watery groans makes one last impression on the Governor's auditory nerves, the noise of the biter stampede engulfing him and drowning the inner voice needling the Governor with the savage truth: *He's gone . . . he's been gone for ages . . . he's in the ground . . . dead . . . gone . . . he no longer exists!*

The Governor barely feels the sensation of being kicked in the small of the back by Lilly.

Her final nudge sends him reeling forward blindly, his one good arm pinwheeling futilely, almost comically, like the fin of a fish, as he plunges into the rotting, desiccated bosom of the reanimated cadavers. The biters practically catch him with their flailing arms and snapping jaws, and he collapses into the throng, writhing in the awful darkness, finding his voice one last time.

"PHILIP BLAKE LIVES!!"

His death cry, albeit hoarse and bloodless and papery thin, is shockingly audible and clear to all those within a hundred-foot radius.

"PHILIP BLAKE LIVES!!" he shrieks as the blackened, slimy teeth descend upon him, driving him to the ground, incisors tearing great mouthfuls of his clothes, burrowing into the soft spots in the seams of his body armor. They go for his exposed neck. They go for his extremities. They go for the concavities of his wounds, chewing through his eye patch, ferreting down into the pulsing meat of his hollowed-out eye socket. They tear through his nose and suck the tissue from his nasal cavity with the vigor of truffle hogs rooting for delicacies. The last warm remnants of the Governor's life flow out of him in one great hemorrhage that inundates his attackers in a baptismal bath until the feeding frenzy begins to disconnect flesh and sinew from bone, drawing and quartering the body into more manageable pieces . . . the last ghostly blips of brain activity like a vinyl record stuck on the same incessant skipping phrase over and over again . . . *PHILIP BLAKE LIVES PHILIP BLAKE LIVES PHILIP BLAKE LIVES PHILIP BLAKE LIVES PHILIP BLAKE LIVES PHILIP BLAKE LIVES PHILIP BLAKE LIVES PHILIP BLAKE LIVES PHILIP BLAKE LIVES PHILIP BLAKE LIVES PHILIP BLAKE LIVES PHILIP BLAKE LIVES PHILIP BLAKE LIVES . . .*

Within moments, there's nothing left but the feeding and the blood . . .

. . . and the eternal white noise of Brian Blake's mind-screen at the end of its programming day.

Now it occurs to Lilly Caul—as she backs away from the horrible scene, bristling with terror, both her Rugers drawn, one in each hand—that the unintended effect of the Governor being devoured by the very creatures he once used as entertainment is a slim opportunity opening up for the survivors—a momentary diversion—as scores of biters engulf the heaping pile of fresh meat. The onslaught has stalled, drawn to the commotion of the feeding frenzy, more and more of the creatures pressing in to get a taste of the still-warm human remains.

The lull in the stampede has left the remaining members of the Woodbury militia standing paralyzed between the herd and the closest building, stricken dumb, staring, watching their leader being reduced to slimy, wet shreds of tissue and clothing before their eyes. Moving on pure adrenaline now, Lilly quickly assesses the situation. In all the excitement, she has momentarily lost track of Austin. But right then, before she has a chance to figure out what happened to him, she sees a clear path to the closest alcove-entrance.

"HEY!" She tries to get the other combatants' attention, gazing across the grounds at the horrified remnant of four men and one woman—Matthew, Hap, Ben, Speed, and Gloria Pyne—as they back toward the building. "LOOK AT ME! ALL OF YOU LOOK AT ME!"

For a single instant, amidst the adrenaline-soaked horrors of that swarming, smoke-bound prison yard, a subtle yet instant shift in power occurs. Lilly finds a voice that she didn't know she had, a strange baritone shout from deep within her—her father's voice, firm but fair, steadfast but humble, and strong enough to shout a coyote off a porch—and she aims it at the group of survivors.

"THAT'S GONNA SLOW A FEW OF THEM DOWN BUT NOT FOR LONG!" She indicates the feeding frenzy in progress across the grounds, and then jerks a thumb at the nearest alcove draped in shadows. "C'MON!—EVERYBODY FOLLOW ME!"

Lilly starts toward the building, the others following her, some of them snapping out of their dazes and firing shots into the swarm. Some of the horde has separated from the feeding frenzy and are lumbering toward the humans, and a series of shots-on-the-fly takes them down in puffs of brain fluid and pieces of rotting skull flying up into the haze. "KEEP MOVING AND KEEP SHOOTING!" Lilly hollers. "I'M ALMOST OUT OF AMMO—WE'VE GOT TO GET—!"

A loud booming blast from behind her cuts off her words, and she whirls in time to see Austin—careening backward to the ground, a pair of biters clawing at his legs—his Glock emptying the last rounds of its last magazine across the tops of the creatures' heads. Unfortunately, the rounds take the male down but just graze the skull of the female. Austin screams a curse and kicks and flails at her. The big-bellied former housewife—still dressed in her filthy terry-cloth robe, curlers in her slimy hair—snaps her rotten teeth at Austin's wrists and flailing legs.

"AUSTIN!!"

Lilly charges toward him, closing the gap between them in mere seconds—maybe thirty feet or so—raising both .22s as she runs, sending surgically precise blasts across the distance at the dead housewife. Direct headshots drive the monstrous woman off Austin in a series of skull-shattering eruptions of meat and glistening gray matter, until half her head is gone. She lands beside Austin, her cranium trepanned open like a hollowed-out gourd, showing a cross-section of her infected cerebrum with the scientific precision of a high school biology class. Gas expels from the depths of her malodorous brain cavity, and Austin rolls over, coughing and gagging.

Lilly reaches him, shoves her pistols into her belt, and latches onto one of Austin's hands with the strength of an iron vise. She yanks him to his feet. "C'mon, pretty boy . . . we're outta here."

"Fine with me," he utters in a strangled voice, levering himself up.

The two of them race toward the alcove, leading the others out of harm's way, through a breached metal door and into the unknown chambers of Cellblock D.

Fueled by the eating frenzy, bolstered by the growing number of walkers hauling themselves through the gaps in the fences, the herd engulfs the prison grounds in short order, until multitudes of ragged, molting figures are clumsily crowding every corner, every square foot of every yard and basketball court and walkway. Some of them find entry into buildings through gaping doorways, left open by the exodus of inhabitants. The incredible noise and stink floods the passageways and echoes up into the impassive gunmetal sky.

From high on the ridges overlooking the property, the last of the fleeing inhabitants pauses to gaze back at their temporary home being overrun by the walking dead.

If there is a more indelible portrait of the world's end, no single soul gazing back at that derelict prison property that day can think of what it would be. The vast compound stretching across several hundred acres of pastureland virtually swims with upright corpses. From such a distant vantage point, it resembles so many black dots in a hellish pointillist painting, the shambling horde filling every nook and cranny, thousands of them, many cocking their dead faces toward the uncaring heavens and letting out yawps and groans as if being consumed from the inside by their overwhelming, cancerous, inescapable hunger. The sight of it brings tears to the eyes of those who lived there in relative safety for many months. The image will live in their minds for the rest of their lives. The prison has become a bellwether of doom.

The last few souls slipping away that day into the adjacent woods stare down at the swarm only briefly, unable to bear looking at it for long before turning away and beginning the next phase of their arduous search for shelter.

A massive thud reverberates the bones of the receiving room, making everybody jump. The prison is collapsing under the weight of the onslaught, the troubling din of thousands of shuffling feet and mortified vocal cords moaning incessantly inside and out, filling the air, as the surviving members of the Woodbury militia huddle in the middle of a desolate, flyspecked, littered foyer, trying to catch their breaths and figure out their next move.

"Austin!" Lilly points at a rack along the room's back wall, upon which are stacked signposts and flagpoles and implements. "Do me a favor and grab one of those sign poles and reinforce that side door!"

Shuffling with a limp, Austin hurries across the room and grabs one of the iron stands. He turns to a side exit situated under a powerless CORRIDOR D-1 sign and slams the object down across the middle of the door, wedging it under the broken bolt plate and a side hinge at the precise moment another muffled thud strikes outside the door.

Austin jerks with a start as plaster dust rains down and metal creaks, the force of multiple walkers outside the door pressing to get in, trying to get to the source of the human smells that are taunting them.

"They're gonna break that fucking door in!" Matthew Hennesey cries out from the front of the room. "There's too fucking many of them!"

"No, there's not!" Lilly rushes over to the front entrance and starts pushing a metal credenza brimming with heavy file folders and directories across the boarded glass of the front door. "C'mon, gimme a hand with this—Matthew and Ben—get your asses over here!"

They heave and push the immense shelving unit across the door.

The room is a little less than five hundred square feet of shopworn tile flooring and painted cinder-block walls scarred with illegible graffiti and the wear and tear of generations of intake procedures. The air smells chalky and sour, like the inside of an old refrigerator. One wall houses the grimy glass-fronted guard desk, elevated to shoulder height, where newcomers became official wards of the state of Georgia. Another wall is gouged with bullet holes and the cracked, dangling, framed portraits of former wardens and state officials. A lack of power has plunged the room into cold darkness, but the ambient daylight from outside the high, barred windows provides enough illumination for Lilly to see the owlish, terrified faces of her contingent.

In addition to Lilly and Austin, the ragtag group of surviving

Woodbury militia consists of the following four men and one woman, now huddled in a tight group in the middle of the receiving room: Matthew Hennesey, the twentysomething bricklayer from Valdosta, now draped in half-empty mag pouches and a sweat-soaked camo jacket; Hap Abernathy, the gaunt, graying, retired school bus driver from Atlanta who currently looks like a candidate for a hip replacement with his pronounced limp and bandaged ribs; Ben Buchholz, a pouchy-eyed man from Pine Mountain who lost his entire family last year in a swarm outside F.D. Roosevelt State Park and now appears to be flashing back to that earlier trauma; Speed Wilkins, a cocky nineteen-year-old high school football star from Athens who, at the moment, looks punch-drunk and dazed by the struggle, all his big-man-on-campus swagger long gone; and Gloria Pyne, her wounded leg wrapped in a crude bandage, her deeply creased, world-weary eyes still glowering out from underneath her I'M WITH STUPID visor, the headgear frayed and spattered with blood and soot.

Another thud makes them all jump. "Take it easy, everybody." Lilly stands before them with her back to the front entrance door. Each of her Rugers is shoved behind her belt on an opposing hip for easy access, but the problem is, she only has about six rounds left in one magazine, and one round in another, with an extra bullet in each chamber. The sound of scraping sets her teeth on edge and the pressure makes the credenza tremble and creak as the swarm shoves against the door. "This is hugely important—that we stay calm and don't panic."

"Are you shitting me?!" Hap Abernathy trains his ancient, gray eyes on her. "Stay *calm*? Did you happen to notice how many of them things are out there? It's only a matter of time before—"

"SHUT UP!" Austin booms at the man with fire in his eyes, his outburst uncharacteristic enough to raise even Lilly's eyebrows. "Just shut the fuck up and let the lady talk or maybe you want to just—!"

"Austin!" Lilly gives him a gentle warning-wave of her gloved hand. She still wears the fingerless driving gloves that Austin gave her the previous night. "It's okay. He's just expressing what everybody's thinking." Lilly looks at all of them, one at a time, that voice of her father coming through. "I'm asking all of you to trust me, and I will get you out of here."

She waits for everybody to get their breath back, get their bearings. Hap Abernathy stares at the floor, cradling his AR-15 as though it were a security blanket. Another thud makes them jerk. A cracking noise comes from the depths of the prison; something falls and shatters above them.

The walkers have gotten inside Cellblock D—one of the back entrances had been left open—but nobody knows how many of them have infiltrated the building or what parts of the prison are still secure.

"Hap?" Lilly speaks softly to him. "You okay? You with me on this?"

He nods slowly, staring at the floor. "Yes, ma'am . . . I'm with you."

A beat of noisy silence follows as the creaking noises and low, ubiquitous drone of walking dead pressing in on them grips the air with unbearable tension. The thing that nobody expresses at that moment—the gorilla in the room that they all try desperately to ignore—is Lilly's assassination of the Governor in plain view of everybody only moments earlier. Deep down inside all of them, they expected it to happen in some form sooner or later. They are all children of an abusive father trying to recover from the inevitable yet logical outcome of situations such as these—and like abused children everywhere, they have already begun to repress their unresolved feelings. They look at Lilly now with new eyes. They wait for her to lead.

"We're safe here in this room," she says at last. "For the time being at least. We'll keep close watch on the high windows, and keep the doors as secure as possible. How much ammunition does everybody have?"

It takes a moment for them to figure this out. In all the excitement, they have lost track. Matthew has the deepest reserve—a couple dozen 7.62 mm slugs in his cargo pocket, and seven more in the AK's magazine—but the rest of them have paltry supplies. Ben's got eleven 115-grain 9 mm rounds left for his Glock 19. Gloria's got a full mag of 305.56 mm slugs for her AR-15, and Hap's got a revolver with six rounds left. Speed's got a Bushmaster with five rounds still in the clip. And Austin has a single round remaining in his M1 Garand—Gloria loans him her spare Glock 17—which makes Lilly wonder how many bullets she has left in two separate magazines for her .22 caliber pistols. She checks them and confirms that she only has four rounds remaining.

"Okay, so we're not exactly loaded to the teeth, but we're safe here," Gloria finally speaks up, taking off her visor and running her fingers through her dyed red hair. "Then what? What's the plan? We can't just stay in this fucking room indefinitely."

Lilly nods. "I'm thinking we wait out the swarm, give them a chance to clear a little bit." She looks at them, giving each of them a respectful look as though offering them an option when they really have none. "We'll stay the night, and then we'll reassess in the morning."

A long silence follows, but nobody argues with her.

Late that night, after each of the six survivors have staked out private little corners and recesses within the confines of the intake room (mostly for the purpose of trying to get *some* semblance of rest), Lilly and Austin find themselves ensconced in the shadows behind the glass-fronted receiving counter. They spread a tarpaulin from the room's storage locker across the floor for a modicum of comfort, and now they sit slumped on the tarp, their guns on the shelf behind them, their backs resting against the file cabinets along the back wall . . . as the relentless drone of walkers continues unabated outside the barricaded doors and windows.

For the longest time, neither Lilly nor Austin says a word. They merely pass the time holding each other, stroking each other's arms and hair. After all, what is there to say? The world has spiraled out of control and they're just trying to hold on. But Lilly can't turn her mind off. She keeps dabbing the pearls of blood oozing from her split lip with a Kleenex and noticing little things around them that don't add up, such as the pine tree deodorizer hanging from the desk lamp above her, or the unexplained bloodstain on the ceiling, or the lump under Austin's sleeve.

"Wait a minute," she says at one point very late that night, her stomach growling from nerves and the empty feeling of not having eaten anything for almost twenty-four hours. She looks at the sleeve of Austin's leather jacket and realizes there are two puncture holes directly over the lump. "What *is* that?"

"Okay, now don't get all bent outta shape on me," Austin says as Lilly reaches down and pulls up his sleeve. Under the cuff, a faded blue bandanna is wrapped around Austin's wrist, the cloth soaked in blood.

Lilly gently pulls the bandanna back and sees the telltale puncture wounds. "Oh God no," she utters under her breath. "Please tell me you cut yourself on the fence."

From the look on his narrow face peering out at her through unruly tendrils of curly hair—an uncanny mixture of sadness, resolve, anguish, and calm—it's clear he didn't hurt himself on barbed wire.

EIGHTEEN

Already beginning to darken and turn livid around the edges with infection, the bite marks are so severe—perhaps deep enough to have nipped an artery—that it's a miracle Austin hasn't bled to death. Lilly springs to her feet. Mind racing, heart thumping in her chest, she yammers for a moment, "Jesus . . . Austin, we have to . . . Jesus Christ . . . the first-aid kits are in the . . . fuck . . . FUCK!"

Austin hoists himself to his feet, replacing the bandanna, wrapping it around the wound. He starts to say something, but Lilly is busily whirling around, madly searching the shelves and drawers of the intake office for something—anything—to stanch the infection. "We have to take care of it immediately before it . . . SHIT!"

She throws open drawers, rifling through old documents, dusty intake forms, office supplies, candy wrappers, empty bottles of booze. She glances back at Austin and blurts out, "A tourniquet!"

"Lilly—"

She reaches down to the tails of her denim shirt, starts ripping off a strip of fabric, her hands trembling. "We need to apply a tourniquet before—!"

"What the hell's going on?!"

The voice comes from the opposite end of the intake counter, a figure standing outside the glass partition, audible through the pass-through slot. Gloria Pyne has a packing blanket wrapped around her, and from the puffy redness underneath her eyes she appears to be half asleep. She knocks on the glass.

Lilly takes a deep breath and tries to appear semi-calm. "It's nothing, Gloria, it's just—"

"What's wrong with Austin?" She notices the bloody bandanna. Two other figures—Hap and Ben—appear behind her, gazing through the glass. "Is that a bite?" Gloria stares at the blood-soaked cloth around his wrist. "Did he get bit out there?"

"No, goddamnit, he just—"

"Lilly, come here for a second." Austin speaks softly to her. He puts his good arm around her and gives her a gentle squeeze. He looks into her eyes and smiles sadly. "It's too late."

"What?!—NO!—What the fuck are you talking about?"

"It's too late, kiddo."

"No!—No!—Fuck no!—Don't say that!" She gazes across the dusty vestibule and sees the entire group now gathered outside the glass, the moonbeams slanting down through the high lintels, silhouetting their tense stares. They're all gaping at Austin.

"Lilly—" Austin starts to say, but she cuts him off with a raised hand. She turns toward the others. "Go back to sleep, goddamnit, all of you—GO ON! GO BACK! GIVE US SOME FUCKING PRIVACY!!"

Slowly, one by one, they turn away from the glass and slip back into the shadows of the foyer. In the silence that ensues, Lilly turns and searches for the right words. She will *not* allow him to give up.

Austin touches her face. "It was bound to happen sooner or later."

"What the fuck are you talking about?!" She blinks away the tears. She can't afford to cry right now. Maybe someday she'll be able to cry again. But not now. Now she has to think of something. Fast. "Okay . . . look. I'm gonna have to do something radical here."

He shakes his head calmly. "I know what you're thinking. Unfortunately, the thing has already gone way beyond amputation, Lilly. I can feel the fever. The thing has already spread. There's nothing you can do. It's too late."

"Goddamnit, would you stop saying that!" She pulls away from him. "I'm not gonna lose you!"

"Lilly—"

"No, no . . . this is unacceptable!" She licks her lips, gazing around the enclosure, thinking, searching for some answer. She looks back at Austin, and she sees the expression on his face, and all at once the fight goes out of her, and she realizes there is, indeed, nothing she can do for him. Like a balloon deflating, she sags, letting out an anguished sigh. "When did it happen? Was it that big lady walker, jumped you before we came inside?"

He nods. His expression remains tranquil, almost beatific, like a person who's had a religious conversion. He strokes her shoulder. "You're gonna survive this thing. I just know it. If anybody can do it, you can."

"Austin—"

"The time I got left . . . I don't want to, like, dwell on it. You know what I mean?"

Lilly wipes the tears from her eyes. "There's so much we don't know. I heard about this one victim, up near Macon, who never turned. They got a fucking *finger* chewed off, and they never fucking turned."

Austin lets out a sigh, smiling to himself. "And unicorns exist."

She takes him by the shoulders, and burns her gaze into his eyes. "You're not gonna die."

He shrugs. "Yeah. I am. We all are. Sooner or later. But you got a good shot at avoiding it for a long time. You're gonna get outta here."

She wipes her face, the sorrow and horror rising up her gorge and threatening to break her into a million pieces. But she stamps it down, shoves it back, swallows it . . . hard. "We're all gonna get out of here, pretty boy."

He gives her another weary nod, and then he sits back down on the tarp, leaning back against the wall. "If I'm not mistaken, I think I saw a flask in one of those drawers you were banging around in." He gives her one of his patented rock-star smiles, brushing wisps of curly hair from his ashen face. "If there's a God, there'll be liquor left in there."

They stay wide awake the rest of the night, sharing the last few fingers of stale hooch in the flask left behind by some overworked intake guard. Throughout the wee hours, they talk softly, careful not to be heard by the others out in the foyer, discussing everything *but* Austin's bite wound. They talk about how they're going to get out of this place, whether they might find any supplies in other parts of the prison, and how they might avoid the infestation of walkers currently skulking around the corridors of the building.

Lilly puts Austin's condition out of her mind. She has a job to do—get these people home safely—and she has assumed the mantle of leadership as readily as slipping into a new wardrobe, as easily as pulling a trigger, as quickly as a shot to the head. They talk about how the people in Woodbury will react to Philip Blake's death. And for a while, Lilly fantasizes about a new Woodbury, a place where people can breathe and live in peace and take care of each other. She wants this badly, but neither she nor Austin can admit to themselves how farfetched it all sounds—how slim their odds are of even escaping this godforsaken prison with their skins intact.

Around dawn, as the high windows turn a luminous gray and begin to cast pale light into the receiving room, Lilly shakes herself out of her reverie. She looks at Austin. He shivers with a worsening fever. His dark eyes—once perpetually alive with mischief—now look like those of an eighty-year-old man. Dark circles rim the lower eyelids, and burst capillaries have turned the whites to a sickly pink. His breathing seems labored, rough and clogged with phlegm, but he manages to smile back at her. "What's wrong? What are you thinking?"

"Listen to that," she whispers. "You hear that?"

"What? I don't hear a thing."

She tilts her head toward the side door leading into the cellblock corridor. "Exactly." She stands and brushes herself off, then checks her pistols. "Sounds like the stragglers have drifted away, gotten bored with the empty hallways." She flicks the safety on her Ruger. "I'm gonna check out the cellblock, see if we can't find anything useful."

Austin stands up and nearly falls over from the rush of dizziness. He swallows the nausea rising inside him. "I'll go with you."

"No, no way." She shoves the gun in her belt, checks the second pistol, shoves it down the back of her jeans. "You're in no shape to go. I'll take the others with me. You stay here and hold down the fort."

He looks at her. "I'm going with you, girlfriend."

She sighs. "Okay . . . whatever. I don't have the energy to argue with you." She goes over to the glass door, pushes it open, and gazes out at the dreary light of the foyer. "Ben? Matthew?"

Out in the reception area, the others are huddled together on the floor. They sit on a blanket after a sleepless night, their eyes red and drawn with fatigue. At first, they appear to be playing some kind of game, the contents of their pockets in a pile on the blanket in front of them as though wagers are being made. But very quickly Lilly realizes that they're pooling the meager resources from their pockets: candy bars, keys, cigarettes, a flashlight, chewing gum, a couple of hunting knives, a scope, a walkie-talkie, handkerchiefs, a canteen, and a roll of electrical tape.

"What's going on?" Matthew springs to his feet, reaching for his ammo belts. "What's happening with junior?"

"I'm right as rain," Austin replies sternly from behind Lilly, his voice sounding as though he's about as right as a whipped dog. "Thank you for asking."

"I need some of you to give me a hand with a quick search of the corridor," Lilly tells them. "Matthew, you come along with the AK . . . just in case . . . and Ben, you too . . . bring those knives." She looks at Gloria. "The rest of you hold down the fort. Something goes awry, fire off a single warning shot. You understand?"

They all nod.

"C'mon," she says to the others, "let's do this quickly and quietly."

The three men follow Lilly over to the side door. Lilly draws her .22, takes a breath, and yanks the iron stand off its temporary mooring. She carefully turns the knob, the door squeaking softly as she cracks it open a few inches. Through the gap she peers out, craning her neck to see down the hundred-foot length of main corridor.

The hallway sits in silent darkness, a few cells along the walls sitting open.

At the far end of the corridor, so far away that they look like indistinct jumbles of clothing strewn across the floor, Lilly sees the remains of the three men sent into the prison by the Governor the previous afternoon. They now lie torn to shreds on the tiles, their torsos and extremities so mutilated that they're unrecognizable as men. Their drying blood coats the floor and walls.

Fortunately, as far as Lilly can tell, the walkers have moved on, despite the fact that their putrid odors still cling to the air.

Lilly gives everybody a nod, and one by one they slip into the corridor.

They get halfway down the hallway, passing empty cell after empty cell, finding nothing but litter and discarded clothing on the floors—people obviously left in a hurry—when Austin suddenly hears a noise behind him. He wheels around and comes face-to-face with a figure bursting out of one of the darker, windowless cells.

Austin jerks back with a start, instinctively raising his Glock at the precise same moment a huge male biter with a wild gray Rasputin beard unhinges its creaking jaws and pounces at him. Jowls hanging in bloody shreds from a recent gunshot wound, milk-pod eyes flashing with bloodlust, the dead old man tries to gobble Austin's face as the Glock's muzzle almost accidentally lodges itself inside the creature's throat. Austin starts to squeeze the trigger.

"Austin, don't fire it!" Ben Buchholz hisses at him from the shadows off his right flank. "The noise!—Austin, don't!"

Blinking with shock, his fever spiking with streaks of painful light across his field of vision, Austin shoves the creature's huge head against the closest wall. The impact cracks the thing's skull, but it keeps chewing furiously on the barrel in its mouth as though trying to masticate the gun.

Austin grunts and slams the skull again and again against the wall when a flash of steel streaks across his peripheral vision and a knife blade embeds itself in the thing's forehead with a watery crunch.

Rotten blood and black fluids gush around the knife's hilt as Ben Buchholz pulls the blade free, and then he stabs it a second time, and a third, until the thing with the beard collapses to the floor in a bloody mass of blubber and escaping gases.

A moment of edgy silence follows as everybody gets their bearings.

They move on. Austin brings up the rear, moving slowly, the nausea twisting his insides into knots, the fever sending clammy gooseflesh down his back. They creep toward the end of the corridor. Ben and Matthew take the lead, each with a buck knife at the ready. Austin sees Lilly pausing in front of an open cell about twenty-five feet ahead of him. She stares at something inside the cell. The two other men pause and look over her shoulder.

Something's wrong. Austin can see it in Lilly's body language, the way she lowers herself to one knee and picks something up off the floor. The other two men wait impatiently for her, saying nothing. Austin approaches and looks over her shoulder.

He sees what has Lilly so transfixed and turns to the other men. "Give us a second, guys," Austin says to them. "See if you can go secure the door at the end of the hall."

The two men pad away, scanning the depths of the hallway ahead of them with knives poised and ready. Troubling scratching noises echo. The distant, omnipresent drone of the herd vibrates in the air. The yards are still rife with the dead, the horde surrounding the cellblocks. At the moment, though, the corridor remains still and silent. Austin crouches next to Lilly and puts an arm around her.

A single tear drops off her chin. Her shoulders tremble as she takes in the former sleeping quarters of a child, its former inhabitant evidently abandoning it in a hurry. Across the cinder-block wall over the cot someone has hung a small banner of letters from the alphabet spelling out the name S-O-P-H-I-A. Lilly cradles a small teddy bear in her arms as if it's a wounded bird—the stuffed animal is missing an eye and its fur is worn down to the nubs from compulsive fondling. On a makeshift dresser of crates in one corner is an old music box.

"Lilly . . . ?"

Austin feels a tremor of fear as Lilly pulls herself away from him and crosses the cell to the dresser. She opens the lid of the music box, and a tinkling melody rattles out of the thing for a moment. *Hush, little baby, don't you cry . . . Mama's gonna sing you a lullaby.* Lilly collapses into a sitting position in front of the music box, her expression crumbling with grief. She sobs. Softly. Uncontrollably. Her body shudders and convulses as she lowers her head. Tears stream down her face, falling to the grubby tile floor. Austin joins her, kneeling next to her, searching for the right thing to say. No words come to him.

He turns away from her, partly out of respect and partly because he can't bear to see her weep like this. He studies the contents of the cell, patiently trying to give her the space and time to let this horrible grief work its way through her. He sees the child's things strewn across the floor, on the bed, and on a meager little shelf nailed into the rotted cinder-block wall. He sees Kewpie dolls, arrowheads, leaves pressed onto construction paper, and books—dozens of them—lined along the shelf and shoved under the bed. He studies the titles: *The Wizard of Oz, Charlie and the Chocolate Factory, Eloise, The Phantom Tollbooth,* and *Matilda.*

His gaze lingers on one of the books. His head throbs. His eyes moisten and his stomach clenches with fever chills as he stares and stares at the book's title. An idea strikes him right then, a way out of this place—Austin's destiny written on the cracked gold-leaf spine of a dog-eared Little Golden Books classic—all of it coalescing in his mind in one great paroxysm of inspiration.

He looks at Lilly. "I promise you, we're gonna get out of here," he says in a low, measured, confident tone. "You're gonna live a long life, have a lot of babies, be a terrific mom, and have a lot of parties with drinks with those little umbrellas in them."

She manages to raise her head and look at him through wet, swollen eyes. She can barely talk. Her voice sounds drained of life. "What are you babbling about?"

"I got an idea."

"Austin—"

"It's a way out of this mess. C'mon. Let's get the guys together, and I'll lay it out for you." He helps her to her feet.

She looks at him, and he returns her gaze, and for the first time since the war began, the love between them returns in earnest. "Don't argue with me," he says, giving her a wan smile and ushering her out of the cell.

But before heading back to the receiving room, Austin throws one last fleeting glance into that sad little child's lair . . .

. . . and takes one final look at the threadbare, split, well-thumbed spine of *The Pied Piper from Hamelin*.

NINETEEN

Less than an hour later, before the sun has even cleared the tall pines to the east, Lilly stands with the others in the musty intake room, waiting for Austin's signal. She can't show any emotion. She can't show her fear, her sorrow, or her anguish over letting Austin execute this insane plan. The five other surviving members of the Woodbury militia—by this point having taken their positions around the room—need to know this is going to work. They are coiled and ready to spring, and each of their frightened gazes rests on Lilly. They need her leadership now more than ever.

Matthew and Speed—the strongest of the six—stand near the giant metal credenza blocking the exit door. Gloria, Hap, and Ben—each clutching their weapons with sweat-slick hands—stand in the center of the room, facing the exit, prepared to move on Lilly's cue. Lilly has a Ruger pistol in each hand, taking deep breaths on the other side of the credenza, a runner in the blocks, muscles taut with tension, as ready as she'll ever be.

Nobody knows about the hushed argument that transpired only half an hour ago between Austin and Lilly behind the shattered glass of the intake desk. Nobody heard Lilly pleading with him not to do this. And no one else will ever know what happened when Austin finally broke down and admitted through runnels of snot and tears that he *has* to do this—he has no choice—because he has always been a coward and a liar, and these attributes only worsened when the plague broke out, and this is the only way he will ever be able to redeem himself, and do something good and right.

He told Lilly then the truest thing—the thing that will live in Lilly's heart the rest of her life—that *she* is the only person that he has ever loved, and he will love her for eternity.

The first shot rings out on the far side of the yard, faint and muffled inside the foyer, dampened by walls of brick and mortar.

Everybody in the room bristles, spines stiffening at the noise. Lilly raises one of her guns at the ceiling, getting everyone's attention. "Okay," she says. "There's the first signal. He needs two minutes, and then we head out. Get ready."

Lacking a stopwatch, Lilly begins counting off the seconds in her head to occupy her thoughts.

One Mississippi . . . two Mississippi . . . three Mississippi.

Austin gets halfway across the exercise yard on the north edge of the grounds—firing off large-caliber attention-grabbers every few seconds in order to draw the swarm away from the cellblocks—when the herd gets too thick.

Dizzy from the harsh sun pounding behind his eyes, in a weakened state from the fever, he manages to kick his way through a cluster of biters on the edge of the fences, but soon the monsters outnumber him three hundred to one. He reaches the mangled wreckage of chain link, taking a few down with headshots—Matthew equipped him with an AK, a full magazine, and a knife—but the moment he plunges into the wall of walkers milling about the tall grass, he gets pinned down.

He spins and strafes a group of ragged monsters coming up behind him, sending flesh and blood into the air in an arabesque of red spray, but when he whirls back toward the meadow, one of the larger males pounces on him and knocks him down. He drops his gun and tries to scuttle back to his feet but the male clamps down on his ankle, rotten bicuspids digging in, latching onto him with the force of grappling hooks. Austin cries out and kicks, to no avail.

Through sheer force of will, he rises back to his feet. With every last shred of strength he can muster, the searing pain spreading through every tendon, every capillary, he starts moving again, the huge male still clamped onto him. He knows, deep down, that this isn't about destroying creatures—it's about drawing them away—so he drags the male as far as he can across the leprous meadow.

It's slow going at first, but he covers nearly twenty-five yards in this manner, hemorrhaging pints of blood, the knife now in his sweat-greasy fist, the pain a living thing inside him, devouring him. He flails and strikes out at more and more attackers coming at him from every direction, screaming as loud as he can, "COME AND GET ME, MOTHERFUCKERS—YOU BUNCH OF STINK-ING, ROTTEN PUSSIES!!—COME AND GET ME!!"

Out of the corner of his eye, he sees the leading edge of the swarm shifting like a black tide rolling back out to sea, many of those who had been snuffling around the buildings now awk-wardly turning, bumping into each other, starting to trundle back toward the meadow, drawn by the commotion of fresh meat in their midst.

Austin's plan is working—at least for the moment. The trick is going to be getting them away from the vehicles. Austin's body be-gins to shut down, the male clawing at the place in his legs where the femoral arteries live, ragged arms tangling with his feet, throw-ing him off stride. He knows he only has a few more minutes left in him, a few more feet, a few more strangled breaths.

"COME AND GET IT, SHITHEADS!! SOUP'S ON!! WHAT ARE YOU WAITING FOR?!!"

He can see the closest vehicle—a military transport truck—its doors still hanging open, the wind blowing through the empty cab. He manages to drag the monster off to the left of the aban-doned caravan another few yards before the pain and the pressure of the creature's teeth and the clawing fingers drag him to the ground.

He crawls another few feet before more rotting teeth close in, a fogbank of noxious black stench engulfing him, the hellish choir of growls contracting around him like a giant turbine turning and turning. The pain steals his breath, makes his vision grow dim and amorphous, makes the growing number of teeth sinking into his flesh lose all meaning. He hears a whisper in his mind, which drowns the horror, numbs the pain, and turns the black inkblots of a hundred cadaverous faces looming over him into a gauzy blur. The whisper carries him over—takes him across a beautiful pristine-white threshold—as the feeding opens him up: *I love you, Austin . . . and I always, always, always, always will . . . I will never stop loving you.* It is the last thing Lilly said to him this morning, and it is the last thing he hears in his mind as his arteries collapse and spill his life-force into the grass, the blood seeping down into the earth. . . .

The giant credenza shrieks across the floor suddenly as the two young men shove it away from the door. Lilly gives Gloria, Hap, and Ben a terse nod—they nod back at her—and Lilly turns to the door, jacks the knob, and throws it open.

The harsh light of a pale sun shines in her face as she steps outside.

Several things register to Lilly as she takes her first loping strides across the concrete deck of the exercise yard—the others following closely, their guns poised, their hot gazes everywhere at once—but she tries to focus solely on the task of getting the group to a vehicle in one piece rather than succumb to the chaotic flow of information now streaming into her brain.

The first thing that occurs to her is the absence of any sign of Austin. She scans the grounds, and then surveys the outer fences, and sees only walkers. Where the hell is he? Did he make it to the woods? She leads the group toward the outer fence.

The second thing that registers in Lilly's churning mind is the dearth of walkers still wandering the grounds. Only a few stragglers still drag across the cement here and there, providing very little threat to a tightly packed group of humans racing across the exercise yard.

Matthew wields the largest knife—and he runs alongside Lilly—keeping an eye on the errant biters that might make note of them.

They cross the sparsely populated grounds in less than a minute, and Matthew has to drive his knife into the decaying craniums of a mere handful of walkers before they get to the pasture.

Which leads to the third thing that registers fully at that point in Lilly's brain: The configuration of the herd has now spontaneously shifted to the north. Like a teeming mass of ants, they swarm around something dark and glistening on the ground fifty feet from the farthest vehicle.

The noise of the feeding frenzy reaches her ears as she leads the group toward her truck—the massive vehicle still sitting with its cab doors open exactly as she left them the day before—and she calls out to the others as they crane their necks to see the gruesome scene along the north edge of the pasture: "DON'T LOOK!"

Lilly's voice sounds almost robotic in her own ears—all emotion blanched out of her now by the scalding rush of adrenaline—as she comes around the driver's side of the cab. She jerks to a stop when she sees the ragged female in a soiled sundress inside the cab, wedged behind the steering wheel, her threadbare dress tangled on the stick shift. Lilly quickly raises her .22 and puts the female out of her misery, sending the back of the girl's skull across the glass of the passenger door.

Dark blood washes the inside of the windshield as the female sags to the cab floor. Lilly kicks the body toward the door, ripping the dress free. Gloria Pyne reaches in from the passenger side and yanks the body out of the cab, dumping it in the grass.

The others rush around to the rear hatch and start climbing onto the truck. First, Hap Abernathy . . . then Speed, then Matthew, and finally Ben. Lilly throws a glance out the driver's-side window and sees—in the cracked reflection of the shattered mirror—that Ben Buchholz has to struggle to heave his way on board. The contents of the truck—crates of ordnance and supplies—have shifted and spilled, and now the four men have to huddle dangerously close to the rear gate in order to fit into the cluttered cargo bay.

The sound of a muffled knock on the rear wall signals they are all safely on board.

The keys still dangle from the ignition, and Lilly kicks the engine to life. Gloria takes her place on the passenger side, shutting the door behind her as quietly as possible. She gazes out her open window. On the edges of the herd, some of the stray biters have noticed them, turning languidly in their direction, starting to drag toward them.

Gloria sticks the barrel of her Glock 19 out the open window, preparing to fire a few suppressing shots as Lilly slams the gearbox into reverse, but Gloria freezes when she catches a glimpse of just exactly what lies on the ground in the heart of the swarm.

Already torn apart and eviscerated beyond recognition, the human remains feature familiar clumps of long curly hair, shredded leather, and an ammo vest now torn to pieces. Two biters fight over a single motorcycle boot, the visible white fibula bone and part of a bloody ankle still lodged inside it. Gloria sucks in a breath. "Oh dear Jesus God . . . what have we done?"

"Don't look," Lilly utters under her breath as she kicks the accelerator.

The gears shriek, and the truck lurches into reverse. The gravitational forces shove Lilly and Gloria forward, nearly slamming them into the dash as the vehicle's undercarriage shudders and threatens to break into pieces. The massive tires cobble and bump over dead bodies—both walkers and humans alike—which still lie strewn across the battlefield. Lilly keeps the foot-feed pinned. A few errant biters get bowled over by the rear bumper in a succession of watery, arrhythmic thuds as the truck careens.

"DON'T LOOK!"

She cries it out in a strangled voice—addressing herself more than Gloria or the others—as the vehicle screams backward, skirting the edges of the swarm. The stench engulfs the rattling truck, the air black with smoke and carbon and gouts of exhaust enveloping the open windows, as the countless creatures flock like carrion crows fifty yards to the north around the pathetic human remains, which are now scattered across an entire square acre of scabrous, blood-sodden, sacrificial ground.

Don't look, Lilly tells herself as she slams on the brakes thirty feet from the edge of the wooded slope, smashing Gloria into the folds of the passenger seat. Lilly wrestles the shift lever into second gear and guns it.

The engine booms and the rear wheels dig into the muddy turf for a moment, spinning in place, and Lilly realizes—for one terrible split second—that she now has a fleeting opportunity to get a good view of the feeding frenzy that saved their lives transpiring right this instant through the blood-slimy windshield. *Don't look, don't look, don't look,* she keeps repeating to herself in her mind as the rear wheels finally find purchase, and the truck plunges forward in a huge wake of dirt and detritus.

She manages not to look for the entire span of time it takes them to circle around the slope to the access road and start to weave headlong up the side of the hill, the engine bellowing.

But just as the vehicle crests the hill, Lilly shoots an involuntary glance out at the hairline fractured reflection of the side mirror.

The first thing she takes in is the entirety of the prison—the grounds now completely overrun, demolished, abandoned of all life, littered with bodies, some of the towers still smoldering faintly with the aftermath of the firefight—and she registers this in a single microsecond of a synapse firing in the deepest part of her limbic brain: *This is both the end and the beginning.*

Then, in that single horrible instant before reaching the road along the edge of the woods, she does the one thing she promised herself she would not do.

Eyes drawn involuntarily to the corner of the mirror still reflecting the swarm of biters to the north, at this distance looking like a million black maggots burrowing into a cairn, she does the thing that will scar her soul forever.

She looks.

"Lilly?—Sweetie?—You okay?—Talk to me." Gloria Pyne breaks the excruciating silence of the rumbling cab about five miles down the road as the cargo truck wends its way along the snaking asphalt highway.

The desolate two-lane cuts a swath through the dense, biter-infested shadows of primordial woods, the blur of ancient pines on either side of them making Gloria feel almost claustrophobic. Lilly just keeps silently driving. They are closing in on Woodbury. The town lies in a valley just up ahead, around a bend in the road, maybe ten minutes away, maybe less.

"Lilly?"

No answer.

Gloria chews her lip. The relief of fleeing the prison in one piece has been short-lived for her, the thing her mother called "woman's intuition" revving now in her brain at the advent of Lilly Caul's stony, ashen, miserable silence. Her hands welded to the steering wheel, her eyes shiny and cratered out with agony, Lilly hasn't said a single word since they escaped the prison.

"Talk to me, honey," Gloria says. "Yell . . . scream . . . cry . . . curse . . . *something*."

Lilly suddenly throws a glance at her, and the two women make eye contact for a single moment. Gloria is taken aback by the clarity in Lilly's eyes. "We were going to have a baby," Lilly says at last in a clear, calm voice.

Gloria stares at her. "Oh my God . . . I'm so sorry, honey. Did you—?"

"He saved our lives," Lilly adds then, as if to put the final punctuation on something.

"He surely did," Gloria says with a nod, her mind reeling for a moment. She looks at Lilly. "So did you, honey. You saved us when you—"

"Oh no." Lilly sees something troubling up ahead of them as they round the bend. "Oh Jesus *no*."

Gloria snaps her gaze toward the windshield, and she sees what Lilly sees as the air brakes kick on, hissing noisily and slowing the truck to a crawl.

In the middle distance, about a quarter mile away, above the tops of the swaying pine boughs bordering the eastern outskirts of town, an enormous cloud of black smoke billows up into the sky.

Woodbury is burning.

TWENTY

The cargo truck thumps across the derelict railroad crossing outside Woodbury's southernmost outskirts. The air crackles with the noise of burning timber, and the acrid stench of scorched flesh and tar hangs thick over the streets. Lilly slams on the brakes a couple hundred yards from the barricade.

In the middle distance, the east wall burns, sending up a noxious, swirling cloud of smoke. Lilly can see the place is under attack—from this distance it looks like a small herd of walkers has pressed in from the south woods—and now the remaining twenty or so townspeople, most of them seniors and children, struggle to stave off the onslaught with torches and bladed weapons.

For a brief moment, Lilly is almost mesmerized by the sight: Some of the biters along the breaches in the barricades have caught fire, and now stumble without direction or purpose, like phosphorescent schools of fish, wreathed in flame, radiant and surreal in the morning sun. Some of the sparks issuing from the creatures are touching off sections of the outbuildings, adding to the chaos.

"Jesus Christ, we gotta help them!" Gloria blurts out, wrenching open her door.

"Wait—WAIT!" Lilly grabs the woman, holds her back. In her side mirror, Lilly can see the others in back leaning out of the rear hatch, their eyes hot and wide with panic, some of them hopping off the gate and cocking their weapons. Lilly calls out to them. "EVERYBODY WAIT!"

Lilly climbs out of the cab. She has two or three bullets left in each Ruger, but Matthew has at least two dozen rounds of armor-piercing slugs still tucked into his gear, and the magazine in Gloria's Glock 19 is nearly full. The other men have a few bullets each, but considering the fact that there appears to be no more than fifty walkers—give or take—engulfing the south side of town, they should have enough ammo to intercede.

Matthew comes around the front of the cab, jacking back the charging handle on his AK. His youthful face furrows with panic, his dark eyes blazing with tension. "What's the plan?"

A gust of wind rife with sparks and death-stench slams into them, and they all crouch down by the front of the cab, each of them starting to breathe faster.

Ben Buchholz speaks up from the other side of the cab. "I say we go in blazing—what other choice do we have?"

"No, we're going to—" Lilly starts to say when a voice cuts her off from the other side of the truck.

"Whatever we do," Gloria Pyne says, gaping at the fires and the monstrous apparitions robed in flame staggering here and there along the crumbling barricade, "we better do it quick. These people can't hold them off much longer with matchsticks and bare hands."

"Listen up, listen up!" Lilly raises her hand, and turns to Hap Abernathy, who crouches behind the truck's fender. "You used to drive buses, right?"

The older man nods furiously. "Thirty-four years and a gold Timex from the Decatur School District—why?"

"You're gonna drive the truck." She looks at the others, making eye contact with each tense face. "The rest of you, how are your singing voices?"

Minutes later, Barbara Stern sprints around the corner of Main and Mill with a chemical fire extinguisher in her arms when she hears the strangest sound warbling on the winds above the chorus of moaning, reanimated corpses.

Her iron-gray hair pulled away from her deeply creased face, her peasant dress and denim jacket soaked with sweat and chemicals, she feels responsible for this disaster. So does David. The Governor thought enough of them to leave them in charge of the town during the battle and now *this*!

All of which makes Barbara Stern bristle when she hears the advent of human voices singing out from the south, ululating like a tribe of Bedouin maidens, their piercing cries rising above the din of burning wood and flesh. Barbara sniffs back the panic and alters her course slightly, charging toward the railroad crossing at the end of Mill Road—the place where the largest number of biters now swarm and press in through the holes in the fortification.

She sees something moving out beyond the blazing inferno, something raising a thunderhead of dust into the sky, and the closer she gets, the more she hears an engine—as distinct as a bell—grinding through its low gears: *a truck!* Her heart beats faster as she closes in on the chaos at the wall. Heat punches her in the face as she approaches the haze-bound corner of Mill and Folk Avenue.

She sees her husband near the abandoned railway office, shouting orders to the others. Some of the older citizens are stationed at key junctures along the tracks, awkwardly flailing torches at swarming biters, fighting a losing battle, the human shouts drowned by the noise. Barbara's eyes water as she closes in on the scene.

Near the office building, Barbara sees three other seniors spraying dwindling amounts of chemical foam on the burning facade. David has a hunting bow in his trembling hands and pulls another arrow from the pack as Barbara approaches. They found the bow in the warehouse with an old quiver filled with a couple dozen arrows, and now David shakily aims one of the last arrows at an oncoming walker.

Flames envelop a huge male in greasy workman's overalls as it lumbers toward David, its flaming face still biting at the air, arms sleeved in flame but still reaching. The arrow pierces its moldering skull between the eyes, and the walker staggers backward in a miasma of sparks, opening its gaping maw of a mouth—smoke curling out of its black gorge—before collapsing to the oily pavement.

"DAVID! LOOK!" Barbara drops the fire extinguisher as she approaches her husband, the tank rolling across the cobblestones of the intersection. "LOOK!—OUT BEYOND THE TRACKS!—DAVID, IT'S THEM!"

David notices what she's babbling about just as a cornerstone collapses and half the railway office caves in on a fountain of sparks. The heat and noise and tendrils of flame spewing out like a particle bomb make every survivor jerk back with a start, some of them diving for cover, falling to the ground on their brittle, aging joints. David stumbles backward and trips over his own feet, dropping the bow and arrows. The flames catch on an oil spill and lick across the road. Voices cry out, and Barbara goes to David.

"Sweetie, this is no time for a nap," she taunts him breathlessly, lifting him up with a grunt. "Look, David!—Look!—They're backing off!—LOOK!"

Sure enough, David Stern manages to get his bearings back and look up, and all at once he sees what she's talking about. In the middle distance, the swarm has changed course, many of the biters still sparking and smoking as they clumsily turn toward the engine noises and howling sounds emanating from the vacant lot beyond the tracks. A large vehicle now slowly rumbles across the lot, drawing their attention. The plumes of black exhaust are visible above the wall, and the clamor of crooning voices fills the air. Barbara and David rise to their feet and scurry across the intersection.

They find a vantage point near the old wooden water tower and gaze through a break in the flaming barricade at the military cargo truck now prowling the hard-packed gravel on the far side of the tracks. "Oh my God," Barbara utters, putting her hand to her mouth. "It's Lilly!"

David gapes at the strange spectacle unfolding in the defunct train yard.

The truck rattles over petrified tracks as the horde of walkers, many of them still smoldering, fuming with smoke and sparks, follow the sounds of human voices trumpeting out the rear of the vehicle. Three men sit on the hatch with guns, yammering and whooping and hollering at the throng, and every now and then shouting out off-key choruses from old Southern rock tunes— "Green Grass and High Tides," "Long Haired Country Boy," "Whipping Post"—and the strangeness of it, the very incongruity of a bunch of good old boys hollering and crooning, mesmerizes every walker and human within hearing distance. Then the shooting starts.

The muzzle flashes from the rear of the truck take down monster after monster. Some of the creatures stagger and whirl in swirls of sparks and blood spume before going down. Others collapse like bags of rocks. One by one, like clay pigeons, they get picked off by the falsetto-howling noisemakers in the rear of the truck.

Lilly stands behind them, holding on to a side brace, overseeing the operation with her laser-focused gaze, until suddenly, without warning, the truck hits a rut. The bump knocks Speed Wilkins— the youngest of the three—off the rear of the truck.

From her vantage point behind the burning water tower, Barbara Stern inhales a startled breath. "Oh Jesus . . . Jesus, Jesus . . . shit!"

Out in the vacant lot, the man behind the wheel of the cargo truck evidently doesn't see the accident and keeps rolling slowly away from the fallen man, who is now rising to his knees just as a phalanx of biters surrounds him. Speed madly searches the ground for his gun, but the biters are pressing in on all sides—at least a dozen of them—most of them still smoking from tufts of ragged clothing that are still on fire. One of them—a wiry female with a scorched face, dead flesh burned as crisp as parchment—unhinges her creaking jaws to reveal rows of slimy, sharp teeth.

Speed lets out a yelp and dives away from her, shoulder-rolling into three more monsters.

This all happens within the space of a few seconds, Barbara and David Stern watching helplessly from behind the tower. David fecklessly raises his bow, thinking he might be able to hit the three attackers now converging on the boy—but he is so far out of range he might as well be in the next county. Just as he stretches a metal-tipped arrow back in the sling, several things transpire with neck-snapping swiftness.

Barbara sees a flash leap out of the truck, vaulting through the air before the other two men even get a chance to raise their guns.

Lilly lands fifteen feet away from Speed Wilkins, just as the three smoldering corpses pounce on him. Wilkins rolls away, flailing wildly, kicking out at the smallest one with his work boots. Lilly charges across the gap, pausing only for a split instant to scoop up Speed's Bushmaster—the rifle has maybe two rounds left, if that, but it's *something*—and she simultaneously raises the .22 in her left hand while tossing the rifle to Speed with the other.

At the last possible instant before the rotting jaws of the closest biter close around Speed's forearm, Lilly pinches off a series of quick blasts at the heads of the attackers, hitting two out of three dead center in their foreheads, sending black fluids skyward and causing the smoldering bodies to deflate into the dirt.

Practically at the exact same moment, Speed catches the rifle, slams it up into the mouth of the third creature, and squeezes off the last round in the chamber. The third biter's cranium vaporizes in a mist of purple-black cerebrospinal fluid, leaving the onlookers across the lot, huddling behind the water tower, utterly breathless as they watch. Barbara holds her hand over her mouth, her eyes wide and hot while David lets out a pained breath.

Now they watch the team in the cargo truck spring into action—muzzles sticking out of open cab windows, men rising up on the edge of the rear gate—emptying the last of their precious ammo into the cluster of biters. Bullets riddle molding flesh and take the ragged figures apart in a gruesome ballet of death—a *plié* of ripping flesh over here, a *jeté* of blood spray over there, a grand *pas de deux* of two sparking, burned figures slamming into each other and going down in a seizure of blood—as the air lights up with the tommy-gun rattle of automatic gunfire.

"Good God," Barbara Stern murmurs in absolute awe, her voice barely audible even in her own ears, as she watches Lilly calmly stride back toward the truck, tear a hank of her shirttail from her waist, unscrew a cap on the truck's rear quarter panel, and stuff the cloth into the truck's fuel tank. Only about ten biters still stand, and now start lumbering toward the truck. Lilly pulls a lighter from her pocket, lights the rag, and then ambles around to the driver's side of the cab to say something to the others.

The four men and one woman all turn and charge toward the barricade as Lilly reaches up and starts honking the air horn—the harsh bleating noise drawing every last biter in the vicinity toward the noise—and finally Lilly turns and runs off as the smoldering rag ignites the diesel fumes and then sparks the contents of the tanks.

Lilly covers about twenty-five yards—nearly reaching the burning wall—when the fuel reservoir explodes. The blast is preceded by a quick and silent flash of magnesium-bright light like a photographer's strobe, making a match-head sound, and then the thing erupts.

The remaining biters are liquefied in the blast, the sonic boom like Vulcan's hammer shattering the entire town, rattling windows for at least three blocks. The shock wave rams into Lilly and lifts her off her feet, sending her careening through the gap in the burning fence. She lands only a few feet away from the point at which the Sterns now gape at the spectacle from behind the water tower.

A black mushroom cloud the consistency of coal dust curls and rises into the sky over the mangled truck, about 60 percent of the frame and superstructure now reduced to scorched wreckage.

The silence that follows is almost as shocking as the explosion. Lilly rolls onto her back and stares at the empty sky, her head spinning, her ears ringing, her mouth coppery-tasting from the split lip opening back up, the small of her back wrenched in the concussion. The other members of her team come out from behind flaming debris and stand staring at her for a moment, as if knocked senseless by the final act of their counterassault.

Nobody says anything for the longest moment as the flames crackle around them. The sun is high in the sky now, the day warming up. At last Barbara Stern steps out from behind the water tower and casually walks over to where Lilly still lies, catching her breath.

Barbara stares down at her and lets out a long, anguished breath, and then manages a weary smile. Lilly smiles back at her—thankful to see a rational face—and the two women communicate volumes to each other without saying a word. Finally, Barbara Stern takes a deep breath, narrows her eyes at Lilly, and murmurs a single word.

"Show-off."

They can't relax—even for the briefest of moments—because the town is vulnerable. They've used up most of the ammunition, and the wall continues burning, throwing sparks, catching other structures. Plus, the pandemonium has almost certainly drawn more walkers out of the adjacent woods.

Lilly takes the reins and starts addressing the issue of the fire. She places her able-bodied men—Matthew, Ben, Speed, Hap, and David Stern—along the breach to guard against further walker attacks with the meager amount of ammunition they have left. Then she enlists the healthiest of the seniors and children to form a bucket brigade along the railroad tracks, using the stagnant well water from behind the courthouse.

They assail the fires with surprising efficiency, considering the varying skills and physical prowess of the weaker citizens now lugging buckets of foul-smelling water and tanks of CO_2 across the south edge of the town. Nobody questions Lilly's authority as she gently but firmly shouts orders from the roof of a semitrailer. People are too shell-shocked and jittery to argue with her.

Besides, most of the surviving Woodbury citizens still expect the Governor to return. Everything will be okay when he shows up. It might be mass chaos now, but when Philip Blake comes back, things will most certainly settle down and return to normal.

By dusk that evening, Lilly finally manages to secure the town.

The fires have all been extinguished, the bodies removed, the barricades repaired, the wounded taken to the infirmary, the alleys cleared of any lurkers, and the leftover provisions and ammunition inventoried. Exhausted, sore, and drained, Lilly makes an announcement in the town square. Everybody should take a quick break, tend to the wounded, replenish themselves, and then meet in the community room in the courthouse in an hour. They all need to have a little talk.

Little does anybody know, Lilly has a bombshell to drop and she needs to do it as gently as possible.

TWENTY-ONE

The entire population of Woodbury—a town that once upon a time was known for being the largest railroad hub in west central Georgia and was referred to in promotional literature and water tower insignias as "A Peach of a Place"—now gathers in the damp, fusty-smelling, cluttered community room in the rear of the modest little courthouse building.

The total number of souls still inhabiting the village—not including the two men currently patrolling the walls outside (Matthew and Speed) or the man presently occupied by some unknown task down in the infirmary (Bob Stookey)—amounts to a grand total of twenty-five: six women, fourteen men, and five children under the age of twelve. These twenty-five people now take their places around the scarred parquet floor on folding chairs, each of them facing the front of the room, theater-style, waiting for the single speaker on the program that night to begin her presentation.

Lilly paces along the cracked, bullet-riddled front wall, where the shredded remains of the state and national flags hang by threads on dented metal standards like totems of a long-lost civilization. Since the plague broke out nearly two years ago, men have lived and died in this room. Unspoken threats have been made, contracts have been sealed, and regimes have changed in the most violent of fashions.

Before speaking, Lilly measures her words silently, her face damp with flop-sweat. She has changed into clean clothes, a color-ful orchid bandanna now battened around her neck. Her paddock boots click on the dusty tile as she paces. She has one Ruger MK II in a new holster on her hip. The wind rattles the high dormers, and the squeak of metal chairs settles, the hushed, expectant whispers fading into silence.

Everybody waits in the stillness for Lilly to say what she has to say.

She knows she has to just come out and say it, so she takes a deep breath, turns to the group, and tells them the truth. She tells them everything.

Bob Stookey trundles down the dark, deserted sidewalk with his sticky, bloodstained biohazard container under his arm, turning the corner at Main Street and Jones Mill Road, when he sees the generators on the courthouse lawn twenty yards across the square. The squat little five-horsepower engines vibrate and puff with exhaust, working busily, making the windows of the annex glow softly with warm yellow light.

The sight of the entire town gathered inside those windows gives Bob pause, and he lingers on the edge of the square for a mo-ment, watching the reactions of his fellow citizens to Lilly's news. Bob knows what happened, knows about Austin and all the others who perished, and he knows what she has most likely just dropped in the laps of these poor people. Late this afternoon, Bob spoke briefly with Lilly, shared her grief, and told her that he would sup-port her in whatever she has planned for this place. He didn't tell her about the Governor's last request, however, nor did he show her the sole occupant of that second-floor apartment at the end of Main Street.

Now Bob stands alone with his box full of entrails, staring through the proscenium of windows into the radiant light of the community room.

He sees Lilly nodding at the folks, and he sees some of the

townspeople raising their hands, speaking up, asking imponderable questions, their faces furrowed with worry. But Bob also sees something right then that makes him furrow his own deeply lined brow with bemusement, maybe even a little dismay. From this distance, hiding behind a skeletal poplar tree with his gruesome chum wafting its stench all around him, he can see some of the faces displaying expressions of . . . what? Hope? Humanity?

Bob's mother, Delores, a former navy nurse in the Korean War, had a word for what Bob is seeing right now through those grimy windowpanes on the weathered, world-weary faces as they patiently listen to Lilly make her case for the future of their little motley hamlet. The word is "grace."

Even in the worst situations, Bobby, Delores Stookey used to tell him . . . *in the midst of death and suffering and, yeah, even evil . . . people can find grace. God made us this way, Bobby, don't you see? God made us in His image. Don't you ever forget that, honey. People can find grace under the rocks of misery, if they have to.*

Bob Stookey watches the faces in the community room, most of them eagerly listening as Lilly Caul explains the road forward. From the expression on *her* face—the way she holds herself, the way she almost imperceptibly squares her shoulders toward her audience despite her battered body and soul, her exhaustion, and her grief—she now looks as though she's closing the deal.

Nobody would ever accuse Bob Stookey of being a trained OB-GYN—although he did treat that poor gal overseas after her miscarriage—but now he is *convinced* that he's watching the birth of another new soul.

This one, a leader.

Standing in that airless room, caught in the feverish gazes of twenty-five expectant, frightened, hopeful faces, Lilly Caul waits for the whispering to quiet down one last time before laying her proverbial cards on the table.

"Let me bottom-line it for you," she says finally. "Whatever you thought of Philip Blake, he kept us alive, and he kept the walkers at bay. It's that simple. But you got used to living under a dictator. We all did."

She pauses for a moment, parsing her words carefully, watching them watching her. The room gets so quiet, Lilly can hear the ticking of the foundation, and the whistling of the breeze through the bones of the hundred-year-old building.

"I don't want to dictate anything," she says. "But I'm willing to take responsibility for this community. We have an opportunity here. I'm not asking for power. I'm not asking for anything. All I'm saying is, we can make Woodbury a good place to live again, a safe place, a decent place. And I'm willing to be the one who . . . you know . . . *guides us there*. I won't do it, though, if you don't want me to. So it's time we took a vote. No more dictatorships. Woodbury's a democracy now. So here we go. All in favor of me taking the wheel for a while, raise your hands."

Half the hands in the room go up immediately. Barbara and David Stern—sitting in the front row, their hands the highest of them all—are already smiling, their sad eyes belying the struggle ahead.

Some of the people in the back of the room look at each other as though searching for a signal.

Lilly lets out a sigh of both profound relief and exhaustion when the rest of the hands go up.

Sleep comes hard that night, despite Lilly's fatigue. It feels as though she hasn't slept in her own bed in years—in fact, hasn't *slept* in years—when, in fact, it's only been a couple of days. She dozes off and on and gets up a couple of times to pee, and while she's up, she discovers Austin's things scattered across the apartment.

With a tenderness and sorrow that sneaks up on her, she carefully gathers all of his personal effects—his lighter, a deck of playing cards, a pocketknife, a few articles of his clothing, including a spare hoodie and a porkpie hat—and puts them in a drawer for safekeeping. She would never throw them out. But she needs to clear the deck for the challenges ahead.

Then she sits down and has a good cry.

When she goes back to bed, she gets an idea—something that she and the rest of Woodbury should do first thing in the morning before they tackle any of the other myriad tasks that need to be done. She sleeps for a few hours, and when she awakens to a room full of sunlight, the rays slanting through the curtains, she feels transformed. She gets dressed and then walks down to the square.

A few of the older townspeople with weaker bladders and aging prostates have already convened in the diner across from the courthouse and fired up the ancient stainless-steel coffee urn by the time Lilly arrives. They greet her with a conviviality reserved for world leaders. She gets the sense that everybody's secretly relieved that the Governor's regime is over, and people are delighted to learn it's Lilly who has stepped up.

She tells them her idea, and they all agree it's a good one. Lilly enlists a couple of the stronger folks to go out and spread the word, and an hour later, the entire town has gathered in the bleacher section of the speedway.

Lilly takes center stage—walking out across the dusty infield, standing in the former fight ring where men and women fought to the death for the titillation of the residents—and she thanks everybody for coming, says a few words about her plans for the future, and finally asks everybody to bow their heads for a moment in remembrance of those among their number who have passed away.

Then she simply lists the names of the men and women who have died over the past weeks and months in the struggle to survive.

For nearly five minutes, the slow litany of names echoes up into the robin's-egg-blue sky. "Scott Moon . . . Megan Lafferty . . . Josh Lee Hamilton . . . Caesar Martinez . . . Doc Stevens . . . Alice Warren . . . Bruce Cooper . . . Gus Strunk . . . Jim Steagal . . . Raymond Hilliard . . . Gabe Harris . . . Rudy Warburton . . . Austin Ballard . . ."

On and on, she recites the names in a strong, respectful, resonant voice, pausing for a moment after each of them as the wind takes them off into the echoing reaches of the stadium. She has memorized most of them, glancing down only occasionally at her crib notes scrawled on an index card nestled in her moist palm for a few last names she never knew before today. Finally she comes to the last name and pauses for a beat before saying it without emotion.

"Philip Blake."

The name has its own echo—ghostly, profane—as it reverberates on the breeze. She glances up at the beleaguered crowd gathered against the chain-link barrier, most of the bowed heads turning upward to look at her. Silence greets the exchange of glances. Lilly lets out a long exhalation of breath and then nods. "May God have mercy on their souls," she says.

A smattering of whispered responses and amens drifts across the arena.

Lilly invites everybody onto the field for the final phase of the ritual. Slowly, one by one, the elders and children and surviving members of the militia file through the gate and onto the dirt infield. Lilly supervises the dismantling.

They take down the post and shackles that once bound walkers to the periphery of the fighting ring. They clean up the vestibules and cloisters, removing the forlorn remnants of torn clothing and spent shells and broken bats and mangled blades that litter the passageways. They clean up the congealed puddles of blood. They sweep the ramps, wipe down the walls, and toss all evidence of the fights into huge garbage bins. A few of the younger men even go down into the catacombs beneath the stadium and destroy the walkers still enclosed in their hellish purgatory, and Lilly begins to feel their housekeeping project is a cleansing of a deeper sort.

The Roman Circus officially closes today—no more gladiators, no more fights other than the collective one for survival.

While they work, Lilly notices something else that surprises her. Very subtly at first, but gathering momentum as the infield transforms, moods begin to lighten. People start talking to each other in positive tones, cracking jokes, reminiscing about the old days, and hinting at better times to come. Barbara Stern suggests that they turn the grounds of the infield into a vegetable garden— the feed store still has viable seeds in it—and Lilly thinks that's a damn fine idea.

And for one brief stretch of time, in the warming sun of a Georgia spring morning—however fleeting it might be—people almost seem happy.

Almost.

By sunset that evening, things have settled down in the new Woodbury.

The barricade has been reinforced on the southeast and north corners of town, a new patrol schedule established—the surrounding woodlands remaining relatively quiet—and the town's supply of fuel, drinking water, and dried goods is accounted for and distributed evenly among the residents. No more bartering, no more politics, no more questions asked. They have enough provisions and sources of energy to keep them going for months—and Lilly sets up a town meeting room in the courthouse, where she begins the process of establishing a sort of steering committee among the elders and heads of families to vote on critical matters.

As the dusk presses in and the air cools, Lilly finally decides to head back home. She's flagging from the pain that lingers in her lower back, and the intermittent cramps that still torment her, but she's as clear-headed and grounded as she's ever been.

Exhausted but oddly tranquil, she walks along the deserted sidewalk toward her apartment building, thinking about Austin, thinking about Josh, and thinking about her father, when she sees a familiar figure trundling along on the opposite side of the street with a dark gunnysack dripping black droplets on the boardwalk.

"Bob?" She crosses the street and approaches him warily, gazing at the blood-sodden sack. "What's going on? What are you doing?"

He pauses in the shadows, a distant sodium vapor light barely illuminating his weathered features. "Nothing much . . . um, you know . . . takin' care of business." He looks strangely nervous and embarrassed. Since he managed to stop drinking, his grooming has improved, his greasy hair now pomaded neatly back away from his deeply creased forehead, accentuating the crow's-feet around his droopy eyes.

"I don't mean to be nosy, Bob." She nods at the sack. "But this is the second time I've seen you hauling something disgusting across town. It's none of my business, but is that by any chance—?"

"It ain't human, Lilly," he blurts. "Got it down by the switch-yard. It's just meat."

"Meat?"

"Pieces of a rabbit I found in one of my traps, just a carcass."

Lilly looks at him. "Bob, I don't—"

"I promised him, Lilly." All the pretense goes out of him then, his shoulders slumping with despair, maybe even a little shame. "This thing . . . it's still in there . . . poor wretched creature . . . was once his daughter, and I promised him. I had to keep that promise."

"Jesus Christ, you're not talking about—"

"You could make the argument that he saved my life," Bob says, looking down at the ground. The sack drips. Bob sniffs miserably.

Lilly thinks about it for a moment, and then says very softly yet very evenly, "Show me."

TWENTY-TWO

Bob turns the key and pushes the door open, and Lilly follows him inside the apartment, crossing the threshold of the Governor's inner sanctum.

She pauses in the foul-smelling foyer. Bob still clutches the sack of meat in his gnarled hand as he scuttles around the corner, vanishing into the living room, but Lilly lingers in that cramped vestibule, taking in the sad remnants of the Governor's private life.

Since arriving in Woodbury, Lilly Caul has been in the Governor's lair only a couple of times, each visit brief and accompanied by a flesh-crawling uneasiness. She remembers hearing those inexplicable noises coming from other rooms—the thick breathing, the faint metallic jangling sounds, and that weird percolating drone of bubbles, as though a meth lab were chugging away in the kitchen—but right now, standing with her arms crossed defensively against her chest, hearing those same noises, she feels very little of the repulsion or aversion she had experienced earlier.

The heartrending sadness of the place calls out to her, and weighs down on her. The scarred hardwood floor, the faded wallpaper, the windows masked with black muslin and threadbare blankets, the single bare lightbulb hanging from the cracked plaster ceiling, the odors of mold and disinfectant thick in the stagnant air—all of it squeezes Lilly's midsection with tremendous sorrow.

She takes a girding breath and tries to push the sadness out of her mind. Bob calls out to her from the living room.

"Lilly, come on in here . . . I'd like you to meet somebody," his voice beckons, wavering slightly as he tries to keep things light and easy. Lilly takes another breath, a strange thought passing through her mind: *The man who lived here lost everything, and that drove him over the edge, and he ended up here, a castaway in this tawdry, lonely limbo of masked windows and bare lightbulbs and no life.*

Lilly walks into the living room, and the tiny figure shackled to the opposite wall stops Lilly cold in her tracks. The sight of Penny Blake sends an icy trickle of terror—most of it involuntary—down through Lilly's bowels. The flesh on the back of her neck prickles. But accompanying these innate responses come stronger and stronger waves of despair, sadness, and even empathy.

Something about the way the accouterments of childhood still cling to this creature sends Lilly's mind reeling—the shriveled, blackened face crowned with ratty pigtails and filthy ribbons tied in bows, the little pinafore dress so inundated with drool and bile and gore that its original cornflower-blue color has now turned earthworm gray. Bob kneels near the creature, close enough to stroke her shoulder but far enough away to be just beyond the reach of her snapping, gnashing, rasping jaws.

"Lilly, meet Penny," Bob says with a tenderness that's almost jarring as he reaches into the gunnysack and pulls out a morsel of purplish-red tissue. The girl-thing gnaws at the air and moans an excruciating moan. Bob feeds her the organ. Her milky-white eyes fill with agitation and something that almost looks like agony as she masticates the offal, fluids leaking through her tiny, puckered, toothless gums and running down her chin.

Lilly comes closer, the sorrow weighing down on her, forcing her to fall to her knees a few feet away from the child-thing. "Oh my God . . . Bob . . . Jesus Christ . . . is this his . . . ? Oh Jesus, Jesus."

Bob gently strokes the child's waxy hair as the thing devours the entrails. "Penny, meet Lilly," Bob says very softly to the creature.

Lilly bows her head and stares at the floor. "Bob, this is . . . Jesus."

"I promised him, Lilly."

"Bob . . . Bob." Lilly shakes her head and continues staring at the floor as the watery smacking noises fill the air. She can't bear to look at the tiny monster. In her peripheral vision, Lilly can see nail marks on the worn carpet, an outline of bloodstains where a panel was hastily driven into the floor. She can also see smudges of stubborn bloodstains on the walls that refused to come out with Comet and elbow grease. The air smells of sour rot and copper.

Bob says something else but Lilly doesn't hear it. Her mind swims with sadness now, marinating in the misery and madness baked into the fabric of this place, festering in the drapes and the grain of the floorboards and the black mold in the seams of the baseboards. It takes her breath away and burns her eyes. The tears come then, and Lilly tries to get breath back in her lungs and stanch the welling of her eyes and the urge to sob. She stuffs it back down her gorge. She clenches her fists and looks back up at the girl.

A long time ago, Penny Blake sat on her father's lap and listened to bedtime stories and sucked her thumb and nuzzled a security blanket. Now she gazes out through eyes the color of a fish belly, insensate as a mole, catatonic with a black hunger that will never fade. She is the living embodiment of the plague's toll.

For an unbearable eternity, Lilly Caul slumps on her knees in front of the girl-thing, shaking her head, staring at the floor while Bob feeds the rest of the chum to the creature, saying nothing, softly whistling as though merely braiding a little girl's hair.

Lilly gropes for the right words. She knows what has to be done.

At last, after endless minutes, Lilly finally manages to look up at Bob. "You know what we have to do, right?" She holds Bob's droopy, red-rimmed, crestfallen gaze. "You know there's no other way to go."

Bob lets out a miserable sigh, levers himself to his feet, shuffles over to the sofa, and plops down as though the stone of Sisyphus rests on his shoulders. He slumps and wipes his eyes, his lips trembling as he says, "I know . . . I know." He looks at Lilly through his tears. "You're gonna have to do it, Lilly-girl . . . I ain't got the heart for it."

They find an ice pick in the kitchen drawer and a relatively clean sheet on the bed, and Lilly tells Bob to wait outside. But Bob Stookey—a man who has ministered to dying soldiers and taken in stray dogs all his life—refuses to dishonor the memory of a little girl. He tells Lilly that he will assist her.

They sneak up behind the girl-thing while she's feeding, and Lilly throws the sheet over her, covering her head and face, trying not to disturb the creature any more than necessary. The tiny monster writhes and struggles in the cocoon of fabric for a moment, as Lilly gently forces the wriggling body to the floor. Pressing her weight down on the shuddering form, Lilly grips the ice pick in her right hand.

The head squirms and flails under the sheet, and Lilly struggles for a moment to position it properly for a clean and decisive thrust. Bob crouches next to her, next to the shivering lump, and begins softly singing to it—an old Christian hymn—and Lilly pauses for a moment, just before plunging the ice pick into the head under the sheet, taken aback by the sound of Bob's voice.

"On a hill far away stood an old rugged cross," Bob croons softly to the thing that was once a child—his gravelly drawl suddenly transformed, turning soft and warm and as sweet as honey. "It's the emblem of suffering and shame, and I love that old cross where the dearest and best, for a world of lost sinners was slain."

Lilly freezes, feeling something extraordinary develop inside the damp sheet beneath her. The writhing and shuddering and growling subside, the creature suddenly and inexplicably growing calm, as though listening to the sound of Bob's voice. Lilly stares at the sheet. It doesn't seem possible, but the thing remains still.

Bob softly sings, "Then He'll call me someday to my home far away . . . Where His glory forever I'll share."

Lilly thrusts the point deep into the cranium under the sheet. And the thing named Penny goes to her home far away.

They decide to have a burial ceremony for the child. Lilly comes up with the idea, and Bob thinks it's a pretty good thing to do.

So Lilly sends Bob out to gather the others, find a wheelbarrow, some tarp, a suitable container, and a proper location for the gravesite.

After Bob leaves, Lilly lingers in the apartment, one piece of unfinished business left to address.

TWENTY-THREE

Lilly finds a box of shells in Philip's bedroom closet, which fit the 12-gauge pigeon gun leaning against the wall behind a stack of peach crates. She loads the gun and carries it into the side room.

All it took was a single glance through the doorway into that shadowy chamber where the ghastly aquariums are still lined along the wall, bubbling and thumping in the darkness, for the mystery of Philip Blake to forever be burned into Lilly's memory.

Now Lilly positions herself in front of the glass containers and pumps the shotgun. She levels the barrel on the first aquarium and fires. The blast nearly blows her eardrums out as the container explodes, sending glass shards through the air and a gush of fluid across the floor. The bloated head tumbles out.

She pumps another shell into the chamber and fires, and she does it again and again, hitting each aquarium dead center, spewing waves of water across the floor at her feet and sending the heads to oblivion. She goes through twenty-five shells, until the room swims with cleansing water, broken glass, and the remains of the Governor's trophies.

She tosses the shotgun to the floor and wades out of the flooded room, her ears ringing and the last traces of Philip Blake's madness exorcised from the earth.

That evening, as the sun begins its descent behind the high tree-tops on the western horizon and the air turns cool and luminous in the lengthening shadows, the twenty-eight surviving inhabitants of Woodbury, Georgia, stand in a semicircle around a freshly turned mound of earth, finishing up their tribute to a lost child . . . and closing a violent chapter in the town's post-plague history.

The spot Bob picked out for Penny's final resting place is outside the wall, shaded by massive live oaks, dappled in wildflowers, and relatively free of the detritus of past skirmishes and attacks.

Everybody stands in respectful silence, heads bowed, mouthing their final whispered prayers. Even the children present stop fidgeting for a moment and look down into the dirt and clasp their little hands together in prayer. Lilly closes the small, dog-eared Bible that Bob loaned her for the occasion, and she gazes at the ground for a beat, waiting for the moment to run its course. She has just finished reciting a brief eulogy for a child no one knew, a child who seems a fitting symbol for the loss of many others, as well as the sanctity of those lives still being lived, and now Lilly feels a profound sort of closure.

"Rest in peace, little Penny," she says at last, breaking the spell and bringing the moment to an end. "Thanks, everybody. Probably ought to be getting back now . . . before darkness rolls in."

Bob stands next to Lilly with a wadded handkerchief in his huge hands, the cloth soaked with his tears. Lilly can tell by the sanguine look behind his rheumy, hound-dog eyes that this little impromptu ceremony has been good for him. It's been good for all of them.

One by one, they turn away from the grave and start making their way across the vacant lot outside the northeast corner of town. Lilly walks in the lead, Bob ambling along next to her, wiping his eyes with his handkerchief. Behind Bob, Matthew and Speed carry rifles on their hips in case they encounter any stray walkers.

The others follow closely, chatting softly, talking idly about matters great and small, when the faint sound of an engine in the distance gets everybody's attention. Most of them stop and crane their necks to see what in God's name might be coming this way.

"If I didn't know better," Bob says to Lilly, reaching for the Smith & Wesson lodged behind his belt, "I'd say that was a car coming down 109."

"Okay, just take it easy—everybody—take it easy," Lilly says to the group, glancing over her shoulder at the column of people behind her and seeing some of them pulling weapons, some of the kids pushing in closer to the adults. "Let's just see what it is before we get all bent outta shape."

For a moment, other than the sputtering sound of a dying engine, all Lilly can make out in the distance is a wisp of black exhaust rising above the tree line and then diffusing in the wind. She keeps her eyes on the bend in the road a couple hundred yards away when a battered station wagon comes into view.

Lilly can tell instantly that the car poses no threat. It appears to be an old, battered, rust-flecked Ford LTD, a late 1990s model, burning oil, with half the wood panels shaved off in side-swipe mishaps, the wheels wobbling as though they might fall off at any moment. "Lower your weapons," Lilly says to Matthew and Speed. "C'mon . . . it's okay."

As the vehicle rattles closer and closer, the people inside come into view—a tattered couple in the front, three small urchins in the back—apparently a family, their engine running on fumes. They pull up to within a safe distance—about twenty-five yards down the road—and cobble to a stop in a cloud of noxious haze.

Lilly raises her empty hands to show the people in the car she's not a threat.

The driver's-side door squeaks open and the father climbs out. Dressed in layers of Salvation Army rags, as malnourished as a prisoner of war, the man is skin and bones. He looks as though he might collapse at any moment. He responds to Lilly's gesture by raising his *own* hands to show that he, too, means no harm.

"Evening!" Lilly calls out to the man.

"Hello." The man's voice sounds hollow, like that of a terminal cancer patient. "Mind if I ask if y'all got any spare drinking water ya might part with?"

Lilly recognizes the faint, urbanized drawl of a Southern city—Birmingham, Oxford, Jacksonville maybe—and she glances over her shoulder at the others. "You folks stay put for a second; I'll be right back." She turns again to the stranger. "I'm gonna stroll a little closer, sir, if that's all right?"

The man turns and looks worriedly at his family huddling nervously in the car. He turns back to Lilly. "Sure . . . I guess so . . . c'mon over."

Lilly walks calmly toward the station wagon, her hands still raised. The closer she gets, the more she can see how badly these people are hurting. The man and his wife look like they have one foot in the grave, their sallow, ashen faces so thin they look cadaverous. In the cluttered backseat, the children are caked with grit and scantily dressed. The wagon is filled with empty wrappers and moth-eaten blankets. It's a miracle these people are still upright. Lilly approaches and stands a few feet away from the father. "My name's Lilly, and yours is . . . ?"

"Calvin . . . and that's Meredith." He points at his wife, and then at his kids. "And that's Tommy, Bethany, and Lucas." He looks at Lilly. "Ma'am, I would be forever grateful if you could maybe part with some food, and maybe any weapons you might be able to spare?"

Lilly looks at the man and proffers a warm, guileless, genuine smile. "I've got a better idea, Calvin. How about I show you around?"

extracts reading groups
competitions books new
discounts extracts
extracts
competitions
books
reading groups
events
discounts
new
events
books
extracts
extracts
new
titles
reading groups
interviews
events extracts
discounts
new books events
events new
discounts extracts discounts
www.panmacmillan.com
extracts events reading groups
competitions books extracts new
books